COUNTED WITH THE DEAD

PETER O'KEEFE

GRENDEL PRESS

Cover Design by Matthew Revert
Edited by Gabino Iglesias

Published April 2024
ISBN: 978-1-960534-11-8 (Paperback)
ASIN: B0D21MCZ28 (eBook)

Written by Peter O'Keefe
www.peterokeefewriter.com

Published by Grendel Press LLC
www.grendelpress.com

COUNTED
WITH THE DEAD

PETER O'KEEFE

For Lesley

The man from whom the joys of life have departed is living no more, but should be counted with the dead.

Sophocles

1

J ACK KILLEEN LEADS THE way, powering through the rough terrain with the assurance of a bike messenger in traffic. His right arm is a rigid tow bar dragging the hooded Victor Moravian by his necktie. Victor's hands are bound behind his back with his own belt. His sweaty face is mummified beneath the thin nylon sack pasted to his features like a death mask. The drawstring is tight around his throat.

The two men are harnessed together in an oddly syncopated lockstep as they move through what—if you squint your eyes—could generously be described as a forest. The trail they follow is a thin crust of weeds and dirt salted with brick shards and broken glass. The trees are exhausted, leafless totems. Bristling clumps of saplings erupt from scattered grassy mounds like the desiccated tentacles of the dead emerging from some bestial burial ground.

Jack's pace is unforgiving and Victor sways in his grip, whipping and wobbling like an oversized trailer as he sideswipes trees and stumbles over obstacles. They leave the shelter of the trees and Jack drags Victor through a gap in a chain-link fence. The ground on the other side of the fence is flat, a bone-dry mosaic of waist-high weeds and crumbling pavement. They walk across the open ground for a bit before Jack stiff-arms Victor to a halt. Ahead of them are the ghostly ruins of a long-abandoned auto factory, Fisher Body Plant 21.

Victor makes a pitiful mewling sound beneath the hood and Jack brings him to his knees with a brutal yank on his necktie. His eyes are still fixed on the wrecked industrial monolith looming over them. Located at either end of the massive pile, the plant's elevator towers are the battlements of a ruined fortress. Between those towers, the factory floors are piled one atop the other, a hulking layer cake of masonry and glass. The vaporous glow from a thin necklace of streetlights—like the smoldering watch-fires of a besieging army—reveal gaping wounds where scrappers and neglect have done the work of cannon fire.

The besiegers and the besieged moved on long ago. Now the plundered ruin is surrounded by a desolate tundra of overgrown parking lots, providing an open field of fire for any spectral guardians that remain.

Jack turns his attention back to his prisoner. Victor rocks stiffly from side to side, all soft contours and sweat, like some grim inflatable toy. The thin nylon over his mouth flexes with each wheezing suck as Jack pulls the Glock from its holster. The weight, the familiar feel of the textured grip against his fingers and palm, gives him a sense of calm; two pounds of lethal worry beads in the hands of a monk. He screws a silencer onto the threaded barrel and charges a round in the chamber. The sharp metallic squawk of the slide snaps Victor out of his stupor.

"Please... Dear god... Don't do this. I have money. I can pay you."

Victor struggles to rise, but Jack forces him back to his knees.

"I won't say anything. I'll disappear. They'll think you killed me."

Jack raises the gun until it is inches from Victor's shrouded head. His finger moves from the trigger guard to the trigger.

"Please... My wife, what will happen to her?"

Jack tenses at the mention of Victor's wife. The gun in his hand suddenly weighs a thousand pounds. It may as well be Thor's hammer as its dead weight wrestles his arm downward until the barrel is pointing at the ground.

Victor, sensing an opening, presses on. "In my wallet... I have a picture."

Jack digs through Victor's jacket until he secures the wallet. He fumbles through it with his free hand and finds a photograph that depicts Victor arm in arm with his beautiful wife. They are a radiant, smiling, odd couple; her supple elegance nestled against Victor's benighted, grinning bulk. Victor is looking into the camera with the bemused confidence of a game show contestant with all the answers. His wife, smiling and rocking a short, pixie-like haircut, is a beguiling mix of luminous warmth and a watchful, feral intensity.

Jack allows the wallet to slip through his fingers but maintains his grip on the photo as he rips the bag from his prisoner's head. Victor, his face drizzled with snot and sweat, is a hopeful penitent studying Jack's face. Jack holds the photograph in front of the condemned man's eyes.

There is the faintest flicker of hope in Victor's voice now. "That's her... My wife..."

Jack finishes his sentence. "Marlene."

"Yes, Marlene... My wife... I don't understand. How did you...?"

Jack meets his gaze and Victor suddenly realizes what this is really about.

"You?"

Jack releases his grip on the photo. Victor's eyes track it mournfully as it flutters to the ground. Then, like a man suddenly reminded of an unfinished chore, Jack raises the gun and shoots Victor in the chest.

The slug slams him backward into the dirt and Jack stands directly over him for the kill shot. A dark, textured bruise is blooming across the expanse of the dying man's chest as the hitman lifts his arm to fire again. He points the gun at his victim's head but finds his aim inexplicably veering away from his target. Perplexed, he grips the gun firmly in both hands. He tries to line up the shot but his aim again skips slightly off target.

Enraged, Jack swivels and fires at the photo, pulling the trigger until the fragile image has been obliterated and the clip is empty.

Jack uses a glove to unscrew the silencer. He drops to one knee and carefully retrieves the shell casings. He jams them into the nylon bag that covered Victor's head and uses his shoe to grind the remnants of the photo into the dirt. He rolls the body on its side to assure himself that nothing has fallen underneath. Then, he steps over the lifeless form of Victor Moravian and begins to retrace his steps to the car.

The path seems to have narrowed—Jack doesn't remember being hemmed in so tightly by tree limbs on the way in. His shoulder skids painfully off the side of a tree trunk and he corrects his trajectory to stay on the rapidly constricting pathway. Skeletal saplings, hard and sharp, lash out at him with the whip-like savagery of scorpion tails. He doesn't care. His thoughts are already on the glassine sandwich bag in the glove box. Thank god he's already rolled one.

2

Victor Moravian is floating serenely on his back. His eyes are shut tight against the brilliant glare of the sun as he contemplates making the effort to open them. Maybe later. He was about forty yards off the beach last time he looked; the one they had all to themselves until the little French family showed up. He smiles at the memory of the French girl, a lithesome, brown faun in a Persian red bikini bottom with perfect, pert little breasts, tossing a frisbee with her brother.

He reconstructs the rest of the pleasant little diorama in his mind, each piece dropping into place like the elements of a Matisse cutout: the flat cerulean blue of the sky, the verdant green of the cliffs, the pale ocher of the sand. Marlene, walking naked into the surf, droplets of water glistening on her flanks, fingers softly trailing the surface, her smooth flesh oh so slowly merging into that tranquil liquid quilt. The goddess, glancing back over her shoulder to bestow a smile upon her loyal subject.

Maybe he should open his eyes now. Does his stomach still peek out from the warm, placid water of the Caribbean like a fleshy pink island? Is she still lying on her towel, soft flesh baking in the sun? It would be so very pleasant to gaze at Marlene in all her naked splendor...

Marlene...

Victor is beginning to remember: The man with the gun. The long, terrifying walk through the woods. Those hideous lips forming that most sacred of words: "Marlene."

Oh, my dear god...

Victor opens his eyes to find himself in the middle of a jungle, a dense, impenetrable jumble of massive tree trunks, vines, and creepers. In the distance, some creature, an enormous, insect-like thing, scuttles through the tangled labyrinth. Wait, it is an insect! Victor realizes that his face is pressed against the ground and the trees are the twigs and blades of grass in front of his eyes.

There are voices now, moving closer. A light sweeps across his little tropical thicket and then is gone. A sense of relief washes over him; someone has come for him. With his ear pressed into the turf he can sense as much as hear their footsteps moving around him. Something makes a scraping sound as it is dragged across the broken pavement. Two voices float far above him. One is older, commanding, confident. The second voice is younger, frightened.

The older man is close to his ear, so close Victor can hear him breathing. His voice, cold and self-assured, fills him with dread. "It seems our unknown benefactors have made another donation to the cause of science."

"What if they ever find out?" asks the younger voice.

The older man's voice is all icy contempt. "What will they do? Call the police?"

"But why here? This is not the same place as before—"

His master cuts him off. "Silence. We haven't much time."

These are not the reassuring, measured tones of first responders. Victor's miniature forest disappears under the dark weight of a planet as one of them crouches beside him. A sweet, musky odor is thick in his nostrils; the familiar smell of cheap cologne he often encounters in the locker room at the plant.

Victor can hear the fabric of their coats swishing together, knees pressing into the dirt around him, a zippered case being opened. Then, a brilliant, blinding light blots out his vision. The panicked voice of the younger man is the last thing he hears. "Oh my god, he's alive! This one is still alive!"

3

H ADDAD IS AT HIS post behind the counter, a benign smile on his face as he watches Jack make his selections. The burly proprietor is on the other side of the floor-to-ceiling plexiglass wall that separates the register from the rest of the store: the dusty shelves of canned goods, pasta and potato chips, the coolers full of beer, soda pop and malt liquor, the customers.

The premium goods, the cigarettes and hard liquor, the razor blades and flashlight batteries, fill the wall of shelves behind him.

Haddad's elderly father is seated on a small balcony at the back of the store, asleep, a shotgun resting on his knees. The dogs can be heard barking in a rear storeroom.

Jack ignores Haddad's eye roll as he sets the six-pack of Stroh's and a bag of chocolate chip cookies into the turntable used to conduct business through the plexiglass. He tilts his head in the direction of the unseen dogs. "Those hellhounds of yours secure?"

Haddad knows from long experience he's not expected to answer. He nods as he rotates the makeshift lazy Susan and silently bags Jack's purchases. He rings them up and Jack drops a fifty-dollar bill into the counter scoop beneath the dingy barrier. Haddad throws him a look and Jack shrugs. "Smallest I got."

Haddad sighs and opens the register drawer.

Jack studies the grimy 1998 Coca Cola calendar, incongruously illustrated by a placid rural farm scene, tacked to the wall behind the proprietor. "I guess that explains all those year-old expiration dates."

Haddad turns briefly to glance at the calendar. "They never sent me one this year." He turns back to the register, shrugging. "Every day is the same here."

He counts out Jack's change and stuffs it into the scoop. He stoops to pick up a dropped quarter and Jack notices the automatic jammed into his pants beneath the stock coat. Haddad used to keep it on the shelf beneath the register but must have realized that was not quite close enough. Or maybe he has two guns now.

Haddad rotates the brown paper bag to Jack's side of the counter. He is shaking his head. "This is not healthy, my friend. Not healthy."

Jack hefts the bag. "How about some sprouts? No? Got some tofu then?"

Haddad gestures helplessly to the contents of the tiny market. There's nothing resembling produce here.

Jack moves to the front door and stops. He studies the rows of cans: SpaghettiOs, tuna fish, pinto beans, pork and beans, creamed corn. "This isn't a grocery store, Haddad, it's a goddamned bomb shelter."

He pushes through the heavily barred door, Haddad's voice trailing after him. "Tomorrow, my friend, a salad bar. And French wine. You'll need a fucking suit and a tie to get in." The door closes on Haddad's final words. "Do you own a fucking tie, my friend?"

Jack crosses to the two-story brick building on the adjacent corner. The windows on the ground floor of the former pharmacy were bricked up decades before. The windows on the second floor on the side facing the market have been filled with glass bricks, leaving only a narrow slit in the center of each for a clear glass pane, like the firing ports in a blockhouse. A bulging band of leaded glass windows over the barricaded front door is all that remains of the original facade.

Jack pauses on the sidewalk before unlocking his door. He looks down the dark residential street at the barred and boarded-up windows, the accordion security grates, the steel doors, the dogs chained in bleak, desolate yards. *This isn't a city,* he thinks to himself, *it's a zoo. A zoo abandoned by its keepers, leaving their charges to fend for themselves as their cages and lairs collapse around them, leaving them to roam free, to forage, to starve, to kill or be killed.*

Once inside, Jack secures the deadbolt on the steel door. He tosses the keys onto the kitchen counter and climbs the creaky stairs to the dark wood balcony that circles the open two-story former retail space like the running track in a gym.

Jack helped evict the previous occupants, artist types who took advantage of the open space and the natural light from the expanse of leaded glass windows over the front door and entryway. From the looks of the paintings they left behind it's no wonder they couldn't make a go of it. They were handy, though, and had modified the office and storage areas in the back of the building into a comfortable living space with two bedrooms upstairs and a kitchen and full bath below. Jack liked it so much he bought it for cash.

Jack never said a word about it at the time, but it was the basement that sealed the deal. Immediately after moving in, acting on his suspicions, Jack pulled down a half-assed false wall in the back. Behind layers of cheap paneling, he uncovered a relic from Detroit's prohibition days: a tunnel going beneath the alley and into the sturdy brick garage behind the building.

The location is perfect for a man who likes to keep to himself. On one side, across a narrow side street, is Haddad's market. In addition to its guns, dogs, and barbwire-festooned roof, it has a proprietor who keeps his nose out of other people's business.

On the other side of the old pharmacy is a long-vacant welding shop, secured with plywood and cinderblocks against scavengers. To the front is Trumbull Avenue, where pedestrians are an endangered species and vehicle traffic is sparse, particularly now that the Tigers have played their final game at the old stadium a mile and a half south in Corktown. On the other side of Trumbull are Wayne State University's athletic fields, extending east all the way to the concrete ditch of the Lodge Freeway. Talk about your open field of fire.

Jack sets himself up on the wide dusty ledge between the second-floor balcony and the dingy leaded glass windows over the boarded-up front door. He sits cross-legged in the dark, staring out across the barren athletic fields to the distant lights of downtown. The beer and cookies are within easy reach. If he paces himself, they should give out at about the same time.

Jack lights up a joint, shuts his eyes, and inhales deeply. Now what? It's done, so why is he still on edge? Usually, by now he's half-crocked, listening to something bluesy at Nancy Whiskey. Afterward, once the mellow kicks in, he'd hit one of the strip clubs on Woodward. It was much easier when he was younger, when he could tap out listening to some shrieking banshees abuse guitars at PJ's or launch himself at the freak-show mob in the pit at Lili's 21. Not so easy when you suddenly find yourself closer to forty than thirty.

Afterward, once the music got him out of his head, once he'd tapped out, he was done with it. It was in the past, just another job, like harvesting deer... No, like harvesting rats. There's no room for pity, for second thoughts. These are men who brought this on themselves, men who bought into the game with eyes wide open. Men like him, completely aware of the risks. They might as well have signed a fucking waiver. This one tonight, he did it to himself. And Jack will never think about this particular job again.

He'll do what he always does when it's over: return to his books. The entire length of the second-floor balcony rail is lined with shelves that once held store inventory. Now those shelves, not visible from the main floor, are jammed with books: yard sale books, junk store books, library sale books. Jack's books.

Some guys drink to fill the void. Some gamble or piss away the hours in pool halls. Others chase women or sit hunched in front of flickering screens playing video games. Jack loses himself in his books. He tries to disappear, to live as if there is no world outside these four walls. Smoking dope. Drinking beer. Hitting the heavy bag. Blasting away in the makeshift gun range in the basement. Eating bad food. Reading. Always reading. Occupying his mind. Leaving no space for pity, no room for second thoughts or regrets. Waiting for the next gig: a debt to collect, some stubborn son of a bitch in need of a little "adjusting," an eviction.

And, sometimes, and always for the Italians, the grinning, backslapping, big-bellied fucking Italians, "a piece of work."

Jack snuffs the joint out against the windowsill. He stares out into the darkness. "What the fuck have I done?"

4

VICTOR IS BEING SWEPT along on an oscillating belt feeder, helpless as a rag doll in an avalanche. He's embedded in a mass of surging rubble, all sharp edges, jagged corners, and hurt.

Then, he hears the whirligig trill of swiveling caster wheels beneath him and remembers being rescued. He opens his eyes to find himself strapped to a gurney. Overhead, instead of the reassuring blandness of a hospital passageway, is a grimy industrial blur of pipes, flaking paint, and rust. His rescuers are running alongside, gripping the side rails like bobsledders preparing to launch themselves onto the track.

The younger one is a skinny Black man in his twenties. His hair is cut short and he's wearing plastic safety goggles over his glasses. As he runs, he bobs up and down as if on a skateboard. His coat is several sizes too large, and he strikes Victor as a manic, scuba diving scarecrow. He's talking to himself as they hustle down the corridor, the way children do to comfort themselves.

Victor's other savior is a stocky white man in his fifties. He's using his free hand to press the business end of a stethoscope to Victor's chest as they roll. He's balding, with a tight, curly beard that frames his face like a wreath. There's something regal about his appearance and Victor is reminded of an ancient bust he once saw. Was it in London? No, maybe the Met... It was the bust of a Greek general. Victor doesn't remember the names of any ancient Greek generals. He decides to call this one Daedalus.

Each bump sends a fresh jolt of pain ripping through the default layers of agony that have colonized Victor's organs. He squeezes his eyes shut and concentrates on the rhythmic *slap-SLAP*, *slap-SLAP*, *slap-SLAP* of the scarecrow's shoes on the hard floor as he struggles to keep up with his colleague. The cart hits another bump and the pain rips through Victor's entire being like the multiple blades of a combine harvester. He tries to scream but finds his mouth crammed full of hard plastic and metal.

Daedalus responds to Victor's smothered shriek by grabbing the gurney's rail with both hands and picking up the pace.

"Faster! We may never get another opportunity like this! We need to harvest the brain tissue and the optic nerves immediately. Do you understand?"

Victor hears the scraping, metallic growl of a freight elevator door being raised. The elevator car is not properly aligned with the floor and the gurney drops several inches as they enter, bouncing violently. Victor braces for a fresh wave of agony, but nothing happens.

Something has changed. Everything has slowed down. He feels as if he's floating. The pain has crossed some sort of a threshold. *Is this morphine? If so, praise God for morphine. Morphine is God. Is this the morphine talking?*

Victor opens his eyes for a few seconds to see he's rolling off the elevator. An industrial control room passes overhead like a rusting, cast iron dirigible. It seems much older than the ones they fabricate at the Piquette Avenue Plant, a relic from another era. He closes his eyes.

Victor is weightless now, impervious to pain. When he opens his eyes again, they are rolling through a forest of concrete pillars. Stalagmites hang from the dingy ceiling like fossilized vomit. Victor allows his eyelids to close again. He remembers walking across the shop floor with Marlene. "That's a bridge crane, for moving the control rooms from one station to the next during fabrication. Over there, that's what we call a gantry crane. There's one at every workstation. That one there, that's a jib crane."

Marlene was impressed. He even talked differently when he was on the shop floor, almost like one of the guys. It was all very manly, very real, very... Christ almighty, he just didn't know when to shut up! He wanted so desperately for her to see what he saw: the breathtaking, brutal choreography of massive steel plates and girders wheeling and dancing across the wide-open expanse of the plant; the panorama of gargantuan welded steel control rooms dangling from chains and hoists. As if some museum curator, tripping on acid, had decided to hang a David Smith exhibit like a group of Calder mobiles.

"Over there, the steel gauge control room being lowered into the paint booth... Can't you see? It's got the compact, coiled weight of a Mark Di Suvero *Snowplow*. And did I tell you about the site visit last week? The basic oxygen furnace? Sexy, undulating, organic, shape-shifting industrial steel. Hello? Ever hear of Richard Serra?"

He can still see the look in her eyes. Like he had just told the woman he married, the woman every other man wants to sleep with, the woman who chose him, that his hobby is pasting postage stamps into an album with tweezers. *Fucking moron.*

Victor senses he is no longer moving. He opens his eyes and looks down on himself from a great height, gazing down at his body strapped to an operating table. Daedalus and the scarecrow are cutting away his clothes, tossing them in a soiled heap inside a canvas hamper.

Victor realizes the bloody mess next to it is the gurney he arrived on when Daedalus gives it a violent shove, sending it rattling away to crash unseen into a distant wall. The scarecrow scuttles around the table with a pronounced limp. His left leg is badly deformed, as if the unbending limb beneath his trousers has been splinted with a pair of warped two-by-fours.

The industrial space where he lies in state has been converted into an operating theater of some sort. The makeshift surgery suite is equipped with a jumbled array of state-of-the-art and jury-rigged medical equipment: gooseneck lamps and magnifier lights, monitors, drills, sterilizers, face shields, instrument carts, and table clamps. Other machines, mysterious devices with articulating arms and swivel mounts, are woven into the array with a web of conduit and cables, binding it all together like the sinews of a flayed, mechanical corpse.

They are covering his bruised, swollen body with a sheet. Then, Victor sees the other body. Victor's disembodied form is lying on an operating table that has been arranged head-to-head with a second, adjoining operating table.

On the other table is a monstrous cadaver, or, more precisely, a monstrous figure fashioned from many different cadavers. The creature has been constructed around an armature of bone, stainless steel, cartilage, and muscle, with the entire assembly bolted together and reinforced with metal straps.

The chest cavity of the misshapen hulk is open and the heart—hooked up to a compact, jury-rigged heart/lung machine on a rolling cart—beats strongly. The difficulty encountered integrating so many diverse elements, so much dead meat, has resulted in a large and ungainly creature, and hydraulic systems assist in the movement of limbs where muscle and tendons no longer suffice.

The head, assembled from pieces of several skulls, is a twisted mass of bone, steel plate, composites, and flesh. The top of the skull is missing and the eye sockets are empty. Like the beast as a whole, it gives the impression of a man pieced haphazardly together from the torn limbs and twisted metal of a plane crash.

Daedalus is busy assembling a tent-like structure around the creature's head, as if preparing it for a surgical procedure, for some sort of brain surgery. The scarecrow is doing the same with the other body. His body.

The room begins to spin faster and faster. The floor below him revolves so fast it becomes a whirring blur as if he's been suspended over the blades of a helicopter. The churning rotors are rising toward him, threatening to annihilate him. The powerful blast of air preceding the seething vortex is warping and stretching the flesh of his face across his skull.

He shuts his eyes tight and turns his face away, but the impact never comes. Instead, Victor feels his body revolving, rapidly at first, then slower, as if he's been fastened to the turntable of a giant lathe that is powering down.

All motion stops. Victor opens his eyes to find himself back on the operating table. The agony is once again unbearable. He tries to focus on the face of Daedalus, looming over him, gazing directly into his eyes. He is not reassured to discover that Daedalus has the dead eyes of a sociopath.

"He's lost a great amount of blood. We must proceed immediately."

The scarecrow is preceded by the overpowering smell of his cologne, unctuous and sweet. He sounds troubled. "We've always worked with cadavers. This man is alive."

Victor tries to make them hear him, to hear the voice bellowing somewhere inside his skull.

Yes, I'm alive! I'm alive!

Daedalus fixes his colleague with a baleful stare. "Nothing is going to stop me. Not now. Do you understand?"

The younger man lowers his eyes and nods his assent.

The scarecrow is fastening a metal cage-like device over Victor's eyes. His mouth is close to Victor's ear as he fusses with a hinge bracket. He's talking to himself. "This is messed up, man. This is so messed up..."

Daedalus joins him. "Silence! How many times have I told you? It's distracting."

The scarecrow stifles and finishes his work on the apparatus. Both men hover over him now like humanoid blimps, their faces hidden behind surgical masks. Victor has found his voice. He's screaming, a banshee's wail. They must hear him now! They must realize he's still alive!

Victor realizes it's not him making the noise—it's the sound of a power tool, a drill. His mind reels in horror as the helix-shaped cutting edge of titanium and tungsten carbide bites into his flesh. He can feel each individual twist and channel in the rotating bit as it is driven into his skull.

Is this what it's like to be dead?

5

J ACK FIRES UP A fresh joint, flicks the match out the car window, and
sucks in a lungful of smoke. He exhales and leans back in the seat
to admire the sunrise. There's a crow on the peaked roof of a carriage
house across from where he's parked, looking down and side to side like
a preacher sizing up his congregation.

The shabby, tree-lined residential street is a ramshackle collection of
urban mansions with turrets, covered porches, wrought iron fences, and
carriage houses. Jack is parked in front of a boarded-up Tudor pile that is
slowly being smothered beneath a dense tangle of feral vines and shrubbery. The house directly across from Jack's parked car is surrounded by
an exoskeleton of scaffolding that seems to have rusted in place. The
plastic sheeting that once sealed the windows has been reduced by the
elements to flapping tassels with the consistency of wax paper.

Many of the other homes on the block are meticulously restored and
occupied. Across the street and several houses down is the blue and green
Victorian confection belonging to Marlene and Victor Moravian. To
Jack, it is yet another baffling choice by the factory owner. *Why would
an old money guy like him choose to be an urban homesteader in Indian
Village when he could afford a mansion in Grosse Pointe or Birmingham
with all the car guys? And if you are bound and determined to live within
the city limits, why not Sherwood Forest, with the Black surgeons, the
rich white do-gooders, the professional basketball players, and the crooked
politicians? Go fucking figure.*

Indian Village is one of the rare, semi-flourishing neighborhoods in Detroit's central city, a magnet for artists, urban pioneers, and home invaders. To Jack, it's all a mirage; your eyes are fooled by isolated streets like this. They are the green, leafy branches scattered across this massive decaying oak of a city. If you look closer, you'll see that the dead and dying limbs far outnumber the living. And the tree itself is rotten and hollow at the core, destined to collapse in some future storm, taking everyone and everything with it.

Jack studies the Moravian home more closely. He can't help but smirk when he spots the two white-faced lawn jockeys flanking the driveway. *Pure, fucking Marlene*, he thinks. He'd love to have seen Victor's face when she brought those puppies home.

Several lights downstairs have been on all night, but otherwise, there's been no discernible movement. *Maybe she's not even there? But where else would she go? Who would she go to?*

Jack remembers when he was the one she would go to, when he was the one she chose. He remembers when they were young, when she'd show up with her hair gathered and tied on top of her head in soft, gravity-defying coils, like some slightly deranged Motown princess. And he remembers what it was like to be with her, the warm, everything-is-possible energy she radiated. That feeling of complete acceptance that enveloped you when you were with her, as if nothing you could ever say or do could possibly be wrong.

And then there were the bad times. With Marlene, there were always the bad times. It would come on suddenly, like a cloud passing over the sun, and then by god, you'd be in for it. But when those clouds parted, when she looked at you, when she saw you, when she really saw you, and then she smiled, it was like a drug. It was like the Big Fat Fuck used to say, something he saw on one of his TV documentaries, something called "intermittent reward."

COUNTED WITH THE DEAD

They'd give these rats in some lab a piece of cheese every time they went through a maze. Then, they'd give these other rats a piece of cheese only sometimes when they finished the maze. The rats that never knew when they'd get the reward, they were a thousand times more fired up to go through that fucking maze than the ones that always got the cheese. *At least that's what the Big Fat Fuck said. Even he was right once in a while. Sometimes, something in that constant stream of bullshit actually made sense. Sure seems like he nailed it with Marlene.*

The rearview mirror reveals Marty's ten-year-old Monte Carlo, looking like it just rolled off the dealership lot, pulling up behind Jack's car. Jack carefully stubs out the joint and slips it into his shirt pocket. He gets out, walks around to the passenger side, opens the door, and slides in beside his brother.

The Killeen brothers are a pair of mismatched mongrels with the same father but different mothers. Marty has black hair and olive skin. He's built like a vending machine and his leather coat is stretched across his bulk like the upholstery on a sofa. A tight, oval mouth punctures the lower part of his flat, rectangular slab of a face like the drain hole in a tub. The early Christians would have encountered guys that looked like him in the Colosseum. Given the choice, they probably went with the lions.

Jack is tall and fair-skinned. His lean, muscular build is the product of generations of digging peat, stoking furnaces, and manhandling sheet metal on assembly lines. Not that Jack has ever done any of those things himself. The thin smile, with just a hint of cruelty, seems out of place on his open, honest face. Until you look into his eyes. Those eyes—blue-gray, hard, and clear as ice—have seen things you don't want to know about.

Marty has come straight from third shift. Jack grabs a lunchbox the size of a piece of luggage off the seat and starts to put it in the back. Marty stops him with a look. "Your mail..."

Jack opens the lunchbox to find his mail inside, neatly bundled with crisscrossing rubber bands.

"Bills mostly."

Jack nods and stuffs the packet of mail into his jacket. Then he sets the lunchbox on the back seat. Turning back, he realizes Marty is still watching him.

"What?"

"You're welcome."

"For fuck's sake, I'll get a PO Box, alright?"

Marty turns and looks straight ahead. "I don't care. It's just..." He sees Jack re-lighting the joint. "I asked you not to smoke in my car."

Jack goes to snuff the joint out in the ashtray, but it's polished like a piece of fine jewelry. He tosses it out the window instead.

Marty's hands are gripping the steering wheel. He tilts his head in the direction of the Moravian home. His voice is flat. "That her house?"

"Yeah, I got something I need to do. Won't take long."

They sit in tense silence, until Jack decides he's had enough. "Spit it out already."

Marty reacts with the fury of a dog hitting the end of its chain. "What the fuck, Jack? We were fucking done with this."

Jack glares at his brother. "You are done. This is on me."

Marty gestures to indicate his surroundings. "I'm sitting here in my goddamned car, at the goddamned crack of dawn..." He glares, wide-eyed, at Jack. "Do I look like I'm fucking out of it?"

Jack slouches down in the seat like an angry child. "I didn't have a fucking choice."

"The fuck you didn't. You been saying no to that son of a bitch for two fucking years. You were done with it. We were done with it."

Jack straightens up. There is a dangerous edge to his voice. "I. Didn't. Have. A. Fucking. Choice. Alright?"

Marty grips the wheel and stares straight ahead. Jack's voice is barely a whisper. "You want I should get somebody else?"

"You haven't got nobody else."

Jack pulls a .38 revolver out of his pocket and holds it out for his brother. Marty looks at it with disdain. "What do I need that for?"

Jack has the barest hint of a grin. "Cockroaches."

Marty's not smiling. "Put it in the glove box."

Jack opens the glove compartment—it's as neatly organized as a NASA first aid kit. He slips the gun inside and shuts it. He nods in the direction of Jefferson Boulevard. "There's a payphone on the corner."

Marty pulls a small Nokia cell phone out of his pocket. It looks like a child's toy in his massive paw. He's clearly enamored with his new purchase. "Already got your number programmed."

Jack is not impressed. "You'll fucking lose that thing in a week. I'll lay money on it."

Marty ignores him and admires the little device in his hand. "Prepaid. I can toss it and buy another one any time I want. And nobody'll be the wiser."

"How the fuck am I supposed to call you?"

Marty, irked, slips the phone back into his pocket. "Same as on the damn payphone: I send the number to your pager, you dial it."

Jack cracks the door and Marty gives him a hard look. "Let her go, Jack. You can't protect her anymore. Not now. Let them fucking have her."

Jack glares at his brother. "Just watch the fucking house." He tilts his head in the direction of the Moravian home. "That motherfucking house; that's your fucking HBO. Got it?"

He closes the door softly on his way out.

6

MARLENE IS SITTING BY the kitchen window in the dark. Her gaze is fixed on the empty spot in the driveway, under the overhang where carriages once unloaded, where Victor's Saab is supposed to be. *What kind of an idiot drives a Saab? In Detroit? A fucking convertible, no less?*

She remembers her father's stories from the auto plants, how foreign cars in the employee lots were keyed and had their tires slashed. Victor owns the company and has his own parking spot. *Even so, there'd been times... For Christ's sake, half his business is with the car guys.*

Marlene used to cherish these solitary interludes before the day begins. It was her daily ritual to sit here drinking coffee from a heavy mug, basking catlike in the security of familiar household objects and the almost sacramental sense of quiet.

She grimaces, remembering her annoyance when Victor started making an effort to come down earlier, just so he could spend more time with her, interrupting her treasured morning routine. God, how she would welcome him blundering in now.

It had taken her a long time to understand how different Victor was from the others. She'd hated the oafish boyishness of the men she'd known before him. To them, she was nothing but a fucking piñata, an interactive sex toy in a game of pin the tail on the donkey. All they cared about was shoving their cocks in her mouth, her cunt, her asshole, any available orifice.

Victor's was a different sort of boyishness. He wanted to please her. He needed to please her. And he seemed to expect nothing in return. For so long she had scorned him as weak before she realized the real problem was her own stupidity, her inability to judge him on his terms instead of measuring him against the others.

No one knew the state she was in when Victor found her. No one knew what he had done for her, and what he had endured from her. In the beginning, she would exhaust herself attempting to penetrate his reserve, to goad him, to humiliate him, to drive him away. But she'd met her match. Nothing penetrated his calm, easy, entitled confidence. Nothing she could do, or not do, could make him go away.

All she wants now is to sit with her knee resting against his, to feel their shoulders touching, to not speak, to just be with him.

On their first date, Victor took her to see a foreign film at the art museum. Born and raised in Detroit, she'd never set foot in the Detroit Institute of Arts. She didn't even know they had a movie theater. She decided to be a good sport—she didn't even say anything about the subtitles. *Hell, Victor was driving a 'Vette in those days.*

Afterward, the only place they could find open on that stretch of Woodward Avenue was this goofy little place called The Gnome. Following dinner, Marlene made a blind stab at sophistication and ordered a Greek coffee with dessert. The waiter grimly informed her they were Turks. She didn't get the distinction. *Besides, since when was a place named after some sort of a fucking mythical midget troll creature considered some kind of ethnic?*

Victor smoothed it over. He had the waiter laughing till tears rimmed his eyes. Afterward, over drinks at a nearby bar, at a place called the Traffic Jam that Victor assured her was in no way related to any particular ethnicity, they giddily discussed the baggage each of them brought to a potential relationship.

Marlene warned him that the baggage she carried into a relationship was like one of those big-ass steamer trunks you see in the old movies.

Victor, refusing to be outdone, described his own baggage as the equivalent of the Titanic, welded to the Lusitania to make the world's biggest pontoon boat, with the Enola Gay strapped to the deck and towing Three Mile Island and Chernobyl behind it on barges. With complete sincerity, he assured her, "I've got some fucking baggage, girl."

She didn't get even half of the references he was making, but the words "fucking" and "girl" sounded ridiculous coming out of his mouth and they laughed. She was beginning to like this guy despite everything. It wasn't as if she hadn't been with white guys before—fucking Jack—but this was one very white guy.

Marlene is suddenly overcome by a wave of nausea. She grips the seat of the chair with both hands until it passes. She attempts to drown out the voice in her head by repeating the litany she's been chanting all night: "Victor is coming back. Victor is coming home. Victor is coming back to me."

Marlene looks up at the clock on the wall. It's almost seven. In another hour she can start making calls again. If only she knew who else to call. She'd kept making calls late into the night, until she got nothing but endless unanswered rings or answering machines. She called everyone she could think of but the most obvious, the police. Victor had told her not to go to the police no matter what happened; he was working things out. He had gripped her shoulders so hard it hurt. He was angry with her for even bringing it up. He never spoke to her like that. It frightened her at the time; it was a side of him she'd never seen before. Well, almost never. He was working things out. The worst thing she could do was call the cops. *Fuck. Fuck him. Why did he have to go and do this? Why now?*

Outside, kids are walking by on their way to the bus on Jefferson. She doesn't know any of them. They're all Black and, aside from her, no one Black, or with kids, lives on this block. The children move past singly, in conspiratorial pairs, in bunches, a thin meandering stream, like the crows flying overhead at dusk, coming from, or returning to, wherever the fuck it is they go to.

The last kid jogs past the house in an effort to catch up with friends. Marlene tries to think of a friend to call. She doesn't have any friends. Marlene has always left people behind. Not on purpose, not by design, it's just that, somehow, each chapter in her life happens to contain new people. Grammar school, middle school, high school, college, nursing school, jobs, relationships, the street—her world has always been that way.

She has moved through life as if she was traversing a towering sky-scraper. Each new chapter has taken her to a different floor. And each subsequent level has had no connection to any of the previous ones. No one, no friend, no lover, no coworker accompanied her when she moved on. Always alone. Always closing the door firmly behind her. You get off the elevator and it's all new, all fresh. Everyone else is in the past, gone. *Except for Jack. Fucking Jack.*

Victor's people accepted her, but that's as far as it went. She was accorded a certain degree of respect due to her husband, to her last name. She was a respected junior partner, but she didn't belong. She wasn't expected to speak at their level, to know about things like art and music. No one embarrassed her, at least not on purpose, and never in front of Victor. No one asked where she'd gone to school. No one asked her about her family, foreign travel, fashion, books, politics. And that was fine with her. That would be just fine until it was time to go, time to move on. But this time she doesn't want to go. She doesn't want to move on.

Suddenly, a snorting laugh bursts from her lips as she flashes on the image of Victor and his brothers and his cousins and their wives and girlfriends at that wedding—the one out in Sterling Heights. *Doing that stupid ass dance... What did they call it? The chicken dance. Victor was off the hook!* He was grinning and tripping, all spastic and goo-goo eyed, like some dorky, supersize Vanilla Ice, making her laugh so hard she had to grab on to her bitch-ass sister-in-law to keep from falling over.

Marlene lurches to her feet, stumbles to the sink, and spews undigested peas and chunks from last night's chicken pot pie all over the dirty dishes in the basin. She stands there, hands gripping the counter, head down in the sink, wiping her mouth with the back of her hand.

Victor isn't coming back.

7

Father Paul is feeling rather melancholy. The scent of his last penitent, a stale, cloying stew of powdered lilac and mothballs, still permeates the air, stirring memories of his grandparents' house on Marlborough Street. As a small boy, his grandparents' decaying east side home had filled him with dread each time he entered. The dark wood paneling, the ponderous furniture, even the drapery, possessed the oppressive weight of a world cast in lead. To his young eyes, it was a massive, airless mausoleum poised to sink under its own weight into the dark earth, like a stone dropped into a marsh.

Father Paul imagines his confessional as a tiny capsule, which the weight of countless sins has compressed into an impossibly dense, dark matter projectile. Some fine day, one final penitent, one final insult against God, against reason, will tip the scales and the incalculable weight of his confessional will punch through the floorboards, through the cellar, through the concrete foundations of the church, through the very crust of the earth: a plummeting, impenetrable cage bearing him to the planet's fiery core.

The priest holds his wristwatch close to the light leaking through the curtained doorway and realizes he has twenty more minutes of this to endure. The usual group of babushkas was already here when he arrived, bunched together in the two pews closest to the confessional, the jury waiting patiently for the court to be called into session. Thank God there were no therapy sessions today—just the usual old ladies with their laundry lists of trivialities and torment—and he was able to dispose of them in less than an hour.

The priest knows his clientele well. The keys to success are patience, an absolute refusal to judge and, critically, the careful calibration of penance. Too much, and you're rewarded with a put-upon sigh followed by the penitent's sudden need to share her fond memories of your predecessor. Too little, and they question if you've been paying attention. It's been years since anyone has questioned Father Paul.

Father Paul suddenly remembers that Rita is warming up the baked ziti for lunch. He is reaching over to turn off the penitent light when he hears the slow, muffled sweep of the imposing church door swinging open. He hesitates, gripping the smooth metal toggle between thumb and forefinger as he listens to the sound of the inner door opening, followed by the echoing plonk of footsteps on tile, turning into the side aisle and approaching the confessional.

These are clearly the footsteps of a man moving at a steady pace, a man who is not supported by a walker or tapping away at the tile floor with a cane. A man who is not even shuffling. *A new parishioner?*

Father Paul releases the switch and settles back onto his bench. He looks to Jesus, nailed to his wee cross and gazing pensively down from the wall. Father Paul winks.

"Relax, I've got this one."

The unseen man's pace slackens as he nears the confessional. When he is several feet away he stops and Father Paul begins to regret his benevolence. Then, with the sound of leather scraping tile, the man's shoes rotate tentatively in place and Father Paul grows hopeful. *Maybe he will turn around and leave? Maybe Rita's made that lovely antipasto salad of hers? Maybe...*

The wooden superstructure of the confessional trembles as the penitent settles onto the kneeler in the adjoining cubicle. The priest slides open a small wood panel to reveal the screened window that allows him to communicate with the penitent in whispered anonymity. He can make out the vague outline of his visitor. He's tall, possibly young, at least younger than the typical occupant of that seat.

The man leans close until his forehead is pressed up against the screen. He does not speak.

Father Paul is thinking about that antipasto salad. "Let's have it, son. I'm all ears."

The man speaks in a gruff whisper. "I'd like to make my confession, Father."

The man lapses back into silence. Father Paul utters an encouraging grunt and the penitent reacts like an actor to his cue.

"My last confession was, I don't know, does it really fucking matter?" Realizing his mistake, he quickly backpedals. "Sorry, Father. It must have been about twenty years ago. More... I don't know... Twenty-five, maybe?"

Father Paul has already pegged this penitent: he is clearly unaccustomed to finding himself on the subservient end of any interaction. He's making an effort to sound contrite, or at least reasonable, but is struggling to temper the arrogance and the sense of menace required to navigate his day-to-day world. The priest knows the type well. Men like this are the reason he no longer hears confession at the annual retreat for senior executives at General Motors.

Father Paul makes no effort to conceal his impatience. "Yes, go on."

"I'm sorry, Father, I don't really know how to start."

Father Paul reaches over and turns off the penitent light to discourage any other stragglers. He laces his fingers behind his neck, arches his back, and exhales.

"After twenty-some years I don't doubt it. Why don't we start with the really big ones and work our way down?"

The penitent's voice is cold, matter of fact. "I just killed a man, Father."

Father Paul is suddenly attentive. His hands move cautiously from the back of his neck to his lap, as if any sudden move will place him in jeopardy.

"More than one, Father. There were others. Seven. Maybe eight."

Father Paul manages to stop himself from repeating the word "Maybe?"

There is another long pause, as if each word is being laboriously excavated from a dark place. "I didn't know the men I killed. I didn't have beef with them. It was just..." He sighs. "It was just a piece of work."

The penitent takes an even longer pause. He's working hard, trying to find a way to polish this massive turd he's dumped into Father Paul's confessional. "What I mean is, the way I always looked at it, it wasn't me pulling the trigger; it was the guy who hired me. I was just the tool he used. You know, like a guy picking up a hammer and pounding a nail."

His voice reflects the confidence of a man who is convinced of the unassailable logic of his argument. "If I didn't do the job, they'd get somebody else. Right? Any way you look at it, the guy'd still be dead. Am I right?"

Father Paul is beginning to regret turning off the penitent light. It would be nice to know there was someone else in the church, even if it was one of his babushkas. He looks to the cross for succor, but the tiny, crucified Jesus averts his gaze. The priest decides to go it alone. "Why are you here?"

The man seems unsure. "For confession, Father. To get your absolution."

Father Paul persists, "But why? Why now? We're not talking impure thoughts here. You didn't hit a car in the parking lot and fail to leave a note."

The man's voice is an angry hiss. "Because I'm supposed to be here. Because I've had it beaten into my head my entire fucking life that I'm supposed to do this, that I'm supposed to feel bad, to feel regret."

Father Paul allows himself the slightest glimmer of hope. "So something has changed? Now you feel something?"

"Now I want to feel something," the penitent says. "I'm done with it, Father. I'm fucking done with it. I told the man to his face I was done with this."

The penitent shifts in his seat and Father Paul thinks he might be leaving. Then he leans into the screen again. "I made my confession, Father. You have to give me your absolution."

Father Paul Mayhew, pastor of St. Stanislaus, bureaucrat, janitor, minister, arbiter of petty disputes, peerless funerary orator, comes to a sudden, startling realization: he is not a coward. The words come out in an urgent hiss. "Bullshit. This is bullshit. You can't dump this on me and walk away without doing something, without at least taking responsibility for what you've done."

The man lurches to his feet. Through the screen that separates them, Father Paul makes out the outline of the man holding the curtained doorway to his cubicle open, poised between attack and flight. In the long, oppressive silence that follows, Father Paul fondly recalls the image of his cubicle plunging deep into the earth. Forcing himself to confront more relevant matters, he tries to remember if he deleted those awful pictures from his computer. *I did, I absolutely did*, he assures himself. *And*, he thinks ruefully, *I'm wearing clean underwear.*

Leaning forward in his seat, Father Paul is impressed by the steadiness of his own voice. "Tell me why you're here, son. Now. Today. After all this time."

The man hesitates before returning to the kneeler with the force of a linebacker pouncing on a fumble. The words come tumbling out. "The last time was different. The man I was hired to kill—I had a thing; I was in love with his wife. I've always been in love with her." His voice softens. "I hadn't seen her in years. Then her husband got mixed up with the people I work for. Used to work for." A note of petulance creeps into his voice.

"She came to me. She fucking came to me. That's how I got mixed up in it. That's how I got back in..."

His voice trails off. Father Paul, uncertain of his ability to produce words in this moment even if he wanted to, waits him out.

"When I did the job, it was just like the others: a piece of work. Until I looked into his eyes. Then I knew. I fucking knew. I wanted that motherfucker dead. Not somebody else. Not the people I work for. Me."

Father Paul instinctively crosses himself, but it is a feeble talisman against the ferocity in the man's voice.

"I wanted him dead because I wanted her. I was responsible."

Father Paul finally finds his words. "Oh my dear God."

The man's voice has grown cold, an impatient diner demanding the check. "I'm sorry for these and all the sins of my past..." He turns dismissive. "I don't remember the rest, how it goes."

Father Paul is silent. His revulsion for this penitent is at war with his duty to uphold the church's doctrine of forgiveness.

"Father?"

The priest's voice is trembling. "If God Almighty in His infinite mercy could forgive the thief on the cross..." He is suddenly, passionately angry. "But he was a thief! Not a cold-blooded killer. And you have done nothing, nothing, to atone for the horrors you have committed."

The man's thin veneer of civility evaporates. "I should have fucking known, coming to a man who's never even been in sniffing distance of a pussy. What the fuck do you know about these things?"

Father Paul decides to turn the other cheek. "I'm... I'm sorry. I think, I think you should go now."

The man on the other side of the screen is an aggrieved shopper about to call for the manager. "I've made my confession, Father. You have to give me your absolution."

Father Paul grabs the sliding wood panel. In his panic, it takes both hands and several stuttering false starts for him to pull it shut. He realizes the futility of his gesture when his antagonist stands and exits the adjoining cubicle. The priest settles back in his seat and braces himself for the bullet or the body he expects to come hurtling through the curtained doorway.

Nothing happens. The man remains motionless outside the confessional. This time, it is Father Paul who can no longer endure the silence. "Please, don't ask me to do this. Not with the blood still on your hands. Please..."

The man starts to walk away. Father Paul calls out to him. "Wait."

The man stops.

"When you're ready... I'll be here."

Father Paul listens as the footsteps move up the side aisle and across to the center interior door. A moment later he hears the dull thump of the heavy outside door falling shut. Then silence.

Father Paul grabs the doorway curtain and uses it to lever himself to his feet. He trips over the threshold on the way out and crashes to the hard tile floor of the side aisle. He grips the edge of a pew and pulls himself to his knees to look around. The church is empty.

8

VICTOR CAN FEEL THE pleasing weight of Marlene's body on his, her head nested into his shoulder. Eyes shut, he methodically explores her naked form, cupped hands moving in slow, sensual counterpoint as he imagines himself a blind cartographer, carefully tracking the soft contours of flesh from her calves to her shoulder blades.

Pity, she's asleep, he thinks. No, she moves, rising up on her knees, her shoulder pressing against his, the fleeting warmth of her breath on his neck. Her entire body surges forward, urgent. Her hips, struggling against his grip in her eagerness, slide smoothly through his hands like two snug brackets. The velvety softness of her breasts skims his chest and gently grazes his face. He kisses them in passing, then her stomach and the solid ridge of her pelvis. His hands move hungrily over the taut curvature of her legs, hips, and buttocks, his hands gripping the firm, arcing contours of her flanks, guiding her—

Her flesh suddenly gives way, muscle, bone, and tendon collapsing under the pressure of his grip like a block of Styrofoam in a vice. Her body is crumbling in his hands, disintegrating in the face of an unseen nuclear firestorm. He struggles to grasp the scattered, tumbling spray of tissue before it dissipates but it is like tackling smoke. He opens his eyes and is immediately engulfed in an explosive, searing flash of blinding light.

Victor's terror slowly recedes as he begins to realize it was all a bad dream. He attempts to rise and finds himself strapped to the operating table with a sheet drawn up to his chin. His head is wrapped in bandages with an opening for his nostrils and a slit for his eyes that is covered with a pair of lightly tinted goggles.

He struggles against the restraints and the sheet falls away from his body. He can see his reflection in the polished metal of an overhead fixture. It's not his body lying on the table; it's the monstrous cadaver that occupied the adjoining table in his nightmare.

He turns to look at that other table and sees his lifeless form covered with a sheet. The monitors recording the vital signs are silent. From the way the sheet falls across the back of the head, it is apparent that a large part of the skull is missing. Horrified, Victor realizes he is seeing the world through the eyes of the creature from his nightmare.

Then, two men in surgical masks hover over him. Daedalus holds a needle-like probe aloft while he studies the image of Victor's brain on a nearby monitor. The scarecrow works the controls of a device that sends massive jolts of power to the probe in the doctor's hand.

The scarecrow is on the verge of panic. "No one's ever done this before. You said yourself: we don't know what damage this might do to the reasoning center. It could be catastrophic."

Daedalus turns to his colleague. "DeRon, look at me."

The scarecrow eyes his master like a chastened dog. "Yes, Professor."

Daedalus's voice is all cold precision. "I will not risk losing him. Do you understand?"

The scarecrow nods.

"Good. He will have no desire to escape if he does not remember what he has lost. Now, do as I say: execute."

Victor attempts to follow Daedalus with his eyes as he moves in close, preparing to insert the probe into the side of his misshapen skull. The scarecrow reluctantly engages a lever and Victor feels the probe slice through bone and tissue as it is driven into his skull. The pain is excruciating but Victor is unable to cry out. He does not even know if he has a mouth to scream with.

He shuts his eyes tight and wills himself to awaken from this nightmare. He tries to focus on Marlene. He concentrates until he is able to see her. She is moving closer. Smiling. Arms open wide in welcome. He can almost touch her...

No... Wait... What? She is with that man... Jack. Her smile is for him. Her arms are open wide... For Jack...

Jack Killeen.

Suddenly, in an explosive, shrieking, sickening rush, Victor feels his entire body collapsing in on itself. He has become a tiny meat planet sucked into an even smaller black hole. Every fiber, every muscle, every inch of flesh is twisting and contorting in agony. His bones are being broken, shattered, and pulverized into dust as they are dragged through an opening the size of a keyhole.

Then, mercifully, nothing.

9

J ACK GRINDS THE REMNANTS of the joint into the ashtray. He's sitting with his back against the door, legs stretched out across the front seat of his car. He pushes the ashtray lid shut and straightens up for a better view of the house. Her car is out front: she's in there. Maybe she's looking out a window, looking for Victor, wondering when—if—he's coming home. Maybe she's thinking about him. Probably wishing she'd never met him, wishing he'd stayed away. But he never could stay away.

He remembers driving through an exotic winter landscape of suburban cul-de-sacs north of Detroit. The big, boxy homes with their vast, snowy lawns and decorative lampposts felt strangely insubstantial, as if they were cruising through a life-size department store Christmas village.

It was Seedy's car, so he was driving. Jack was riding shotgun. Marty and Calvin were in the back seat. Jack, Marty, and Seedy had hair down to their shoulders. Calvin's hair was decked out in disco-era jerry curls, which made him as much a pariah in the neighborhood as did his white friends. They all wore steel-toed boots, jeans, and army surplus fatigue jackets. They all had box cutters. Calvin liked to keep a metal pipe stuffed down his boot and up under his pant leg. Sometimes, closer to home, Blacks from the Jeffries projects would mistake them for hippies, pegging them as a soft touch. "Hey, give me some weed, bro. Hey mothafucker, you deaf? I said give me some fucking weed." That didn't always end well.

They found the address listed on the xeroxed flier. Bob Seger's "Turn the Page" was blasting through the car speakers, the sullen fury of the lyrics stoking their inchoate sense of alienation.

They were ready to explode. Not for any particular reason, but because they were young, and horny, and broke, and angry at the fucking world.

Earlier in the day, they'd stolen some random boxes off an unattended delivery van. One of the cartons contained a shipment of Afro wigs intended for a beauty parlor. They'd spent the afternoon in Seedy's basement smoking dope and drinking 40s while giddily modeling the wigs and miming the Jackson 5.

Now, no longer concerned that some frightened suburban cop would spot their silhouettes and call in the National Guard, they put the wigs back on and piled out of the car.

The living room was full of white, suburban, high school kids with razor cuts, jocks with letter sweaters, and cheerleaders in pleated skirts. Someone shouted something about Halloween being over but quickly stifled under the glare of the hard-eyed quartet from Detroit, at once imposing, and jarringly alien, in the misshapen wigs.

Jack spotted Marlene in an adjoining room, making out, perched on the lap of the only other Black kid in the house, a clean-cut jock in a letter sweater. Marlene glanced in their direction and went right back to sucking face, dismissing Jack as if he was some kid delivering pizza. A glowering, puffed up kid with a thick neck and a varsity jacket got in Jack's face. He told them to leave. Jack sneered and the jock struck a pose, like some old-timey boxer on the back of a cereal box.

Jack grabbed the lamp off the table next to him, jerking the plug from the wall and flinging away the shade in one violent motion. The heavy metal base felt good in his hands as he swung it like a baseball bat. The impact on the boy's skull, of metal on bone, was thrilling. And there was blood, a lot of blood. Head wounds always did that. And people were always freaked out by the blood. They screamed. They jerked around like spastics. And they did nothing constructive.

One guy though, a beefy lineman, had better instincts than most. He charged Jack, but Marty, moving impressively fast for a guy his size, body-slammed him into the wall. Jack picked up the end table and whacked the downed lineman across the head a few times for good measure.

Calvin had the steel bar out. Seedy was blocking the door with a box cutter. Some blonde girl was screaming at Jack now, her face contorted, all incomprehensible noise. A lanky, mop-haired kid in a necktie approached him, arms outstretched in the universal language of the peacemaker. He was saying something about "being cool." Jack gripped the end table by two legs and smacked him across the face with it. The boy, his nose a bloody wreck, stared at Jack like a stunned slaughterhouse steer before sinking to his knees.

Jack was in his element. He felt good, he felt solid. He wanted more. He was invincible. He wanted to take on all comers. He wanted to see ten, twenty, a hundred bodies hurling themselves at him.

Then he saw that the chair Marlene and her boyfriend had occupied was empty. Calvin was screaming something about the cops. Marty was bum-rushing him to the door. Outside, Seedy had pulled the car up onto the lawn. Both passenger side doors open wide, flopping on their hinges.

They piled into the car and Seedy took off, tires spinning, flinging divots of snow and sod, and almost ran her down. The front bumper was right up against her legs, and she had to lean forward, gloved palms on the hood, to keep from falling.

Everyone in the car was screaming bloody murder, everyone but Jack, as Marlene calmly straightened up, brushed the snow from her coat, and walked around to the passenger door. Jack opened the door to let her in. He wouldn't slide over so she climbed onto his lap. She ripped the Afro wig off his head and threw it into the back seat. "You're such a fucking asshole."

Seedy floored it and the car's momentum swung the door shut.

Jack glances in the mirror to see Marty's Monte Carlo approaching. He swings his legs off the seat and settles in behind the wheel. He starts the car, pulls forward, and makes a U-turn as Marty glides to a stop at the curb.

Jack pulls up alongside and Marty rolls down his window. "We can't keep meeting like this. People will talk."

Jack ignores him. Marty reaches into the back seat for his thermos. "It's been over a week. Nothings gonna happen."

"What do you care? You're on hiatus. Collecting a paycheck for sitting on your ass all day."

Marty starts to crank up his window. "Says the man who never collected an honest paycheck in his fucking life."

Jack drives away without another word.

10

H EAD DOWN, LIMPING AND in pain, DeRon allows the leashed dog to pull him up the gentle slope of the driveway to the house. His fist is wrapped around the bundle of keys on the retractable chain attached to his belt. His fingers are gripping the house key.

Reaching the front door he releases the deadbolt. Before he can get the key out of the lock the German shepherd, O'Jay, pushes past him and inside. DeRon unhooks the straining dog from the leash before accepting the enthusiastic greetings of one of his other roommates, Babyface, an elderly, short-legged mutt that could be a cross between a dachshund and a potbelly pig. Gladys, a slender black cat, dodges Babyface to glide between DeRon's legs. A second cat, a big orange tom named Marvin, is curled up on the couch, feigning indifference.

DeRon secures the deadbolt and tosses his jacket over the back of a chair. He lives in a state of perpetual chaos and every available surface is covered with the detritus of his avocations: mechanical and electrical engineering books, science magazines, technical manuals, soldering irons, circuit boards and computer chips, socket wrench sets, dog-eared crossword puzzle books, computer monitors, and music CD's.

He goes to the kitchen and takes a frozen dinner out of the freezer. A Hello Kitty refrigerator magnet falls to the floor as he shuts the freezer door and DeRon stares at it. His leg is a pulsating bundle of agony, and he is helpless to pick it up. He sighs, gives Hello Kitty one final mournful glance, "Welcome to your new home," and turns away. He hobbles to the stove, sets the oven timer, and shoves the TV dinner inside. Responding to an urgent whine, he goes to the back door to let Babyface out.

Before releasing the heavy chain lock and the deadbolt he grabs the .22 rifle leaning against the wall. He opens the door and Babyface scurries out to do his business in the tall grass. A decade and a half earlier, DeRon's tidy bungalow had been nestled in the middle of a cluster of small brick homes bordering an industrial zone of machine shops and repair garages. Now, as the only remaining structure on the block, it's been transformed into the Little House on the Prairie. But this little house has bars on the windows. And the prairie consists of a sea of vacant lots peppered with clumps of junk trees, the weathered foundations of demolished homes, and the burned-out carcasses of abandoned cars.

The gun nestled in his arms gives DeRon a rare sense of authority as he leans against the doorframe, scanning the darkness beyond the fenced yard for packs of wild dogs. Around him, outside the barbwire-topped chain-link fence, beyond the sea of vacant lots, are the twinkling dots and constellations of light marking the other isolated homes and settlements of Detroit's east side. On clear nights when the stars come out, he likes to imagine his little home as a lonely outpost on a meteor-scarred asteroid.

Babyface scurries back inside the house but DeRon remains outside. Directly behind his home is the dark hulk of a refrigerated truck trailer with a generator running, a generator that can never be allowed to stop, a generator that provides the relentless, 24/7 soundtrack to the nightmare he is living.

In the beginning, the Professor's angry vision had seemed to mesh seamlessly with DeRon's own dark forebodings. Since childhood, DeRon had imagined a murky cloud mantle encircling the globe. Each act of violence, every killing, every hanged cat, every beating, every slap to the face or hurt feeling, added to the density of this poisonous, black vapor that was slowly, relentlessly, smothering life on earth. The deadly process had been ongoing for thousands of years but was now accelerating at a dangerous pace. Only an act of fierce, terrible violence; a blast of unfathomable savagery could generate a countervailing force with the power to shatter this noxious shell. *And only the Professor has the capability to...*

DeRon finds himself shaking his head. No. He's not so sure anymore. He has exhausted his anger. The blind, mindless rage is gone. He doesn't hate other people now. He doesn't even hate his own existence anymore. Well, at least not the part he spends with his four-legged tribe. The rage has withered away to desperation, to need—he desperately needs to be fixed. He would happily settle for being like everyone else. Even kind of, sort of, like everyone else. *If only the Professor would do what he has promised so many times...*

If only.

DeRon pulls a five-gallon gas can from behind the cinderblocks that prop up one end of the trailer. He sorts through the keys on the ring and opens the padlock securing the trailer door. He allows the dense clump of keys to slither back to his belt and stands motionless in the darkness. Then, finally, he wills himself to go inside.

Afterward, after hunching beneath the shower for a long time to wash away the smell of the lab and the memory of the trailer, he returns to the living room. The other residents of this peaceable kingdom are already gathered, waiting as DeRon sinks into the lumpy couch. Around him, everything is in its place. Arrayed on a side table to his immediate right and the coffee table in front, within easy reach, are his TV dinner, a malt liquor, the remote for the stereo, the TV remote, the new Mechanics Illustrated, the phone, the CDs and the mix-tapes—X Clan, Dr. Dre, Public Enemy—and, of course, his meds.

DeRon props his legs up on the coffee table. On cue, the German shepherd tunnels beneath them and collapses to the carpet with a sigh. Babyface clambers onto the couch and snuggles up against DeRon's hip. Gladys stretches out on the back of the couch, pressed against his shoulders like a furry black headrest. Marvin, his favorite, sits on the coffee table and glares at DeRon.

"Right, sorry..."

DeRon pulls the thin blanket out from beneath the dead weight of the already sleeping Babyface. He carefully drapes it across his knees, creating a proper perch in the hollow between his good leg and the damaged one. Marvin executes a surprisingly dainty leap from table to lap and curls up, already purring.

DeRon smiles and reaches for the stereo remote.

The phone rings. Only one person ever calls him. He doesn't want to answer it. He knows that is not an option.

11

JACK IS WELDED TO the front passenger seat of the cherry red 2000 Ford Mustang. He knows he needs to get up. If he stays where he is, if he allows his eyes to close, he will fall into an exhausted slumber. Through the windshield he can see that Rhonda and his daughter Monica are heavily engaged. The salesman in the plaid sports coat attempts to interject but quickly backs away, hands raised in surrender, momentarily content to be a bystander.

Rhonda, her blonde good looks hardening into middle age, looks exhausted as she argues with their daughter. Monica—*Jesus, can she really be sixteen already?*—debates her mother with the stubborn entitlement of a teenager. The salesman, pushed completely out of the orbit of the arguing mother and daughter, moves hopefully toward the Mustang's open window. "Whaddaya think, chief?"

He is forced to backpedal out of harm's way when Jack flings the car door open. He ignores the salesman and strides over to his daughter.

"This is way too much car for you, Monica. You just touch the pedal on this bomb and it takes off like a damn rocket."

Monica is indignant. "Dad! You didn't even give me a chance. We didn't even go on the freeway."

The salesman attempts to reassert his relevance. "I'm sure the young lady has a light touch on the pedal."

Jack responds angrily. "Who you tryin' to bullshit? She's a kid. Any kid's gonna put their foot through the floor in a bomb like this."

The salesman beats a tactical retreat while Rhonda steps between Jack and his daughter.

"She doesn't need a car—she hasn't even got her license yet. What she needs is braces. And clothes for school." She gestures back to the Mustang. "She's only sixteen. I never had a new car my whole life."

Monica, ignoring her mom, continues to work her dad. "I got my learner's permit. I need a car to drive."

Jack tries his most honeyed tone with his ex. "C'mon, I had my own car when I was her age."

She's not having it. "You were stealing cars when you were twelve."

Jack glares at Rhonda but speaks to Monica. "Go look at that car over there."

Monica glances over to the car in question, then turns to her dad pouting. "But I don't like the Escort."

Jack is still in a stare-down with her mom. "I said go look."

Monica slouches over to the Escort. Rhonda moves to stay between Jack and their retreating daughter, arms crossed defiantly across her chest. Her gaze holds Jack in place as they wait for Monica to move out of earshot. There's a lot of history in those eyes, pent up, angry, smoldering history.

Jack's voice softens. "C'mon, gimme a break. I'm just trying to do something nice for my little girl."

Rhonda is unmoved. "And I'm trying to teach her to be responsible."

"Fine. It doesn't need to be the Mustang. We can look at—"

She cuts him off. "How come every six months when you're feeling flush, all of a sudden, she's your little girl? The rest of the time I've got to sic a lawyer on your ass to get a fucking check."

"That's not gonna happen anymore. Things are gonna be different."

Rhonda's tone is sarcastic. "Been there, done that."

Jack reaches into his pocket for the wad of fifties. He starts to count out some cash. "Here, let me give you for next month—"

Rhonda pushes his hand away. "You gave me money already."

He hesitates, then pockets the bills. "Just trying to make a point here. Things are gonna be different now—"

"Been there—"

Jack, grinning, completes the sentence with her. "Done that."

Rhonda finds herself suppressing a smile. She moves away, embarrassed by how easily Jack can get to her.

Jack follows and steps in front of her. He takes both her hands in his. "So what's with this hundred feet bullshit?"

He starts slow dancing with her. Rhonda is flustered and angry at the same time.

"No... Jack..."

Jack is moving her easily across the showroom. "Can't do this from a hundred feet apart. Hundred feet apart... That's how those young kids dance."

She's going with it, smiling in spite of herself. Then, her resolve stiffens and she pulls away. "No, Jack. Not this time."

Jack starts to argue but the defiant set of her jaw silences him. He sees Monica has drifted back to the Mustang. She opens the driver's side door and Jack shouts, "Get it out of your head. Take you two minutes to wrap that car around a goddamned tree."

Monica angrily slams the Mustang's door shut. Her mother walks over and grips her by the arm. "Let's go. You have homework."

Monica yells over her shoulder to her dad. "Don't forget you're supposed to take me driving so I can get my license!"

Jack raises his hand in acknowledgment. Monica pulls away from her mother and exits. Rhonda turns back to get the last word. "Pick her up on the corner this time. Court order says one hundred feet. Don't think I won't call the cops."

Jack meets her gaze. The look in her eyes does not match the anger of her words.

Rhonda realizes—with Monica gone—she no longer has any excuse to stay. She strides to the door, turning to the salesman on her way out. She nods in the direction of the rack of car keys on the wall. "Better count those when he leaves."

12

M ARLENE IS NOT SURE how far she's driven. She glances at the passing scenery and recognizes the suburban office parks of Southfield. Another ten miles and she'll be home.

She continues to silently berate herself. *This did not go well.* She should never have gone to her sister-in-law for help. *Barbara and her goddamned stupid, moronic boots and riding breeches. Pretentious fucking bitch! Too fucking busy to sit down and talk. In a fucking chair. Like a normal fucking person.*

Marlene grips the wheel, mimicking, "Walk with me, Marlie. We can talk along the way, Marlie."

Marlene glares into the rearview mirror. "Walk with this, you fucking bitch."

They'd walked across the pasture so Barb could visit with one of her precious horses. As she watched Barb stroke that massive head, Marlene realized she was terrified to be so close to the enormous beast. It was more like a fucking dragon than a domesticated farm animal, with great, billowing nostrils and big, menacing, flat, black eyes. *Am I nuts? Who's afraid of a fucking horse?*

But that animal, so big, so close, without a bridle, saddle, or rider to manage it, suddenly seemed fucking scary. Not like when they're riding around in movies, up on the screen with cowboys and shit. Or even when you see those police horses at the Thanksgiving Day Parade with the big cop straddling it. With a big fucking bridle. And boots. This horse was completely unrestrained, with no boundaries, with no fence or trees in sight, with no way to escape, no place to run. Unless it went through her. Or over her. Or chomped down on her arm with those big, damn, brontosaurus teeth.

She lost it. *I goddamned told her I was afraid of horses. Who the fuck is afraid of a fucking horse? God, I could have smacked her when she started laughing.*

Why didn't she tell Barb she hadn't heard from Victor? That she has no fucking idea where he is? Why does she keep covering for him? *And what's with all the questions about money? About accounts payable, trust accounts, receivables, partnerships, shares? I thought my husband ran a fucking factory?*

I'm not dense. I'm not fucking stupid. I could understand these things if he'd just explained them to me. If he'd fucking let me in. But he never brought his work home. That job ceased to exist for him as soon as he pulled out of the parking lot. It might have been the family business—his business—but to him, it was just a job. At least it used to be.

The anonymous glass office towers of the suburbs have given way to the endless rows of single-family brick homes that carpet Detroit's northwest side. The freeway cuts through the city like a concrete moat, keeping drivers safe from the mayhem beyond the service drives.

As she drives, the neighborhoods get grittier, the houses closer together, the storefronts more likely to be boarded up, the graffiti more prominent, more profane, more fucking idiotic. Somewhere in that passing landscape is the house where she grew up. That is, if it hasn't been torn down or burned out by drug dealers. *Good fucking riddance.*

Crossing I-94, spotting the signs for Wayne State, Marlene realizes she can't bring herself to go back to the house. Not yet. She pulls off the freeway at Warren and heads over to the Detroit Institute of Arts.

Marlene parks her car in the underground garage off Farnsworth and enters the museum. After flashing her membership card, she walks briskly through the Great Hall. She doesn't bother to look at the silent honor guard of knights in their gleaming armor. Eyes down, she doesn't glance at the vast interior courtyard beyond with its gargantuan Diego Rivera murals. Turning to her right, she moves into the adjoining gallery and descends the circular stone staircase to the Kresge Court.

She goes directly to the echoing indoor garden atrium and takes a seat, exhaling as she settles into the wire mesh chair. This is her oasis. She loves everything about it: the stone tile floor, the ferns, the brick, the milky glass skylights high overhead. This is the one place where things are clean, maintained. Where people speak in hushed voices. Where, sometimes, a lady plucks a harp. A fucking harp!

This is where she drinks bad coffee or nurses a glass of cheap wine. This is where she waits for Victor while he looks at art.

Without her.

She'd found herself staring at the sleek, unfamiliar piece of mechanical equipment in one of the contemporary galleries. She was confused, not sure if it was part of the exhibit of whirring gee-gaws, blinking lights, latex, plexiglass, and god knows what else. Then, she realized Victor was at her side. She was forever grateful to him that he did not laugh, or even acknowledge what they both knew: she'd mistaken the mechanized floor cleaner for part of the exhibit. He took her hand in his. "That's enough art for one day."

"That's enough art for a fucking lifetime" is what she wanted to say. She didn't.

After that day she'd wait for him in the atrium, drinking coffee and flipping through old Cosmopolitan magazines. Listening to a woman play the harp.

The piercing shouts of children bring Marlene back to the present. A group of hyperactive students is surging through the adjoining corridor on their way to the auditorium. Once they've gone, she finds herself following the progress of a tiny ladybug as it creeps across the pebbled glass tabletop.

For some reason, the tiny, jewel-like insect's survival this far into the fall annoys her. "Aren't you supposed to be fucking dead already?"

Growing impatient, she flicks the insect from the table with a snap of her finger. She grabs her purse and rises. Then she looks down to see the ladybug stubbornly traversing one of the stone tiles at her feet. Before leaving, she grinds the bug into the tile with her shoe.

13

DeRon HAS BEEN ON his feet for fourteen hours. He desperately wants to sit, to rest his throbbing leg, but he knows better than to neglect the responsibilities the Professor has tasked him with. He can see the great man moving back and forth in the adjoining room, monologuing to himself as he sterilizes his instruments. There will be more surgery. The motor cortical circuits have not been completely purged. The cerebral cortex is not yet the blank slate Drettmann requires for his work. This hell has no end.

DeRon turns his attention back to the entity strapped to the operating table. *The creature is already off the ventilator! How can that be? How can an organism experience such massive trauma and not only survive but seemingly thrive?* The readings on the cardiac monitor and the pulse oximeter aren't just strong; they are off-the-chart strong. He zeroed out and refreshed the pulmonary artery catheter because the pressure waveforms were too good to be true. They turned out to be true.

DeRon stares at the web of hydraulic lines that power the beast's massive frame. The Professor's work has come a long way since he developed the primitive apparatus that replaced DeRon's missing leg, his poor, pathetic, dearly departed limb.

The bones in DeRon's leg were pulverized to powder by a seafoam wave of Detroit steel tumbling across the asphalt like an asteroid. Seven botched operations followed. *All for what*, he wonders. *Did they at least harvest the titanium rods, screws, clips, and metal plates before his*

mangled limb was finally tossed into the furnace? My god what I would
give for a real leg. What I wouldn't give to hurl this Rube Goldbergian
mess into the flames. The Professor will get it right next time. He promised.
He may be crazy, but he is a man of his word.

After that day, after the accident, the hospitals, and the surgeries, there
were the group homes and foster homes. It's one thing to be a pathetic,
painfully shy, geeky Black kid named DeRon Dempster—all too often
transformed to "Dumpster" by guffawing classmates—with a pocket
protector and the social skills of a brick. It's entirely something else to
be a pathetic, painfully shy, geeky Black kid, named DeRon Dempster,
with a pocket protector, the social skills of a brick, and one good leg.

DeRon realized he needed an edge so he determined to become the
master of the cliché. As a ten-year-old, he created a Rolodex in his brain
he could flip through to come up with the appropriate response to
respond to any situation, conversation, or tongue-tied silence: "That's
for me to know and you to find out. Let's not reinvent the wheel. It's
not rocket science. The fool speaks, the wise man listens. A hard head
makes a soft behind. Money talks, bullshit walks. Life is short and full
of blisters. Everything happens for a reason. Good fences make good
neighbors. When you get lemons, make lemonade. The blacker the berry,
the sweeter the juice. A bird in the hand is worth two in the bush. What
goes around comes around. Nice guys finish last. Haste makes waste.
Time heals all wounds. You haven't got a leg to stand on."

The last two proved problematic for a one-legged kid on crutches.
They were quickly eliminated from the repertoire.

Friendships remained elusive. The foster placements invariably failed.
DeRon Dempster wasn't remotely popular. In fact, the pathetic crippled
kid who spoke in clichés was barely tolerated. So DeRon doubled down,
he went negative: "Don't let your mouth write a check your ass can't
cash. I used to have a coat like that... Then my old man got a job. The
lights are on but there ain't nobody home. I'm going to memorize your

name and throw my head away. You're so ugly you make blind kids cry. Girl, have several seats."

You'd think nobody would dare punch a one-legged kid on crutches. You'd be wrong.

DeRon eventually came to the realization that there were two things he could control: animals and machinery. As a ward of the state, he couldn't have a pet, so he focused on machinery. He read wiring diagrams like most kids read comic books. His discovery of the main library's collection of Chilton auto repair manuals rivaled Heinrich Schliemann's descent into the Tomb of Agamemnon. There, arranged by make, model, and year were dense, detailed repair manuals for every car on the road. DeRon ogled the technical illustrations and diagrams like a hormonal teenage boy with a Playboy centerfold. And, as he devoured the dry, matter-of-fact text that took him calmly, step-by-step, without drama or emotion through the process of understanding and repairing complex machines, he found his purpose in life.

Then he ended up in a foster home with a rusting 1962 Corvair sitting on blocks in the garage. The car had a blown engine and his foster dad let him have it. DeRon purchased his very own Chilton's 1962 Chevrolet Corvair Repair Manual. He scoured junkyards for parts. Using his foster dad's tools he got the Corvair running. At sixteen he had his own car. Eventually, guys from school came to him for help with their cars. He'd found his niche, something he could do well. He'd found something he could actually talk to people about. Well, other gearheads, but that was okay; gearheads only talked about cars.

DeRon turns away from the monitors. He has a general understanding of what they signify, enough to report any aberration to the Professor. His real love is for the machines themselves, the complex array of devices he has engineered, machined, soldered, and assembled under the Professor's direction. They are a known quantity: predictable, reliable, unthreatening. They are not people.

And, thankfully, this place, this hellish lab—he shivers involuntarily at the memory of his endless hours there in the frigid dampness—at least it's not the trailer.

Prior to bringing the entity into the operating room, DeRon had spent hour after hour, day after day, week after week, chilled to the bone, peering through a magnifier light stitching together muscle and blood supplies, embedding tiny electrodes into muscle and nerve tissue. He was always cold, surrounded by corpses, everything drenched in polyethylene glycol. The skin peeled away from his fingers even with the latex gloves. And he's never been able to completely wash away the smell of glycol and death.

DeRon tried not to think about the bodies, the pieces of bodies, as people. He imagined himself working on upholstery or, when he could no longer deny the nightmarish reality of his gruesome task, as meat. He was good at it, with a steady but delicate touch, much better than the Professor. By now, he muses, he could probably get a job as a master tailor or upholsterer. Or he'd be the star in any surgical suite where the patients were actually alive.

In his fugue state, DeRon has not noticed that the Professor has joined him, peering over his shoulder at the gauges and monitors. DeRon steps aside to give his master unimpeded access to the readouts. The Professor ignores the machinery and stares at him, his smile cold, eyes impenetrable.

DeRon stammers, "You... You want I should do something, Professor?"

The Professor takes DeRon's hand in his strong, clammy grip. "Now, you can rest."

DeRon nods and starts to turn away. The Professor kicks him in the knee, his one good knee, and DeRon hits the floor hard.

The Professor's foot is on his throat, pressing against his Adam's apple. "Do not ever question me again."

DeRon nods his feeble assent. Drettmann removes the foot from his throat and extends a hand to help him up. DeRon ignores the outstretched hand and struggles to rise on his own. By the time he manages to rotate onto his good hip and leverage himself to a seated position, the Professor is gone. But DeRon can hear him shouting.

DeRon twists around to see that the monstrosity, the thing with the brain of Victor Moravian, is convulsing violently and the Professor is struggling to hold it down on the table. A strap holding one of the beast's arms gives way and the creature flails wildly, knocking the Professor to the floor.

The beast contorts and twists until it manages to rip out the wires and catheters. Then, it breaks free from the remaining restraints and topples to the floor with the dead weight of an automobile falling from a lift.

DeRon slithers beneath a steel workbench on his belly. The beast continues to writhe about on the floor, knocking over tables of instruments and monitors, until it manages to claw its way to its feet.

The creature has little control over its limbs and veers spastically through the room with the destructive force of a panicked steer. DeRon wraps his arms around his head and curls into a fetal position as the creature careens into walls and racks of electronics, wrecking everything in its path.

After several minutes of carnage, the beast manages to gain some control over its powerful limbs. A frightening hybrid of human, raptor, and robot, the creature's bulk and lurching gait create the impression of a monstrous, meaty, Rock 'Em Sock 'Em Robot in the form of a man.

Legs churning, it staggers across the lab and slams into the opposite wall. Leaning against the wall for support, the creature surveys the wrecked lab, its labored breathing escaping in raspy spurts like the bellows of a furnace.

DeRon curls into an even tighter ball as he watches the beast stutter-step over to the rolling factory door that blocks its escape. It picks up a heavy instrument console and hurls it at the door. The steel door is dented but does not give way.

The beast grasps a heavy steel workbench in both hands and hammers the door with it. The steel plate gives way, warping and tearing as the blows splinter the wood beneath it. Striking blow after blow, the beast drives the increasingly deformed door so far into the opening that the rollers are ripped from the overhead track and the entire assembly crashes to the floor. The beast staggers across the wobbling pile of wreckage and escapes.

DeRon struggles to his feet. He joins his master who is standing in the doorway watching as the creature disappears into the darkness.

DeRon is horrified. "What have you done, Professor? What have you done?"

The Professor's face is radiant as he turns to place a paternal hand on the younger man's shoulder. "What have *we* done. What have *we* done."

14

THE KITCHEN IN MARTY'S apartment is an art deco throwback from the 1930s. At first glance, the only concessions to the present are the boxy black microwave mounted under a cabinet, the electric coffee grinder, and the gleaming French press featured prominently on the counter.

Jack is seated at the round coaster table with the chrome rim, drumming his fingers on the polished white surface. He checks his watch and yells impatiently over his shoulder. "Marty, what the fuck?"

Marty shouts from the other room. "Gimme a minute. Gotta take a dump."

"For Christ's sake, Marty, I'd a brought a fucking gas mask."

The only response is the sound of a slamming door and Jack smacks his hand on the table in exasperation. He gets up and opens the fridge. He pulls out a bottle of Mexican beer and examines it skeptically. He peers back inside to confirm this is his only option, grabs the opener from a drawer, and returns to the table.

Jack settles back into his chair and grips the bottle like a gearshift as his mind drifts back to the priest in his confessional. That fucking priest was supposed to give his absolution. He was supposed to make it so he doesn't have to think about this shit anymore. *That fucking son of a bitch!*

He opens the beer and flings the cap to ricochet across the spotless kitchen. *Fuck him, it doesn't matter.* He takes a long swig from the bottle. His world is solid, untouchable, organized into separate, secure, watertight compartments, like a submarine gliding beneath the surface of Detroit. The job, the blood, the fear, the stink, the night terrors; all that is sealed off in one impenetrable chamber. None of it touches any other part of his life. None of it touches anyone else.

Marty is in one compartment. His daughter and Rhonda inhabit another. *And Marlene... What about Marlene?* "Fuck!" Jack slams the bottle down on the table. *Marlene is sitting in that fucking barn over on Seminole Street. Alone. A sitting duck. This is one big royal fuckup.*

Jack stands abruptly, tipping over his chair.

Marty shouts from the other room. "Hey!"

Jack stands the chair back upright. Marty enters, tucking in his shirt. Jack returns to his seat. "I saw a cockroach."

"Fuck you. Where?"

Jack indicates with a tilt of his head. "Under the sink."

Marty, looking suspiciously at Jack, opens the cabinet doors beneath the sink.

Jack is staring at his beer. "Might have been two. Two fat fucking roaches."

Marty opens both cabinet doors wide. The storage space under the sink could be the cleanroom in a biotech lab. Marty closes the cabinet and straightens up. He spots something and walks across the room to pick the bottle cap off the floor. He throws an accusing look at his brother before dropping it into the trash. He moves to the fridge. "You want one for the road?"

Jack stands. "We got business." He looks around the room with disapproval.

"Nobody in Detroit lives in a fucking apartment, Marty."

Marty is puzzled by the accusation. "What about you? Your fucking Fortress of Solitude?"

"That's not an apartment; I own the building."

Marty shrugs and puts on his coat. "We lived in apartments. The Big Fat Fuck always had apartments."

Jack puts on his jacket. "Retired old fucks who sit at the bar all day drooling on themselves live in apartments. Welfare mommas with twelve kids from twelve daddies live in apartments." He fixes his brother with a hard stare. "The faggots in Palmer Park, they live in apartments."

Marty, looking like his head is going to explode, moves to block his brother. For a moment it looks as if they will come to blows. Then, Marty grins. "You saying the Big Fat Fuck was a fag?"

Jack smiles and shakes his head in bemusement. "Even they wouldn't take that asshole."

Marty's grin freezes in place. Jack pushes past him and out the door. Marty hesitates a moment, then follows. "Fucking asshole."

———————— • ————————

Magoo leads the two brothers out onto a wide cedar deck at the back of the sprawling faux villa of a house. The bald, bullet-head bodyguard is a walking grain silo with thick, metal-rimmed glasses.

Two additional bodyguards stand off to the side smoking cigarettes. One of them, Borneo, with a thick shock of unruly red hair, is the woolly bookend to Magoo's skinhead droog. Grinning broadly and speaking in a deep baritone, Borneo plays ringside announcer as the brothers enter. "The Kille-e-e-e-n K-uh-rew..." A nod to Jack in passing. "Ladies and gentlemen, in this corner: the Gollum. Out of the shadows and into the ring for all the marbles. Now ya see 'im, now ya don't."

He turns his attention to Marty. "And Fr-r-ench P-p-press-s-s-s..." With a sneer. "Gonna make us a pot, love?" He blows Marty a kiss as they go by, holding his thumb and forefinger to his lips as if taking a dainty sip from a cup of tea.

Marty ignores him, hissing angrily to his brother. "One fucking job! I took it to one fucking job!"

It's impossible to tell if Jack cares.

The deck overlooks a small private lake surrounded by dense woods. Pompey is standing with his back to them, leaning on a railing overlooking the lake. He's a wiry piece of gristle in an untucked, button-down dress shirt with the folds from the dry cleaner still visible. He could be a pharmacist dressed for a night out on the town. That is, if it wasn't for the mirrored aviator sunglasses and the Sig Sauer P220 he fires from time to time at an unseen target somewhere between him and the lake.

Jack looks bored as he takes a seat at a canopied table. Pompey continues blasting away until he empties the clip. He racks the slide to clear the chamber and seems to notice his guests for the first time. He removes the shades and stares at them with dead eyes that reflect nothing but a heart filled with metal shavings. "Well, if it ain't the Killeen crew."

Pompey moves to the table. He reloads the gun with a clip from his pants pocket and sets it down on the table before taking the seat across from Jack. Marty looks to make sure the gang boss has no objections before pulling up a chair.

Magoo sets a drink on the table in front of his boss. Pompey taps the gun with his finger. "Your body is like a tea kettle. Pressure builds up, you gotta release it or you blow your fucking top."

He turns his attention to Marty, staring at him with contempt. The attention makes Marty uncomfortable. He looks to his brother for support. "What? I got a fucking booger on my face?"

Jack ignores his brother. Pompey smiles and shakes his head. He turns to Magoo, gesturing back to Marty. "What I tell ya? Put a wig on him and he's fucking Martha Washington." He turns back to Marty, chuckling. "Martha Washington, I swear to god, fucking Martha Washington."

Pompey eyes Jack with a smirk. "Get the lean, mean, killing machine here something to drink. Martha too."

Marty gets up and stalks over to the railing. Jack, seething, sees several shadowy figures in the periphery of his vision. He decides he doesn't give a shit. He looks hard at Pompey. "Say that to me."

Pompey eyes him warily. "What?"

Jack nods in Marty's general direction. "What you just said to my brother. Say that to me."

Pompey's smile would freeze the Detroit River solid. "Why? You don't look nothin' like Martha Washington."

Magoo slaps two whiskeys down on the table in front of Jack. Marty, still sulking, returns to take his drink but remains standing.

Pompey takes a sip from his glass and turns his attention back to Jack. "So, how're things in niggertown?"

Jack takes a drink before responding. "Things in Detroit are just fine."

Borneo, off to the side, swaying and making inane hand gestures, is a dancing bear with delusions of Eminem. "He's living in the D. representin the 313."

One look from Magoo is enough to send the redhead back into hibernation. Pompey completely ignores the interaction. His tone is mournful. "Fucking Paris of the Midwest."

Jack doesn't react.

Pompey's countenance softens as he begins to reminisce. "Fucking Paris of the Midwest: that's what Detroit was when I was comin up. Orchestras, nightclubs, classy restaurants, wide fucking boulevards—you could eat off the fucking streets."

Jack has heard this before. "Can't do that in Paris from what I hear. Unless you got a thing for dog shit."

Magoo and the two other soldiers now flank the brothers. Pompey has his index finger poking through the trigger guard of the Sig Sauer and pressed against the tabletop. With his other hand on the grip, he slowly rotates the gun around his finger. He's talking to himself. "Can't do that in fucking Paris. Fucking wiseass."

He lifts his finger and slides the gun off to the side. Magoo and the two bodyguards are three linebackers waiting for the snap. Marty grips the back of a chair. He looks like a lion tamer waiting for the big cats to be released into the ring. Jack, hands flat on the table in front of him, could be meditating.

Pompey moves his drink around the tabletop like a chess piece. "Tell me this, wiseass: I been watching the TV news all week. I like the kind of stories where they find some guy stuffed into the trunk of his car with a bullet behind his ear. Usually, some putz who welshed on a debt."

Jack is nonchalant. "Sometimes, they never get found."

Irritated, Pompey slams his glass down on the table. "So how do you figure that?" He chooses his words carefully. "How come nobody can find this stiff when even—from what I understand—the guys that wanted him dealt with want him found?"

Jack leans back in his chair and looks out on the lake. "Maybe they aren't looking hard enough."

Pompey leans back in his chair while Magoo refills his glass. "Or maybe he's sitting in a room someplace talking into a tape recorder. I hear you got the hots for his old lady. Maybe you worked something out."

Jack bristles at the accusation. "He's gone. Problem solved. What does it matter if he never gets found?"

Pompey leans back in. "I'm running a fucking business. These old money guys, these Grosse Pointe cunts, they think they shit vanilla ice cream. They think they can just walk away from a fucking debt. Nobody walks away. And when they do, we gotta make an example. Or all those fucking Grosse Point, silver spoon cunts will think they can just walk."

Jack starts to respond. Pompey raises his hand to stifle him. "You need to fix this. It's your fucking job to fix things."

Jack takes a sip from his glass before responding. "You got nothing to worry about. Victor Moravian is dead."

Pompey is becoming agitated. "I have to be sure. There has to be a body." He begins to tremble.

Magoo, concerned, moves closer. "Boss?"

Pompey swats at him like a fly. "Get away from me. Christ! You're like a fucking old lady." His gaze remains fixed on Jack. "If you can't give me Victor Moravian, I want his family, his wife, his jigaboo fucking cunt of a wife. And this time I want a body. I want to be sure."

Jack gets up from the table. "I did your piece of work for you."

Pompey leaps to his feet in a rage. He's breathing fast and hard, as if his sunken chest is struggling to operate on half a lung. Suddenly, he grasps the edge of the table with both hands, in the grip of an epileptic-like attack. He speaks to Jack through gritted teeth. "You don't say no to me—"

Pompey grips the table so hard the veins bulge in his neck. Magoo, obviously an old hand at this, wraps his employer in a bear hug and throws him down on the table. Jack and Marty watch as the bodyguard pulls a mouthpiece out of his pocket and forces it between the gangster's teeth to keep him from biting his tongue.

Pompey continues to convulse violently, eyes bulging, arms stiff at his side. The massive bodyguard keeps him pinned to the table until the attack subsides.

Pompey recovers quickly and Magoo helps his boss back into his chair. Pompey pats him affectionately on the arm. "I'm okay... I'm okay."

Magoo hands Pompey his drink and hovers protectively nearby. Pompey takes a sip. His voice is barely a whisper. "Doctor says I shouldn't get excited. Can't get worked up about things no more. No more pussy. Can't even think about pussy no more." He shakes his head sadly. "That's no way for a man to live."

His eyes narrow as he looks at Jack. "You don't answer your pager no more."

Jack meets the gangster's angry glare. "Tossed it in the river. I don't work for you no more."

There is a tense silence as Pompey digests this information. Then, he shrugs it off. "Don't matter, cellphones better anyhow. That way, I can always reach out and touch ya." He smiles coldly and turns to Marty. "Ain't that right, French Press?"

Marty, embarrassed, looks down at his hands. Jack, clearly surprised at the apparent contact between Marty and Pompey, throws his brother a hard look.

Pompey seems pleased by Jack's momentary discomfort. Then he turns to Marty and his eyes grow cold. "You... You talk to your brother."

Pompey turns away, dismissing them. Jack walks off the terrace, followed by his brother and Magoo.

Pompey picks up the automatic and returns to the railing.

The sounds of gunshots follow the brothers down the long circular drive to the car. Jack tilts his head back in the direction of the house as they walk. "You got him in your phone too?"

He opens the driver's side door. Marty stands there looking uncomfortable.

Jack slides behind the wheel. "You walking back to Detroit or what?"

Marty hesitates, not ready to face his brother's wrath in the confined space of an automobile. Jack closes his door and starts the engine. "Get in the fucking car already."

Marty does. Jack burns rubber getting out of there.

15

THE BEAST'S EARLIEST MEMORIES are of constant, frenzied motion, of utter darkness, piercing cold, and pain. But, mostly, he remembers the ravenous, all-consuming hunger that raged inside him. In the beginning, he was nothing more than a lumbering, yawning chasm of need on two legs. His entire existence had been reduced to a desperate search for sustenance.

There was water from a powerful, churning river, but it did nothing to satisfy the insatiable vacuum that seemed to hollow him out. Driven berserk from hunger, he clawed at the ground, choking on dirt and breaking his teeth on rocks. Then, cold and wet, careening between the frigid water and the shore, he stumbled into a massive nest of twigs and tree branches.

Digging through sticks, mud, and murk he was gouged and bitten by fierce, furry things that crawled and scurried in the darkness. He tore through fur and flesh and sticky warmth until they were still, reduced to blood and viscera, bone and stink, to be consumed with greedy bliss.

Now, satiated, the beast lurches from shadow to shadow, pinballing off walls and ripping up fences or any other obstacle that blocks his path. He's driven by the pain, trying, somehow, to outrun the torment that permeates every inch of him like a frost. To do that, to keep moving, he needs every ounce of focus to control this mad, morphing stew of body parts. Each limb, each organ, every digit, every orifice, is its own raging, snarling entity, stitched, bolted, welded one to the other, pulling, ripping, tearing in all directions at once.

As he moves, shards of awareness emerge, surfing on the brief moments of clarity that punctuate the cresting waves of misery. Objects seem to leap out at him, their images colliding with the jumbled torrents of words in his brain. But nothing sticks. The pain makes it impossible to think clearly. Each tiny eddy of consciousness is quickly submerged beneath another tidal wave of agony.

The beast finds his path blocked by a white wall of steel. He totters back a few steps and finds himself facing an enormous fuel storage tank. Enraged by the obstacle, he pounds it with his fists. Each blow makes a satisfying dent in the metal and the beast redoubles his efforts. He quickly discovers that the shock of flesh and bone against the metal skin of the tank allows him to focus all of the pain in his body on the point of impact. Working himself into a frenzy, the creature suddenly finds his voice. But no words emerge, only a chaotic stew of bellows, blubbers, screeches, and howls.

The beast picks up a jagged piece of concrete and punches a hole in the storage tank. He stumbles back in alarm as oil gushes from the ruptured metal. His fear quickly gives way to fascination when he discovers that the sight of the black liquid spurting from this towering white shape creates a pleasant sensation that briefly distracts him from the pain.

Mesmerized, eager for more, he punches additional holes in the tank at various levels and steps back to watch the streams of liquid spurting and spraying, curling and crisscrossing as they form a web of lines against the sky. It is all somehow weirdly calming.

A word bubbles into his consciousness: pretty. He forms the word with his lips: "Pretty." He turns and slogs through the rising pool of oil for a better view. He turns back to take in the result of his efforts. *Yes. It is pretty.*

The respite is brief. His brain, hammered by the relentless waves of agony, is blistering and swelling, threatening to burst his skull like an eggshell. And there are the piercing sounds of sirens. He must keep moving.

16

V IEWED IN THE DAYLIGHT from above, Fisher Body Plant 21
is the hollowed-out shell of a volcano dominating a tiny desert
island of broken pavement, scrub trees, cinderblock, and graffiti. The
ruined factory and the acreage of vacant land and overgrown parking
lots encircling it is one small part of the relentless algae bloom of urban
decay that is slowly enveloping the surrounding grid of surface streets
and freeways.

Jack and Marty are tramping through tall grass in the shadow of the
plant. Marty stops and turns to his brother. "You sure this is the right
place?"

Jack ignores him and continues to search. His brother makes another
circuit of the area before stopping again. "Maybe he was wearing a vest."

"He wasn't wearing a vest."

"Maybe you missed it. Guy wasn't exactly a fashion model, you
know."

"He was bleeding like a goddamned pig."

Marty makes an abbreviated sign of the cross. "Abuon-anima, Victor
Moravian."

Jack turns to his brother in disgust. "What's with the 'abuon-anima'
shit?"

Marty is insulted. "What? My mother was Italian."

"How do you know? D'you ever meet her?"

"Yeah, sure..." Marty hesitates. "Probably. I don't remember."

"She ever cook rigatonis for you?"

"No."

"Meatballs?"

"No."

"Sing some Ginzo lullaby to put your fat ass to sleep at night?"

This is not the first time they've had this debate. Marty is staring at his shoes. His beefy hands, fingers spread wide, are pressing hard against an invisible force field. "My. Mother. Was. Fucking. Italian."

Jack winks at his brother. "The Big Fat Fuck liked fucking Italians. I'll give you that."

Marty can't stop himself from sharing Jack's grin. "Whatever. Dolores is Italian."

Jack's voice is all snark. "Yeah, how'd that work out for ya?"

Marty shrugs. "I'm still close with her people." He glances over at his brother. "Sometimes I think that's the only fucking family I got."

Jack ignores the dig. They resume searching but Marty's not ready to let it go.

"How do you know you're fucking Irish? You never set eyes on your old lady either."

"The Big Fat Fuck was Irish."

Marty is unconvinced. "The Big Fat Fuck was Irish on St. Paddy's Day. Everybody's Irish on St. Paddy's Day."

"We grew up in Corktown, you fucking dope."

"I don't know about you, but I grew up sleeping on couches all over the fucking west side."

Jack spots something. He crouches to examine the marks made when Victor was dragged off. He is not happy. "Somebody found him."

Marty joins his brother to examine the marks. "What would anybody want with a stiff?"

Jack doesn't have an answer. Marty gazes nervously at the hulking Fisher Body Plant. "Don't you usually do it, you know, inside?"

"You heard what the man said: I left him so he'd get found."

"Well, somebody fucking found him."

Jack looks toward the factory. "I guess we better check it out."

Marty stares at his brother, "What do you mean 'we,' white boy?"

Jack is not amused. "That's fucking funny. I swear t'god, he found you in a goddamned pet store." He tosses Marty his car keys. "There's a bag in my trunk."

Marty is annoyed. "What am I, the fucking butler?"

Jack's voice has a dangerous edge. "If I fucking say you are."

Jack trudges off in the direction of the abandoned factory. Marty, mumbling angrily under his breath, turns and heads back to the car.

Inside the plant, the imposing space the brothers move through could be mistaken for a ruined cathedral. They pick their way through scattered mounds of rubble as daylight floods in through mammoth constellations of windows, each a titanic mosaic consisting of scores of intact, broken, cracked, and missing panes of glass.

A concrete forest of pillars, with bell-shaped tops, supports the plant's vast interior. The men move through these industrial-age colonnades like miners exploring a cavern of fossilized tree trunks.

Jack slaps at one of the concrete pillars in passing. "All these places were built by the same guy: Albert fucking Kahn."

Marty is not impressed. "He told you that, right?"

Jack is offended by the insinuation. "Big Fat Fuck didn't tell me nothin'. I saw it on TV. A documentary."

"Didn't know you had a TV in that dump."

"With Rhonda."

"Oh."

"He did thousands of em. All over the fucking world. Designed half the buildings in Detroit."

Marty is dubious. "Guy named Albert?"

"That's right."

Marty is trying to puzzle this out. "Everybody must have called him Al, right? I mean, nobody on a job site's gonna listen to a guy named Albert... Right?"

Jack is undeterred. "Dodge Main, Packard Plant, GM Building, Parke-Davis, Burroughs, Ford Highland Park..."

Marty still can't get his head around the name. "Guy's name was Albert? For real? Like Fat Albert?" He has a sudden inspiration. "Hey, don't tell me he was a fucking Moolie?"

Jack's voice takes on an edge. "Moolie? What's with the fucking Moolie shit now?"

"You know what I mean. Name like that, musta been a Melanzana. A porch monkey. A spook."

Jack eyes his brother "Maybe you are fucking Italian after all."

"Since when'd you get so fucking sensitive?"

"You talk like a fucking Guinea."

"Whatever."

Jack stops and glares at his brother. "What's your fucking name?"

Marty does not like where this is going. "Killeen."

"I can't hear you."

"Fuck, Killeen. Okay? You fucking happy now?"

Shaking his head, Jack turns and continues through the ruins, talking over his shoulder to his brother. "Melanzana... Abuon-anima... Fucking Christ, what's next? You gonna start wearing gold chains and wife beaters?"

Deep inside the plant, they come upon a row of rectangular concrete pits, the access bays to long-vanished assembly lines. Each chamber is roughly the size of a grease pit at a muffler shop. Some are partially filled with brackish water, others with rubble.

Marty moves past his brother and stands staring at the row of gaping holes. They could be a series of open graves prepared for a race of giants. There is fear mixed with awe in his voice. "This where you do it?"

Jack doesn't answer. He moves to the edge of one of the pits. He kicks a piece of rubble inside and it lands in the darkness below with a splash. He stands there for a moment looking down before speaking. His tone is somber. "You know, I never wanted you to be a part of this. That's why I never brought you in on, you know, on this."

Marty walks along the row of access bays. He stops and kicks a piece of angle iron into one. It lands with a muffled splunk into the mud below. He takes a few more steps and kicks a paver into the third pit. It lands with the dry clack of brick on stone. "This one's dry." He kicks in a few more pavers for good measure, staring intently into the void as he does so. "You fucked up, Jack." He turns to look at his brother. "You just don't know when to stop."

Jack pushes past his brother and goes to one of the pits that's still relatively intact. He tosses the duffel bag into the void. It lands somewhere below with a dull thump on dry ground. "Here."

Marty joins him on the edge and peers down. "You make the poor sons a bitches climb down in there?"

"So?"

Marty is genuinely perplexed. "What if they don't fucking wanna go?"

Jack gives him a shove and Marty tumbles into the pit. He nearly recovers before landing but skids hard on his knees and hands. He climbs to his feet in a rage. "You fucking son of a bitch!"

Jack drops in beside him. He glares at Marty, challenging his brother to respond. "I did what I had to do. You got a fucking problem with that?"

The two brothers stand at the bottom of the shaft glowering at each other. Marty finally looks away. Jack picks up the duffel bag and shoves it into his brother's arms. He turns and ducks his head under the concrete rim at one end of the pit.

In the gloom beneath the ledge is a large wood pallet leaning against the wall. Jack wrestles the skid away from the wall to reveal the rusted steel access door behind it. There is only a black void where the door handle used to be. Jack unzips the duffel and takes out a steel pry bar. He jams the hooked end into the hole and uses it to drag the heavy steel door open. He reaches into the bag for two flashlights and hands one to Marty. He turns his on and leads the way inside.

A narrow concrete staircase takes them down into a subterranean service tunnel beneath the plant. The darting beams from their flashlights reveal an arched brick ceiling, silted mounds of debris, and pools of standing water.

Marty shines his light around the tunnel. His voice is a solemn whisper. "Where are they?"

Jack keeps moving. "I leave 'em here to…" He searches for the right word. "*Settle* for a while. Kind of like an Indian graveyard, you know?"

Marty hurries to keep up with his brother. "You come back for em? Jesus, you're creeping me out."

Jack stops. "Don't have to." He shines his light across the sides of the tunnel. "Why do you think this is still clear after all this time? All the storm drains for blocks lead in here. When we get a big storm, water goes through here like flushing a giant toilet. Washes everything into the river."

He shines the light back in the direction they came from. "When I first started coming down, there was a dumpster over there." He plays the beam of the flashlight over an empty stretch of tunnel. "You see a fucking dumpster now? It's on the bottom of the river."

Jack continues down the tunnel. Marty follows, still skeptical. "You don't know for sure they end up in the river."

"They sure as fuck aren't here, are they?"

"Maybe they get hung up somewhere along the way?"

"You worry too fucking much."

Marty is still unconvinced. "You sure nobody else knows about this? Scrappers are all over these places. And those kids, what the fuck do they call em? Spelunkers or something? They think this is a fucking amusement park."

"Nobody knows about this place. At least not that's still able to talk about it."

The beam from Marty's flashlight playing along the tunnel wall reveals a glimmer of blue in a niche between two rows of bricks. He slogs through six inches of standing water to the wall. He reaches inside the niche to find a cardboard box filled with disposable latex gloves. The box is as fresh and dry as the day it was purchased.

Jack wades over and snatches the box from his brother. He stares at it for a long time before he finds his voice. "Fuck me."

17

DeRon hobbles down the sidewalk on a single crutch with O'Jay dragging him by the leash. His throbbing leg feels like a marble statue that has been shattered and put back together with white glue and battery acid. The street they are on is a desolate vista of vacant lots and burned-out homes and DeRon occupies himself searching out the ghost gardens along the way.

The quest is a bit more difficult this late in the fall, but he quickly spots the tiny purple splotches of Russian sage in the sea of waist-high weeds that have colonized a string of vacant lots.

On the next block, he finds a ragged border of white and yellow chrysanthemums struggling to emerge from beneath the charred bed of a burned-out pickup truck.

These are the artifacts of another time, reminders of the house-proud residents who toiled in backyard gardens when this was a dense neighborhood of brick homes. When this was a community of porch swings, photo albums, Sunday dinners, backyard barbecues, basement workshops, La-Z-Boy chairs, TV consoles, and pot roasts.

DeRon stops to let O'Jay sniff some dubious object in the tall grass. Standing there, he sees that the skeleton of an abandoned bicycle frames a patch of reddish-pink sedum. The bike and the sedum are more relics of the before time. The time before the jobs went away and people left. Before the homes were abandoned and overrun by drug dealers. Before they were burned out and bulldozed. Before it was all reduced to this, a weed-choked urban prairie where even the street signs have been lost to scavengers.

Until recently, this particular block was one of DeRon's little secrets: the rare city street still lined with mature elms. For DeRon, it was like stumbling on a grove of towering, Jurassic-era ferns, or pulling a prehistoric Coelacanth out of the Detroit River. Dutch elm disease swept through this city like a biblical plague decades ago and the trees are virtually extinct now in this part of the world. In most neighborhoods, they disappeared long before the houses and people did. It was almost as if their demise was a harbinger of things to come, the first of the many biblical plagues to ravage this doomed city.

Here, somehow, the trees hung on long after the neighborhood itself was erased. No more. The block was recently clear-cut, and the once majestic canopy of trees has been reduced to a sad procession of stumps.

One of those fresh stumps it patrolled by a disoriented, chirping squirrel. DeRon attempts to maneuver around the stump and its guardian, but the squirrel launches itself at O'Jay.

DeRon uses his crutch to fend off the crazed rodent and drags his puzzled dog into the street. "C'mon O'Jay. Let's go."

The squirrel follows, undeterred, lunging, teeth bared, keeping just out of reach of the flailing crutch.

DeRon drags the dog to the other side of the street with the squirrel in manic pursuit. A car approaches and the squirrel, instead of retreating back to the opposite curb, charges the vehicle and is immediately crushed beneath the wheels.

DeRon stands on the curb for a long time afterward staring at the pancaked creature. The dog begins to whine its impatience and DeRon realizes what he's doing; he's searching for movement, waiting to see if the dead creature comes back to life. He grips the leash, swivels on the crutch, and soldiers on.

DeRon ties the dog to the metal signpost outside the Dunkin' Donuts. O'Jay is accustomed to the routine and settles sphinxlike onto a patch of yellow grass while DeRon goes inside.

DeRon goes to the counter and orders his usual. He limps over to the hard Formica table-bench combination overlooking the intersection and leans the crutch against the wall. He nods his thanks to the girl who brings him his black coffee and powdered sugar doughnut and settles into the bench.

DeRon sips his coffee and stares out the window. He watches the light change from green to yellow to red to green again. He watches cars speed through the intersection, the homeless with their shopping carts, the rumpled men in tracksuits and knit caps, the diesel-spewing city buses, the pigeons, the stray newspapers cartwheeling in the wind.

Long after his coffee has gone cold DeRon sits staring at the reflections in the glass, at the ghostly avatars of cars and trucks moving through the intersection. Sitting there, watching, remembering, is like pressing his tongue against an aching tooth. It hurts, but he can't stop himself from doing it.

Then, an ambulance races by, siren shrieking, the driver slouched casually behind the wheel, as if in his easy chair at home in front of the TV.

And DeRon remembers.

He remembers his childish surge of excitement: *I'm gonna see a car crash!* He remembers the big green Buick in the left turn lane, blocking the crosswalk they were waiting to cross, inching impatiently forward as the light turned yellow.

The opposite left turn lane was occupied by the massive, gray bulk of a city garbage truck, which blocked the Buick's view of the black Ford Bronco coming fast from the opposite direction, racing to beat the light.

The light turned red, and the Buick made the turn at the same instant the Bronco accelerated through the intersection. Six-year-old DeRon

Dempster was not disappointed. The speeding Bronco never braked as it T-boned the Buick. The collision was explosive.

DeRon's brain replays the event in remorseless slow motion: the implacable wave of metallic green steel hurtling toward their little family grouping on the sidewalk; Mom, prim and proper in the cloth coat with the faux leather collar; little sister Khaliq gripping Mom's coat pocket; baby brother Damon in the stroller, chubby legs dancing on the footrests.

And DeRon, fingers tight around the stroller handle, fixated on the broad, dreadnought flank of the Buick, throwing off sparks like a bulldozer blade as it swept across the pavement.

The last thing he remembers is releasing his grip on the stroller. Starting to run. Abandoning them. Leaving them there, forever frozen in time, like a diorama in the Museum of Natural History: the Cro-Magnons butchering a woolly mammoth; the Plains Indians weaving baskets; the Pygmies of Africa on the hunt; the Egyptian Pharaoh and his attendants...

The Dempster family on an east side Detroit street corner. Waiting for the light to change. Still waiting.

The rest he can only imagine. And he does. Repeatedly. Four thousand pounds of Detroit steel moving at high velocity to collide with three perfect, fragile bodies. Flesh and bone. Sinew and blood. Teeth. Limbs. Eyeballs. Eyeglasses. A purse. Bonnets and cloth coats. Six shoes, seven if you count the one DeRon left behind. One secondhand collapsible stroller.

And the merciless seafoam green tsunami sweeping them all away, erasing them from the physical world, plunging DeRon, who even in his blind panic was a step too slow, into a dark, endless planet of pain.

18

B ILL IS STANDING BY the Mister Coffee, waiting impatiently for it to finish brewing. The windowless room is clad in dingy ceramic wall tile. It looks like someone drained the deep end of a YMCA swimming pool and equipped it with overhead fluorescents and stainless-steel autopsy tables. Bill turns at the sound of the door to see the Killeen brothers walk in.

Marty closes the door behind them. He takes a rubber doorstop out of his pocket and uses it to wedge the door shut.

Bill watches nervously as his two ominous visitors stroll casually around the space.

Marty picks up a pair of calipers and drops them into the white porcelain butcher's scale used to weigh human organs. He watches until the vibrating pointer on the dial comes to rest and then nods sagely, as if he knew all along what the weight would be.

Jack circles the room, making his way to where Bill is standing. He stops and leans against the edge of an autopsy table, his gaze fixed on Bill.

There is something about the look in Jack's eyes that has the morgue attendant contemplating the narrow membrane that separates the living from the cold meat he examines each day on the autopsy table. He pours himself a cup of coffee. His hands are trembling. He tries to sound relaxed. He doesn't succeed. "Hey, I'm up to date. I swear."

Bill flinches as Jack reaches over to take the coffee cup from his hand and set it on the counter. "We're not here to collect."

"Cool. That's cool."

Marty is fiddling with a tray of knives now. "They taking you along to the new joint? The one they're building up there on Warren?"

Bill turns his attention to the larger of the Killeen brothers. "Sure, why wouldn't they?"

Jack grabs Bill's face and turns his attention back to him. "You guys ever run into any competition?"

"Competition? For what?"

Marty has lost interest in the cutting implements. "For stiffs."

Held tight by Jack, Bill tries to follow Marty with his eyes. "C'mon..."

Jack releases his grip, takes Bill by the shoulders, and guides him back onto a stool. "Never get a call, show up with your kit and your body bags and your spatula, but there's no body?"

Bill does not like where this is going. "You should ask the cops. They'd know about that sort of thing."

Marty is now standing on the other side of Bill. "What about John Does? Anybody ever come around looking to claim em?"

Bill's lips form a tentative smile. "Mrs. Doe?"

It's clear that his feeble attempt at a joke has fallen flat. Bill is confused about which brother he should be answering to.

Jack leans in close from the other side. "He asked you a fucking question."

Bill seems relieved at the possibility of actually being able to give them something. "Come to think of it, there was this guy, came around a few years back. He was from the medical school. Wayne State. Wanted cadavers for the students to practice on."

Jack decides to give him a little space. He backs off and leans against the autopsy table again. He takes a glassine bag of rolled joints out of his shirt pocket. "Yeah, so?"

"Didn't work out. I only remember cause there was a big stink about it." He lifts his eyes to the ceiling. "Upstairs."

Jack takes out a joint and fires it up. Bill looks like he's about to complain but thinks better of it. Jack inhales deeply, holds it in for a moment, and then releases a thick geyser of smoke. He offers the joint to Bill, who shakes him off.

Marty kicks the stool. "C'mon, spit it out. Suspense is killing me."

"It actually kind of worked out, at first. One of my colleagues—former colleagues—fudged some paperwork, diverted some stiffs from Potter's Field to the med school, even though he didn't have the proper releases."

Bill pauses, hoping this will suffice. He is met with hard stares, so he continues. "This doctor was apparently very persuasive. And my former colleague... Well, let's just say he should never have taken a job right down the street from a casino. Anyway, there's a process in place: protocols, paperwork, the med school, the morgue, medical examiner, next of kin... Doctors don't just go around freelancing for cadavers."

Jack takes another long toke. He's speaking through gritted teeth. "So, he wasn't a real doctor?"

"Sure he was. Some kind of surgeon. But after all the hullabaloo, he got canned. Something about his credentials, or malpractice." A mystified shrug. "Or something."

Marty places one of his large hands on the back of Bill's neck. "We need a name, Billy boy."

Bill tries to pull away, but his neck may as well be caught in a vice. His eyes look as if they're going to pop out of his skull. "How the fuck would I know? I never met the guy, just heard it all, you know, secondhand."

Jack stubs the joint out on the side of the steel autopsy table. He wanders over to the tray of knives and picks out a large one. "Coulda used one of these at Thanksgiving. Bet it cuts through bone like nothin'."

Bill finds his voice again. "There was this guy used to hang around when we'd come to a scene to collect the remains. Squirrely little fuck. With a leg..."

Marty squeezes Bill's neck. "No shit. I got two of em."

"No, I mean, his leg was all jacked up somehow. He kinda dragged it around, you know, like a pirate... like a peg leg or something, you know?"

Jack returns the knife to the tray. He moves back to Bill. "Long John Silver, he got a name?"

"Not that I know. Haven't seen him in a while. Last time was, you remember the frozen guy at the old Packard Plant? Last winter? Was all over the frigging news."

Jack is impassive. "I don't watch TV."

Bill continues, "Fucking icicle. Had to jackhammer him out of the elevator shaft. He looked like Han Solo." In response to their blank looks, "You know, frozen in that block of carbonite?"

Still nothing. Bill shrugs and continues, "That was the last time I saw the guy. One of the techs got suspicious and took his plate number. Cops went out and talked to him. Spooked him, I guess. Never saw him again."

Jack gets right in his face. "I need a name."

Bill, at the end of his rope, is defiant. "Ask the fucking cops."

Jack straightens up. He and Marty exchange a glance. Marty releases his hold on Bill's neck and pats him on the shoulder. He walks over and sorts through several trays of instruments. "Hey, you remember that guy, the dentist, used to come around the center when we were kids?"

Jack scowls at the memory. "Yeah, filling cavities for poor kids. Hands like a goddamned gorilla. Hated that son of a bitch."

Marty finds something to his liking. He approaches Bill, toying with a large syringe used in removing fluids from cadavers. "When he was about to drill your ass, he'd say, 'You may experience a little discomfort, son.'"

Jack grabs Bill's collar with one hand, the stool with the other, and drags him over to the autopsy table. Marty plants himself directly in front of Bill. He's still reminiscing about the not-so-good-old-days. "Discomfort? Fuck, I think I ripped the arms off the damn chair." Eyeing Bill, he slowly works the plunger on the syringe. "You may experience a little discomfort, son."

Bill is panicking. "Hey, c'mon. Guys'll be back any minute now."

Jack grabs Bill by the hair and drags him backward across the table. Bill fights him and Jack slams his head against the steel surface. Marty holds the syringe a fraction of an inch from Bill's open eye. He looks to his brother. "Bet this baby'd suck that eyeball right out of there."

Jack is skeptical. "No way."

"No, really." Marty makes a sucking sound with his tongue and lips. "Like a shop vac."

Bill looks nervously from one brother to the other. "C'mon, this isn't funny."

He detects no hint of humor. Marty moves the point of syringe closer. Bill's resistance collapses. "Wait... Wait... Wait."

Jack looks to his brother. Marty pulls the syringe away from Bill's eye.

Jack releases his grip on his hair and the words come pouring out of Bill's mouth. "One time, there was a lady turned up stuffed in a freezer. In her garage. Eastside, over on Coplin. By... By Lozier. I'll never forget it—body was mummified by the time she got found—scrappers I think. Anyway, he was there, he was walking his dog, big-ass German shepherd."

Annoyed, Jack grabs the syringe from Marty. "I haven't got time for this shit."

Marty grabs Bill in a throttlehold. Bill's talking fast now. "There's not fifty occupied homes in a square mile of that place. It's like the frigging Rapture took the people and then came back for their houses."

Jack grabs Bill by the hair. "Fifty? Do I look like a fucking Jehovah's Witness? I haven't got time to go knocking on fifty fucking doors."

"No, you don't understand..."

The Killeen brothers do not look kindly on this attack on their cognitive skills. Bill tries to dig himself out. "What I mean is, people with dogs, they got a routine. Right? Same time. Same route. Every day. And

this guy, with his messed-up leg, he can't live too far from there. Right?"
He's desperate to get an Amen here. "Right?"

Jack nods to Marty and his brother releases Bill. The attendant lifts
himself off the autopsy table, warily eyeing his two unpredictable guests.

Jack gets the details from Bill while Marty dutifully returns the syringe
to the tray where he found it. He stoops to reclaim the rubber doorstop
and pockets it.

Jack opens the door and holds it for his brother. He nods in the
direction of the now extremely pale morgue attendant. "Kinda high
strung for somebody in this line of work. Doncha think?"

Marty grins. He gestures magnanimously for Jack to exit first, then
follows. "Fuck him if he can't take a joke."

Jack stops in the corridor. He tilts his head to indicate the ornate
corbeled ceiling overhead. "Albert Kahn." He moves on, shaking his head
sadly. "They're just gonna tear the sucker down."

19

MARLENE IS ALREADY ON her third glass of wine. She thought the server gave her a funny look when she ordered the last time. After all, the Kresge Court at the Detroit Institute of Arts is not the sort of place people come to in the middle of a weekday afternoon to get high. Or maybe she's just paranoid. She can't shake the feeling she's being watched, followed. This morning she thought she saw Marty Killeen's car behind her on Jefferson. *But Christ, if anyone's got the right to be paranoid...*

She checks her watch again. The cop she made the appointment with would have been at the house over an hour ago. What's this Detective Chambers going to think when she realizes she's ducking her? Why does that detective want to meet her at the house anyways? *Doesn't she have a fucking office? Isn't that what police stations are for? I mean, besides locking people up? Does she know something about Victor?* How can she tell a cop that she helped her husband hook up with a guy like Jack? Not to mention whatever the hell it is Victor is mixed up in?

She needs to go home. That detective must be gone by now. She can't ignore the phone calls much longer: her sister-in-law, Victor's parents, the accountants, the guys at the foundry, the lawyers. The floor beside the fax machine in Victor's home office is littered with faxes she's afraid to look at. The machine is now, blessedly, out of paper.

She drains her glass and sets it back on the table. *Take it, take it all: the house, the cars, the business, the fucking art. Pile it all into one big fucking bonfire.* She'll even light it. She'd trade it all just to have Victor come striding in through the archway to meet her, grinning and goofy, satiated, for the moment at least, with his fucking art.

She remembers the disastrous brunches, the arduous dinners, and her own stilted, self-conscious timidity at the lakeside home of Victor's elderly parents. Even now she can feel her face warming as she recalls her humiliation when she offered to help with dinner and worked furiously to saw through the middle of an avocado. Before her incredulous host took the knife from her hand. "Haven't you ever seen an avocado before?"

Well, actually, no. Not unless it was in the fucking dip that came with my happy hour—two for the price of one—fucking margaritas. Thank you very fucking much.

The last time, this past summer, his parents served dinner in the gazebo overlooking the water. The air had been heavy with tension the entire day. She constantly found herself excluded from conversations that moved just out of earshot as she approached. And Victor had completely shut her out. She felt like a tourist in some exotic land, completely isolated when the trusted tour guide suddenly forgets how to speak fucking English.

Fuck him, she thought, *two can play this game.* So she checked out. While polite conversation went on around her, she focused on the life and death drama unfolding in the latticework of spider webs that stretched between the vertical posts supporting the deck rails.

As the dinner wine splashed into her glass her eyes were fixed on the delicate threads glinting in the glow of the ornamental lights. The web was completely empty then, floating lazily in the gentle breeze, harmless as a gossamer bed sheet on a clothesline.

Her miso-squash soup grew cold as she watched the first of several gnats become entangled in the web. By the time Ana, frowning, took away the untouched fennel-Asian-pear salad, that lethal netting had snared a dozen unwary gnats and moths.

Dinner was roasted lamb with rosemary. Victor, concerned by her silence, squeezed her leg and smiled. She repaid him by carving off a delicate forkful of lamb. But her attention was fixed on the railing, on one particular moth, yellow and purple and much larger than any of the previous casualties. It drifted in and out between the rails, oblivious to the web and its quivering victims displayed like alien sea creatures in a tiny fisherman's net.

Marlene gripped her fork and waited for the inevitable. She nearly gasped out loud when one of the moth's fluttering wings brushed against the web and stuck fast. For a moment it looked as if the struggling creature would break free. Then, the other wing made contact and the panicked, flailing moth was engulfed in a tight, murderous cocoon of webbing.

Dessert was served: champagne-poached pears with chocolate sorbet. Marlene waved off the coffee. When the spider came to claim its trembling prize, she stood up and excused herself from the table.

In the car, Victor turned and looked at her, all soulful innocence. "July, she will fly. And give no warning to her flight."

She was in no goddamned mood. "What is that? A fucking poem you wrote?"

He looked wounded. "Simon and Garfunkel."

"Simon and whofunkle?" She let out an exasperated sigh and carefully calibrated the lack of enthusiasm in her voice. "Don't worry. I'm not going anywhere."

He started the car and accelerated, gravel ricocheting off the trees lining the drive. His face was a steely mask, eyes fixed on the road ahead, hands gripping the wheel. Dull vanilla voices were droning away on the radio and Marlene turned it off. "I hate fucking NPR."

His lips barely moved. "Whatever."

Marlene decided she didn't have the patience for forty minutes of sullen dead air.

She poked and jabbed at her husband's hard shell of silence until, all at once, it collapsed and Victor flew into a rage like nothing she had ever seen before. How could she disrespect his parents like that? Disrespect him? After all they'd done for her? After all he'd done for her?

His anger was so all-encompassing, such a force of nature, so out of character, that, for a moment, she was convinced he was going to stop the car and throw her out.

She managed to calm him down and they drove on in silence for a few minutes. Then, he pulled off the highway. She was startled out of her funk. "What are you doing?"

He ignored her, searching for a place to pull over. Then, he made a screeching U-turn, drove over a curb, and pulled into a gas station. He slalomed through the cars jockeying for position at the pumps and parked on the side of the building near the restrooms. He turned off the car and rested his forehead on his knuckles for a few seconds.

When he finally turned to her, he looked terrified. "We might have to sell the house."

"What do you mean sell the house? You love that house."

"We're broke. I'm hanging on by a thread."

"But you're busy. I don't understand. You're working all the time."

"Doesn't matter if we can't get paid." He reacted to her confused look. "Most of our jobs, we're the sub of a sub of a sub of the prime contractor. And the prime contractors, they pay when they feel like paying."

"The company's been in business fifty years. You've been doing this for fucking forever. How can this happen? How can you let this happen?"

"We live in a different world now. There was a time..." He jerked his head, as if shaking off a suggestion from an unseen adviser. "What was once thirty days payable became sixty. Then it became ninety. Then six months. Now, sometimes, it's an entire year. Meanwhile, I have payroll, vendors, taxes, the vehicles, insurance; I have to keep the bloody lights on."

She couldn't hide her astonishment. "But they have to pay you. Isn't that the law? Don't you have lawyers?"

Victor took a deep breath. "They have more lawyers. They will always have more lawyers." His hands were slightly apart, thumbs pressed to index fingers, a conductor struggling to find the right notes. "They stiff their sub. That sub stiffs their subs. One of those subs stiffs us. And the big guys, the clients, they practically dare you to sue them. They know we can't afford to do that. And even if we did, they'd just find another vendor."

His delicate, careful handling of her naivete was infuriating, but she tried to keep the anger out of her voice. "There's got to be something…"

Victor exploded. "You don't think I'm trying everything I can? What in god's name do you think I'm doing?" He gripped the wheel as if he wanted to pull it off the steering column. Then, he quickly regained control of his emotions. "I'm sorry, I didn't mean that."

A skinny white guy in greasy jeans so low they revealed his ass crack had paused in front of the car on his way to the restroom. He was staring at them. She flipped him the bird and Victor grabbed her hand. "What are you doing?"

She ignored him, glaring at the man as he pushed through the door of the restroom, grinning over his shoulder at them as he disappeared inside.

"Fucking asshole."

Victor started the car and pulled out of the parking lot. "You know I don't like it when you speak like that."

She spoke to the passenger side window. "Get a fucking grip."

They rode in silence. All she could think about was the art. The fucking art. For years he'd been buying art like crazy. "Cass Corridor art" they called it. A fucking Detroit thing. Art made by artists who looked like homeless bums and streetwalkers. Art made in storefront studios, in derelict hotels and abandoned warehouses. Ugly, angry, incomprehensible objects made from house paint, scavenged lumber and plywood, cardboard and chicken wire, polyester resin and sheet metal.

The walls of the house are covered with that art. It hangs all over the foundry. He's got storage facilities filled with even more art. And still, he keeps buying.

They drove in silence the rest of the way home. But then, stepping into the entrance hallway, with the John Egner whatchamacallit on the wall, that Gordy Newton monstrosity visible from the living room, the colorful splotches of the tiny Barbara Greene watercolors in the kitchen, she lost it. She couldn't hold it in any longer. "Sell the fucking art."

"Marlene, it's not that simple."

"Am I speaking fucking Greek? Sell the fucking art. You paid a fortune for it. Sell it to some other..." She bit her tongue, avoiding the word she wanted to use, "Collector."

"You have to understand, there aren't a lot of people like me, people who appreciate this work as much as I do."

Marlene's heart sank. She moved into the kitchen and collapsed into a chair at their vintage midcentury table. "Oh fuck. Oh, dear fucking Jesus."

Victor took the seat opposite her. She threw him a challenging look. "Sorry, I'll watch my fucking language."

He didn't take the bait. His voice was once again calm, reassuring. "It's an investment, a long-term investment. I've supported a lot of artists during some rough times in their careers. It's going to pay off... in time."

"What about us? You're supposed to be supporting us. Aren't we having a fucking rough time?"

"If I sold it all now, we'd be flooding the market. Prices, such as they are, would collapse. I've got to hold onto it. I just need something in the interim, a bridge loan. I'm still talking to the banks."

"Go to your family."

"I can't do that."

"What do you mean you can't do that?"

He was choosing his words carefully now. "They won't understand the situation I'm in."

"The situation *we're* in. *We're fucking in.* Fuck your family's delicate sensibilities."

"That's not it. I've spent money I wasn't supposed to touch. I need to get that back first." He brightened. "We've got some enormous payables out there. There are some real good projects on the horizon. I just need some time."

That's when it hit her: she could help him. She could contribute. She could be the one to fix things for a change. "I know someone."

He looked at her through narrow lids, like she'd announced she was joining the circus. "What do you mean?"

She reached across the table to grasp his hand. "I know someone who can help you—us."

He stared at her in disbelief. "What? C'mon, who do you know with that kind of money?"

"I know someone. I mean, I used to know someone."

He was listening intently now. His voice was a whisper, as if someone might be listening. "What are you talking about? Who do you know?"

"I know someone who knows people, people who can get you the money so you can pay everybody back. So you don't have to sell the art." She quickly corrected herself. "Not all of it anyways."

Victor was wavering between hope and disbelief. "I don't get it. What's the catch?"

Even as she spoke the words, she was already regretting it. Why hadn't she just kept her fucking mouth shut? "These are not nice people."

He smiled. The way you smile at a child who just offered to buy you a new house with her next allowance. "Sweetheart, I deal with people like that every day of the week."

Marlene twists the stem of the empty wine glass in her fingers. Torrents of rain are sweeping across the glass roof panels overhead. Maybe she should go to the police? Can she meet with a detective when she's drunk? No, that's crazy.

She looks over to the young man standing, fidgeting, behind the bar. Will he sell her yet another glass of wine? Maybe if she smiles at him real nice...

20

THE BEAST SLOGS THROUGH a heavy downpour as it traverses a bleak industrial landscape of rusting steel girders, twisted rebar, broken concrete, and empty warehouses. There are 19th-century iron train trestles nearly obscured by weeds the size of men. Silent brick smokestacks tower over broken factories that are slowly receding into the landscape like the terraced ruins of ancient citadels.

Desperate to free himself from the pain welded to him like a second skin, he tears through them, one after the other, legs churning, arms pumping, moving faster and faster.

He exults in the mastery of his limbs, the power of his body, the violence he inflicts on these sagging carcasses of brick, masonry, and rebar. He is a heat-seeking projectile bursting through timber barriers, cinderblock walls, and steel grates. He is invulnerable. He is unstoppable. He is like a god.

He breaches the thin brick outer membrane of one structure and comes up against a concrete rail abutment that is impervious even to his raging fists. The beast stops. The deity is exhausted. He can go no further.

Then, he hears a soft, rippling sound, a cluster of musical notes that penetrate his brain like a key slipping into a lock. Fascinated, he stares at the dense shrub where the sound resides. The sound is so soothing and familiar it momentarily calms the frenzied racket in his brain.

He struggles to put words to it. "Tweak... Squeak... Squeaking... Squeakering... Klee... Kleeing?" Then, his lips shape themselves into something like a smile. "Twittering! Twittering tree! Klee! Paul Klee!"

He reaches out to touch it and a gust of tiny sparrows explodes into the air. The beast laughs and claps his hands like a child as the breeze carries the birds away like winged confetti. He shouts eagerly at the now silent shrub. "Again! More! More!"

He waits. The birds are gone. The bush is silent. Angry, he grapples with it, his flesh punctured by the sharp edges of a hundred tiny, jagged branches. Enraged, he tears it out by the roots.

The beast continues moving. His brain is struggling to make sense of the unrelenting barrage from a thousand shrieking nerve endings. With each step, he struggles to map the geography of his body by the nature of the pain each individual organ endures. He is certain of only one thing: if he stops moving, he will become just one more lifeless shell slowly merging with the earth.

Then he sees it.

Nestled among the other industrial temple mounds is the squat brick redoubt that is the Piquette Avenue Plant. The beast topples the chain-link fence in his path and stumbles across the gravel lot to lean against the outside wall of the building. As he presses his body against the brick exterior, he has a fleeting moment of peace. There is warmth here, this is, somehow, inexplicably, a living body in the midst of this field of corpses.

The beast puzzles over the concept of a lock and key before battering down a steel service door. Inside, the silence is shattered by the ear-splitting shriek of an alarm. The beast answers the shrill screech with an angry roar. He lifts a trash bin and uses it to hammer the alarm box mounted on the wall until it is as silent as the uprooted shrub.

The beast shuffles onto the immense shop floor. The familiar surroundings put him at ease and he luxuriates in the pungent smells of carbon and steel, machine oil and ash. Around him, neatly stacked pallets and hand trucks await the arrival of the morning shift. Overhead there are welded steel control rooms the size of mobile homes dangling from winches.

He roams the plant floor, slapping aside dangling hoist chains and batting away heavy gauge steel plates like laundry hanging on a line. The howling storm of words and images in his head continues to intensify, but he is powerless to master it. There is one thing he does comprehend: he belongs here. There is an answer here, something that will make things clear, make things right.

A furnace-like gust of pain propels him up a flight of metal steps. Reaching the top, he finds a long corridor lined with small cubicles. Inside them are drafting tables, desks, water coolers, and whiteboards. To the beast, they are a puzzle, cages too flimsy to contain even the most pitiful creature.

He makes his way to a much larger room at the end of the hallway. There are words on the door, words that shape an image in his mind. It is the image of a man, a man called "Victor." In his head, there is another word attached to that name, to that man. Briefly closing his eyes, he glimpses a slender, brown body walking into the waves, and he experiences a brief moment of serenity.

But that image and the sense of contentment accompanying it is snatched away, sucked back into the dark, roiling murk of his brain. He pries the nameplate off the door in a desperate effort to bring it back. Finding nothing on the other side, he hurls it away and kicks the door in.

Inside, the walls are covered with large, colorful objects and he has a brief moment of clarity. These are things that are not really those things: "pictures." Words bubble into his brain and burst from his gaping mouth. "Still life. Color. Calm. Parish. Sestok. Pletos. Luchs. Mitchnick. Beauty."

Then, another word forms itself inside his mouth. He parts his lips, and it escapes, softly, pleasantly, like a delicate bubble: "art."

He is drawn to one of those things on the wall that are not really those things. There are two creatures. A man. A woman. Teeth. Smiles. Flesh. Hands. Hair.

One of these creatures, the man, has that word entangled with it: "Victor."

The other, the woman, is that companion word. The smile word. The slender, brown body walking into the waves word.

His tongue snares that elusive word and it bursts from his lips in a shout, "Marlene!"

The power of that word knocks him back into the desk. He leans against it to steady himself and catches his reflection in a mirror on the wall. He does not see a man. He sees a monstrosity.

The beast turns and shoves the steel desk across the room. Drawers are spit out, vomiting files and papers onto the floor.

He paws through them until he finds one he knows: the red file folder. He recognizes this red thing. It is all about pain, searing, unimaginable pain. He grasps the file folder clumsily and sheets of paper erupt into the room. He tries to snatch them from the air but only succeeds in batting them further away.

The sheets of paper spread across the room like the singed flotsam from a bonfire and he crawls from one to the next. There are papers with words. There are pictures of Marlene. There are pictures of Marlene and a man.

His eyes settle on the image of the man with Marlene. He remembers that face, those eyes. He remembers looking down the barrel of a gun. He remembers Jack. And he remembers them together. Those words spoken together are absolute, unendurable agony. "Jack and Marlene. Jack and Marlene. My Marlene."

He shuts his eyes and slams his head repeatedly against the floor until those awful words are swept away by the pain. Opening them again, he sees the red folder. He uses it like an oven mitt as he crawls around the room snatching up the images. He crumples the whole mess into a dense red wad of cardboard and paper and stuffs it into his coat pocket.

The beast climbs to his feet. He returns to the picture on the wall, of the man and the woman. Victor and Marlene. He reaches out for Marlene, cautious—he does not want to break her. His fingers encounter a thin, smooth coating of something... Ice? No, glass covering it. He pokes the image again and the glass shatters, the tiny, jagged shards puncturing his flesh.

The beast pulls the painting from the wall. He holds it up in front of himself as he strides out of the office. He starts down the stairs, but his jury-rigged body has not yet mastered the task and he stumbles forward, careening all the way down the flight of steps. His momentum carries him across the shop floor until he slams into a bin of metal rods, driving the heavy container into the tall steel cabinet behind it.

He leaves the canvas there, spiked on the metal rods. In a titanic rage, he veers violently around the room. He is a man engulfed in fire attempting to smother the flames by contact.

He batters and rams and destroys until every part of his body is unified in achieving its ultimate level of agony. Even so, he cannot drive out the images seared into his brain. The images of them, together. Of Marlene. Smiling. Laughing. With him. With Jack.

He returns to the bin. The not-real Victor and Marlene have been impaled on a dozen metal rods. The rods pierce their faces, eyes, throats, arms, torsos, and lips. Liquid from a toppled container above the bin has washed across the canvas and the faces melt in front of his eyes until Victor and Marlene are hideous, monstrous, and alike. Like him. The beast exults. "Now she is like me!"

His brain is melting in the heat of madness. His mouth distorted into a hideous grin. The words that escape his lips are embedded in a cackling laugh. "Marlene. My Marlene. She is my Marlene. Mine."

Later, after the rain, he strides across the soggy urban prairie with the tattered painting catching the wind like a sail. He stops beneath a rail abutment to admire his prize. He studies the smeared colors, the tangled swirl of features, Marlene's distorted face, and his mouth shapes a word he does not understand. But for some reason it makes him smile: "Dekooning."

21

MARLENE IS SITTING IN the chair by the bedroom window when she wakes up. She closes her eyes again and listens to the creamy licking of the cat grooming himself. Then she remembers they no longer have a cat. She opens her eyes and realizes there's a soft rain pelting the window glass.

She tries to remember her dream. Yet another, disjointed, harrowing ordeal that involved rescuing one of her childhood pets from some calamity. She has a vague, fading memory of her cat Coco attempting to snatch a piece of chicken off the stovetop and searing her paws in the process. She'd rushed over to find the kitten's front paws not just seared, but actually in flames. The last thing she remembers before waking up is snuffing the twin conflagrations out with her bare hands.

The therapist Victor sent her to had some trippy explanation for these recurring nightmares. According to her, these frantic efforts to rescue a beloved pet were actually, somehow, all about Marlene trying to rescue herself. She'd explained that as a child Marlene had desperately wanted someone to come and rescue her. But no one ever did. Now, in her dreams, she's not trying to save those long-dead pets; she's trying to save herself.

"Ain't you something?" Marlene says aloud. "Can't even get it right in your fucking dreams."

She notices movement across the street. The Morgans' housekeeper is hurrying back after walking their Airedale, thrashing a soggy umbrella into submission before going inside. Marlene finds herself smiling at the irony: she's gone from neighborhoods where dogs lived their lives chained in backyards, to neighborhoods where dogs are actually walked by their owners, to this, a place where the family dog is walked by the fucking maid.

She fingers the knob on the radio by the bed. She remembers standing in the kitchen in her pajamas as a little girl, slowly putting on her coat and hat. She'd stand there watching her dad in his work coveralls, gripping the folded newspaper in his free hand, eating his fried eggs and ham. She'd try to look as pathetic as possible, knowing it was pointless. Knowing he would not even look up, even as her mother scooped more eggs out of the heavy black frying pan onto his plate. Finally, defeated, she'd take the keys off the hook by the door and trudge out to his car.

She remembers those frigid winter mornings sitting in that clammy seat with the engine running and hunks of snowmelt sliding off the roof, waiting for the car to warm up so her dad could be nice and snug on his drive to work. She'd hug herself, shivering, desperate for the trickle of warm air coming from the vents to turn into a gust so she could go back inside and eat her cold cereal.

She remembers reaching over to turn down the volume on his old-school soul music and accidentally changing the station. She remembers her panic as she searched desperately for the right station, her terror of his monumental rage, her relief, and her tears, when she finally found his music again.

Then she smiles, remembering the time she finally drove away in her father's car.

She lands on Victor's radio station. Men are doing some sort of chanting in a language she doesn't recognize. *Is this that, whatchamacallit, Latin Mass stuff? That Kevorkian chanting?* She doesn't understand this music, never did, but listening to it now, with Victor gone, makes her feel happy somehow.

The announcer comes on to detail the particulars of the Gregorian chant the audience just heard. Marlene realizes this is not Victor's NPR; it's one of the university stations. She sighs and keeps looking.

She's thinking about her dreams again. About rescuing the cats. There was a time she'd counted on Jack to rescue her. *Yeah, that went fucking well.*

She remembers how it ended. The first time it was a stop sign. At first, she thought Jack was just trying to scare her. He sped up as he approached the intersection, completely focused, hands gripping the wheel like he was in some kind of a trance. She kept waiting for him to hit the brakes as they approached the four-way stop with two cars already there. Instead, he hit the accelerator and blasted through the intersection like a rocket. A car that had started through the intersection slammed on the brakes, fishtailing, missing their rear fender by inches.

Afterward, she screamed at him. She called him a fucking asshole and told him if he wanted to kill himself, he could do it without her in the car. He didn't seem to hear her. His eyes were shining. He was talking to himself like she wasn't even there. "Nobody fucking touched me... Went through there like a missile. A fucking guided missile..." The look on his face was pure exultation.

She eventually forgot about it. Until he did it again. A red light on Woodward Avenue. He stomped on the accelerator as they approached the intersection and she screamed, ducking beneath the dash, head wrapped in her arms, flinching at the shrill braying of horns and shrieking tires.

Afterward, after cheating death—no, not cheating death, embracing it—Jack was in a weird mental state. He was unreachable, beyond words. It was like he felt invincible. Like he thought he was some kind of a fucking superhero or something. Not her. She nearly threw up. She made him pull over. She was shaking so badly she almost tripped getting out of the car. "Fuck you, Jack! Fuck you! Fuck you!"

It was years before she finally understood what really made her get out of that car. It wasn't because of how frightened it had made her, although it did. It was because of the way it frightened her. The way being with Jack had always frightened her. It was the kind of fright you got on the roller coaster at Edgewater. It was the kind of fear that you wanted to experience again and again. It was a fucking rush, a drug.

It was like heroin, but better, because you didn't need to stick a fucking needle in your arm. Or someone's dick in your mouth. You didn't need to endure the humiliation of getting busted raiding the hospital pharmacy cabinet. And you didn't need to worry about the chucks or the night sweats or the terrors until you could get your hands on another hit. But once you did it, you needed to do it again. And again. And again. That's why she couldn't stay. That's why she had to go. That was the end of her and Jack.

She finds Victor's station. It's a fucking pledge drive. She turns the radio off. *Maybe it's time I looked out for my own damn self.*

———— • ————

Jack and Marlene fucked up against the wall in the front entrance hallway, his jeans down around his ankles, her pressed against the wall, legs clamped tight around his waist, arms wrapped around his neck. They were too drunk to care.

Afterward, they didn't move for a long time. He could hear snatches of Johnny Carson's monologue from the TV in her roommate's bedroom upstairs. Everything felt right: her supple weight balanced between him and the wall, the smell of beer and stale cigarettes, the softness of her cheek, her breath, against his neck. He could have stayed there like that until morning, not moving, his ass hanging out. He didn't care. He just wanted to hold her.

But, as time went by, as he got older, as things got serious working for the Italians, to be with her became increasingly dangerous. When he was with her, when he had her, the anger that drove him like a relentless, dogged force of nature, simply faded away. That bottomless, frenzied rage was his gift, his talisman; it protected him, drove him, made him fearless. His constant, white-hot fury was like the magical amulets worn by African tribesmen charging into battle. Like them, he believed he was protected against bullets.

But with Marlene that anger was extinguished. With her, he was disarmed. With her, he could walk away from it all, be like other people. With her, in his line of work, he was a dead man walking.

Jack shakes off the memory. He's sprawled across the front seat of his car with a clear view of the Moravian house across the street and further down the block. The upstairs bedroom lights are on. He props himself against the passenger side door to wait. He's not sure what he's going to say to her, not that it matters. He simply won't take no for an answer.

He checks his watch: 2:12 am. This is as good a time as any—there's no one on the street and no traffic on nearby Jefferson Boulevard. Jack cracks the door to dump the piss out of the Maxwell House coffee can. He positions himself behind the wheel and prepares to start the car. He'll go through the alley and pull her out through the backyard, just in case there's any drama.

Before starting the car, he surveys the block one more time. Then he pulls the key from the ignition. He has a vague sense of unease that something's not right. Somehow, something is different, out of place. He just doesn't know what.

Jack exits the car and carefully shuts the door so as to not make a sound. He moves to the trunk of a nearby tree for cover and examines the opposite side of the block, house by house, porch by porch, parked car by parked car, trying to determine what set him off.

And then he sees it: the darkened carriage house behind the boarded-up Tudor. Every night he's been here there's been an ornamental lamp between the two garage doors, on a timer that goes on at dusk. Tonight, the carriage house is dark.

Jack studies the dark silhouette of the carriage house until he spots a slight halo of light reflected onto the bricks below the soffit above the garage door. The light is on, but something is blocking it.

Crouching behind parked cars, he moves in the direction of the carriage house. He stops one house down and peers out from behind the hood of a car. He realizes that the garage light is being blocked from his line of sight by an SUV parked in the driveway. There are two dark shapes in the front seat.

Jack pulls out his gun. He makes a wide circuit to avoid the SUV before crossing the street and entering the alley behind the Moravian home.

He enters the Moravian yard from the alley and goes to the covered back porch. He feels around beneath the wood steps until he finds the house key hanging on a nail. Muttering to himself at Victor's carelessness, he goes to the back door and lets himself in.

Jack locks the door behind him and moves noiselessly through the dark kitchen. He makes a quick sweep of the ground floor and then moves cautiously up the stairs to the second floor. Reaching the landing, he sees light coming from the partially open door to a bedroom in the front of the house. He moves stealthily down the hallway and pushes the door open. Marlene is standing at the window with her back to him. Jack watches her for a moment before speaking. She is even more beautiful than he remembers.

"You should stay away from the windows."

She turns, startled, and then realizes who it is. Her voice is like ice. "I told you never to come here again. You promised."

Jack strides across the room and takes her by the shoulders. He moves her away from the window. "This isn't safe."

She pulls away from him. Her body is rigid, recoiling at his touch. Jack closes the window shade. "You can't stay here. They'll kill you."

Marlene, stricken, turns back to face him. "Then he is dead."

Jack takes her arm but she angrily shakes him off. "Tell me. Tell me what's happened to Victor."

He grabs her roughly by the wrist and pulls her to the door. "Later."

Jack starts to drag her down the stairs but she grabs the banister. Her voice is a panicked shriek. "I have to wait for him. I have to be here when he comes home."

Jack looks her in the eye. "He's not coming home."

She studies his face and sees the certainty there. Her whole body sags. Jack's grip on her arm is all that's holding her up now. His voice softens. "Do you have someplace to go? Someone you can stay with?"

She shakes her head. "No."

Jack guides her the rest of the way down the stairs and into the kitchen. There is a phone on the wall and Jack cradles the receiver to his ear while dialing. He keeps one hand on her shoulder.

Marlene is suspicious. "Who are you calling?"

"My brother."

Marty's machine picks up and Jack slams the receiver back into the cradle. "We'll go to my place for now."

She tries to pull away from him, but he maintains a grip on her wrist. "I'm not leaving."

Jack hears something and gestures for her to be silent. She starts to protest but he pulls her close and stifles her with a hand over her mouth. They stand in the middle of the dark kitchen and listen. There is the creak of timber as heavy footsteps mount the back steps. Jack takes out the Glock.

The intruder is on the back porch now. Jack pushes Marlene back into the hallway and gestures for her to stay there. He moves across the dark kitchen to the back door.

Jack presses himself against the wall to one side of the door. The hulking shape of a man is silhouetted against the door's curtained window. An unseen hand twists the doorknob to find it locked, then shakes it violently. Jack smiles as he slowly raises the gun: he has this sucker dead to rights.

Suddenly, the door, together with the entire doorframe, explodes inward. Jack takes a step back to avoid the wreckage and the indistinct shape of a man's head juts into the room, bulky and formless under what appears to be a ski mask. Jack gets a whiff of something like diesel as he puts the gun barrel against the side of the intruder's head. "Surprise, asshole."

The intruder turns to face him with an animal-like bellow of rage. There is no ski mask, just the monstrous, freakish face of the beast. The creature's speed and power are beyond anything Jack has ever encountered and he has the gun ripped from his hand. He tackles the hideous apparition but it's like grappling with a forklift and he is hurled across the length of the kitchen. He slams into the opposite wall and slides painfully to the floor. Before he can roll away, the demon is on him, raising him up and pinning him to the wall with one powerful hand. Jack pummels the giant with his fists but his blows have no effect.

At the sound of a woman's scream, the beast turns to see Marlene standing in the kitchen. The monster drops Jack like a child distracted by a new toy.

Jack screams, "Marlene! Get back!"

Marlene tries to get away from the horrifying creature but is cornered. It reaches out with a massive hand to touch her face. Stupefied with fear, she slides to the floor, covering her head with her arms.

The monstrosity's malformed lips are trying to shape a word, spitting and sputtering, until it manages to produce a guttural, growling croak: "Muh... Mur... Marl... een..."

Jack grabs a newspaper from the table and lights it off the burner on the stove. He shoves the fiery brand into the monster's face and it backs off in fear. Jack starts to drive it out of the house but the creature, flailing wildly, manages to bat the flaming torch away.

Marlene quickly lights another newspaper off the burner. She uses it to drive the howling beast back through the door and onto the porch. The creature attempts to stand its ground and Marlene gets a good look at the monstrous features by the light of the torch.

Something in the beast's eyes causes her to lower the flaming brand. Those two eyes, a frenzied mixture of pleading and pain, are the unexpected windows on a tortured soul.

Jack grabs the torch from Marlene and jams it into the creature's face. The monster crashes through the porch railing, struggles to its feet and runs shrieking across the yard.

———— • ————

The dark SUV is stopped at the far end of the alley with the lights out. One of Pompey's hoods stands by the open passenger door checking the silencer on his gun. He looks to the driver and gestures toward the alley. "Pick me up at the other end."

The driver merely grunts. They hear a muffled cry and look down the alley to see a dark figure stumbling toward them, hands covering its face. The hood squeezes off a shot that seems to have no effect other than to cause the onrushing figure to veer angrily in his direction. Before he can get off another shot the enraged beast is on him. The impact is like a speeding truck eviscerating a hapless deer.

The panicked driver struggles to remove his gun from its holster. The fiend tosses the first hood's broken body aside, rips the door from its hinges, and hurtles inside the car. The scream never makes it out of the driver's throat.

22

J ACK AND MARLENE SIT side by side on the dusty second-floor ledge overlooking Trumbull. They are staring through the bulging array of leaded glass windows in stunned silence.

Marlene's gaze is fixed on the emerging sunrise softening the horizon. "There must have been something in the water, right? I mean, you hear about those things all the time: stuff leaching into the groundwater, messing with people's heads. There are all those old factories around the house. Chemical plants. Hazardous waste..." Her voice trails off. Even she doesn't believe it.

Jack is holding a cold can of Schlitz to the side of his face. He looks like he went ten rounds with Robocop. "Wasn't a figment of my imagination threw me across the goddamn room."

She studies his face, desperate for some sort of an answer. "Then what... What was it?"

He shrugs. "I don't know. I don't fucking know."

Marlene shakes her head. Jack lights a joint. He takes a long toke and holds it in, speaking through gritted teeth. "Then what? You tell me."

There is wonder in her voice. "The eyes... The eyes were so... I don't know..." She trembles at the memory. "He... Somehow..." She looks at Jack in astonishment. "He knew me! He knew my name!"

Jack exhales a cloud of smoke. "You don't know what you're saying. I mean, c'mon, that was rough, even for me."

He takes another drag off the joint. "What we need to do now is make a plan."

She shakes her head, as if to dislodge the horrible image in her mind. "I could see it in his eyes: He knew me. He knew my name."

Still gripping the glowing stub, Jack pops the beer tab and takes a sip. "Let me take you to the airport. You need to go somewhere. Anywhere."

She turns on him, fierce. "That's your fucking plan?"

He takes another toke, scowling, leaking smoke. "Yeah, that's my fucking plan. Unless you got a better one." His tone softens and he tries to sound encouraging. "You got skills. You were a nurse for fucks sake. You can probably do that anywhere."

She grabs the joint from him. He takes hold of her wrist to stop her. "You sure about this?"

She pulls free of his grasp. She takes a drag on the joint, her eyes daring him to do something about it. She inhales deeply and holds it in, speaking through pursed lips. "I'm not going anywhere. I want to know what happened to my husband."

She exhales a cloud of smoke. Then, she leans back against the wall, eyes wide, looking stunned. She stares at the joint in her hand. "What the fuck is in this? PCP?"

He reaches for the joint. "You don't wanna know."

She holds on to it, so he takes a slug of beer instead. He swallows and sets the beer down on the floor. He's watching her intently for her reaction. "He's dead. Victor is dead. That happened."

Marlene lights a match and holds the flame to the stubby remnants of weed and paper. It glows red-hot while she sucks out every last vestige of smoke. She finally exhales, eyeing him fiercely. "Fuck you. You don't know. You don't fucking know anything." She pauses, sounding troubled. "Do you?"

He shakes his head. She looks around for an ashtray. There isn't one so she jams the joint into Jack's open beer. He's pissed at first, then smiles and reaches for her. "God, I missed your fucking ass."

She pushes him away and clambers to her feet. She is forced to crouch in the tight space of the alcove. Her voice is an angry hiss. "This is on you. Whatever's happened to Victor is on you. These are your people. They hurt people. They kill people." She glares at him. "You hurt people. You..." She doesn't need to complete the sentence.

Jack takes a sip of beer in spite of the weedy detritus floating in it. "He knew what he was getting into. You both knew."

Marlene picks up her purse and stares at him, looking for some hint of understanding. "I loved him, Jack. And I never even had a chance to say goodbye."

He remains stone-faced. She turns away from him and goes out onto the balcony that runs the perimeter of the loft.

Jack climbs to his feet and follows. "Where do you think you're going?"

She's defiant. "I'm going to find out what happened to my husband."

He steps in front of her. She tries to go around but he blocks her. He takes her purse, opens it, and removes her keys and wallet. He pockets them and hands the purse back to her. "There's nothing you can do. You wouldn't even know where to start."

She looks him in the eye. "You would."

He can't meet her gaze. "Look, I know I fucked up. I should have been looking out for you."

She's not having it. "Like hell. There was nothing for you to be looking out for. There never was anything between us. Ever."

His look says differently and she's not about to let that stand. "I wasn't planning to leave Victor. I fucked you. Rinse and repeat. End of story."

"I don't believe you."

Her voice is cold. "You weren't sure you could help my husband. I fucked you and you were sure."

He can't believe what he's hearing. "What about all the other..."

She cuts him off. "Insurance."

"No, I know you. I've known you fucking forever. You're not like that."

She eyes him with contempt. "I let a guy pick me up once when I was pumping gas..."

He interrupts, "That was a long time ago."

She doesn't allow him to sidetrack her. "He was driving a Bentley. We had dinner at the Chop House first. That was back when it was still good."

His voice softens. "Everyone wants to be with you. That's your gift."

She's practically spitting. "Everybody wants to fuck me. And it's no fucking gift, believe me."

Jack gets in her face and backs her up. "What makes you think Victor was any different? He wanted you because every other guy wanted you. You were just another piece in his collection: world's best piece of ass. Why do you think he never let you go back to work?"

She's momentarily caught off guard. "That was my... I never wanted to be a nurse in the first place. It just... happened." She's sputtering now. "I don't need to justify myself to you. You're pathetic." She thrusts out her hand. "Give me back my keys."

He doesn't move. "Give me a list and I'll have my brother pick up some things for you."

She clearly doesn't like the idea. "Why him?"

"Because I trust him. Because maybe he's the only person I can trust."

Marlene does not look convinced. Jack flares with anger. "What? You think you're fucking better than him because he's a..." He can't go there.

She can. "I don't care who he fucks. I'm not some goddamn church lady." She continues, dismissive, "He's just fucking weird, that's all. I

COUNTED WITH THE DEAD

mean, Jesus, he goes around kicking that, that whatchamacallit, that icy gray sludgy stuff, out of the wheel wells of parked cars." Her voice rises in astonishment. "Other people's cars. Who the fuck does that?"

Jack looks at the floor, fighting off a smile. "What can I say? Marty is fucking Marty."

Marlene takes his hand in both of hers. There is a single tear sliding down her cheek. "I need you to find Victor. I need you to do that for me."

Jack pulls his hand free and takes a step back. "You don't know what you're asking."

There is the deep rumble of an engine, a car idling outside on the side street. Jack reaches into his jacket and pulls out his gun. Marlene takes a fearful step back. He's shocked by her reaction.

"What? You thought...?"

He listens as the car turns onto Trumbull and pulls away. He checks the clip and returns the gun to its holster. She continues to eye him warily and he grows annoyed. "If you feel that way, why did you come to me in the first place?"

She sounds wistful. "Because... Because I remembered you from before, from when we were kids." She can't help but smile. "You were a bastard then too," she sighs, "but such a beautiful fucking bastard." She grows serious. "And there was still a part of you that was good, that was real."

He can't believe what he's hearing. "I thought we were good together. This time."

She gapes at him in astonishment. "Jack, there was nobody fucking there."

He protests, "We couldn't keep our hands off each other."

She leans back against one of the bookshelves along the railing and eyes him warily. She's not sure how far to push him. But she can't help herself. "You fucked me. That's all you did: you fucked me. It was like being fucked by a goddamn machine. You weren't there anymore." She waves her hand dismissively at him. "You aren't there anymore. I don't fucking know you."

Her voice softens, for a moment. "When I saw you again, I was fooled, at first. I mean, I saw two arms, two legs, a face... There was something there that looked like an actual human being standing in front of me." Her eyes are hard now, remorseless. "I didn't know then what I know now, what you'd become."

He can't hide his astonishment. "You make it sound like I'm some kind of a fucking monster."

It's clear from the way she's staring at him that she's not going to argue the point. Jack flies into a rage. "I should've known. I should've known never to fucking trust you."

He turns and starts to walk away. Then, he does an about-face, as if he's come to a decision. "I'm gonna fix this. I'm gonna fucking fix this. I swear to god."

Marlene is puzzled. "Fix what? What has this got to do with Victor?"

He's already moving to the stairs. "You just stay put." He stops and jabs his finger in her direction. "You don't fucking leave this place unless it's with me or Marty. You got that?"

She nods.

He turns and charges down the stairs.

23

THE BEAST SITS WITH his back against a tree, exhausted by the hours of aimless, bitter wandering. His misshapen form is partially obscured by the overgrown weeds and saplings on the perimeter of a city park. The pain that engulfed his face like an angry swarm of bees has subsided to a dull throb.

Thirty yards away a young father is alternately tossing two tennis balls in opposite directions, expertly keeping a toddler and a dog entertained and on completely separate trajectories.

The creature marvels as the dog and the small clumsy human—pure, rapturous joy in motion—retrieve and return the bouncing objects over and over again. They are two miniature, hyperactive satellites, resisting and responding to the gravitational pull of the adult at their center. The beast finds the symmetry of their movements somehow satisfying, calming even. He's mesmerized. He doesn't want it to stop. Ever.

The dog is tireless, completing two trips to each one for the child. After a while, the toddler—not so single-minded as the dog—tires of the game and wanders off.

The child wobbles in his direction and the beast rises to his feet in anticipation. He wonders what it would be like to touch someone, to be touched. Not in anger, not with blows, a scalpel, or a drill, or fire. How would it feel to be touched by this tiny, fragile, harmless creature? Are there sensations beyond pain? Beyond loss? Beyond confusion?

The father calls to the child but is ignored. Then, heaving the ball one last time to the dog, he goes in pursuit of his son. He trails happily behind the toddler until he sees the beast. Realizing that this frightening creature is the child's destination, he shouts and quickens his pace. The dog, still gripping the ball, follows.

The child stops just short of the beast. His father is frantic, screaming, "Stop! Don't touch him! Don't you fucking touch him!"

The behemoth drops to its knees in front of the child. He attempts to communicate with this tiny being but in his excitement only manages a few guttural croaks. The child stares wide-eyed at the freakish ogre and then falls back on his butt, wailing. The dog outpaces the out-of-breath dad, drops the ball and barks furiously at the creature.

The father arrives, panting, falling forward like a sprinter at the wire, and lunges for the child. The beast intercepts him, shocked at the speed of his own reflexes. He holds the man at arm's length while reaching out with his other hand to the child. The father is making odd, gurgling sounds. The fiend releases him, and he falls to the ground, neck crushed, legs fishtailing in the grass.

The child is shrieking now, and the dog is barking maniacally. The beast reaches out to soothe them both and the dog latches onto his hand. The sharp jolt of pain acts as a catalyst, jump-starting the chain reaction of agony that suddenly erupts in every part of his body. The child is wailing, his father gurgling, the dog growling, jaws clenched onto his hand.

Enraged beyond comprehension, beyond understanding, the creature grabs the child by the legs and uses the tiny, compact object to bludgeon the dog. Again. And again. And again. Until both are still.

People in the distance are shouting. A few take tentative steps in his direction before thinking better of it.

There are sirens.

24

MARTY TURNS ON THE brights as they cruise slowly along yet another desolate side street. They pass the occasional lone survivor of a house, sometimes two or three in a row, separated by wide swaths of grassy steppe where neighboring homes once stood.

They see a Black man in a long coat and a wide-brim campaign hat. He's walking a brindle pit bull. He moves briskly, without a limp and Marty nods in his direction. "Don't think that's our guy."

"No shit, Sherlock."

The man and dog move out of sight. Marty pulls over to the curb. He grips the wheel and squirms in his seat. "How much longer? My ass is sore."

Jack ignores his brother, and they sit in silence for several minutes. Then they see an elderly Black woman walking a small poodle mix the color of wet playground sand. She's clutching a bulky purse under one arm.

Marty follows his brother's gaze. "No way that's a shepherd."

Jack ignores him. He waits until the woman is almost alongside the car and pops the door. The woman stops when she sees him. She grips the purse tight to her body and pulls the dog close.

Jack shows her his hands. "Sorry, lady, didn't mean to scare you."

"Who says I'm scared?" She eyes him suspiciously. "You the po-lice?"

Jack takes a step forward and she takes a corresponding step back. "You don't look like a policeman." She eyes Marty's Monte Carlo. "And that sure don't look like no police car." She shifts the purse to get a better grip. "But nowadays, you never can tell."

Marty leans out the car window. His smile is about as reassuring as a dental drill. "We found this dog, German shepherd. We're trying to find the owner."

The old lady says nothing. Jack realizes she is staring at the empty back seat of Marty's car. He gestures in the general direction of downtown. "We dropped it off at the city shelter. But we wanna find the owner before, you know..."

She's appalled at their apparent cluelessness. "You took that dog to the city? To animal control?"

Jack nods. "Sure. Why not?"

"The Humane Society will try to adopt it out. The city, they just gonna kill it. You should never take a dog to the city shelter."

Marty gets out of the car. "Yeah, well, that's why we need to find the owner. He's got a bad leg. Lives around here."

Marty moves to a position flanking the lady and her dog. She pulls the dog closer with one hand and slips the other into her bag. She looks suspiciously at Marty. "How do you know this man has a bad leg?"

Jack takes a step toward her. His tone is menacing. "You have a piece in that bag?"

Marty moves around behind her. She steps to the edge of the sidewalk and swivels her head back and forth in an attempt to keep tabs on both of them. ".44 Magnum. Put a hole in you big as a damn pie plate."

Marty moves closer. She turns her body toward him, holding the bag in front of her like a shield.

Marty raises his hands, palms up. "Look, lady, we just wanna get this guy his dog back."

She reacts to the sound of a round being chambered. She turns to find Jack's gun pointed at her head. His eyes are hard. "Nobody points a fucking gun at me."

Marty edges out of the line of fire. He holds his hands out to his brother. "It's okay, I got this." He turns his attention back to the woman. "Look, lady, take your hand out of the purse and set it on the ground. Please."

"The hell I will," she says, eyeing Jack. "He's not gonna do nothin'." She glares at Jack. "Why don't you just go ahead and shoot?" Her expression changes when she sees the look in Jack's eyes: he will shoot her. She gestures with the purse in Marty's direction. Her voice has lost its bravado. "I was pointing it at him. Honest to god truth: I was aiming at the big fella here."

Both Marty and the old lady are staring at Jack now. His face is unreadable, his voice barely a whisper. "I'm not gonna shoot you, lady." He lowers the gun until it is pointing at her dog.

Her eyes are tearing up now. "Why would you go and do that, mister? He hasn't hurt nobody."

Jack is unmoved. Marty takes another step back. "Lady, he's not playing."

The woman carefully removes her hand from the purse. She bends at the knees to set the bag on the sidewalk. She remains in a crouch, holding the dog close, and looks to Jack. "We good now?"

Jack is still pointing the gun at her dog. "Who's the guy with the shepherd?"

"The young man with the German shepherd sounds like that boy DeRon. Over on Scott Street. Right off Grandy."

"Which house?"

She stares at Jack like he's an imbecile child. "The only house."

Marty reaches into her bag and removes the gun. He empties the bullets into his hand and tosses them into the surrounding brush.

The woman rises to her feet, indignant. "Those don't grow on trees, you know."

Jack is already getting back into the car. Marty returns the gun to her purse and sets it back on the pavement. "In this town? I wouldn't be so sure." He sighs, turns, and returns to the car. "Have a blessed day."

Marty slides behind the wheel and looks at his brother. "For shit's sake Jack, it's a poodle. Who shoots a fucking poodle?"

Jack is watching the old lady scrambling in the undergrowth for her bullets. "We better get out of here before Annie Oakley reloads."

Marty starts the car. He can barely contain his anger. "Right, Kemosabe."

25

MARTY PARKS THE CAR down the street and they approach DeRon's bungalow on foot. His is the only house still standing in an expanse of urban prairie that extends several blocks in any direction. There is a battered white panel van in the driveway. The portion of the backyard fence visible from the front of the house is an eight-foot chain-link topped with coils of razor wire. Floodlights mounted under the bungalow's eaves and atop the garage create an illuminated island in the middle of a dark and desolate no man's land of overgrown vacant lots. It could be a checkpoint in the middle of the DMZ.

They pause on the sidewalk in front. There is a steel front door and bars on the windows. Jack is impressed. "Fucking Fort Apache."

Someone with some carpentry chops has rebuilt the porch and railing recently. Lumber and paving bricks are stacked neatly on the porch in preparation for additional projects. The steps are lined with empty clay flowerpots. A shovel used to mix mortar leans against a railing.

The German shepherd sleeping on the porch beside a pile of lumber springs to its feet. It charges down the steps and onto the lawn but is jerked to a stop by a chain bolted to the porch rail. Barking furiously, it lunges at the two strangers as DeRon stumbles out the front door with his rifle. He's unsteady and has to grasp the banister for support. "This is private property. You're trespassing."

Marty moves across the lawn to the left side of the porch, drawing the raging dog after him. Jack moves to the right and the dog, moving in a wide arc at the end of its chain, pivots angrily from one to the other. DeRon mirrors the dog's movements, swinging the barrel of the rifle back and forth like the needle of a compass.

Marty suddenly yells and charges the dog, which quickly backpedals, recovers, and rushes forward with increased fury. Marty backs hastily out of reach and the dog hits the end of the chain with such force it nearly snaps its own neck.

DeRon is distraught. "What's wrong with you? Stop that! He's gonna hurt himself."

Jack takes the opportunity to grab a flowerpot and fling it at DeRon. The little man stumbles backward, drops the gun, and drapes his arm over the railing to keep from falling. Jack vaults the porch railing and grabs the shovel. The dog scrambles up the steps after him and Jack greets it with the shovel, slamming the steel blade violently against the floorboards as he advances.

The dog skids to a stop and then retreats in the face of Jack's ferocity. Jack continues to pound the shovel blade savagely against the floorboards and the cowering dog backs into the far corner of the porch.

Jack raises the shovel over his head and prepares to strike the cornered dog. He freezes at the sound of his brother's alarmed shout. "Stop! Jesus..."

Jack lowers the shovel.

"Cool it, alright? Just cool it," says Marty.

The shepherd eyes Jack warily while attempting to make itself one with the floorboards. Marty continues to speak soothingly. "Let's just do what we gotta do and get the fuck outta here. Alright?"

Jack continues to brandish the shovel like a batter waiting for the pitch. His brother's voice, even softer now, is tinged with anxiety. "Alright?"

Jack drops the shovel and turns away from the cowering animal. DeRon makes a fumbling effort to recover the gun but Jack grabs him by the collar. Marty grabs the rifle and Jack sneers at his prisoner. "If you can't bite, don't bark."

He shoves the little man off the porch. DeRon falls into the shrubbery, thrashing about like a drunk in a wading pool. Jack takes the rifle from his brother and pumps out the shells. He wedges the gun between the lower porch rail and the edge of the porch for leverage and leans on it until he separates the stock from the barrel.

DeRon, still flailing in the bushes, yells at him. "What are you doing? I need that."

Jack tosses the remains of the weapon onto the lawn. "The hell you do. You'd be dead if I didn't need to talk to you."

DeRon manages to get a grip on the railing. He levers himself out of the bushes and onto the steps. Jack goes inside the house while Marty hauls DeRon to his feet and brings him along. He gets the full jolt of DeRon's cologne and holds the little man at arm's length. "Jeezus! You smell like Liberace's dressing room."

The dark shape of a cat slinks into the bedroom as Jack enters the house. Babyface sorties out from under the coffee table to bark shrilly at the intruders. Jack takes one look at the ancient mutt and dismisses it. He begins ransacking the house while the dog harries him from a discreet distance.

Marty kicks the front door shut. He starts tossing things around in another corner of the room. Neither one of them knows what they're looking for. DeRon leans against the doorframe and watches them with alarm. He is obviously drunk.

"This is private property. You're trespassing."

The brothers ignore him.

DeRon starts to hop in the direction of the phone. "I'm going to call the police."

Marty grabs him by his shirt and deposits him into a chair. Jack, growing frustrated, kicks over a stack of cannibalized computers. Babyface
slinks over to DeRon and cowers behind his chair.

Marty goes to the back door, opens it and quickly scans the yard. He
glances at the derelict truck trailer up on blocks and shuts the door. He
rejoins his brother. "There's nothing here."

Jack tilts his head in the direction of the coat closet by the front door.
"Check the closet."

Marty spreads his arms in frustration. "For what?"

"Just do it."

Marty flings open the closet door and sweeps aside the motley collection of coats and jackets hanging inside. Gladys leaps out from hiding
and Marty steps back in alarm. "Jesus fuck!"

Jack kicks at the cat as it ricochets around the room in terror. Marty
opens the front door and DeRon springs to his feet in alarm. "No! She's
an inside cat!"

The traumatized cat escapes and Marty slams the door shut behind it.
"Not anymore." He pauses to examine several freshly installed deadbolts
in the doorframe. He eyes DeRon suspiciously. "You dealing out of
here?"

DeRon can't meet his gaze. "I need those for protection."

Marty latches and unlatches one of the heavy-duty deadbolts, clearly
designed for a much larger door. "From who? Godzilla?"

Jack moves into the kitchen and stops to check out the assortment
of photos taped to the refrigerator. The photos are candid shots taken
in what appears to be a lab or medical research facility. The images de-
pict various employees gathered to celebrate birthdays and other casual
events.

DeRon appears on the fringe of several photos, seemingly out of place
among the grinning professionals. Jack focuses on the one photo that
clearly features DeRon. He's smiling happily, posing with a bearded,

middle-aged white scientist who has draped his arm around DeRon's shoulders. Both are wearing powder blue lab coats.

Jack peels it off the fridge and returns to the living room. He shoves the picture in DeRon's face. "Who's this clown?"

"The Pro... Professor... Doctor Drettmann, I mean. We worked together."

"What'd you do?"

DeRon pushes the photo away. "I don't have to talk to you."

The German shepherd on the porch begins to bark and DeRon glances nervously toward the window.

Jack moves to the window and looks out. "Expecting somebody?"

DeRon's first instinct is angry defiance and he turns to glare at Jack. "Kicked dog's gonna bark."

The dog continues to bark and his resolve softens. He suddenly decides he might actually like some company. Any company. "I worked for the Professor in the vascular bionics lab at the university medical center. It was my first real job after aging out of foster care."

Jack moves away from the window. "I don't need your fucking life story."

DeRon is determined to say what he has to say. "Sweeping floors at first. Cleaning test tubes. Taking care of lab animals. I liked it. Liked it a whole lot. Then, the Professor realized what I could do, what I was capable of."

Jack and his brother exchange dubious glances.

DeRon is insulted by their obvious skepticism. "I can fabricate anything. Anything." He smiles broadly. "Others fake it. I can make it."

Jack studies the little man, intrigued. "Make what? What'd you do? You and this Professor guy?"

DeRon is losing faith in his audience. "You wouldn't understand."

Jack leans menacingly over DeRon. "Try me."

DeRon isn't sure where to start. He's never spoken to anyone else about the work before. "The Professor—Doctor Drettmann I mean—his work is... was, focused on the remote manipulation of inert muscle tissue with electrical current. At least at first. Then BMI. Mostly BMI."

"Speak fucking English."

DeRon stares at his interrogator as if it's all completely obvious. "BMI: Brain-Machine Interface."

Now he's met with two blank stares. He soldiers on, not so sure of himself now. "I just know about it from watching the Professor. And reading about it. Surface electrocorticography arrays are implanted during open brain surgery. They control—"

Jack is not waiting for the punch line. "Fuck that. What did he need the stiffs for?"

"Cadavers have always been used in medical research. Since... forever."

Jack barks at him, impatient. "What did Doctor Demento need the stiffs for?"

DeRon reaches behind the chair and grabs a fistful of dog to calm himself. He takes a deep breath and continues, "In the beginning, when we started, the goal was to find a way to treat stuff like physical disabilities, extreme physical trauma, neurological disorders..." His mood darkens. "Then... then the Professor started working with human cadavers."

This is clearly not a good memory. He's talking fast, like he wants to get it over with. "He had some sort of a—you know—a breakthrough. And his work, his work seemed to go in a whole nother direction."

He stops, attempting to shrug it off. "I'm just a lab tech. I don't always understand these things. I did what I was told." He shakes his head. "But the Professor, he changed. He was obsessed. You know what I'm saying?" He smiles weakly, staring at the floor, his voice lower. "I guess he kinda left me in the dust."

COUNTED WITH THE DEAD

Jack gets in the little man's face. "Where is he now? Where is this Professor?"

"I don't know. Like I said, I was just the lab tech." There's bitterness in his voice. "Now that the Professor's gone, they treat me like the janitor. I'm not even full-time staff anymore."

Marty is flipping through the stack of Popular Mechanics magazines on the coffee table. The German shepherd is barking again. Marty moves to the window to look out. "What's with the dog? Your closest neighbor's gotta be fucking Windsor."

DeRon eyes him anxiously. "You see something?"

Marty turns away from the window. "Whole lotta nothin'."

"Probably scrappers. They come around here all the time. That's why I had..." DeRon tilts his head in the general direction of the porch. "The rifle." He reaches around to comfort the dog behind his chair but keeps glancing nervously toward the window.

Jack isn't finished. "So what happened with this Drettmann guy? Why'd he get shit-canned from the hospital?"

The German shepherd has gone quiet again. DeRon can't decide if he's more afraid of what's outside the house or inside it. "I don't know. Nobody ever told me anything."

Jack pulls him roughly out of the chair. Babyface commando crawls underneath the coffee table.

DeRon, balanced precariously on his good leg, realizes his best strategy is to keep talking. "The Professor, he had this dream: to make the crippled walk again, to give hope to the paralyzed. He was obsessed. There was almost nothing he wouldn't do." He catches himself, "No... that's not true." His voice is hard now, bitter. "There was nothing he wouldn't do. Nothing."

Jack eyes a half-empty bottle of vodka sitting on a table. DeRon meets his gaze. "You think I'm juiced up?"

Jack eyes the assortment of crutches and walking sticks leaning against the wall by the back door. He turns back to DeRon. "Why do you douse yourself in all that fucking cologne?"

He pushes DeRon back into the chair and rips the pants covering his bad leg open from ankle to crotch. The leg underneath is wrapped in a black plastic trash bag held in place by Velcro straps. Jack rips the plastic covering from the leg and steps back in horror at what he finds underneath.

Marty, disgusted, is flapping his hand in front of his nose to block the stench. "Jesus..."

Jack is equally at a loss for words. "Jesus fuck..."

DeRon's leg is a gory assemblage of sausage-like chunks of rotting flesh, bone, tendons, and composites; all stitched, bolted, wired, or stapled together. The whole bloody mess is interlaced with hydraulic lines and held together by metal straps. It looks as if a flayed cadaver leg had been put through a hay baler together with a grab bag of recycled electronics.

DeRon is trembling with emotion. "I... My leg... It was gonna be his proof of concept."

Marty keeps his hand over his face and takes another step back. "Dude, I'd ask for my money back."

"It was too soon. I shouldn't have... I shouldn't have begged him like that. It didn't take. He wasn't ready." He shrugs. "Careful what you wish for."

Marty perks up, pointing a knowing finger at DeRon. "Cause it's always darkest before the dawn."

DeRon replies with the slightest hint of a smile. "Behind every cloud, there's a silver lining."

Marty is grinning now, "Hey, let's make sure we're not making a mountain out of a molehill here..."

Jack angrily cuts them off. "Jesus fuck! Enough already."

Marty winks at DeRon. "Now he's gonna rain on our parade."

Jack glares at Marty, who keeps his mouth shut.

DeRon picks up the torn plastic bag and wraps it loosely around his deformed leg. "He's gonna try again. He promised. Once he perfects the technique."

Jack eyes him suspiciously. "I thought you didn't know where he was?"

DeRon attempts to backtrack. "I don't. He said he'd find me. You know what I'm saying?"

Jack pulls out the Glock. "This is getting us fucking nowhere."

Before Marty or DeRon can react, he chambers a round and splinters the top of the coffee table with a half dozen shots.

DeRon is screaming. He goes after Jack but Marty knocks him to the floor. He looks at his brother. "What the fuck was that?"

Jack glares at his brother. "Proof of concept." He flips the table with his foot to reveal the bloody carcass of the dog beneath. Torn pages from the Popular Mechanics magazines drift down into the blood pooling across the throw rug.

Marty releases his grip on DeRon and allows him to crawl over to the dog.

Jack clears the chamber. He gestures in the direction of the door. "Now, I'm gonna take care of the other one."

DeRon is rolling back and forth on the floor with the dead dog in his arms. Tears are streaming down his face. He's on the verge of hysteria. "What do you want? What do you want from me? What? What?"

Jack rolls the edge of the rug up with his foot to keep from walking through the blood. "Tell me what happened to this Drettmann guy. Why'd he get shit-canned? Was he stealing bodies?"

DeRon continues to rock the dead dog. "I don't know... I don't know..."

Jack moves toward the front door, gun ready. DeRon cries out to him. "Wait! Wait! Please!" His voice is reduced to a whimper. "Please..."

Jack turns away from the door.

DeRon struggles to a seated position and pulls the lifeless dog onto his lap. His eyes are open, but he is no longer there in the room with them. His voice is a dull monotone. "The subject was a teenage girl. She lost her arm at the shoulder in a car crash, so regular prosthetics weren't gonna do much." He shrugs. "We, I mean the Professor..." He shakes his head as if to clear it. "We built an articulated arm for her. It was designed so that she could manipulate the limb using her brain... Her brain waves."

He takes a moment to collect his thoughts before continuing. "It wasn't working. I mean, after weeks of work, the best she could do was maybe wiggle a finger. Maybe. It was hard to tell. The movement, it was nearly imperceptible. He was furious, the Professor."

The sense of aggrievement is clear in his voice now. "He was convinced that I'd messed up with the power source I'd fabricated, that the limb wasn't getting enough current to power it. He told me to splice the inverter into the backup generator for the demonstration." He shakes his head at the memory. "That's two hundred thousand volts, you know what I'm saying?"

He looks to Jack as if he must understand the insanity of the request. Jack looks back with dead eyes.

DeRon takes a deep breath and continues. "I warned him: it wasn't the power; it was the signal strength. I just needed time to tweak it, to figure something out. I don't think he realized how much torque..."

His narration is interrupted by an involuntary sob. It takes him a moment to compose himself; then the words spill out of his mouth. "There were sparks. Smoke. The girl, she panicked, she went crazy, and I wasn't able to cut the power in time."

DeRon is there now, in that lab, watching in horror as it all unfolds in front of him. "The limb, her new arm, it started moving under its own power. Gyrating. Then it started rotating like a propeller. Faster and faster and faster. So fast it was a blur, like a broken fan belt."

He grips the dog tightly in his arms and rocks back and forth. "So fast... Oh my Lord, so fast. And the screams..." He swallows a sob. "There was blood and tissue... The walls... The floor... The monitors... My eyes." He stares blankly at his hands. "Everywhere."

DeRon topples sideways onto the bloody carpet, still cradling the dead dog. He is sobbing uncontrollably. Marty looks at his brother. "I think we're done here."

Jack takes one last look at DeRon before leaving. Marty looks at the dead dog lying in a pool of blood before following his brother out the door.

———— • ————

Outside, the German shepherd is straining at the end of its chain, ferociously attacking the surrounding darkness. Jack stops on the porch to holster his gun. Marty, still in a state of shock, stares at him. "What the fuck, Jack? I mean, what the fuck?"

Jack jerks his head toward the house. "Get the shells."

Marty ignores his order. "You just wanted to shoot a fucking dog."

Jack stares off into the darkness. "I wanted an answer to my fucking question. Now get the fucking shells."

Marty hasn't moved. Jack turns on his brother, seething. "Whatever it takes, Marty. Whatever it fucking takes." He glares at his brother. "And nobody, and I mean nobody, better get in my way."

Marty is stunned almost speechless by Jack's threat. Almost. "Fuck you, Jack."

Jack gets right in his brother's face. "No, fuck you. What do you care? You got nothing at stake here. You got nobody depending on you. Dolores and the boys are in fucking Vegas."

Marty is livid now. "You don't think they got their people in Vegas? You don't think they got their Jack Killeen in Vegas?"

Realizing he's pushed his brother too far, Jack turns away from the confrontation.

Marty flings the door open and stomps back inside the house. Jack watches the barking dog for a moment. Then, sensing something, he steps off the porch. The dog stifles when it sees Jack approaching.

Jack moves across the lawn, scanning the surrounding landscape for any sign of movement. Marty comes out of the house and joins him. His brother is still staring out into the void. The dog, crouching by the steps, is growling at something unseen.

Marty is holding the shells wrapped in a sheet of paper ripped from a magazine. "You see something?"

Jack shakes off his feeling of foreboding. He turns and takes the packet of shells from his brother. "Get 'em all?"

"No, I left him one for his fucking charm bracelet."

Jack's tone is suddenly friendly. "I'm gonna fix this, Marty. I'm gonna fix everything. You wait and see."

Marty eyes his brother warily. Jack slaps him heartily on the shoulder, then turns and heads off in the direction of the car. He's already fishing in his shirt pocket for a joint. He calls back over his shoulder as he walks. "Fuck him if he can't take a joke. Am I right? Am I right?"

Marty remains silent watching his brother walk away. All around him, the rusted hulks of burned-out cars are ominous shapes in the darkness. Behind him, the dry leaves blowing across the sidewalk are a thousand tiny, scrabbling claws on the concrete. Then, the dog resumes its manic barking.

Spooked, Marty hurries to catch up to his brother. When they reach the car Marty gets behind the wheel. Jack slides into the passenger seat beside him, defiantly sucking on a joint.

Marty eyes the glowing end of the blunt with annoyance. Jack responds with a challenging look and Marty looks away. He starts the car, then remembers something. "What about the trailer?"

Jack has no idea what he's talking about.

"The one behind the house."

Jack is dismissive. "More crap, probably."

"He's got it hooked up to a generator."

Jack stares at his brother in amazement. "Running?"

"Yeah, it's running."

"What would he... Why the fuck didn't you say something?"

Marty, annoyed, turns off the ignition. "Last I looked, you got two fucking eyes."

Jack flicks away the joint. He starts to open his door but Marty stops him. He gestures in the direction of a police car creeping down a parallel side street. Jack stares at the patrol car in surprise; police patrols are a rare sight in this part of the city. "What are the fucking odds?"

"Probably just looking for a place to coop."

Jack's not taking any chances. "Leave it. I'll come back." He nods in the direction of the trailer. "Not like it's going anywhere."

Marty starts the car and pulls away from the curb.

"What about Marlene?" asks Marty. "D'you hear from Pompey yet? She off the hook?"

"She's gone."

Marty is puzzled. "Gone where?"

Jack, lighting another joint, tries to make it sound like no big deal. "She's got family down south somewhere. Didn't give me a name. Anyway, I figured it's better we don't know."

This is making Marty anxious. "We gotta call Pompey. Let him know."

Jack is holding in a lungful of smoke as he speaks. "What? That we helped her skip?"

Marty pounds the wheel in frustration. "Shit! Fuck! Fuck! Fuck!"

Jack, gripping the joint in his teeth, tries to calm him down. "Just let me worry about it. Alright?"

Marty is having a meltdown. "We're fucked. We are royally fucked." He turns to scream out the window. "Fucked! We're fucked! FUCKED!"

Jack allows his brother to blow off some steam before responding. "I'm working on something. Alright? I might have an angle."

"What angle?"

"I know some people. Maybe we can still work something out with the Italians. Alright?"

Marty has a death grip on the steering wheel. "You're blowing smoke up my ass."

Jack grins. "Is that a thing?"

"Fuck you."

Jack's already limited patience is nearing an end. He can no longer hide the edge in his voice. "Just sit tight. Alright?"

Marty remains grimly silent. Driving.

Jack stubs the joint out in Marty's pristine ashtray. "What the fuck? You gonna clam up on me now?"

Marty responds, exasperated, "I'm driving. I'm fucking driving."

"What? You can't drive and talk at the same time? Afraid you're gonna hit a fucking deer or something?"

Marty is stubbornly silent. Jack softens his tone. "Actually, there's deer all over the place nowadays. Even downtown. Skunks, possums, coyotes, all kinds of wildlife in this city nowadays."

Marty shakes his head in despair. "Now she's gone, we got nothin'. We got fucking nothin'." He jabs a finger at his brother. "We got to sit down with Pompey. We gotta talk."

"About what? Unless you got Victor Moravian wrapped around the spare tire, we got nothin' to talk about."

Marty slams on the brakes at a stop sign. He erupts. "This is on you, Jack! You got us into this! You gotta give me something. Right now, we got nothing."

Jack's not having it. "The hell we do." He pokes himself in the chest. "We got me. We got Jack Killeen."

Marty pulls away from the stop, grimly concentrating on the road. Jack turns and rolls down his window. He takes the packet of spent shells out of his pocket and tosses them from the moving car. Marty is annoyed by this act of littering. "What the fuck?"

Jack rolls up the car window. "What? I'm gonna go looking for a fucking trash can? The whole damn city's a goddamn trash can."

He rolls up the window.

26

THE BEARDED GUIDE IN the pith helmet is leading his little group through the ruined lobby. The only light comes from high above, leaking through the occasional window where plywood barricades have been ripped away. There is rubble underfoot and dark marble walls on either side. Craning their necks to gaze at the ornate, barrel-vaulted ceiling, they could be mistaken for a party of archaeologists exploring the ruins of an ancient Roman temple.

The guide stops and the group gathers around him. He gestures grandly at their surroundings. "David Broderick Tower. Built in 1927. Thirty-five stories. One of the tallest abandoned skyscrapers in North America."

The two French tourists adjust the telephoto lenses on their cameras in an effort to capture the neo-classical details beneath the grit.

"Magnifique!"

"Incroyable!"

The girl with the long, straight black hair and headphones sets her knapsack down on a chunk of fallen architectural detail the size of a small desk. She raises her camcorder and begins recording. "This is pretty badass."

The guide turns and gestures for the group to follow. "It's best we keep moving. All sorts of unsavory characters hang out in these places."

The beefy guy with the puffy jacket and surfer shorts looks around apprehensively. "What about the police?"

The guide is already mounting the central staircase. "I'm talking about the police."

His comment is met with nervous laughter from the others. Surfer shorts and the two French photographers clamber up the stairs behind him. The girl with the headphones grabs her knapsack and hurries to rejoin the tour.

The little group slogs up a seemingly endless sequence of staircases. Each successive flight leads to yet another maze of ravaged corridors, empty office suites, desolate retail spaces, and abandoned showrooms. Everywhere they go there is graffiti clinging to every surface like a turbo-charged strain of invasive mold.

A half hour later, they are gathered in a rubble-strewn corridor on the 28th floor. The guide checks his watch while his charges study the graffitied walls as they recover from the climb.

Surfer shorts, hands on his knees, is gasping for breath. "How many more floors?"

The guide paces, anxious to keep moving. "We'll go to the roof next." He glances over and sees surfer short's look of dismay. "Trust me, it's worth it. Incredible view: Metropolitan Building, Wurlitzer Building, David Whitney, Statler Hotel, United Artists Building... It's the freaking Grand Canyon of abandoned skyscrapers."

One of the Frenchmen is approaching the partially open door to a nearby office. "What eez the odeur?"

The guide cautions him. "Better not, might be squatters—"

Too late. The Frenchman, joined by his compatriot and surfer shorts, has already entered the room. Inside they find a rubble field of toppled file cabinets and moldering heaps of soggy file folders. Then they discover the source of the odor: the office has been used as a toilet and coiled mounds of shit are scattered throughout the room. Although the excrement appears to be human, it is massive, nearly bovine in scale.

The adventurers push past each other to get through the door and back out into the relative sanity of the corridor. Before they can process what they've seen, they hear headphones girl cry out from another office further down the hall. "Hey everybody, in here..."

When the group joins headphones girl in the ruined dental office, she is circling the room with her video camera. A red file folder goes unnoticed as it is trampled underfoot. Headphones girl is excited by her find. "This is badass. This is pretty frigging badass."

Someone has clearly been squatting in the space. The patient treatment chair is fully reclined and covered with a knotted assortment of blankets. A bedraggled canvas with the barely discernible images of a man and a woman is pinned to the wall opposite the chair and positioned so that the chair's occupant can study it at leisure. Badly stained, torn, and peppered with holes, it could be an ancient icon rescued from a ruined church.

There are the charred remnants of a fire in the sink. And there are the remains of a partially eaten meal in the dental spittoon next to the chair: the singed carcass of a small animal.

Headphones girl gingerly approaches the carcass with her camcorder. "Oh my god! Is that a dog?"

The guide takes a close look at the remains. "No, look, here's a piece of the fur. It's a possum or something."

Headphones girl zooms into the grizzled carcass with her camcorder. "Look at those claws; it's like a gigantic rat." She turns to the guide. "What are those things in South America? You know, those rats the size of pit bulls?"

The guide is looking anxiously at his watch. "No, I don't think it's a capybara."

Dozens of 8x10 photos have been pinned to the walls with rusty nails that look to have been driven into the plaster with a sledgehammer. The multiple images appear to be surveillance photos capturing the same man and woman at various locations around Detroit. The man is white, handsome, and thuggish. The woman is a beautiful, light-skinned African American. Headphones girl marvels at the images. "It's like an art installation. Like some homeless private eye is recording the lives of the lost Detroiters." She frames her next shot. "This is so badass."

They all freeze at the sound of loud noises coming from the direction of the stairs. The guide attempts to sound reassuring. "Probably just scrappers."

The noises are moving closer and they all turn to watch the door. The Frenchmen train their cameras on the entrance. Headphones girl is setting her camcorder up on a small pocket tripod.

Surfer shorts turns to their guide. He's holding a small folding knife in his fist like a child's crayon. "I've got a knife."

The guide gestures for him to put it away. "That's just gonna piss em off." He puts on a brave front. "Relax. I'm pretty good at rapping with these cats. We'll be fine."

Something large is moving closer, slamming into walls like a battering ram, and they each take an involuntary step back from the doorway. Surfer shorts is puzzled. "What? Did they haul a dumpster up here?"

Headphones girl focuses her camera on the entrance. "This is so frigging badass."

They are all watching the door when the beast comes through the wall.

27

VICTOR REMEMBERS LAUGHING WHEN she told him he had to kill the spider before she would join him in the shower. Grinning, playing it as a goof, he'd assured her that the insect would retreat into the gap near the ceiling as soon as the water was turned on. She had insisted but he remained firm, refusing to kill any creature, even a spider, for no good reason.

He leaned into the shower stall and attempted, unsuccessfully, to shoo the critter up the tiled wall. He turned back around to find her standing there, naked, splendid, with the pouty smile of a mischievous child. "Pretty please..."

He killed the spider.

Victor smiles at the memory, eyes shut tight against the water streaming over him. He is beginning to feel vaguely uneasy, trying to understand how he could still be in the shower. It all seems so long ago...

Then, he is plunged into a deep black void. He thrashes and kicks against the turbulence, his body tumbling and spinning, until he manages to arrest his descent. Flailing desperately with both arms, he struggles to make headway through the suffocating miasma he's become immersed in; so heavy he can't open his eyes against it. Then, as he begins to lose hope, his arm manages to break the thick, greasy surface.

Gasping, he opens his eyes to find himself staring at the plaster ceiling above his head. Something is dripping. Did he leave the shower running?

How long has it been leaking? Must be bad, the water is rusty. These old houses...

"Oh my god..."

Victor realizes it's blood dripping from the ceiling. He fights off the urge to panic as he struggles to understand where he is and how he came to be here. At first, he can't even grasp how his body is oriented in space. Then, as he slowly gains control of his emotions, he comes to understand that he's on his back in some sort of a chair. The ceiling and the walls around him are spattered with blood. Reaching out, he finds a pair of armrests and attempts to pull himself to a seated position.

Then he sees his hands; deformed talons gripping the arms of the chair.

The horrors of the preceding weeks—now a fiery, tumbling projectile formed from the shards of countless memories—slam into Victor's consciousness like a meteor. He screams and topples from the chair, landing hard on his shoulder and thrashing about in a panic on a floor sticky with blood.

After a moment he settles and grows still, trying desperately to remember how he came to be in this place. He reaches for the bloody pith helmet lying by his side. Puzzled by its weight, he turns it over to discover the wearer's bearded head still strapped inside, the mouth contorted in fear.

Then he sees it, the one thing that makes sense to his frenzied brain: the painting of Victor and Marlene. The images on the canvas are stippled with sprays of blood and his gaze follows rivulets of the dark fluid down the wrinkled canvas to the dead, staring eyes of a girl wearing headphones.

He uses the arm of the dental chair to pull himself off the ground. As he rises to his feet, the force exerted by his bulk levers the chair from its base and it crashes to the floor. Fighting for balance, he leans against the nearest wall for support, his massive paw dwarfing the bloody handprints there. Scanning the room, he encounters a charnel house of viscera, blood, and body parts.

Then his eyes find the photo of Jack and Marlene on the opposite wall, one of the few that has survived the carnage. The beast bellows with rage and lurches across the room, ripping the dental spittoon stand from the floor in passing.

Victor stops, frozen, the metal spittoon raised above his head. He stares at the photo. Who is that creature with his arms around his Marlene?

The words are expelled from his lips with the explosive force of a gunshot, leaving behind the taste of vomit. "Jack. Jack Killeen."

He drives the head of the spittoon through the photo and the wall behind it. He does not stop his assault until the room itself begins to collapse around him.

28

D RETTMANN IS SEATED AT a workbench surrounded by the wreckage of his lab. He tosses the screwdriver aside in disgust. The NIBT monitor, like so much of the equipment, is beyond repair.

The television propped up on a nearby chair plays without sound. A reporter is conducting a stand-up in front of an abandoned building somewhere downtown. The camera pans to reveal a disordered scrum of police and emergency vehicles with flashing lights. Crime scene tape flutters in the breeze. The on-screen graphic identifies the building as "The David Broderick Tower."

The sliding steel warehouse fire door—off its tracks since the beast's escape and now merely propped up to block the doorway—suddenly crashes to the floor with explosive force.

Drettmann swivels in his chair and watches in astonishment as his creation strides across the fallen portal. The beast's hulking form is shrouded in a hooded jacket the size of a pup tent and he is dragging a heavy object wrapped in a grimy canvas tarp behind him.

The scientist rises from his chair and approaches the creature. He talks to himself as he inspects his creation, "Bipedal mobility is excellent. Good fluidity. Obvious interaction with the environment." He turns to look at the fallen door. "Some limited indication of dynamic processing."

He moves closer to examine the creature. The beast, gazing around the lab, stops him with an upraised hand. "Where is the other one? The little one?"

"DeRon is gone. I don't think he's coming back this time."

Drettmann follows as the beast drags his sodden load into the surgery suite. The scientist's excitement is growing. "Speech is clear. Coherent. Clear indication of integrated natural language comprehension."

He grabs a clipboard. "I need to ask you some questions. I need to establish a baseline as soon as possible. You've already made so much progress. I need..."

Drettmann stifles when he realizes that the beast is staring at one of the operating tables. He cautiously approaches his creation. "Do you have any recollection of what happened to you?"

The beast ignores him.

Drettmann persists. "Do you remember this place?"

The beast rests his hand on a tray of surgical instruments. His voice is cold. "I remember."

Drettmann is not so sure that's a good thing. "That's good. Excellent. Do you have a...? What do you call yourself?"

The beast releases his grip on the canvas bundle. He indicates the spider web tattoo on his right elbow. "I am Joey Tiepolo."

Drettmann allows the clipboard to fall from his hands. "This is not possible..."

The beast indicates a different body part for each name: "I am Tito 'Big Kitchen' Munos. I am Marcus 'Bonedigger' Washington. I am Alex Bronzino. I am Hank Cooney. I am Lonnie Porter. I am Bud 'The Stud' Denker."

The creature lowers the hood to reveal his face. The conglomeration of flesh, bone, and composites has been singed and melted by the flames from Jack's newspaper torch. The beast presses the tips of his fingers against the ugly scar from the brain surgery. "I am Victor Moravian."

Drettmann stares at the creature in astonishment, attempting to make sense of this turn of events. "How do you know this? You can't possibly know all this..."

The brute grabs the canvas bundle from the floor and heaves it onto the operating table. The canvas partially falls away and the pale, limp arm of a woman flops over the side of the table. The beast returns the woman's arm to her side with a level of care that borders on tenderness. There is a tinge of regret in the creature's voice as he looks down on his grim handiwork. "The dead, they speak to me."

The moment passes. The creature turns back to the Professor and angrily peels a piece of charred flesh from his face. "And I have not forgotten you. I am a monster. I am your monster."

Drettmann stays clear of the beast as he moves to the table and carefully removes enough of the canvas to reveal the battered body of the headphones girl. He turns to the beast. "Why have you brought this here?"

He quickly backs away as the creature grabs the canvas shroud and rips it out from under the corpse, like a magician yanking a tablecloth from beneath a dinner setting. But there is no magic here. The girl's body rolls off the table and hits the floor with a dull thud.

The fiend raises the bloody tarp like a pirate's treasure map. It is the painting of Victor and Marlene.

Drettmann stares dumbly at the distorted images on the ruined canvas. "I don't understand."

The beast points to the corpse on the floor. He is gripped by a frenzy of excitement and can barely get the words out. "I want another. I want... I want one like me."

Drettmann attempts to calm him. "Of course, there's no question. This is my life's work."

The beast spreads the canvas out on the floor. Then he walks over, grabs the corpse by the arm, and drags it across the room. He deposits the girl's body on top of the canvas so that it covers the image of Marlene. "You will make another like me. A woman. A wife. She will be mine. She will belong only to me."

Drettmann dismisses the battered body with a wave of his hand. "I can do nothing with that."

The creature's voice is the roar of an enraged beast. "You will do this for me!"

Drettmann backs away, frightened. "I did not say it couldn't be done." Keeping a careful watch on the beast, he moves over to the corpse. "But my work requires the proper materials. I require suitable subjects. And, in the end—and the timing is critical—I must have a viable, living subject."

The beast points at the corpse resting on the canvas. "You will make me a wife. Mine is in the arms of the man who plunged me into this living hell. She will be like me. You will do this for me."

Drettmann uses his foot to lift the girl's lifeless arm. "You do understand the difference between this specimen and a living subject?"

The beast lunges forward and grabs Drettmann by the hair, lifting him so that he has to dance on his tiptoes. "I know living." He releases his grip and the Professor stumbles back a few steps before regaining his balance.

The beast crouches beside the girl's corpse. He lifts the body and sets it back on the table. "And I know dead."

Drettmann keeps his distance. "As I said, I require the raw materials..."

The beast turns to face him. "I will provide."

Drettmann takes an involuntary step back. "I will require the services of my assistant. DeRon. The little one."

The beast takes an angry step toward Drettmann. "No. You... You will do this for me."

Drettmann quickly moves to put the operating table between himself and the enraged beast. "It is not possible." He gestures around at his wrecked lab. "He is the only person who can restore this lab to full functionality."

The behemoth snorts like an angry bull facing a matador. Drettmann is not sure he understands. He gestures again to the wrecked lab. "The little one... I cannot do what you want without him."

The beast relents. "I will provide."

The creature stands over the canvas image of Victor and Marlene in happier times. "My loving wife. She looks at me as if I were some disgusting insect. When I am finished, she will see that look in his eyes. Then I will destroy him and she will have only me. She will once more be my loving wife."

Drettmann stands behind the flimsy protection of a chair and gestures to the corpse. "Leave it. There might be some elements I can work with. Perhaps." He realizes that the creature is staring at him. "Is there something else?"

The fiend moves to the open doorway. "You will take me to the little one."

29

J ACK PAUSES IN FRONT of Haddad's. The lights are out and the scissored steel gate over the door is padlocked. He can hear the muffled sounds of dogs barking from somewhere inside. He studies the front page of the newspaper in the battered Detroit Free Press vending box on the sidewalk. The headline is "Mad City!" The subhead is: "4 Dead in New Atrocity." Beneath it is a photo of the headphones girl with the additional caption: "Missing."

Jack reaches the top of the stairs to find Marlene sitting on the floor of the balcony that circles the loft space. There are several empty beer bottles by her side. She lifts the bottle in mock salute. "I took the last one."

Jack grimaces. "Haddad's is closed."

She's a bit tipsy. "Then I guess you're just shit outta luck."

Jack drapes his jacket over the railing. "Don't sweat it."

She smiles without warmth. "Do I look worried?"

Jack slides to the floor next to her with his back against one of the balcony bookshelves. He takes a joint and a book of matches out of his jacket pocket and lights up.

She eyes him with disapproval. "You shouldn't smoke so damn much."

He takes a deep toke as if to spite her. Holding in the smoke, he speaks through gritted teeth. "And you should mind your own fucking business." He exhales a cloud of smoke and his mood softens. "How come you're not sleeping?"

She slaps her beer down on the floor. "How can I sleep knowing he's out there somewhere?"

He's got no answer to that. He offers her the joint. She eyes it warily, seemingly tempted, but then waves him off.

The space between the balcony rail and the floor is lined with shelves containing a hodgepodge of books. She looks through the books on the shelf closest to her. "If I didn't know better, I'd think this was some little kid's library."

Jack scoffs. "Right. Professor Marlene in the house."

She riffs on the titles as she sifts through books: "Treasure Island. Kidnapped. Robinson Coe-roo-so. Ta-wenty Thousand Leagues Under the Sa-sa-sea." She does a bad imitation of a pirate. "Shiver me timbers. Do I detect a pattern here, Matey? Ahrrgggg..."

He stays focused on the joint. She moves to the next shelf, speaking through pursed lips. "Not so fast, girlfriend. Lord of the Ri-ings. The Deer-suh-laya. The Pie-oh-neer."

Jack points to another shelf. "There's a whole bunch of history books there. Mythology..."

She ignores him and continues with the books in front of her. "The T-t-t-t-time Machine." under her breath, "where can I get me one of them? K-k-k-king Solomon's Mines. King Arthur and the K-k-k-knights of the Round Table." She glances his way. "Rescue any fair maidens there, homie?"

He blows smoke in her direction.

She continues the inventory, sotto voce. "Prince Charming in the house, ladies. If you want my advice, go with the toad."

Unfazed, he reaches for her beer and takes a slug. "I like to read. Keeps my mind off things."

Her voice is dark with suspicion. "What things?"

He ignores her and absently fingers the spines in a row of books. "I don't play cards. Don't shoot pool. Don't watch sports. And I like to drink alone." He sets the beer back in front of her. "Mostly."

She flips through a large book of Greek mythology, looking thoughtful. "What was that word you used to use all the time?"

He smiles at the shared history this represents. "Autodidact."

She looks up from the book. "Self-taught, right?"

He nods. She studies him thoughtfully before continuing. "Teaching yourself stuff. Isn't that kinda like, what is it they say?" She attempts to smother a smirk. "A lawyer representing himself has a fool for a client?"

She pushes forward in spite of the fact he's no longer smiling. "How do you know all the stuff you taught yourself isn't just a load of crap? I mean, how would you know?"

His eyes are hard. "Got me this far."

Warned off by the intensity of his stare, she turns back to the book in her lap. It's open to the photo of a bronze statue depicting a naked Greek goddess. She studies the image. "Reminds me of Victor's 'Tiny Dancer.'" She smiles at the memory. "That's what he called her." She holds her hand about eighteen inches off the floor. "Little bronze lady about yay high. He was real proud of it. Been in the family forever." There's admiration in her voice. "She was this tiny little bronze lady in a toga thingy. Holding this big-ass bronze bowl up over her head." She raises her arms in imitation. "Looked like she was holding up the whole damn planet."

Jack corrects her. "They thought the world was flat in those days."

She lowers her arms. "Well thank you, Professor Killjoy." She snorts happily at the memory. "Bottom of this bowl wasn't flat, it was round. Round like the head of a giant circumcised cock. A giant circumcised cock, big as a damn house, pressing down on that itty-bitty, teeny tiny little lady trying to hold it all up. I told Victor it was Tinkerbelle, about to be smooshed by some giant asshole's ginormous cock." She smirks. "He said maybe I had a future as an art critic."

Jack retreats behind the security of his glowing joint.

Marlene closes the book over her hand to save her place. "One day, when he was at work I took it to a shop in Birmingham. Thought I might get enough money for it to start over someplace else. The man told me it was a reproduction. 'A very nice one,' he told me. 'Very old. You can probably get enough, young lady, for the down payment on a new car.'

I told him I lived in Dee-troit." A mirthless smile. "Probably be enough for a down payment on a goddamn house. That is, if I wanted to be in Detroit." There's a tinge of regret in her voice. "But it wasn't enough money to start the hell over. So I stayed." She smiles softly. "After a while, realized I'd be a goddamned fool to leave."

She brightens at another memory and reopens the book to study the image again. "Then, one day, I realized I was looking at it all wrong: Tiny Dancer wasn't a statue of Tinkerbelle, she was Wonder Woman." She raises her arms and holds the book high over her head in imitation. "Wonder Woman swinging some giant asshole around by his dick, about to send him flying off into outer space. Burn his hinky ass up in the sun." She brings the book back to her lap. "Now... Now I got a big-ass grin on my face every time I see her."

Jack snuffs out the joint and climbs to his feet. Marlene looks up at him. "You said Marty was gonna pick up some things for me."

"Tell me what you need, I'll take care of it." In response to her look, "I'm gonna keep him out of this."

She slams the book shut, alarmed. "Why? Is it because of what happened to Victor?"

He tries to sound reassuring. "We don't know what happened to Victor."

She's practically sputtering in anger. "You said he was dead. You said..." Her words are choked off by a sob.

Jack grabs her hand and pulls her to her feet. She stumbles forward, into his chest. When she doesn't immediately bolt, he wraps her in his arms and holds her, lips pressed softly against the top of her head. His voice is a whisper. "Maybe I got it wrong. I mean, what the fuck do I know?"

They remain like that for a moment before she abruptly pulls away.

Jack raises his hands as if from a hot stove. "I'm sorry."

She lurches back to the railing for support, silent. She steadies herself and turns to face him. "What am I doing here?"

"I'm keeping you safe."

"Maybe I should go to the police."

He looks at her in astonishment. "And tell them what? What happened at the house the other night? They'll think you're back in the game. They won't believe a fucking word you say. Before you know it, you'll be back in Plymouth, eating off a goddamned paper plate with a plastic spoon. That's if they don't ship you direct to the nuthouse." She's staring hopelessly at the floor. "Get some sleep. Alright?"

She looks up at him. "What about you?"

"You know me, I don't sleep. Not really."

"Still the same... You know?"

"Mostly." He shrugs. "Sometimes I wonder what's fucking real and what's, you know..." He shakes his head.

She eyes the joint in his hand. "Might have something to do with living your whole damn life in an altered state."

He raises the remaining nub to his lips. Eyes fixed on hers, he takes a long, deep toke.

She goes to the bedroom door and stands there gripping the knob. Her eyes are fierce. "My life is a goddamned nightmare. All I want is to wake the hell up."

She goes inside and slams the door shut. Jack turns and goes slowly down the stairs.

30

J ACK HAS NO CONCEPT of how long he's been holding on. His hands are locked together in a death grip behind Marty's broad back as he fights desperately to keep his brother from being pulled under. His shoulders are on fire. He long ago lost the feeling in his arms, wrapped around Marty in an awkward bear hug, one wedged beneath his brother's armpit and the other around his neck. The croc, or whatever the fuck it is, has his brother's lower half engulfed in its massive jaws and is trying to pull him down into the murky depths.

Jack stares into the cruel, patient eyes of the beast, not even sure if Marty is still alive. Then, with one massive gulp, the creature's jaws thrust up out of the water to engorge Marty all the way up to his shoulders.

Jack feels Marty's bulk slipping out of his grasp. He can only watch in despair as the croc disappears beneath the water with its prize.

Soon, all that remains is the thin gossamer mesh of blood on the placid surface.

31

J ACK IS DRINKING ALONE in the deserted barroom. There are
several empty bottles of Stroh's on the table in front of him. The
table centerpiece is a squat wine bottle in a wicker basket.

Jack studies the reflections in the glass bottle. He knows that,
on closer examination, each glimmering highlight, each fractured
glint of light, will reveal a perfect, miniature reflected image from
the surrounding room: the TV mounted on the wall in the corner,
Leon, the bartender, standing behind the counter washing glasses,
the jukebox, cigarette machine, and pinball machines, all in a row
along the side wall of the long, narrow space. And in the back, the
two indistinct figures circling the pool table.

More than once the reflections in a bottle have allowed Jack to
watch a man move across a barroom behind him. But that's not
the only thing that separates him from other people. He could pick
up a bottle and end the life of a man sitting, unsuspecting, in the
next chair. No hesitation. None. That is his gift. Others might think
about it. Others might rage and threaten and shout, but he acts.
Without hesitation. Without warning. Without remorse. At least
that's how it's supposed to be.

But he's no sociopath. No fucking way. No sociopath would have
suffered such gut-wrenching misery when he was unable to take care of
his own family. No sociopath would have felt that utter sense of dread
when the bills came due, when the refrigerator was empty, when the

phone didn't ring. And no sociopath would have endured the anguish he felt when he left.

That's what men do: they leave. They've been doing that for thousands of years. The knights in the Crusades, the Vikings, Christopher Columbus, Lewis and Clark, Robinson Crusoe, they all left. For fuck's sake, even Jesus and his apostles left their goddamned families in the lurch. They had a job to do. And they didn't want the people they cared about to face the consequences.

Everyone but the Big Fat Fuck. He never left. The Big Fat Fuck was a giant, immovable object, a mountain packed full of steaming, liquefied shit. From one of those movies he saw as a kid, where the top blows off the volcano and the towering wave of scalding lava spreads out across the landscape, destroying those too old, too young, too slow, or too stupid to get out of the way.

No, Jack assures himself, he's nothing like the Big Fat Fuck. No child has ever flinched when he raised his hand. No one has sat listening to his endless stream of bullshit and wished someone would put a bullet between his fucking eyes.

Jack smiles. Lots of people probably want to put a bullet between his eyes, but not because he won't shut his fucking mouth. That's something.

Then, he realizes that the banter from the pool table has gone quiet. He looks over his shoulder to see that the pool players are gone and a man is standing in the rear doorway they just exited through, watching him. Another man, a stranger, has replaced Leon behind the bar. He too is staring at Jack. Jack looks over to see Borneo, stationed by the front door, grinning at Jack as he holds it open for Magoo.

Magoo weaves his way through the jumble of small round tabletops like a duck plowing through a clutch of lily pads. He's carrying a large white envelope that he tosses onto the table in front of Jack. He stands for a moment and glances around the bar at his various associates before settling into a chair with all the grace of a garbage scow backing into a berth.

Once seated, he takes another dismissive look around before turning his attention to Jack. "Not gonna buy me a drink?"

Jack doesn't bother answering. He shifts in his chair so he can keep tabs on Magoo's men.

Magoo drums his fingers on the envelope, but Jack doesn't take the bait. The overhead light shining down on the thug's bald scalp reveals a long-healed dent in his skull, like the divot left by the head of a hammer. One of his ears is nothing more than a button-like nub of scar tissue, with the rest bitten or sawed off.

Magoo pushes the envelope forward. Jack opens it and allows the contents to slide out onto the table. They are photo proof sheets depicting a pretty teenage girl in a Catholic school uniform. Monica.

Jack slips the photos back into the envelope. He refuses to give the human refrigerator seated across from him the satisfaction of a reaction.

Magoo taps the envelope with a finger. "Figured I'd save you a trip. With that court order, you got to keep your distance from the house. The one over there on Fourth Street."

"Am I supposed to be impressed you can read a street sign?" Jack nods toward Borneo, still manning the door, grinning. "Or did he do it for you?"

Magoo ignores him. "And that school... What can I say? Security at that place is pathetic. Not like the public schools—they don't even got metal detectors."

Borneo gleefully interrupts. "That's cause they got nuns."

Magoo turns angrily toward his subordinate and Borneo backs off, contrite. He makes a zipping motion with his fingers across his lips.

Jack can feel the weight of the Glock pressing against the small of his back. He's trying to calculate how long it would take him to get his hands on it, aim, and fire. Magoo would definitely be a headshot. Nothing else is gonna stop him. And the others? Who the fuck is he kidding?

Magoo moves his hands until they are gripping the edges of the small round table, as if he is contemplating flipping it over. "I know what you're thinking, Jack. You're thinking you can take me out." He shrugs. "Maybe. Maybe not." He tilts his head in the direction of the pool table. "Take down my guys? No fucking way. This ain't some fucking movie. And you sure as fuck ain't Charles Bronson."

"Get to the fucking point already."

Magoo does his best to sound solicitous. He shouldn't have bothered. "You can take care of yourself, Jack. We know that. But everyone else, they're out there flapping in the breeze." He turns to address Borneo. "What's the name of that dump downtown? Where his old lady works?"

Borneo is grinning like the know-it-all second grader who just earned another gold star. "Garth. Artist. Supply."

Magoo turns back to Jack. "Right: Garth's Art Supply. What a fucking dump. I'd be embarrassed to let my wife work in that shithole."

"Ex. And we were never married. And I doubt if anyone married to you could hold down a fucking job."

Anger flashes in Magoo's eyes but he remains outwardly calm. "And your brother..." He shapes his lips almost into a kiss as he enunciates the next two words: "French Press." He continues, grinning, "That degenerate's the reason you don't have any fucking friends in this town. You shoulda kicked him to the curb a long time ago."

Jack just stares. Magoo leans back in his chair. "So, you cutting him loose too?" He smiles. "We know all the fag bars on Six Mile."

Jack matches him, smile for smile. "Yeah, I bet you do."

Magoo has both hands, fists clenched, in the center of the table now. The muscles in his jaw are twitching.

Jack is undeterred. "By the way, what does my brother's dick taste like?"

The table creaks under the downward pressure of Magoo's powerful fists and forearms. It's a struggle, but he eventually regains his composure. He unclenches his fists and backs his chair away from the table. "You're lucky the boss has a soft spot for you."

Jack doesn't sound the least bit concerned. "He didn't look so good last time I saw him."

Magoo does not seem entirely pleased by the thought. "That rat fuck's gonna live forever."

Jack shrugs. "I wouldn't wanna live like that." He carefully edges his chair away from the table, eyes fixed on Magoo. "And I'm not the only one with family."

Magoo's goons are reaching into their jackets. Magoo keeps his eyes fixed on Jack, pondering, calculating. Should he end it here and deal with the consequences later? He snorts, smiles, and waves his men off. "Nah, that's not your style, Jack."

He gets to his feet. "You got twenty-four hours to fix things."

Jack's hands are grasping the back of his chair, inches from the Glock. "Or what?"

Magoo nods in the direction of the photos. "Those'll come in handy at the memorial service."

He turns and exits, followed by his men. A moment later, Leon slinks out of the storeroom and reappears behind the bar. "Everything okay, Jack?"

Jack hurls a beer bottle that shatters against the shelves of liquor bottles behind the bartender's head. By the time he hefts the wicker wine bottle, Leon has retreated back into the storeroom.

32

J ACK SITS IN HIS parked car on a residential side street. He's smoking a joint and staring blankly at the sloping hood of the Taurus. Marty thinks the car is a joke. "You bought a fucking Taurus? What, there weren't any minivans on the lot?"

Jack doesn't give a shit about cars. Cars exist to get you from point A to point B, to start when you need them to start, to run when you need them to run. A radio is good. A lighter even better. And heat. Can't forget the heater. End of story. Who gives a shit what brand it is? Besides, the Taurus is a car nobody pays attention to. And he needs a car nobody pays attention to.

Jack takes a long, greedy hit from the joint. He wonders why he's always driven Fords. Even when he stole a car it was a Ford. He grimaces at the realization: *didn't the Big Fat Fuck always drive Fords?* He stubs the glowing nub out in the ashtray. There's no point going there: he's nothing like the Big Fat Fuck.

Jack hates himself for what he's about to do. Monica's always been the one normal thing about his life. Having a kid, Christ, just being with your kid, in the grocery store, sliding into a booth in the Big Boy on Jefferson, walking down the fucking street, made it feel like you were a regular person. People looked at you different. Other parents talked to you about things normal people talk about. Hell, even he saw himself differently when he was out with Monica, just being a dad, just being a normal human being.

Gazing at the block of dowdy bungalows he imagines the people inside, the families, the moms, dads, kids, grannies, sisters, and brothers who inhabit those brick shells. He can no longer get his head around the concept of two people or more living in the same space. Even though he did it himself a lifetime ago, the thought of multiple bodies occupying, moving around in, eating, sleeping, shitting, sharing the same collection of rooms, is beyond his comprehension.

Something he can't quite put his finger on broke inside of him a long time ago. He's spent the intervening years isolating himself, slowly reducing his world to the building on Trumbull Street, inhabited by a population of one. But now that his life is spinning out of control he needs to cut his family out of the picture. Completely this time. He needs to do it for their own good.

The light is starting to fade as Jack starts the car and pulls away from the curb. He turns the corner onto Fourth Street to see Monica already seated on the curb in front of the house, waiting. *She's wearing that goddamned Mickey D outfit. Christ, I'm not raising my kid to flip burgers.*

The black Escort from the dealership that Monica hated is parked in the narrow driveway and he pulls up in front, blocking it. Monica walks over and leans in the window. "You can't park here, Dad. I can't get my car out." She sees the bruises still visible on his face from the encounter with the beast. "What happened, Pops? D'you get fresh?"

He ignores the question. "Look, I came by to let you know I can't take you out driving today. I got something I have to do." He ignores her look of disappointment. "As a matter of fact, you're probably not gonna see me for a while."

She hits him with her most earnest look. "I can drive you. I have my learner's permit."

He ignores her suggestion. "Where's your mom? I need to talk to her."

Monica shrugs.

He doesn't like where this is going. "You here by yourself?"

"She usually..." She catches herself. "Sometimes, she stays at Eric's during the week."

"Right. Eric. The clerk."

"Sales associate, Dad."

He grips her shoulder and sniffs her hair. "You smell like a goddamned french fry."

She pulls free, grimacing. "Thanks a lot, Dad."

"Don't I give your mother enough money so you don't have to work?"

She indicates the Escort. "Mom says I have to pay the insurance. And gas." Another shrug. "Says I need to develop a work ethic before it's too late."

Jack doesn't like the inference. "You don't think I worked for a living when I was your age? Me and your Uncle Marty—"

She cuts him off. "Dad, we get ancient history in school."

"Watch your mouth, smartass."

She's rocking on her heels, not the least intimidated. "You thought it was funny."

He's fighting off a smile. "Fucking smartass."

She's turned serious. "Mom says you did stuff."

Jack doesn't like what he's hearing. "What do you mean 'did stuff'?"

She can't meet his gaze. He makes another stab at connecting. "What're you reading these days?"

"Stuff. For school."

"Like what?"

She shrugs again.

He's annoyed. "You're not gonna be a fry cook for the rest of your life. Or a sales clerk."

She's defiant. "Sales associate. And he gets real good employee discounts." Her best winning smile. "C'mon, Dad, how'm I gonna pass the driving test if nobody takes me driving?"

He starts the car. "Another time, sweetie. I promise."

She's pissed now. "Mom says you and Uncle Marty are not role models. That's why I gotta work this stupid job."

There's resignation in his voice. "You listen to your mother."

He pulls the car into the driveway to turn around. He pauses there, leaning out the window. "Tell your mom I need to talk to her. It's important. Alright?"

She stares at him, arms folded across her chest. He points to the Escort. "By the way... You're welcome."

He pulls back into the street and she shouts after him, "You know who is a good role model, Dad? Eric."

Jack shakes his head and drives away.

———— • ————

Jack is driving along the desolate street leading to DeRon's house when he sees a pair of headlights in the rearview mirror. He takes out the Glock and sets it on the seat beside him.

Jack parks down the street from DeRon's bungalow. The house and the surrounding yard are cloaked in darkness. There are no lights inside or out. It looks like a power outage. He watches in the mirror as the trailing car, now with its headlights off, comes to a stop about thirty yards behind him.

Jack takes the gun from the passenger seat and gets out of the car. He walks purposefully toward the other car with the gun pressed against his leg. He realizes who it is and quickly holsters the weapon.

Monica rolls down the window as her father approaches the Escort. She's grinning, pumped up with excitement and talking so fast the words are running together. "Pretty good, huh? Just like you taught me. You never would have seen me if it wasn't so dead around here."

Jack leans on the car, seething. He's angry at her but even more angry at himself for leading the kind of life that puts his family at risk. "What the fuck do you think you're doing? Turn this goddamned thing around and get your ass home!"

She's rattled by his vehemence. "I'm sorry... I just..."

Jack grabs her face and forces her to look at him. "You ever do something like this again and goddammit I'll fucking... I'll fucking..." He releases her, frightened by his rage.

Monica, terrified, tries to start the car but only manages to flood the engine. She keeps grinding away until her father reaches in and stops her. "Alright. You gotta let it sit now, sweetie."

Monica is gripping the wheel with both hands, trembling. Jack leans into the open window. His voice is soothing. "I want you to stay in the car. Okay? I'm gonna go talk to this guy for a minute. Just for a minute. Then me and you are gonna have us a little talk. Okay?"

Monica nods.

"Lock the car and stay inside. You understand?"

He motions impatiently for her to lock the doors. She sticks her tongue out but complies. Then she rolls up the window. Jack taps on the glass and she rolls it back down. "Wait another minute and start it up again," he indicates, "then pull up behind my car. You see anybody, you lean on that horn big time. Okay?"

"Alright already."

He gestures and she rolls the window back up. He turns and cuts diagonally across the intervening urban tundra to DeRon's home.

As he approaches the house Jack sees that the steel door has been battered down. He takes out his gun and cautiously mounts the porch. There is no sign of the dog. The post the German shepherd was chained to has been torn away from the porch railing.

Jack looks over his shoulder to see that the Escort hasn't moved. He decides the trailer can wait. As he turns to go back to his daughter, he hears a soft thud from inside the house. He goes and peers inside the front door, gun at the ready. "Hey... Doctor Dolittle... That you?"

Jack steps inside to find the interior has been trashed. Doors are kicked in, furniture splintered, and fixtures ripped from the walls. Entering the kitchen he finds the German shepherd hanging lifeless from the ceiling, hog-tied in its own chain.

"Goddammit."

Jack hears the Escort's engine kick in and realizes he has to get back to his daughter. He turns to go but finds the beast's hulking form blocking the doorway. The hooded jacket conceals most of the deformities but there is no hiding the ravaged, death's head of a face.

Jack raises the gun. "Who the fuck are you?"

The beast tilts his head like a curious dog. His voice is a guttural hiss. "You don't know me, hitman?"

Jack, recalling their previous encounter, takes a step back. "Get away from the door."

The creature moves closer, crowding him. Running out of room to back up, Jack fires. The fiendish behemoth shudders from the impact, then lunges forward to knock the gun from Jack's hand. He grabs Jack by the collar and drags him to the back door. "Come. I will show you. Hitman."

The beast pulls him out the back door and into the yard. Jack struggles to keep pace as the creature drags him over the uneven ground to the trailer. The padlock is gone and the trailer door is ajar. The fiend rips the metal door from its hinges and tosses it aside. He lifts Jack like a rag doll and hurls him inside.

Jack struggles to his feet and the entire structure rocks as the beast climbs inside after him. The compressor is no longer running the refrigeration unit and he is forced to cover his face against the overpowering stench. As he adjusts his eyes to the dim light, he begins to make out large metal bins lining both sides.

The beast lifts the cover on one of the bins. Inside, still recognizable beneath heavy wrappings of gauze and cellophane, are human body parts: a torso, an arm, hands. Jack tries to back away, but the monster grabs him and forces his head inside the bin. "See the results of your work. Hitman."

He picks up a gauze and plastic-encased arm and holds it in front of Jack's face. "Have you already forgotten the men you have killed?"

Jack tries to turn away, but his captor keeps a firm grip on him. He drops the cadaver limb back into the bin and lifts a torso. "Have you forgotten the flesh your bullets have ripped? The bones they have shattered? The souls you have damned?"

The creature dumps the torso back into the bin and pulls a soggy cardboard shoebox down from a shelf. He paws through the contents, a tangle of wallets, drivers' licenses, car keys, holsters, and guns. He pulls out a driver's license, grabs Jack by the hair, and holds it in front of his face. "Lonnie Porter. Dead. By your hand."

He shoves the laminated license into Jack's mouth. Jack tries to spit it out, but the beast's powerful fingers jam it further down his throat. Before he can deal with the first one the beast shoves another license into his mouth. "Joey Tiepolo. Dead. By your hand."

Jack collapses to his knees, choking, as the beast crams yet another license into his mouth. "Tito Munos. Dead. By your hand."

No longer bothering with the names, the demon jams more crumpled driver's licenses into the hitman's mouth. Jack is gagging, pawing desperately at the wad of stiff plastic blocking his airway. When the beast finally releases him Jack rolls on the floor, coughing and spitting as he struggles to clear the compacted clump of laminated plastic from his mouth.

The creature dumps the remainder of the wallets and holsters over Jack's prostrate form. "The bodies of the dead were used to create the monster that stands before you."

The beast squats awkwardly in front of Jack. He grabs him by the scruff and pulls him close so that they are eye to eye. "Do you not know me, hitman?"

Jack stares into the eyes of the monster and is horrified to discover the eyes of Victor Moravian. "Mother of god... Victor?"

The beast releases him and Jack scrambles on all fours to the door. He tumbles out of the trailer to the ground and tries to scuttle away on his knees and elbows. The beast leaps from the trailer and follows. He moves to block Jack's path. "Butcher. You have no stomach for the fruits of your own labor."

Jack fumbles for a piece of scrap metal to use as a weapon but the beast kicks it away. Jack tries to crawl after it but his tormentor steps in front of him, like an adult toying with a toddler. "I'm not going to kill you. Not yet. Your pain is a drop in the ocean compared to mine. I will destroy everyone around you. Only then will I come for you. And Marlene, my wife, my loving wife: she will be mine once more."

Jack grabs a rock. He climbs to his knees and takes a wild swing at the creature. "You fucking bastard!"

The creature knocks Jack down and stands over him. "She will envy even you, hitman."

The beast turns and strides away. Jack climbs to his feet and shouts after him.

"I'll kill you! I swear to god, I'll fucking kill you!"

The creature turns back to face the hitman. "I am already dead."

The beast strides off into the darkness.

Jack climbs to his feet, spitting out bits of laminate as he walks unsteadily over to the trailer. He spots a can of gas by the generator and splashes it over the trailer. He throws a match on it and the vehicle bursts into flames.

Jack returns to the house and retrieves the Glock. Then he hears the car horn. "Oh my god... Monica..."

Jack bolts from the house and runs like every demon in hell is after him. The horn stops and Jack pushes himself harder.

Jack finds the Escort parked directly behind his car. The driver side door has been ripped from its hinges and Monica is gone. Her learner's permit has been pinned to the car with a rusty railroad spike driven through the sheet metal roof.

Jack screams and batters the roof of the car with his fists. He rips out the railroad spike and repeatedly punctures the sheet metal to the point of exhaustion.

Looking out across the vacant fields Jack spots two fire trucks that have stopped several blocks away with their red warning lights flashing.

Jack knows they will not approach a fire in this part of town without a police escort. His instinct for self-preservation kicks in and he stumbles back into the yard to retrieve the gas can. He hurries back to the Escort and douses it with gasoline. He throws the empty can into the front seat and follows it with a lit match. By the time he gets into his own car the Escort and the trailer in DeRon's yard are both fully engulfed.

A light rain begins to fall as Jack drives away from the twin infernos.

———— • ————

Jack drives recklessly through the deserted nighttime streets in search of his daughter. He moves in increasingly wider concentric circles with the burning car and trailer always at the center, fishtailing, running stop signs, and occasionally veering off the road.

In time, he can no longer see the glow from the fires or the distant blinking of emergency lights. He knows he should stop to think, smoke a joint, make a plan. He's looked into the remorseless eyes of the beast and knows what he's doing is pointless, but the rage, panic, and desperation won't allow him to stop moving.

A steady rain is falling when he finally stops. He can't decide where to go next. Downtown? The riverfront? East again? West, toward Woodward? To the police? To Pompey?

He comes to a decision and drives until he spots a payphone outside a liquor store. He gets out of the car and fumbles through his pockets for change to call Marty. The phone is out of order and Jack stands in the pouring rain and repeatedly slams the receiver against the phone box until the casing shatters. He stumbles back to the car and continues driving.

Jack is now driving through a torrential rainstorm, his damp clothing clammy against the vinyl upholstery. The wipers, flailing, full tilt, can't keep up with the sheets of water breaking over the windshield and he's driving nearly blind. Squinting, wiping away the condensation with his fist, he peers into the void on the other side of the glass and attempts to get his bearings.

The beams from the headlights dissipate rapidly in the torrent, revealing only enough to confirm that he is in unknown territory. Streetlights are rare and most of the street signs are gone. It's clearly a former residential area but pools of standing water have merged much of the overgrown street grid into the surrounding urban prairie, making it hard to determine where one starts and the other ends. It takes every bit of concentration to stay on the road.

The car slams into an unseen object with a jarring impact and Jack stomps on the brakes. He steps out into the maelstrom to discover he has struck a shopping cart sitting in the middle of the street, nearly invisible in the dark and the downpour. The homeless man who had been pushing the cart stands in the pouring rain staring blankly at Jack. His worldly belongings have been hurled from the cart and are now a sodden mass on the pavement. His thin jacket, trousers, and shabby gray watch cap are a wrinkled second skin beneath the downpour.

Furious, Jack grabs the battered shopping cart and flips it out of the roadway. He turns and takes an angry step toward the man, his hand reaching instinctively for his gun. "You stupid son of a bitch!" He raises the gun to the man's head.

The homeless man, water gushing over his gaunt features, stares at him. Something about the man's face, the look of absolute defeat, makes Jack lower the weapon. He holsters the Glock and makes a futile effort to shake the water from his clothing. He may as well be standing fully clothed in the shower.

Jack gets back into the car. He sits there, dripping water onto the steering wheel and dash, and stares at the drenched scarecrow of a man standing motionless in the headlights. The man he almost killed. The man he could have killed but didn't.

Jack shuts off the engine and kills the lights. All around him is nothing but an endless, black torrential void. He leans his head against the steering wheel and sobs.

33

J ACK CAN SEE HER through the windshield of the police car. Her shrouded corpse is cordoned off with bright yellow tape. The morning sun reflects off the tiny glass shards littering the topsoil so that the patch of urban prairie surrounding her body glitters with the sparkling residue of long-vanished structures. From the outline of the form beneath the rumpled tarp it's obvious that the body is not complete.

Several other squad cars and a morgue wagon are parked haphazardly around the crime scene. A knot of somber detectives and crime scene techs hover nearby. One of the detectives, a stocky African American woman, breaks away and approaches the patrol car where Jack is sitting.

Jack does not react as Detective Ruth Chambers slides into the back seat beside him. She is a stout, world-weary woman approaching middle age without grace. Her face is puffy from lack of sleep and her eyes are bloodshot.

"You over that case of lockjaw yet? You know we're gonna have to talk about where you were last night." She eyes his bruised and battered face. "Or maybe I should just ask Mike Tyson's people what he was up to?"

Jack remains grimly silent. His conscious mind is consumed with a seething rage that blocks out everything else. Chambers, intense and outwardly sympathetic, isn't giving up. "Who did it, Jack? Who wants you so bad they would do something like this?"

Jack continues to stare at the pitiful shape beneath the plastic shroud. Chambers grabs his arm. "Goddammit, Jack! We want the son of a bitch as bad as you do."

Jack turns his focus to the detective. Chambers, struck by the ferocity of his gaze, releases her grip on his arm but presses on. "I promise you, Jack... You help us get this sick animal off the street, I swear to Jesus—my hand on the Holy Bible—I will put you in a room with him. Alone. And nobody will interfere. Nobody."

Jack studies the detective. All that matters to him is whether or not she can be of any use in getting to Victor Moravian. That seems unlikely. He turns back to stare at his murdered daughter.

Chambers starts to get out of the car. Jack realizes there is one thing he does need from her. "I want to see her."

The detective's stony exterior momentarily cracks. "No, Jack, I can't let you do that. Your brother's coming down to do the ID."

"I want to see what he did."

Chambers perks up at the assurance in Jack's voice. "What *who* did, Jack?"

Jack stares at the shrouded body. The detective shakes her head and sighs. "I'm sorry, but that's not gonna happen."

He turns to meet her gaze. "I want to see her. I have the right. She's my kid." His voice breaks. "She's my baby."

Chambers takes a long time before answering. Finally, she comes down on the side of what might be construed as mercy. "Alright."

They get out of the car. Jack approaches the body with Chambers trailing reluctantly behind. The patrolman standing guard looks askance at the detective and she gestures for him to let Jack through.

Chambers hangs back. She speaks sotto voce to the patrolman as Jack approaches the body. "Chickens coming home to roost."

The patrolman shakes his head. "That's cold, detective. Even for you."

Chambers shrugs and moves forward. A crime scene tech, wearing a paper hazmat suit, is crouched next to Monica's shrouded form. He gestures for Jack not to come any closer. Jack drops to his knees. The tech lifts the tarp and Jack takes a long, hard look beneath.

His daughter's body, or what's left of it, is wrapped in the same clear plastic as the body parts in the trailer. Even with the tarp raised, her face is obscured by a scrap of nearly opaque plastic sheeting. Jack can't quite grasp how the rigid object beneath the plastic—butchered meat encased in shrink-wrap—could be his daughter. "I want to see her face."

The tech reaches to pull the plastic sheet away from the dead girl's face but a look from Chambers stops him. The detective grips Jack's shoulder. "That's enough. Your brother..."

Jack shakes her off and glares at the tech. "I want to see her. Before you butchers get to her." Chambers gestures for the tech to go ahead. He raises the plastic sheet just enough to reveal the girl's face.

Chambers backs away as Jack studies Monica's lifeless features. His daughter's eyes are open, angry, staring. At him. He lurches to his feet and stumbles back into the detective, who steadies him. "You alright?"

Jack pulls away from her. She studies his face, concerned. "Is that her, Jack? Is that your daughter?"

He nods and turns away. The tech pulls the plastic sheet back over Monica's face. Her eyes are closed.

Jack walks slowly back to the patrol car. He is struggling to maintain control, trying desperately to ignore the jagged chunks of rebar, brick, and concrete emerging from beneath the weedy ground all around him, like shards of glass erupting through the skin years after a car accident.

He somehow, intuitively, knows that he has to make this stop. It's only a matter of time before the buried relics of this lost city are followed by corpses, clawing their way to the surface, demanding to be seen, to be heard, to be avenged, or, at the very least, to be remembered.

Jack leans on the hood of the patrol car and slowly wills the apparitions back into the earth. He stares at the pitted glass of the cruiser's windshield for a moment before looking around to ensure himself that the landscape has returned to its original, desolate reality. Instead of relief, however, he finds himself overwhelmed with a wild-eyed fury and he pounds the hood repeatedly with his fist.

Chambers takes a step forward, as if to restrain him, but stops. It's not clear if it's out of sympathy or because the patrol car, like most city vehicles in Detroit, already resembles one of the participants in a demolition derby.

Jack regains control and straightens up. His face is once again unreadable. Chambers opens the back door of the patrol car. "I'll need to take you downtown for a statement."

Before he can respond, another car comes to a lurching stop near the patrol car. Rhonda gets out of the passenger seat. She's distraught. "My baby! Where is my baby?!"

A patrolman restrains her before she can approach the body. Chambers attempts to calm her from a distance. "Please, ma'am, you shouldn't be here."

Rhonda sees the tarp-covered body and screams. "My baby! Oh my god! What have they done to my baby?!"

Rhonda catches sight of Jack and struggles to break away from the cop. "It should have been you; goddamn you! It was you they wanted!"

The patrolman does his best to coax her back inside the police car but she continues to scream at Jack. "You gonna fix this? You gonna fix this, you fucking piece of shit?"

Jack says nothing. He gets into the car and Chambers closes the door behind him.

34

O'JAY AND BUSTER ARE romping happily through the sunny backyard. The two dogs are evenly matched, alternately wrestling, chasing, and yapping as they dart in and out of the dappled shadows along the back fence.

DeRon smiles as he watches the dogs gnawing on each other's shoulders. He always knew they would be good together, that they would be friends.

Too bad Buster died when DeRon was still a small boy, years before O'Jay was even born.

And O'Jay... Well, O'Jay...

DeRon is startled awake by a clamorous racket as an avalanche of broken furniture, bricks, and lumber cascades into the steel bed of a dump truck. Opening his eyes, he finds himself seated at the table where he'd been working on the damaged lab gear. His exhaustion allowed him to drift off to sleep despite the searing pain from his leg.

DeRon tries to focus his attention on the tools and electronics spread across the table in front of him. He is determined not to look across the expanse of the loft to where the Professor is hunched over the operating table, working doggedly on some fresh new horror. The Professor's monstrosity, the beast, will be there with him, eagerly awaiting the command to retrieve yet another grisly trophy.

DeRon attempts to console himself: at least he's back with his machines. The endless hours in the cold room working with the cadavers are over for now, a receding nightmare within the framework of this larger one.

The racket from outside continues and DeRon peers through the bent metal tines of the exhaust vent cut into the wall. There is a demolition in progress further down the block and a skid steer loader is waggling the last bits of rubble out of its scoop and into the bed of a dump truck. The sturdy little machine rotates on its stubby wheels and chugs across the vacant lot to rejoin the demolition bulldozer that is methodically collapsing the brick shell of an abandoned warehouse.

A combination of dingy cab windows, protective cages, diesel smoke, and billowing clouds of dust obscure the operators of all three vehicles and DeRon attempts to imagine them as autonomous machines, going about their business without the complications or pain that afflict the living.

Tears roll down his face as he remembers digging the hole in his yard to bury Babyface, the torn body swaddled in an old sweatshirt as he is set into the moist, dark dirt. He remembers the hard pitiless eyes of the man with the gun. He remembers the malevolent, taunting sneer of the beast, twisting the life out of a squealing O'Jay, like a man squeezing the excess water out of a sponge. And he remembers those same cruel hands, crushing the delicate frame of Gladys like some furry black eggshell.

Mostly though, he remembers feeling paralyzed by the chilling gaze of the Professor as he followed the beast into his home. It's almost impossible now for DeRon to believe that he'd once been impressed by the openness and the promise of that gaze. That he'd once been dazzled by the imagined warmth of the Professor's melodious radio announcer voice. That he'd been seduced by the compliments and the encouragement from this powerful and accomplished man.

He remembers his early days in the medical center lab. How touched he was to see the imperious Professor, unaware anyone was watching, tenderly scoop a tiny kit from a scale and delicately return the rabbit to its cage. DeRon can't keep from snorting as he recalls the countless times since when he has seen the Professor exhibit that same level of warmth and delicacy with a cadaver limb.

Now, too late, he's come to realize that the Professor's gaze was not so much open as it was vacant. Behind those eyes was a void that DeRon had filled with his own neediness. Those eyes, empty of all meaning, allowed him to discern compassion where there was only cruelty, acceptance that was closer to contempt, and admiration where there was nothing more than calculation.

In that moment, in his ruined home, he had realized that the man who stood before him was a cold, soulless vessel hollowed out by a relentless, tireless ambition unleashed in pursuit of a goal that had long ago lost any coherence or reason for being.

The Professor's looming presence brings DeRon back to reality. The beast towers a few steps behind him. The Professor follows DeRon's gaze to the growling demolition machines in the distance. The skid steer is delivering another load of rubble to the dump truck. Drettmann watches for a moment and then turns to DeRon with a smile. "Reminds me of you. Maybe just a little."

DeRon grasps the X-Acto knife he'd been using to strip wires and drives the blade into the Professor's shoulder. The beast braces to launch himself at DeRon but the Professor stops him with an upraised hand. "No. We need him."

The Professor calmly removes the blade from his shoulder. He rolls up the sleeve of his surgical smock to cover the wound and applies pressure. He stands there for a moment studying his assistant. He seems almost impressed. "I'll need you to stitch this up." He turns and strides back to the operating table. The beast, fixing DeRon with a final, threatening glare, follows.

DeRon leans back in his chair with a gasp as the grinding agony of his damaged leg momentarily takes his breath away. He reaches out to grip

COUNTED WITH THE DEAD

the nearest segment of the taut rope line he has strung throughout the lab, allowing him to pull himself from station to station in the wheeled office chair.

Another lightning bolt of agony has him instinctively looking to his leg. DeRon is surprised, yet again, to discover that the limb is no longer there. He shakes his head sadly. This is going to take some getting used to.

35

J ACK IS LEANING AGAINST the brick wall of the funeral home sucking on a joint, waiting. Across the parking lot, two uniformed cops
are leaning against the side of a police cruiser smoking cigarettes and
staring at him.

Marty comes out of the low-slung brick building with a giant floral
wreath that looks like it belongs draped over the saddle of the Kentucky
Derby winner. He tosses it into a dumpster and strides across the asphalt
lot to join his brother, shaking his head. "Nerve of that fucking guy."

Jack takes one last hit from the joint, then stomps it out on the
pavement.

They stand there, not speaking until Marty is compelled to fill the
void with words. "I hear Pompey's in the hospital again." He gives the
nearby cops some nervous side-eye. "Not for his fucking heart, that's
for sure."

Marty reaches into his coat pocket and hands him an envelope stuffed
with cash. His brother ignores the money and Marty sighs. "She won't
have nothin' to do with it." He tries to make light of it. "I think she
taught the folks in there a few new words while she was at it."

Jack stares sourly at the envelope, then jams it into his pocket. He
gestures angrily toward the funeral home. "How's she gonna pay for
this?"

Marty tries to sound reassuring. "We can come back later. We'll take
care of it."

Jack, staring malevolently at the nearby cops, pulls another joint out of his pocket. "She's my fucking kid too."

"I know." Marty shifts, uncomfortable, before continuing, "He thinks Victor Moravian is still alive."

Jack, restless, seething, has a change of heart and stuffs the joint back into his pocket. "So? Fuck him."

"There something you're not telling me?"

Jack, glaring into the middle distance, gives no indication he heard the question.

Marty takes another nervous look at the cops, then at passing traffic. He's looking over his shoulder a lot these days. "So what are we gonna do?"

Jack is about to get into his car. "About what?"

Marty can't hide his anger at Jack's response. "About that rat fuck Pompey. About what he did to your little girl."

Jack grips the door handle. He seems more distracted than angry. "Wasn't him."

Marty can't hide his astonishment. "What do you mean it wasn't him? He thinks it was us took out those two guys of his. He's looking for payback. He's looking to put us in the fucking ground."

Jack is losing patience. "What happened had nothing to do with Marlene. Or us. They probably walked into the middle of a drug deal or something."

Marty is still uneasy. "We're running out of time, Jack."

Jack gestures angrily in the direction of the funeral home. "I'm gonna find the son of a bitch that did this. And I'm gonna take care of him. And then I'm gonna deal with Pompey. I'm gonna fix it. All of it. Alright? So give it a fucking rest. Okay?"

Marty is not convinced.

"What? What, Marty? Fucking spit it out already."

Marty hesitates, concerned about his brother's reaction to what he's about to say. "The reason they think Victor Moravian is still alive... They think, maybe, you and him... maybe you got something worked out."

"What do you think?"

"I think we're fucked. That's what I think."

He turns and heads back to the funeral home. Jack calls after him. "They don't want us in there, Marty."

Marty turns half around, hardly breaking stride. "For such a smart guy, Jack, sometimes you're dumb as a goddamned fucking rock." He pushes through the glass door and disappears inside.

Jack straightens his jacket, takes a deep breath, and follows in his brother's footsteps.

36

M ARTY IS STANDING ON the sidewalk beneath the bright blue awning as Timothy exits Menjo's. Timothy, tanned, with a razor cut, and buffed in an oddly un-athletic manner, is unapologetically gay. He's loosening his tie as he approaches Marty. "You know you can wait at the bar. We don't bite." He flashes a sly smile. "Well, only on request."

Marty shrugs. "Just not my thing. Clubs."

"Gay clubs."

Marty reaches out to fix Timothy's tie, but the smaller man bats his hand away, annoyed. "Jeez Louise, Marty, I'm off work now."

Marty backs off. "Looks sloppy."

Timothy sighs dramatically and yanks the necktie through his collar. He stuffs it into his pants pocket. "How's your brother?"

Marty starts to walk and Timothy keeps pace. "Not good."

"Sorry. How are you holding up?"

Marty acts as if he didn't hear the question. "I've got a couple steaks I took out of the freezer this morning."

"I don't want you to go to any trouble. How about Greektown?"

"Nah, I really don't want to run into anybody I know." Realizing the implications of what he just said, Marty stops in his tracks. "Not because, you know... It's because of my niece. And Jack. Jack's fucking losing it."

"Well stop the presses!" Timothy smiles, shaking his head in bemusement. "You just figured that out?"

Marty keeps walking. "I'm around the block."

Timothy follows. "Don't tell me you're afraid to even park on the same street?"

"Cops write too many tickets on Six Mile. I don't need the aggravation."

Timmy is skeptical. "What cops? I see more stripper cops these days than real ones."

Marty grins. "What kind of joints you hang out in?"

By the time they turn the corner and approach Marty's car Timothy is a step in front. "One of these days we're going to go on a real date."

Marty doesn't respond. Timothy stops in his tracks. There is broken glass on the sidewalk and the side window of Marty's car has been shattered. "Somebody broke into your car..." He turns to see Marty with a gun to his head.

———————— • ————————

Marty is on his knees in hell. The air around him shimmers in the intense heat. The steel girders framing the enormous space are blackened by decades of smoke and ash. The throbbing, percussive beat of Black Sabbath's "Iron Man" is blasting out of a nearby boombox. The grisly bass notes reverberate through the space like some satanic symphony, ten thousand madmen scratching and scrubbing on ten thousand punch presses.

Marty's hands are bound behind his back. Powerful hands are gripping his shoulders.

Directly in front of him pale blue flames surge and swell behind the grillwork of an industrial furnace. Marty rocks back and forth, mumbling to himself, "Mea Culpa, Mea Culpa, Mea Maxima Culpa."

Figures in bulky protective gear trudge through the space like deep-sea divers. Several men with heavy asbestos gloves and aprons hover near the furnace mouth, averting their faces from the stinging heat. Others, wielding shotguns and keeping a wary distance from the industrial inferno, are half-hidden in the shadows.

A pair of work boots move into Marty's line of sight. He looks up to see Magoo towering over him. The thug grabs Marty's face and turns his head so he can see Timothy, who is in the process of being duct-taped standing to a wooden ladder by Borneo and another man. Timothy's frightened eyes peer out from beneath the tape that covers much of his face.

Magoo holds a photo of Marty's two boys in front of his face. "These your boys, Marty? They faggots too?"

"Fuck you."

Magoo's voice is almost tender as he pats Marty on the cheek. "No Marty...Fuck you."

Marty bucks and twists fiercely against the men restraining him until they force him to the ground, his face on the floor, their knees pressed against his back. He spits out gravel as he rages futilely against his captors. "You sick fucking sons of bitches. He hasn't done nothin' to you. He doesn't deserve this. Nobody fucking deserves this."

At Magoo's signal, Borneo picks up a grappling hook and pries the furnace door open. The flames are a luminous orange curtain and Marty and the others turn instinctively from the blinding heat. Several men in protective gear carry the ladder like a stretcher and rest its feet on the lip of the open furnace. It takes some effort to hold it steady as Timothy struggles desperately to free himself from the grotesque duct tape cocoon. His shoes are starting to smoke and the tape around his ankles is blistering and scorching from the heat.

Responding to another nod from Magoo, the stretcher-bearers slide the ladder and their squirming victim into the fiery furnace. They quickly back away as a billowing jet of flames erupts from the furnace mouth. Borneo uses the grappling hook to slam the furnace door shut. He is forced to open it and slam it shut several more times to finally force the butt end of the ladder all the way into the flames.

Marty is released and lies sobbing in the dirt. All around him, Magoo's thugs casually discard gloves and protective gear as they file out.

The boombox shuts off. Magoo stoops to lift Marty's head by his hair. "You know what you need to do." He releases his grip and allows Marty's face to flop back into the dirt.

Footsteps recede into the distance. Somewhere far away a steel door slams shut. Digging his shoulder into the ground and using his bound arms for leverage, Marty struggles back to his knees.

He remains perfectly still, on edge, listening. All around him is the complete silence of the tomb, but he has the uneasy sensation of someone else there with him. He intuits as much as he hears motion behind him, a movement so subtle he's not sure if he's imagining it. He remains perfectly still, afraid to turn his head to look behind him, terrified of what he might see.

Then, a hand comes to rest on top of his head, the unexpected touch nearly taking his breath away. The gesture is reassuring, affectionate even, and Marty, against his own every instinct, breathes an involuntary sigh of relief.

Then, darkness.

37

THERE IS A TAXI idling in front of the building when Jack gets home. He parks behind the cab and gets out of his car. He strides over to the driver's side and raps on the glass with his knuckles. The cabbie lowers the window. "Already got a fare, chief."

Jack nods in the direction of Haddad's. "Where? The party store?"

The cabbie indicates Jack's building. "No, here. What's it to..."

Jack pulls back his jacket to reveal the butt of his gun. "Get the fuck out of here."

The cabbie throws the car into gear and pulls away.

Jack opens the outside door as Marlene is coming out. He shoves her back inside and shuts the door behind them. "What the fuck do you think you're doing?"

She's clutching a plastic shopping bag with a few belongings. She's been crying.

She's still crying. "They killed your little girl because of me, Jack. Because you tried to help me."

Jack grabs her shoulders. "What happened had nothing to do with you. Nothing. You understand?"

She stares at him, baffled. He releases her and turns back to lock the door. Then he leads her to the couch and sits her down. "You can't leave. If something happens to you it'll be on me."

He takes a seat next to her on the couch. She wipes her eyes, her resolve stiffening. "You don't owe me anything, Jack. We're done. I'll find Victor on my own."

Jack scoffs. "There's no fucking way—"

"I'll hire a private investigator." A mirthless smile. "That's what he did. That's how he found out about us."

Jack doesn't react. She stares at him in amazement. "You knew?"

Jack responds with a shrug. "He'd have found out eventually." He sags back into the couch cushions, suddenly tired. "I should have known he'd go after her. I should have fucking known."

She's suddenly alert, confused, and suspicious. "What are you talking about?"

He looks away, realizing he's said too much.

She's on her feet now. "Goddammit, Jack! What's going on? Why is all this happening? Has it got something to do with what happened to Victor?"

Jack cradles his head in his hands for a moment and then looks up to meet her gaze. "I was supposed to kill Victor."

Marlene's legs can no longer support her and she slumps back down onto the couch.

Jack tries to explain himself. "Look, I..."

She stifles him with an upraised hand. They sit in silence for a moment before she manages to speak. She can't look at him. "Who did they get... to do it?"

"I don't know." He tries to sound hopeful. "Maybe nobody."

Marlene uses the arm of the couch for support as she stands. She's wobbly at first but steadies herself and begins pacing the room, picking up random objects and setting them down again.

She moves into the kitchen and stops. She grips the back of a chair, her back to him. "I was always waiting for him to let me in." She's suddenly angry and jams the chair violently into the table leg. "I should have beat the goddamned door down myself. I should have insisted that he let me in, that he tell me what the hell was going on."

She turns to face him. She's furious. "The door I should have closed is you. We would have found a way without you. Without your..." Her lips curl in disgust. *People.*

She starts to laugh, softly at first, then building to shrill, hysterical gulps. "Victor... Poor slob couldn't buy a break. He borrows money from some psycho and the next thing he knows, the guy's his fucking partner. Then—to add insult to fucking injury—he finds out his wife was fucking one of his new business associates."

Jack moves to her. "Marlene, please..."

She jerks away from him. "Don't you touch me! Don't you ever fucking touch me!"

He backs off. "I'm sorry."

"I fucked you to help him. Do you understand? This is on you. You are responsible. You have to fix this."

Jack has nothing to say. He knows he can't fix this. Nobody can fix this.

She sags into a chair at the kitchen table. He gestures to a nearby chair for permission to sit.

"Just... Just don't touch me. Okay?"

He sits. "I'm sorry. I really am sorry."

She reaches across the table as if to grab his hand, but stops short. She pulls her hand back. "You have to bring my Victor back to me." She reaches out again and grips his hand tightly. "Promise me." Angry now. "Promise me!"

He pries his hand from her grip and stands. She looks him in the eye. Her voice is cold. "I hope you fucking rot in hell."

It's near dawn when Jack finishes installing the padlock on the inside of the main door. He drops the tools into the tackle box and picks up the phone on the end table by the couch. He dials Marty's number. He gets the answering machine and slams the receiver back into the cradle. "Where the fuck are you?"

He unplugs the phone, wraps the cord around it, and locks it in a file cabinet.

38

THE SPRAWLING SITE OF the abandoned Packard Automotive Plant is a jumble of ruined and collapsed factory buildings covering eighty acres. From the air, the long, narrow expanse of ruins resembles a decaying shipwreck on the sea floor, a shipwreck the size of a small city. The scores of interconnected structures that make up the immense complex have been degraded and rearranged over the decades by human activity and by nature. Many of the individual buildings have been reduced to their foundations or empty brick and concrete shells. Others are still relatively intact.

Jack is moving through a vast rubble field dominated by orderly rows of burly pillars with bell-shaped capitals that march across the landscape like the columns of a ruined Greek temple. He clutches the railroad spike in his pocket as he walks. He doesn't trust the Glock to do the job on Victor. And he relishes the thought of jamming the iron spike into the fiend's beating heart.

He leaves the rustbelt colonnade behind and explores the network of gutted structures that once housed the plant's multi-story assembly lines. Mature trees are growing in the shafts where the cars being assembled were hoisted from one floor to the next. In the giant rail shed, he encounters scrappers working to excavate steel rods from the concrete, like whalers slowly wringing every ounce of value from a rotting carcass. They do not even look up from their blowtorches as Jack moves through the space.

Jack enters a relatively intact assembly building. Sunlight streaming in from banks of windows on two sides reveal a heavily graffitied space the size of an airplane hangar. Stately rows of pillars continue to bear the weight of the concrete ceiling and the dirt floor is remarkably rubble free.

As he moves farther into the building Jack discovers the reason for the lack of debris. In the center of the cavernous space, where hundreds of men once toiled at long-vanished assembly lines, some artful scavenger has built a massive pyramid from loose bricks and rubble. The dry-stacked ziggurat rises all the way to the ceiling.

The broad expanse of windows on the east wall of the plant is a vast conglomeration of individual glass panes. Many are missing but each of the thousands of surviving panes of glass is degraded, discolored, cracked, crazed, or stained in its own unique manner. The sunlight passing through this woven curtain of glass casts a stippled medley of light and shadow on the monolith dominating the interior, creating the aura of a sacred space.

As Jack studies the squat brick edifice, he can't shake the feeling that it is a living presence, like some watchful rustbelt sphinx. Spooked, he takes a wide detour around the pyramid as he moves on to the next abandoned structure. He grips the iron spike in his pocket. "Where are you, you fucking son of a bitch? Where are you?"

Hours later Jack returns to his car on a nearby side street. He gets into his car and watches a crew of scavengers fill the groaning bed of a stake truck with scrap metal. The battered truck looks like it belongs in the salvage yard together with its load.

The scavengers pile into the cab and the truck wallows on its springs like an overloaded barge as it's driven over the uneven ground to the nearest street. Jack starts the car. There is too much activity in and around the Packard site. The beast will not be found here.

———————— • ————————

Jack listens to Marty's phone ring a dozen times before slamming the receiver back into its cradle. He walks away from the payphone and gets back into his car.

Jack pushes the seat all the way back as he prepares to settle in for the night. Further down the block and across the street he can see the diffuse glow from a lamp shining through the glass brick windows on the second floor of the Trumbull building. The light is coming from inside the room where Marlene is staying. He can't decide if he's watching over the place to keep her safe or to make sure she doesn't leave... or both.

Jack gazes across the passenger seat. He remembers the time, long after she was gone, when he discovered the denim jacket forgotten beneath the seat of a previous car. On first impression, it was so small it could have belonged to a child. But the embroidered flowers, butterflies, and bumblebees were a dead giveaway. This was Marlene's jacket. Left behind when she'd bolted from his car and disappeared from his life.

He spent weeks looking for her, but she was gone, a ghost, haunting the streets and the drug houses of Brightmoor, always slipping away just as he got close. Until she found him all those years later. Looking for a favor. For her husband. For Victor Moravian.

He opens the glove box and takes out the glassine bag of dope. He has a new plan for tomorrow.

39

THIS LOOKS LIKE THE place where broken appliances come to die. The vast space is crammed to the rafters with the city's flotsam: worn-out stoves, antiquated machinery, salvaged auto parts, bike frames, file cabinets, televisions, radios, microwaves, and just plain junk. At a table off to the side, a gnarled old woman in a striped red and white babushka sorts through boxes of dusty radio tubes. The dingy window behind her frames a dystopian landscape of scrap metal dunes, tire mounds, and junked cars.

Jumbo Jablonski is popping the tabs on two cans of Schlitz by the time Jack reaches the counter. The salvage yard proprietor is basically a stationary object and the mounds of yellowing newspapers, magazines, and parts catalogs surrounding him are slowly dissolving into a wood pulp bunker. The junkman's beer-belly is so pronounced it could be a massive tumor beneath his shirt. The gray stubble on his unshaven face gives his skin the pallor of weathered wood. He could be Hispanic, or Black, or Middle Eastern, or White, or any combination of the above.

The two men drink in silence. Jack knows better than to be in a hurry. Finally, Jumbo sets his beer on the counter. "Long time."

Jack takes in his surroundings before responding. It's not a question. "Business is good."

"I just keep on keepin on. How's French Press?"

"Tired of people calling him that."

Jumbo snorts into his beer. "Yeah, and I'm tired of people always calling me Mr. Universe." He raises his eyebrows. "We all got our cross to bear."

Jack's voice is tinged with regret. "Seems me and Marty run in different circles these days."

Jumbo tents his fingertips together over the beer can. It's difficult to tell if he's smiling, grimacing, or squeezing out a fart. "I been thinking about what you said on the phone..."

"Yeah? "

"You want to find a guy that hides out in abandoned buildings?"

"Yeah?"

Jumbo makes no effort to hide his skepticism. "In Detroit? Detroit, Michigan?"

Jack has to work to tamp down his growing annoyance. "Is there another one?"

Jumbo takes off his spectacles. They look like something rescued from the recycling bin. He rubs his eyes before continuing. "Detroit. Let me draw you a map..."

"I don't need a fucking map, JJ, I want information."

Jumbo is undeterred. "Woodward Avenue cuts the city right smack down the middle, like somebody split it with a goddamned meat cleaver. All the way from the riverfront, out to Eight Mile Road." He gestures, first with his right, then with his left hand. "Eastside. Westside."

Jack lays his palms flat on the counter and stares at his beer.

"On your east side, for the most part, you got your industry. Or used to, anyway. The rail lines going through the Dequindre Cut used to serve hundreds of factories."

Jack takes a slug of beer and sets the can down on the counter with a little more force than necessary. Jumbo stops and stares at him, like a teacher facing down a fidgety student. Jack does his best to look attentive.

Jumbo nods before continuing. "Back when you and me were still in diapers, those freight lines were busier than the goddamned New York subway. That was before it all went to shit. Before the politicians and the gangsters and the car guys squeezed the last drop of blood out of this turnip and skedaddled off to the suburbs."

He looks to Jack for his response. Jack doesn't seem to have a problem with this particular narrative so Jumbo moves on.

"Packard shut down, biggest abandoned auto plant in the whole goddamned world. Dodge Main, Fisher Body, Uniroyal, Continental, a hundred more I forget the names. Trains stopped running sometime in the eighties. Dequindre Cut's still there. Only now, it's the Appalachian Trail with muggers."

"For fuck's sake, JJ, tell me something I don't already know."

Jumbo takes a slug from his beer before continuing. "Sitting on the riverfront, you got your downtown. Such as it is. Taking the scenic route through downtown you got your dirty dozen of abandoned high-rises: Metropolitan Building, Farwell, Book-Cadillac, Statler Hotel, United Artists, David Whitney, Broderick Tower, etcetera, etcetera."

He drums his fingers on the counter for emphasis. "Not just vacant and waiting for someone to come along and sign a lease. Abandoned. And that's just the tip of the iceberg. What happened downtown..."

Jumbo gestures with his arms in imitation of a breaststroke. "The ripples, they go out across the whole damn city. All of a sudden, there's a half-million, three-quarter million—who the hell knows how many—people that don't live here no more. So now, on top of all the rest, you got ten, twenty thousand abandoned houses."

Jack wants this to end. "Christ, get to the fucking point already."

"Right. So now, it's not just houses and factories, not just art deco office high-rises downtown... Now you got your thousands of abandoned structures: warehouses, machine shops, garages, apartment buildings, party stores, bars, churches, synagogues, schools, libraries, hospitals, even police stations." He fixes his gaze on Jack. "For people like me, it's a goddamned gold mine. For you..." He shrugs. "Take you a lifetime to search 'em all. You got a lifetime?"

"I did before I fucking walked into this dump."

Jumbo's not done. "Not to mention, your guy, if he's got half a brain, he's not gonna stay in one place for long. Put that in your pipe and smoke it."

Jack glares at Jumbo. "What I got is you. You been strip-mining this city for years."

Jumbo sighs. "Then you got nothin'." The spark of anger in Jack's eyes gets his attention. "Jack, buddy, I'm strictly a cash and carry business. I pay by weight: copper, iron, aluminum, reclaimed beams, windows, doors, doorknobs, whatever comes off the truck." He gestures to a ledger book. "I put their name, such as it is, in the book, so the city's happy. And I don't ask questions. For all I know, for any particular load, it could come from the Statler Hotel or it could come from the goddamned Vatican."

Jack's not having it. "People talk. People always talk."

"Yeah, people talk. Some of em never shut the fuck up." Jumbo holds his hand close to his ear, mimicking a pair of flapping lips. "All day. Every day. They tell me all kinds of crazy shit. Bat-shit crazy shit." He sounds almost apologetic. "I got guys telling me about space aliens, about rats the size of cocker spaniels, and about the Cowardly Lion, or maybe it was the Tin Man, living in the basement of an abandoned middle school." He spreads his arms wide in a gesture of defeat. "Whata you want me to say?"

"Any sites not pulling their weight these days? Maybe someplace your guys don't wanna go no more?"

Jumbo shrugs. "This business, sometimes the vein just taps out. Used to get elevator motors by the dumpster load from the hotels downtown, from Michigan Central Station, from the hospitals. Paid top dollar for the copper. Haven't seen one in over a year now."

Jumbo smiles at a particular memory. "There was this one guy... Guy with a pickup full of scrap, mostly shit. One of these crusty old negroes grew up in the south before beating his brains out in the auto plants. Still had some skills, I guess. Anyway, he tried to sell me some beaver pelts."

"You got guys scrapping the zoo now?"

"There's a goddamned beaver dam on the river now. Down by the old ironworks."

Jack's getting ready to go. "Don't know it."

Jumbo is more than happy to fill him in. "Detroit Gray Iron Foundry. East Jefferson. By the old Uniroyal site. Been mostly abandoned for years now."

"I don't think my guy is a fucking trapper."

"It was in the paper: first beaver dam on the river this far south in over a hundred years or something. Goddamn city's going back to nature." He suddenly has another thought. "Hey, you should sign up with one of those guys that gives tours of all the abandoned buildings. That's a thing now."

Jack shakes his head. "I don't need a fucking tour guide. I grew up in this city."

Jumbo crushes his empty beer can. "Not your city no more." He grins. "White boy."

Jack tosses a couple of fifties onto the counter. "Let me know if you hear something."

Jumbo pushes the bills back across the counter. "I'm not taking your fucking money. I owe you. I owe you big time. Only reason I'm still in business..." He shrugs. "You know... You took care of that thing for me."

Jack pockets the money. As he turns to go, he nods in the direction of Jumbo's enormous gut. "You should get that looked at."

The old lady sorting radio tubes swivels away from the table as Jack goes by. She's eyeing his beer can. "You done with that?"

40

THE BEAST THAT IS Victor Moravian raises his arms in triumph. He tilts his ravaged face upward, twisted mouth agape, and glories in the morning sunlight streaming in from windows high overhead. Finally, blessedly, the clouds have parted. The capricious swarms of consciousness have somehow fused themselves into one coherent, earthbound reality. He can see things clearly now. He can finally take stock of where he is.

The creature lowers his arms and surveys his surroundings. He studies the marble floors, the vast, echoing rotunda, the majestic columns, the barrel-vaulted ceilings, the soft light streaming in from windows high above. This can only be one place... He is in Rome! And this is his favorite place on this planet: the Baths of Diocletian!

The beast shuts his eyes, delighting in the blissful, hushed tranquility of this sacred space. He savors the memories of the visual treasures that await him: the tombs, the paintings, the sculptures, the Basilica, the Michelangelo murals...

But no... Wait... Arms spread wide, unexpectedly a surfer, Victor is forced to brace himself against the warping and wobbling of the suddenly gelatinous ground beneath his feet.

No... God no... Please... No... He fights to control his panic as the kaleidoscopic lens that has hijacked his conscious mind pivots once more, plunging him back into the maelstrom to be pummeled by the shrapnel of splintered memories. He flails hopelessly at the streaking images of light and color that bombard him, desperate to contain the chaos of myriad, shifting perspectives that threaten to drive him insane.

Or maybe he already is insane?

But no, not this time! He clenches his fists. Fighting for control, he plants his feet and wills himself to solid ground. He is an immovable object, unyielding, unalterable, a rock. He is the calm at the center of a whirlwind, a whirlwind that, through sheer force of will, slowly decelerates into nothingness. The chaotic deluge breaks over him and subsides. The unrelenting barrage decays until it is nothing more than a velvety, pelting breeze. He is himself again.

He opens his eyes to discover that the monumental space he occupies has been desecrated with graffiti. The polished marble floor he remembers has been ground into dirt and pebbled crumbs. There are no statues. No murals. No tombs. No chapel. No Michelangelo. And this is not Rome. This is the living nightmare he has tried so desperately to escape. From which he cannot wake.

He rotates slowly in place, a monstrous, hobbled marionette. The vaulted chamber is an impressive work of architecture. He marvels at the soaring rotunda and the thick Doric columns, eighty feet high if they're an inch. But this bleak monument, gutted and stripped of all ornamentation, feels more like a storm-ravaged cavern than a man-made structure.

The beast continues to rotate in place, a shuffling mule patiently turning a millstone, iron-shod feet churning marble fragments into dust. He continues to study his surroundings as he turns. This is a monumental ruin. And, despite the graffiti marking every surface like the work of an army of deranged cave painters, it reminds him of the Pantheon. But, unlike the Pantheon, unlike the Baths, this place is not merely abandoned; it has been emptied of all meaning. In the process of being discarded and forgotten, its soul has been extinguished. There are no ghosts here, no memories, just rats, pigeons, and desolation.

Turning faster, the beast's lips curl into a smile of recognition; he knows this place! This exquisite beaux arts mongrel is the old train station. *Michigan Central Station! My, how the mighty have fallen.*

The creature grows agitated. He turns faster, around and around, wobbling like a faltering top, until the windows overhead merge into one continuous sky-blue gash. Something is terribly wrong, but he cannot put a name to it. He is missing something. Not the statues, murals, or chapel. No, something important, a vital piece of himself, has been taken from him, ripped violently from his flesh. And he must—he will—have it back.

He stops, steadying himself, almost too dizzy to stand. Now he knows who he is. He is Victor Moravian. He is the beast, a monster.

The yawning space reverberates with his howls of rage as he rushes from the rotunda. He hurdles up a dozen flights of stairs, his momentum sending him crashing into walls at each turn. Still dizzy, he hobbles down a long, empty corridor to an empty office high above the vaulted waiting room. He stands in the middle of the room and gapes, his breath erupting in staccato bursts.

Spiked to the wall in front of him, like the pelt of some mythic beast, is the ragged piece of canvas that bears the disintegrating images of Victor and Marlene Moravian. The beast lurches over to the wall and slaps both hands against the canvas. This will have to do for now. He presses his ruined face against that of Marlene. *Mine. She will be mine, always and forever.*

41

J ACK IS ON THE roof of the abandoned GAR Building, a triangular five-story structure just northwest of downtown. Built by a society of Civil War veterans a century before, the GAR has a foreboding stone facade and round towers topped with gap-tooth battlements at all three corners. All of the windows in the structure are boarded up, reinforcing its fortress-like appearance.

Jack leans against the parapet in the south tower. Downtown is directly in front of him and the west side to his right. To his left, his view is mostly blocked by taller buildings, but he can catch glimpses of the east side, where the leafy forest canopy is perforated by the ragged brick outcrops of abandoned factories.

Jack tries to imagine the beast hiking alongside the overgrown tracks of the Dequindre Cut. The below-grade rail cut could serve as a corridor where a man, or something like a man, could move undetected between the gutted industrial hulks of the east side and the abandoned office towers of downtown Detroit.

Traversing the rail cut, the beast would find himself moving through thick undergrowth, flanked on either side by an industrial ghost town of crumbling loading docks, warehouses, and chimneys, every surface ripe with toxic blooms of graffiti. But that's as far as Jack's imaginary journey can take him. *Where is he going? Where does he sleep? Where does the creature rest and recover when he is done killing?*

From his perch, Jack has a nearly unobstructed view of downtown Detroit. The thicket of office towers between him and the river stands out in this mostly low-rise city like a grove of sequoias on a prairie. To the west, separated from downtown by a mile or so of urban tundra, is the massive brick and masonry pile that is Michigan Central Station. The entrance to the train depot is a sprawling faux Roman temple with three arched doors, each flanked by marble columns and topped by a triangular pediment. The depot itself is dwarfed by the attached office tower that rises eighteen stories behind it like a broad-shouldered urban butte. The abandoned train station is surrounded by a flat, empty landscape of grassy fields and gravel lots, creating the impression of an isolated citadel guarding the western approaches to downtown.

Jack remembers it from better days. As boys, he and Marty had roamed the sepulchral interior spaces of the depot in search of mischief. The depot was already in decline and the massive, echoing space of the lobby rotunda was often deserted, reminding young Jack of the forsaken strongholds of men and dwarves from *the Lord of the Rings*. There were dangling bronze chandeliers the size of phone booths, ornate brass elevator doors, and a massive clock high above the ticket windows that had stopped working sometime in the '60s. Mostly though, he remembers the smooth marble floor, vast as a parade ground, and the polished Corinthian columns on square pedestals that seemed to rise up into the clouds.

Jack grips the iron spike in his pocket and pushes himself away from the parapet with his other hand. This is no time for nostalgia. He's made up his mind. Downtown is where the demon will be found.

Built in 1915, the Farwell is a stolid, eight-story brick wedding cake of a building, with a facade bisected by horizontal Greek friezes and framed by Ionic pilasters at the corners. The long-abandoned office building sits at about the halfway point on the west side of the triangle that is Capital Park, a once-stately promenade now completely given over to pigeons and panhandlers.

It's dark by the time Jack pulls into the alley behind the Farwell and the flashlight casing beats a rhythmic staccato against the doorframe as the car bounces over the rutted surface. He's come prepared with bolt cutters, but the skittering spot of light reveals that the chain and padlock securing the heavy steel door off the alley are no longer in place.

The peculiar tribe of squatters that has colonized the Farwell is a hard lot and Jack takes out the Glock before going inside. He makes his way through a series of utility rooms, mounts a flight of concrete steps, and walks out into the Farwell's once genteel lobby. The ornate brass elevator doors are long gone. The marble walls are scarred with graffiti and there are gaping craters in the Tiffany mosaic ceiling.

Moving to the adjoining atrium, he looks up into the grimy skylights high overhead. Eight floors of octagon-shaped balconies frame the rotunda, their wrought iron railings creating the impression of an abandoned steampunk missile silo.

A honeycomb of wood-paneled offices surround each of the central rotunda's balconies and Jack searches them one by one. Most of the suites adjoining the balconies are deserted and trashed but some—one or two on each floor—have been turned into living and workspaces by a hardy group of artists. Lengthy extension cords lead from pirated electric power cables and snake through corridors to power hot plates and stereos. Strings of tin cans that once served as an early warning system for intruders lie in crumpled heaps. No one seems to be home.

Like solitary monks in some desert monastery, each individual artist has colonized a space isolated from the others. The makeshift studios are silent chapels where the occupants worship at worktables cobbled together from salvaged doors and plaster the walls with frenetic drawings.

Jack is confused by much of what he finds there, wondering what sort of artists these must be. There are pipe benders, handsaws, welding torches, and more cans of metallic spray paint than any ten auto body shops. There are vividly painted sheets of hammered steel the size of wading pools and sculptures fashioned from reclaimed wood, tarpaper, and wire mesh. There are no easels or pretty pictures. And no artists.

There is food rotting in picnic coolers, rumpled sleeping bags, and open cans of paint sealed by the blistered skin that has formed over their contents. One of the stairwell landings is littered with spent shotgun shells.

Jack holsters his gun. The artists, this fierce tribe of survivors in this fierce city, have abandoned the Farwell. And they did so in a hurry.

Jack walks across the soggy surface of Capital Park, playing the beam of the flashlight in a wide arc as he goes. The air is damp, and the temperature is in the mid-forties and dropping. A grizzled derelict, encased in plastic trash bags and curled up on a park bench awakens in the glare of the light, shielding his eyes. "Hey!"

Jack is already moving on. He searches the rest of the muddy triangle and stops to zip his jacket against the chill as he considers his next move. Behind him, the hulking Farwell Building is a lifeless void. The other shabby mid-rise buildings surrounding the park are mostly dark, their poor and elderly tenants teetering on the brink of joining the homeless man on the park bench.

Jack suddenly turns and strides back to the bench. Seeing Jack approach, the derelict covers his face with his arms to protect himself.

Jack takes a fifty out of his pocket and drops it on his chest. "Get your ass inside before you freeze to death, you stupid son of a bitch." Jack hesitates, then turns and walks down the middle of the triangle to the row of payphones at the base of the park. He's trying to understand what he just did. He's never given money to a panhandler before, not even spare change. He decides not to think about it.

The first three phones are out of order. One consists of a ragged cable without a receiver hanging limply from a gutted steel frame that no longer contains a phone or a coin box. The fourth is filthy but operational, so he drops in a quarter and dials his brother. The phone rings unanswered and Jack slams the receiver back into the cradle. "Son of a bitch!"

———— • ————

Jack drives a few short blocks north to Grand Circus Park, a sprawling half-circle of grass, walkways, and statues. The park is hemmed in by a glass and masonry Stonehenge of occupied and abandoned buildings and bisected by the city's main north/south thoroughfare, Woodward Avenue. Once the pride of the city, the park's somber constellation of statues and fountains now serves primarily as the grassy lid to the parking structure beneath.

Jack drives slowly up Woodward to the park. Downtown Detroit after dark is desolate, with little traffic and no pedestrians. He can see the David Whitney Building on his left, its nineteen vacant floors secured by dogs and armed guards. On his right, directly across Woodward from the Whitney, is the Broderick Tower, its freshly barricaded entrance still festooned with crime scene tape. Overhead, the raised track of the People Mover railway, supported by fat, round concrete columns, sweeps around the corner like a crumbling Roman aqueduct in some back-water province.

The streets radiating out like spokes from the hub of Grand Circus Park intersect the concentric rings of avenues to create roughly triangular urban islands. The block-long urban wedge to Jack's right is dominated by the Broderick Tower, which commands the narrow point of the triangle. The three sides of the wedge are framed by Woodward Avenue to the west and Broadway to the east, with a street named John R. providing the broad base.

Jack crosses in front of the Broderick and turns right onto Broadway. Most of the block is dark at this hour and, aside from the large neon sign outside Simmons and Clark Jewelers, it's difficult to distinguish the occupied storefronts from the vacant ones. He pulls over at the far end of the block in front of Garth's Artist Supply. The nondescript two-story brick building, wedged in between taller structures, is easy to miss. There are no signs of life aside from the dim glow from security lights behind the grid of steel grates and tattered product posters covering the display windows.

Jack gets out of the car and continues the search on foot. Standing between Garth's and the corner of Broadway and John R. is the ghostly wreck of the Wurlitzer Building. The abandoned fourteen-story tower is narrow—the front is only five windows across—but deep, its wide brick flank looming over Garth's like a sheer canyon wall.

The first two floors are completely obscured by wood scaffolding erected over the sidewalk to protect pedestrians from chunks of the facade. The top four floors resemble a Roman temple, with a facade of stone blocks framed by granite columns and topped with a triangular pediment. This faux temple sits atop a ten-story brick base, as if an office building had erupted out of the ground beneath the temple and lifted it skyward.

Jack squeezes through a gap in the scaffolding. He peels back the corner of a sheet of plywood covering a window and pokes the flashlight through the opening. The beam of light reveals that decades of water damage have turned the Wurlitzer's once elegant lobby into a bleak scene of ruin and decay. The narrow lobby staircase, its railings dripping with a greasy layer of fossilized, moss-like glop, corkscrews up into darkness. Jack turns off the flashlight and climbs out from the scaffolding. This is a project better left for daylight.

Directly around the corner on John R., separated from the back end of the Wurlitzer by an alley, is the long-abandoned Metropolitan Building. The fifteen-story structure is crowned by a center tower section that rises several stories above two bulky shoulders and dominates the base of the wedge like a petrified gothic robot. The structure's intricate facade, as wide as the Wurlitzer is deep, is a complicated mélange of cornices, masonry shields, checkerboard Moorish tiles, and ornate windows. The main entrance, as well as the windows on the first two floors, are securely boarded up.

The building occupies the midpoint of the triangle's wide base and there are alleys leading from the street on either side. Jack enters the alley that separates the Metropolitan from the Wurlitzer. The Metropolitan's triangular footprint mimics that of the larger, block-long wedge it occupies. As a result, the twin alleys come together behind the wedge-shaped building to form a long triangular canyon that dead-ends at the rear of the Broderick Tower.

Jack stops in the middle of the asphalt clearing at the center of the block-long triangle and looks around. The three abandoned towers, the Metropolitan, the Broderick Tower, and the Wurlitzer, loom over this mostly low-rise urban island like three dark citadels. On either side of him are the dumpsters, loading docks, and service entrances for the various businesses on the streets that make up the two long sides of the triangle: Woodward and Broadway.

Jack is struck by the close proximity of the three derelict structures, something not evident to someone driving by on one of the flanking streets. From where he stands, the back sides of the three deserted office towers and every other business on the block are separated by no more than seventy-five or eighty yards of asphalt. One of those businesses is Garth's Artist Supply. Jack pulls his collar up against the chill and heads back to his car. He desperately needs a joint.

42

MARLENE IS SITTING ON the floor in the tiny alcove above the front door. A college marching band is practicing on the school field directly across Trumbull. It's just noise to her: tubas, horns, flutes, and drums, lots of drums, accompanied by confusing swarms of high-stepping bodies. And then there's some guy prancing around with a baton, wearing what looks like Fred Flintstone's water buffalo hat.

She watches the musicians advance and retreat in ragged formation while a guy on a stepladder flaps his arms at them like he's standing on the deck of an aircraft carrier directing traffic. Marlene feels a twinge of envy watching the bandleader's gesticulations. *He's so out there, so comfortable being the center of attention, not afraid of looking the fool. If only...*

Marlene rotates away from the window on her ass. She's confused. What sort of kid decides to join a marching band? Does Wayne State even have a football team? What does Victor see in her? Why are they even together? There is so much in his world she will never understand. And what about her world, her life, her dreams, where she comes from? How could he possibly get his head around any of that?

But the big question, the one she doesn't like to think about, is: What to do now? Should she stay or go? Where would she go? Who would help her? Who can help her? *Besides Jack. Fucking Jack.*

It's always been easy to leave, to start over again. Why is it so hard now? Why is it so hard to leave a guy who's probably already dead? Why is she so determined to hang on to any tiny sliver of hope, however remote?

Why is it that the possibility that Victor still exists makes it bearable to
still be in this shithole of a city? The city she should have left in the
rearview mirror as soon as she learned to drive.

She has to admit, she does have pleasant memories of the house on
Seminole. She'd waste hours on the couch, entranced by the gentle play
of light and shadow as intricate patterns of leaves and branches shim-
mered across the surface of drawn window shades. She was waiting. She
was always waiting. But waiting for what? Writers and artists, they talk
about waiting for inspiration... What was she waiting for? Up to now
her life has been nothing but waiting, preparing, planning, researching,
gathering... and then bailing out before she has to do something, before
she has to make a commitment. *Maybe this time, maybe with Victor...*

She remembers that time in New York City. They were on the Upper
East Side and Victor wanted lunch. He was wearing those awful shorts,
the ones with all the pockets, a baseball cap, sandals, and that ugly,
honkie-ass Hawaiian shirt. She cringed when he insisted on going into
that little French restaurant. It was like something out of a movie, with
the maître d', stiff white tablecloths, and the glossy white people that
made even Grosse Pointe feel provincial. She felt certain that every eye in
the restaurant was fixated on them.

But Victor strolled in like it was his living room. And when that
patronizing ass of a maître d' tried to tell him they needed a reservation,
he smiled. He was calm, relaxed, and didn't take no for an answer. And
that maître d', he turned on a dime. His attitude changed as soon as he
realized Victor was one of them. It was like some sort of gaydar, except
for rich people. That's when she realized, this was a tribe, like the ones
Jack always talked about: the Blacks, the Whites, the Chaldeans, the
Hispanics, the Italians, the Irish. But this tribe, Victor's tribe, this one
was special. Being part of this tribe meant something. It got you places,
got you things. It got you respect from people that mattered, not just the
losers in the Checker Bar.

She thought about how Jack would have handled it. She always felt safe with Jack. He had a stillness that even complete strangers did not mistake for timidity. He would have given that maître d' a couple of fifties from the roll in his pocket. And when that didn't work, he would have gotten pissed and things would have gone wrong in a hurry. Very wrong.

Not Victor. She felt like royalty as they were escorted to their table. This was Victor's tribe. And she was his queen. And, despite the shirt, sandals, and baseball cap, he was recognized as one of them.

He even turned down the first table they were offered. Too close to the kitchen.

Marlene scrambles to her feet and crosses the balcony to the railing. She doesn't have to make a decision right this minute; it's all out of her hands. *Right?* She's almost grateful for the padlock Jack used to secure the outside door. *What is it about Jack and padlocks anyways? And that stupid wad of fifties always jammed into his pocket. I thought it was supposed to be all about the Benjamins, not the... Who the fuck is on the fifty-dollar bill anyways? Oh, yeah, the old guy with the beard and the funny first name.* She always liked the way Jack said it. "You-liss-eez, You-liss-eez ess Grant."

43

S T. STANISLAUS IS AN echoing catacomb as Jack enters. Flickering candles provide a bare minimum of illumination, leaving most of the alcoves and recesses cloaked in darkness. Jack dips his fingers into the holy water font and executes a prizefighter's abbreviated sign of the cross before moving slowly down the main aisle.

A looming shadow cast by someone standing near a rack of votive candles spans the length of one of the side aisles. The dark figure steps into the main aisle. It's Detective Chambers.

"Didn't you see the sign out front, Jack? Padre Pio's not hearing confessions today."

Jack reacts to her presence with nonchalance. He moves into one of the alcoves and stops in front of a religious painting that seems to float above a wreath of flickering votive candles.

"What are you doing here, Jack? Guy like you?" Her gaze encompasses the entire sacred space. "Praying for the dead?"

He's staring at the painting. "I like to look at the pictures."

Chambers joins him. She studies the image for a moment. It's an icon of the dead Christ, head slumped, naked from the waist up to reveal the gaping wound in his side. "Man of Sorrows," she says.

Jack is unimpressed. "Looks like plain old ordinary Jesus H. to me."

"Same guy. It's Greek. An icon." She responds to his look. "I walked a beat in Greektown when I was a pup. Back when there were still Greeks in Greektown." She continues to study the image. "Too bad it's not an original. According to some of those Greek OG's, just setting eyes at one of them is a Heavenly get out of jail free card." She looks at Jack as if this should mean something to him. "One look and you'd get all your sins forgiven."

Jack meets her gaze. His eyes give away nothing.

She smiles. "That'd be a heavy lift."

He turns away from the image. "If you say so."

"Don't know why these Polacks got it here at St. Stanislavski."

Jack corrects her. "Saint Stanislaus. Patron saint of Cracow."

"Did some time in Corktown too, you know. They were still telling stories about your old man."

Jack is determined to shut the door on this particular line of conversation. "That son of a bitch has been in the ground a long time now."

"I heard there was a twenty-one gun salute, him being a Vietnam vet and all." She delivers the punch line with a grin. "Only, way I heard it, they were all pointing their guns at the casket. Just to make sure."

The detective settles into a pew. She takes out a cigarette and prepares to light it. "Can I smoke in here?"

Jack shrugs and Chambers lights up. "I also seem to recall meeting this skinny as fuck little white kid. Hardcore little shit. With a mouth on him. Lord Jesus and his blessed apostles, what a mouth! Hustling. Doing whatever it took to survive." She takes a drag from the cigarette and fixes her gaze on Jack. "Tried to help him out. Tried to cut him a break. Almost cost me my badge."

There is a brief flicker of something in Jack's eyes, something almost tender. Then it's gone. His eyes are hard. Pitiless. "You knew I was a snake."

She leans back in the pew, blowing the smoke back over her shoulder. "I know that now. Wasn't always so."

He snorts at the absurdity of what she's saying.

She shakes her head in protest. "No, not from the get-go. I was young but I wasn't stupid."

"Is this going somewhere?"

"I thought maybe you might feel like getting a few things off your chest." She smiles. "Been told I'm a good listener."

"Like you said." He tilts his head in the direction of the confessionals. "Shop's closed today. Gone fishing."

She continues as if she hasn't heard him. "Word on the street is, you haven't been a good little soldier, that you've got a big fat juicy bulls-eye painted on your back."

He's sarcastic. "You do the weather too?"

Her voice has taken on an edge. "That's right, I forgot. You got out. Right?"

Chambers gestures at the array of flickering candles. "You can light all the damn candles in the world, Jack, but nobody crosses Pompey."

She leans forward, serious now. "What the hell is going on, Jack? Bodies are piling up all over the damn place. They're trying to say it's gang related." She clearly doesn't think so. "All these people being turned into roadkill, they got nothin' to do with gangs. Most of em, far as I can see, they got nothin' to do with nothin'."

Jack shrugs. "Folks'll surprise you sometimes."

She looks at Jack appraisingly. "Didn't you get the memo, Jack? Even the mob has moved out to the burbs. Me, I got myself a nice bungalow in Ferndale. Got a cat. Got a lawn I can't get my kids to mow. Even got a Starbucks on the corner. You ever seen a Starbucks in Detroit, Jack? You ever seen an actual grocery store in Detroit?"

He doesn't bother to respond.

She's not done. "How does a city without a fucking grocery store afford a high-end hitman? There are kids on every street corner who will do what you do for twenty bucks. Hell, they'll do it for free just to watch some poor son of a bitch bleed out on the sidewalk."

Jack just looks bored. "I wouldn't know."

"Yeah, you're just a fucking altar boy."

Jack turns to gaze at the altar, smiling at the memory. "Actually, I was an altar boy. For a minute. Marty too."

She spreads her hands in mock horror. "No, no, no, no, I refuse to even listen to this. God's lightning's gonna strike my Black ass for even imagining you in that altar boy rig."

Jack is mildly offended. "What? You can't see me as an altar boy?"

Chambers sighs and takes a long drag on the cigarette.

Jack sounds almost wistful. "Didn't last very long."

"What happened? Get cornholed by some pervert priest?"

Jack bristles at the suggestion he would let anyone put a hand on him. Then he shrugs. "Pounded one of the other kids." He almost seems embarrassed. "Put him in the hospital."

Chambers seems genuinely interested. "Have something to do with your brother?"

He gives her a look. She smiles in return. "I am a detective. Decorated even."

Jack shrugs like it's no big deal. "Called Marty a fag."

Chambers searches for someplace to stub out her cigarette. She leans across the aisle and drops the butt into one of the votive candleholders. She shakes her head in amusement. "The things that come out of a child's mouth."

She shifts in her seat, eyeing him coldly. The convivial air between them has taken on a darker, dangerous edge. She nods to indicate the bulge underneath his jacket. "You're a felon. I could haul your ass in for carrying a piece."

Jack stiffens.

She smiles. "I'm not gonna bust your balls, Jack, I need you. I need you out there doing your loose cannon shtick. Stirring things up." She settles back into the pew. "So I can just sit back and see what comes crawling out from under all those rocks you keep turning over."

"Careful what you wish for, detective."

She stares coldly at him. "Harm reduction, Jack. Drug rehab do-gooders are all over it nowadays." She shifts her weight and raises her arms so that both elbows are straddling the backrest. "You don't waste your time trying to get a junkie to go cold turkey, Jack, you try to get him to do less drugs. You try to get the crackhead on methadone. You try to get the speed freak to light up a Mary Jane once in a while. He does less drugs, less hard drugs, he has to rob fewer people. He does less drugs, he doesn't need to jack so many cars. He does less harm."

Jack is unimpressed. "The lesser of two evils. That's just life."

She's nearly off the bench now, pissed. "Right now you are the lesser of two evils, Jack. That's the only reason your ass is still out on the street. And I'm gonna ride your sorry ass till I find the son of a bitch leaving body parts all over my goddamned city." She regains control and settles back into the pew. "And then, Jack, me and you, just for old time's sake, we're gonna have us..." She stops, momentarily at a loss for words as she struggles to conjure up the right image. "You ever see Godzilla versus Mothra?"

Jack reveals the barest hint of a smile. "Am I Godzilla? Or Mothra?"

Chambers responds with a sneer. "Neither, Jack. You're one of those little people running around screaming just before they get turned into toe jam." She realizes she likes that image. "Yeah... toe jam. That's deep. I like that."

He eyes her with cold calculation. He seems to be measuring the distance between them. Their détente has clearly ended. "St. Stanislaus was killed in a church."

Chambers instinctively moves her hand to her holstered gun. Then she thinks better of it. "Like I said, I need you out there."

Jack turns to go but Chambers isn't finished. "I'll say one thing for you... You may or may not be good at what you do, Jack Killeen, but you sure as fuck have got a talent for getting everyone around you good and dead."

Jack walks to the door without looking back. He doesn't want her to see how close to the mark her words have struck.

She calls out to him as he pushes through the heavy front door of the church. "Just think about this, hotshot... Who they gonna go through next to get to you?"

44

JACK IS HUDDLED IN a dark doorway kitty-corner from Garth's Artist Supply. He's sucking on the glowing nub of a joint cupped in the palm of his hand. A light snow is falling, the season's first, softening the harsh silhouettes of the city's fading skyline. Overhead, the moon is the steel slug from a punch press embedded in a frozen gray curtain of translucent clouds.

Jack holds in a lungful of smoke as the People Mover, empty as always, churns by overhead, a graffiti-embossed pillbox on wheels. He tries to imagine himself in Pompeii, and the wispy shower of white flakes as the volcanic ash destined to bury this dying city. He can't decide if that's a good thing or a bad thing.

As the dark blur of the People Mover disappears into the distance, Jack's eye is drawn to a faint, shimmering glow that briefly illuminates one of the shoulder-like roof terraces of the Metropolitan Building. The glimmer of light is quickly snuffed and Jack can't be sure what he saw. He wonders if it might have been the reflection from a scrapper's torch, but it's hard to believe there's anything of value left inside that plundered wreck. He tells himself the dope is making him goofy and grinds the joint out against the bricks.

Jack sees lights going off inside Garth's. He backs out of sight as the owner and two employees exit the front door. The owner stops to lock the door behind them. Then, shoulders hunched against the weather, the trio heads east on Broadway, veering into the street to avoid the

Wurlitzer barricades. Two of them cross John R. to a surface lot across from the Metropolitan Building and get into their separate cars. The third continues south on John R. at a brisk pace, on his way to a bus stop or a bar.

The headlights from the two cars exiting the lot glide across the lower facade of the Metropolitan Building as they pull into the street. A few minutes later, Rhonda exits the artist supply store. She reaches into her purse for keys and locks the door behind her. Then she just stands there, looking forlorn and staring blankly at the falling snow. After a moment, she snaps out of it and walks west on Broadway in the direction of Grand Circus Park.

Jack follows, crossing the street diagonally to come up behind her. "Rhonda..."

She turns toward him, startled, then quickens her pace. "Get away from me. Haven't you done enough?"

Jack moves alongside. "Please. Just give me a chance to explain."

Rhonda stops. She's consumed with grief and rage, and it takes her a moment to form the words. "Don't you understand? There are no more chances, Jack. She's dead. My baby is dead." She turns and continues walking. Jack follows. She sees her car up ahead and quickens her pace. He does the same.

"Please, Rhonda. We gotta talk. It's important."

Rhonda reaches her car, parked on Broadway just short of the park. She moves into the street, to the driver's door, and reaches into her purse for the keys. She's glaring at him across the hood of the car. "Can you give her back to me? Can you do that? Can you fix that?"

There's nothing Jack can say.

"Then we got nothing to talk about."

She tracks down her keys but her hands are shaking and she drops them on the pavement. She stoops to pick them up but Jack gets there first. He grabs the keys and unlocks the driver's side door. He slides behind the wheel and reaches over to unlock the passenger door. "Get in. I'm taking you home."

Rhonda fumbles in her purse for change. "I'll take the bus." She crosses the street to the opposite sidewalk and begins walking toward Woodward. Jack starts the car, makes a U-turn, and follows her.

Jack leans across the seat to roll down the window as he creeps alongside. "Rhonda, please, get in the fucking car."

She stops. Then she moves to the open window. Her eyes are unforgiving. There is steel in her voice now. "If there is a God, you will burn in hell, Jack. You will fucking burn in hell."

Rhonda turns to find the beast blocking the sidewalk up ahead. She'd scream but the shock has literally knocked the wind out of her.

Jack stomps on the gas pedal. The car jumps the curb and plows into the beast, slamming him through the plate glass window of a storefront. Rhonda is frozen in terror so Jack scrambles across the seat, pops the door, and drags her into the car.

The creature quickly recovers. He grabs the passenger side door and rips it from its hinges. Jack drags Rhonda out the opposite door as the beast hurtles across the seat for her. He slams the door and the window glass shatters on the enraged creature's head. The beast lunges at them and his massive bulk becomes wedged in the window frame.

Jack hustles Rhonda down the sidewalk toward the park while the beast struggles to free himself from the car door. Jack hustles Rhonda past a startled parking attendant and into the underground garage beneath the park. As they stumble down the ramp, the terrified screams of the parking attendant echo through the tunnel behind them, before being cut short with brutal finality.

The garage is nearly empty and they sprint through the low-slung concrete catacombs until they stumble into a locked steel door at the back. In the distance, they can hear the sounds of crumpling sheet metal as the beast shoves parked cars aside in his furious pursuit. Jack takes out the Glock and shoots the lock off the door.

Jack holsters the gun. He flings the door open, and they enter what appears to be the subbasement to one of the buildings flanking the park. They hurry down a corridor lined with steam pipes and valves until it dead-ends at another steel door.

Jack pulls the heavy steel door open and they find themselves in a basement boiler room dimly lit by a bare overhead bulb. Jack realizes there is no other way out, so he slams the door shut. He finds a heavy piece of lumber and wedges it between the door handle and the concrete floor. He spots a fire axe mounted on the wall and grabs it.

They instinctively back away as the beast approaches and slams into the door. Rhonda is terrified and moves behind Jack. "He's gonna get in! Jack, he's gonna get in!"

Jack is standing over a steel plate in the floor that serves as an access hatch for the steam tunnels below ground. He hefts the axe, confident. "That's the general idea."

The beast stands on the other side of the steel barrier for a moment, his breath coming in raspy gulps. Then he shuffles away and out of earshot. Jack and Rhonda remain motionless in the concrete cell, straining to hear the beast's movements over the dull rumble of machinery and the hissing of steam pipes.

Jack turns to look at Rhonda. She's in shock. Her lips are moving but she's not making a sound. Jack grips the axe with one hand and goes to grasp her shoulder. He's still trying to catch his own breath. "I'm sorry, I should have..."

The steel plate beneath Jack's feet erupts from the floor—the beast has found a way into the underground steam tunnels. Jack is thrown to the ground and loses his grip on the axe. The beast shrugs off the steel plate and grabs Rhonda by her ankle. Jack hurls himself at the creature but the creature knocks him aside.

The hitman scrambles across the floor on his hands and knees to retrieve the axe. By the time he returns to the work hatch the demon has disappeared into the tunnel with Rhonda. Jack jams the axe handle into his belt and descends feet first into the darkness, feeling his way down the metal ladder.

The axe handle catches on one of the rungs and Jack tries to wrestle it out of his belt so he can drop it to retrieve at the bottom. The axe head snags on his coat and, too late, he feels the flashlight sliding out of his pocket. A moment later he hears the lens shatter on the concrete below. "Fuck!"

He drops the axe to be retrieved at the bottom and clambers down the ladder into a pitch-black tunnel. He pulls out a pack of matches and lights one. It barely makes a dent in the murk, but it allows him to recover the axe. He lights the whole pack but only makes it a dozen yards further into the gloom before the flame fizzles out.

45

J ACK POUNDS ON THE door to Marty's apartment. "Marty, open the fucking door! Marty!" There's no answer and he searches under the mat for a key. Nothing. He is bracing to kick the door in when someone cracks open a door further down the hall. An elderly woman with gossamer strands of white hair falling over her face peers out at him. "Go away before I call the police."

Jack pulls out his gun, swivels, and points it at her head. "You go ahead and do that. Cause I know where you fucking live." She shuts the door. Jack holsters the Glock and kicks Marty's door open.

Jack careens through the apartment but there is no sign of his brother. He returns to the living room to check the answering machine but it's unplugged. Moving into the kitchen he opens the fridge and looks inside. The milk is past its due date and the veggies are wilted. He goes into the living room, picks up the white pages and flips through the book until he finds the number he's looking for. He dials and the phone is answered almost immediately. "Homicide."

"I want to speak to Detective Chambers."

"What's your business?"

"Detective Chambers."

Maybe there's something I can—?"

"Tell her it's Jack Killeen."

"Hold tight." Jack is put on hold.

Cradling the phone, he wanders into the bedroom to study the array of framed photos carefully arranged on the dresser. There are pictures of Jack and Rhonda at their wedding; of Marty holding toddler Monica on his lap, so tiny against his bulk she looks like a hand puppet; the brothers leering into the camera, stupid drunk at a Tigers game.

Chambers comes on the line. "Jack? Where the hell are—"

He cuts her off. "Where's my brother?"

The detective sounds puzzled by his demand. "I was gonna ask you that."

He's not sure if he should be alarmed or relieved. "You haven't picked him up?"

"No. Should we?" There's a note of suspicion creeping into her voice now. "You got anything to do with this business going on downtown?"

Jack is silent for a long time. He knows he should just keep his mouth shut. He knows he should hang up the phone. But he needs to talk to someone. Anyone. "He's got Rhonda."

Chambers can't hide her interest in this revelation, particularly his willingness to admit it to her. "Who, Jack? Who has her?"

Jack is holding the receiver against his forehead like a cold compress. "I don't know. I don't fucking know."

Chambers is stunned by the admission. "How could you not..." She does an emotional backflip in mid-sentence and is suddenly sympathetic. "You don't sound so good, Jack. Why don't you come in? Or I can come to you."

Jack sets the receiver down on the table as if he no longer has the strength to hold it. His voice isn't much more than a whisper. "No, it's all on me now."

Detective Chambers' voice is now a tinny murmur in the earpiece. "Give me a hint, Jack. Where do we start looking?"

Jack is already pressing down the plunger to disconnect the call. "I wish to god I knew." He sets the receiver down on the table. He stands there in a disoriented funk. He doesn't realize he's listening to the dial tone until it finally cuts out and is replaced by rapid beeping. He slams the receiver back into the cradle.

46

DeRon stares into the lens of the magnifier light as he carefully stitches the tiny threads of muscle tissue to the microscopic ends of the capillaries that will provide the blood supply to reanimated flesh. He's shivering despite the wool cap and the heavy jacket over his lab coat and pauses from time to time to clench and unclench his fists to keep his hands from cramping.

The Professor used to insist on doing this tedious work himself. But in recent months this delicate task has fallen entirely to DeRon. The original plan was for DeRon to do the work in the refrigerated trailer behind his house. That is no longer an option. DeRon sets the surgical needle holder down on the table and pushes the magnifier light away. He swivels the chair away from his work and grimly examines his surroundings.

The frigid cold room is a ghoulish pantry stocked with plastic-wrapped slabs of flesh and bone. In the past he could console himself with the knowledge that this gruesome inventory was assembled from the bodies of killers, violent men meeting violent ends and undeserving of his pity. But he can no longer distance himself from the inert lumps of carrion on his workbench. These are innocents: women, girls even, butchered like livestock for their organs, flesh, and limbs.

Adding to his confusion, DeRon no longer knows what to make of the Professor's original creation, the fiendish beast that has turned the entire city into the kill floor of a slaughterhouse. What is this thing, assembled from the bodies of killers, Black and white and brown? Is it a scientific breakthrough? The prototype for a new species? Or a sick joke? A madman's twisted idea for uniting the races? *What has this crazy white man done?*

And, somehow, it matters more and more to DeRon that Drettmann is white. In DeRon's life, the people who know things have always been white: the doctors, scientists, lawyers, and judges. And the people with money, real money, legit money, are mostly white. That's just the way it is: White people run things and white people make the rules. But the people who enforce those rules, the foot soldiers for the people who know things, for the people with money, they are allowed to be Black: the school resource officers, teachers, principals, cops, EMTs, social workers, lab techs... sometimes even the foster parents.

DeRon sighs and swivels back to the workbench. When it came to foster parents, he preferred the white ones. Unlike the Black fosters, they didn't always call you on your shit. They were too afraid, or oblivious, didn't care, or cared too much, particularly about things like race, to ever get real with you. That, at least, was something.

DeRon repositions the magnifier light and reaches for the surgical needle. But then he stops, pressing his thumb and forefinger together, remembering the texture, like newsprint, of the paper bus transfer gripped between his fingertips.

He remembers the salty, sweet scent of fried food, grease, and hamburgers. And he remembers the vague, peripheral blur of anonymous bodies moving in space around him. He'd stormed into Mickey Ds with time to fill before the next Jefferson bus. He was distracted, raging, in pain. And he didn't even realize the booth was occupied when he plopped down opposite a white kid eating a Big Mac and fries.

The limp, the grimace, and the relentless, muttered self-recriminations endowed him with a ferocity he could never own in real life. He could see the white kid, older, bigger, shrink into himself, avoiding eye contact. And DeRon, seething over yet another failed placement, did something unimaginable: he reached over and took a french fry.

The white kid studiously avoided DeRon's challenging stare as he chewed on it. Emboldened, still staring, he took a handful of fries from the thin paper pouch and set them on an open napkin. The white kid quickly wrapped up his half-eaten Big Mac and left, tossing it into the trash bin on his way out. DeRon pulled the fries across the table to his side. They were completely tasteless. But, for maybe a minute, one glorious minute, he felt good. He felt really good.

DeRon is once again exhausted and beyond caring. He's chilled to the bone and every molecule in his body is steeped in the glycol that permeates the dead tissue he works with. He imagines the glycol fusing his nerve endings in much the same manner it does those in the inert limbs on his bench. He smiles grimly to himself: if he stays here long enough, he'll be nothing more than a frozen, one hundred and forty-five-pound nervesicle.

DeRon is startled by a dull pounding noise coming from somewhere outside the cold room. He reels his chair to the door and releases the latch. The heavy insulated hatch swings open like the door to a safe and the pounding grows louder. DeRon rappels his rolling office chair along the corridor rope line and back into the lab.

By the time he gets there the pounding has stopped and Drettmann is rolling the factory door open to reveal the beast framed in the entrance. The creature holds a woman's lifeless body in his arms. He carries his grisly burden into the lab and Drettmann drags the wheeled door shut behind him. He trails after the beast, eager to examine the corpse, but Victor ignores him and moves to the operating suite. DeRon follows as well, hauling himself along the rope line in the office chair.

The beast sets his prize on the operating table adjoining the one where the early stage of the second creature—the "mate" being created for Victor—lies covered with a sheet. Drettmann moves around to the other side of the table and begins to examine the corpse. DeRon can only stare forlornly at the bruised and battered body. He shakes his head in dismay. "No more, Professor. Please, no more."

Drettmann ignores his complaints. He speaks over his shoulder to his assistant as he works. "Excellent. Structure is excellent..."

Victor takes the dead woman's arms and attempts to wrap them around his shoulders in an embrace. The lifeless limbs fall back on the table and the beast clumsily caresses the dead woman's hair.

Drettmann, engrossed, does not look up from his work. "You must be patient. She is not Marlene."

The beast turns his attention to the shrouded corpse on the adjoining table. "When? When will I have my Marlene?"

The Professor grabs a pair of scissors and begins to cut away the woman's clothing. "Soon, Victor. Soon."

The beast turns impatiently back to Drettmann. He grabs the table and threatens to overturn it. "Now. You will do it now."

Drettmann presses his hands against the dead woman's flank to keep her from sliding off the table. "I need one more, Victor. One more and I will be ready." His eyes lock into those of the beast. "I will give your Marlene back to you. She will be like you. She will not turn away from you."

The beast releases his grip and moves away from the table. He finds his path back to the door blocked by DeRon, who is gripping the rope line and glaring at him. The beast grabs the rope with such force he rips out one of the eyebolts securing it to the wall. He takes the now slack length of rope and wraps it around DeRon's neck.

Before he can tighten it Drettmann turns and shouts at him. "No! We need him." The beast hesitates. There is the sharp clang of metal on metal as the Professor slams the scissors down on the table. "I cannot do this without him."

The beast glares at DeRon for a moment and then releases his grip on the rope. He shoves DeRon and his chair aside. The chair topples and DeRon crashes to the floor. Victor turns his fierce gaze on Drettmann. "I will bring you another. And you will give me back my Marlene."

The beast strides out of the lab.

Drettmann pays no attention to DeRon who is on the floor struggling to right the chair. He proceeds to cut the rest of the clothing from the corpse and toss it into a nearby hamper. Then, he resumes the physical examination. "The pelvis is too narrow. We'll have to split and widen it..." He turns to DeRon, who has managed to climb back into his chair and is gazing mournfully at Rhonda. "Prep her. We have much to do."

47

J ACK MOVES CAUTIOUSLY THROUGH the alley between the Metropolitan and Wurlitzer buildings. There is an enormous police presence downtown and he tries to use the flashlight as little as possible. He stops, turns the flashlight on beneath his coat, and quickly skips the beam of light along the outside wall of the Metropolitan. All of the windows within reach are securely boarded or bricked up.

He kills the light and moves toward the back of the alley where the building narrows. A dumpster pressed up against the brick wall of the Metropolitan, a building that has stood empty for decades, makes him suspicious. He boosts himself onto the bin to see if it was used to climb into an open window. Once he gains his footing on top of the trash receptacle a quick scan with the flashlight reveals nothing but more barricaded windows.

He is about to pocket the flashlight when the reflected glow spilling across the bricks reveals a dark recess behind the dumpster. He kills the light, rests his free hand on the rough iron lip of the dumpster, and drops back into the alley. He wrestles the heavy steel container away from the wall and finds a recessed opening with a weathered wood frame and a service door. He taps the door with his foot, and it swings open to reveal a black void. Jack goes inside, Glock in one hand, flashlight in the other.

Jack finds himself at the rear of the building where it narrows like the prow of a ship. He could be a deep-sea diver exploring a sunken wreck as the darting flashlight beam pierces the gloom, revealing dark wood ceiling beams and arched doorways framed with ornate plaster scrollwork leading to unseen corridors and arcades.

The structure widens as he moves toward the front and a partially frozen slurry of ice and broken glass crackles beneath his feet. Most of the walls and ceilings have been stripped to bare concrete by a generation of scavengers, but sporadic patches of intricately patterned cobalt blue and blood-red wall tile drift through the flashlight's beam like coral blooms.

Jack's interest lies in the upper terrace where he saw the brief flash of light. He spots a concrete staircase with the decorative wrought iron railings still in place. He mounts the stairs and sets out to explore the upper floors. He uses the flashlight sparingly as he moves through the first dozen floors. Each level he passes through has been gutted to the bare plaster walls, some even to the studs. Ceilings have been stripped to reveal the undersides of the wood plank subfloors from the floors above.

As he ascends into the upper levels the flashlight's beam reveals enormous cast iron radiators lying where scrappers, unable to manhandle them down to the street, abandoned them. Encased in chalky layers of grit and plaster dust, they could be the fossilized remains of ancient sea creatures resting on the ocean floor.

Jack stops when he reaches the twelfth floor. He's now level with the shoulder-like terraces flanking the central tower and he can see that one of the windows overlooking the north shoulder is completely open to the elements. Leaning on the sill, he looks out on a small grove of spindly trees that have taken root and grown to heights of twenty feet or more.

He climbs over the marble sill and finds himself on a desolate platform high above the street that resembles a long-abandoned garden courtyard. The terrace is bordered on three sides by a chest-high parapet wall with massive terra-cotta urns at the corners. The facade wall of the central tower looms over it all with its checkerboard Moorish tiles, horseshoe arches, and lavishly detailed terra-cotta facing.

In one corner, shielded from the street below by the parapet wall, is a concrete planter containing the remains of a small campfire. A fragment of ornamental iron grillwork has been set on top to serve as a cooking surface. A filthy sleeping bag lies nearby, completely unzipped and apparently used as a cloak. Jack knocks the improvised grill cover off and pokes around inside the blackened urn with a stick. Mixed in with the ashes are the bones of several small animals.

Jack goes back inside and climbs one final staircase to the top of the central tower. From there he scales a metal ladder that clings to the wall of the building's turret like the conning tower ladder in a submarine. He flings open a hatch at the top of the ladder and climbs onto the roof of the Metropolitan Building.

The wind is fierce at this exposed height and Jack grips the metal flagpole mount, a welded tripod made from I-beams, for support. To the west and south are the abandoned Broderick and Book Towers, dark, menacing precipices among the lighted towers of downtown. Through the gaps between buildings, Jack can make out the patchy quilt of streetlights defining the flatlands of the near west side and Corktown.

Jack is about to climb back into the hatch when something catches his eye. In the midst of the lighted streets of Corktown is a dark void, like a black hole at the center of a thin blanket of stars: the abandoned Michigan Central Station. In the midst of that emptiness, or what should be emptiness, is a tiny, flickering light, like the signal fire atop a besieged Crusader castle. Jack realizes that the light, perhaps a cook fire, is coming from somewhere in the upper reaches of that deserted wreck.

48

J ACK PARKS ON A deserted side street several blocks west of Trumbull. He walks the rest of the way and then circles the block to make sure his building is not being watched.

Once inside, Jack padlocks the steel door behind him. He can hear music, something Motown, coming from Marlene's room upstairs. He starts up the stairs and detects the pungent odor of marijuana. As he nears the top, he can see the sliver of light peeking out from beneath her door. She must still be awake.

Jack sinks to a seated position on the steps. He can't bring himself to talk to her. Not now. Not with everything that's happened. Rhonda... his daughter... the trailer full of corpses... his brother. Not with everything he's seen. Not with what he has to do now. He has to kill Victor. He has to kill Victor again.

He takes a joint out of his pocket and fires it up. He needs Marty if he's going to pull this off. *What the fuck is up with Marty?* It takes several deep, lung-expanding sucks off the joint before he manages to stop thinking about his brother. He leans back on the steps and listens to the music: The Temptations, "Can't Get Next to You."

He silently mouths the lyrics coming from the other side of the door. He finds himself smiling as he recalls those long-ago drunken, clowning, hand-clapping, soul train strutting nights. His mind drifts back to those electric moments when the world stopped, when he danced with Marlene in those crowded, west side basements.

He was usually one of the few white people there, often the only one. But it didn't matter. Not with Marlene. Marlene had this aura of confidence and warmth that disarmed even the most sullen hard case. Her poise, beauty, vitality; that was the price of admission. Marlene, a grin, and a fist bump got you into any party, made you welcome with any crowd, allowed you to be an unofficial member of any posse. And, as for being the only white guy, that was okay too. Usually. He knew the drill.

Jack had learned at an early age that, if you were to be outnumbered, it was best to be massively outnumbered. When you were the extreme minority you were no threat. Everything was cool as long as you kept your head down and didn't make waves, the extreme exception to that rule being prison. That was a vicious lesson, one that Jack learned fast and well as a teenager during brief stints in DeHoCo and Riverside. But in the neighborhood, in school during his short time at Murray Wright, and at basement dance parties, he seldom had a problem. There were times when it felt as if Black folks actually became somewhat protective when you were the only white face there. That's not something you can get out of a book.

The worst situation to be in was one where the two sides had near equal numbers. Or when the smaller group was large enough to be a potential threat to the dominant group. That's when things got tense. That's when folks got chippie and you had to watch your back. He remembers the Big Fat Fuck's stories about the pitched battles between the races at Cooley High School when the Black/white mix hit the tipping point. That doesn't happen much in Detroit these days. Not for a long time.

Jack leans back on his elbows and sucks in a lungful of smoke. He remembers that glorious feeling of invulnerability as he danced with Marlene, all alone with her in the press of that hot, frantic jumble of bodies. He was lost in the music, energized, powerful, feeling every muscle and tendon as he spun and hopped and whooped, rolled and coiled, twisted, swayed, contorted, and thumped in this exhilarating form of choreographed violence.

Afterward, sweating, eager, they playfully bumped hips as they walked arm in arm to the car. They opened the doors simultaneously, he the back driver's side door, her the front passenger door. Laughing at their disconnect, they lunged into an embrace over the seatback, with Jack dragging her into the back with him. They tore at their clothes like two magicians struggling free of their restraints. Before it was too late. Before this steel coffin plunged to the bottom of the river with them inside.

Jack gets a few hours of fitful sleep on the downstairs couch. He opens his eyes when the morning sun shining down from the leaded glass windows on the balcony warms his face. The place is quiet as he struggles to maneuver his aching body to a seated position so he can light a joint. After filling his lungs full of soft smoke, he feels almost human again. Then, joint clasped between his lips, he climbs stiffly to his feet and peers up to the balcony to see that Marlene's door is closed. He checks to make sure there's food in the fridge and goes into the bathroom. He takes a piss, washes his hands, throws water on his face, and stops to study his reflection in the mirror.

He looks like hell, haggard and exhausted. His mouth is a hard crease, and his face is all raw stubble with patches of sallow, discolored skin still healing from bruises. But it's the eyes that are freaking him out. The eyes looking back at him in the mirror are cold, lifeless, and somehow disturbingly familiar.

Jack shudders with the realization that he's staring into the cruel, implacable eyes of the Big Fat Fuck. He turns abruptly from the mirror and drops the joint into the toilet. Maybe this really is getting to be a problem.

Jack takes the phone from the file cabinet where he'd locked it up. He goes to the door but hesitates before leaving. He stares up at the door to her room, willing it to open, willing her to give him some kind of a sign. He wants desperately to go to her, to convince her to leave with him before it's too late. And if she doesn't want to go? Then to hell with her, he'll make her go. She'll be fucking pissed but she'll come around eventually. There's no fucking reason to stay. Except Marty. *Where the fuck is Marty?*

Jack goes to the door and peers through the peephole. Who's he kidding? He can't leave. He can't go anywhere until he's fixed this.

Jack puts the padlock back on the outside of the steel door on his way out.

———— • ————

Marlene is peering through the rectangle of clear glass at the center of one of the glass block windows in the second-floor bedroom overlooking Haddad's. She sees Jack walking away with the phone tucked under his arm. *That son of a bitch! Where was he hiding it?*

Jack drifts out of view at the end of the block and Marlene returns to her task from the night before: chipping away at the cement between the windowpane and the glass blocks with a kitchen knife. She's not quite sure what she's going to do when and if she manages to remove the glass. Even if she wasn't on the second floor, the opening wouldn't be large enough for her to climb out. And she's not sure if she wants to be a lady in distress shouting down from a window in this neighborhood. There's no telling how that might play out. And she doesn't want to talk to the cops. At least not yet. She just needs to get away, to figure things out. She needs to come up with a plan.

She stops working when she sees a man walking fast on the opposite sidewalk, shoulders hunched, a hoodie obscuring his face. She intuitively recognizes the furtive, purposeful stride of an addict who has just scored.

She can feel her heart beating in her chest. She can almost taste his anticipation, the frantic impatience to get inside, close the door to the outside world and tear into that little foil packet. She grips the window frame with both hands as she watches him climb the steps to one of the dreary houses down the street from the liquor store. After a quick, feral glance in either direction, he puts the key in the lock and slips inside. Once the door closes behind him Marlene has to remind herself to breathe.

Driven by a fresh surge of anger and adrenaline she hacks away at the cement with the dull knife. She's mostly angry at herself. She was so over Jack. She'd walled herself off from him, brick by fucking brick. Until she'd built a towering fortress, surrounded by a fucking moat, with sharks in it. Then he touched her. He placed the flat of his hand between her shoulder blades and it all came tumbling down like the goddamn walls of Jericho.

She shouts, her breath clouding the unforgiving glass. "I am such a fucking moron."

She turns and tosses the knife onto the bed. This isn't going to work. She needs better tools. She needs a better fucking plan.

49

J ACK OPENS THE CAR door and slides behind the wheel. He drops the phone on the seat next to him and slips the key into the ignition. He starts the car but, before putting it in gear, reaches over to replace the receiver that has fallen off the phone base.

A voice comes from the back seat, Marty's voice. "That's not how it works, you know? You gotta buy a special phone. And a plan."

Jack's right hand is still resting on the phone. His left hand is slipping into his jacket. "Yeah? No wonder I can't get any fucking reception."

There's a mixture of menace and fear in Marty's voice. "Don't do it, Jack."

Jack removes the hand from his jacket. He turns his head just enough to see the gun in Marty's hand. "You gonna whack me, Marty? I'm your brother."

Marty leans forward, gripping the seatback with his free hand. The entire side of his face is bruised and swollen where he was bashed with a metal pipe. "Take your gun out and drop it behind the seat."

Jack does as he's told. He studies his brother in the mirror. "You alright, Marty? You look like you got kicked by a fucking horse."

"Start driving."

Jack puts the car in gear and pulls away from the curb. He glances into the rearview mirror again. "You're shit-faced, Marty. A pro never drinks when he's doing a piece of work. Throws off your timing."

"Shut up!" Marty settles back in the seat. "What the fuck do you know?"

Jack's voice is pure, wicked nonchalance. "You taking me for a ride, Marty? Where we going? The airport? You gonna stuff me in the trunk like a piece of luggage?"

Jack takes another look at his brother in the rearview mirror. His voice drips contempt. "You don't know where the fuck you're taking me, do you? You haven't fucking thought this through. You haven't got a fucking plan. How many times have I fucking told you—"

"I told you to shut the fuck up!" Marty taps the passenger window with the barrel of the gun. "Get on the freeway."

Jack turns onto Rosa Parks, headed for the service drive for I-94. "What do you think, Marty? One right behind the ear? Nice and neat. Like a pro." He starts to turn around. "This is me, Marty, your fucking brother."

Marty presses the gun up against the back of his brother's head. He is growing edgier in direct correlation to Jack's calm. He struggles to produce one coherent word. "Don't."

Jack turns his attention back to the road. He turns right onto the service drive. Marty leans forward again. His voice is anguished once he manages to find the words. "They came for me, Jack. They did things..." He chokes off a sob. "I don't want that to happen to my boys."

Jack turns down a side street and Marty becomes alarmed. "What the fuck are you doing? Get back on the service drive."

Jack ignores him. His manner is placid. He could be discussing the best place to purchase floor mats. "Don't do it inside the car, Marty. Car goes to you. Did you know that? Get blood, brains, all over the fucking place."

Marty thrusts the gun to the side of Jack's face. "Jack, I swear to god..."

Jack casually raises a finger to silence his brother. "Hold on... Just ten more payments." His face scrunches in concentration. "No, wait a sec... nine. I think. Brakes squeak though." He gestures in the general direction of the passenger side wheel well. "Maybe you should have somebody take a look—"

Marty's eyes involuntarily follow the gesture and Jack stomps on the brake pedal. The car slams to a stop and Marty's momentum sends him halfway into the front seat. Jack grabs his brother and drags him all the way over the seatback.

Marty still has the gun, but he's face down with his head wedged beneath the dash by the passenger door. He twists his shoulders and tries to raise the gun, but Jack grabs the phone and smacks him on the back of the head with it. Marty is momentarily stunned and Jack twists his arm behind his back until he screams in pain and releases his grip on the weapon.

Jack takes the gun and tosses the phone into the back seat. "Try doing that with your fucking cellphone."

Jack leaps out of the car. He goes around to the passenger side and pulls his brother out. He drags Marty across the sidewalk and slams him into a wall. Marty crumples to the ground, cowering and whimpering as Jack pummels him about the head and shoulders with his open hand. "You gonna whack me, Marty? Huh? You gonna whack me? Your brother? Your fucking brother?"

Marty is sobbing uncontrollably now. The wound from the previous day has re-opened and blood is trickling down the side of his face. "They're gonna go after my family, Jack. What else could I do? I didn't know what else to do."

Jack stands over his brother, rigid with rage. Marty eyes the gun he still clutches in his hand. "You gonna kill me?"

Jack seems surprised to find the gun in his hand. He pockets it and his manner softens. "You're my fucking brother." He grabs Marty by the shoulder. "Get up. You look fucking ridiculous."

Marty climbs shakily to his feet and Jack helps him brush himself off.

"I'm sorry, Jack. I don't know what to..." Marty waves his arms help-lessly, at a loss for words. He looks like he is going to start blubbering at any moment.

Jack looks at him for a long time before finally speaking. "I know where he is." Marty just looks at him in confusion. "The guy that's doing all this, I know where he's fucking cooped."

Marty eyes his brother in disbelief. "Pompey?"

"No, not fucking Pompey." He straightens his brother's jacket. "Look, you want to whack somebody so bad, we'll whack somebody."

"No."

Jack can't believe what he's just heard. "What do you mean 'no'?"

Marty's voice is steady now, determined. "There's something I gotta do first."

———————— • ————————

Jack and Marty are standing by the side door to Magoo's Livonia condo. Marty is eyeing the two baseball bats gripped in his gloved hand with a great deal of skepticism. "I'm not here to fucking play games, Jack."

Jack shushes him and finishes picking the door lock. He slips the tools back into his coat pocket and pulls on a pair of gloves before carefully nudging the door open. Satisfied they have not been detected, he takes one of the Louisville sluggers from his brother. Jack examines the barrel, studded with nicks and gouges, with grim amusement. "Trust me, Mar-ty, these puppies have never made contact with a baseball." He eyes the bloody bandage wrapped around his brother's head. "Just don't fucking bleed all over everything. Alright?"

Magoo is standing in the kitchen in his bare feet and a polyester tracksuit when the brothers enter. He's holding a tiny plastic carton with a basil plant and carefully pressing a thick finger into the soil. He acts as if it's perfectly normal to see two large men with baseball bats stroll into his kitchen. He's reading the little instruction placard planted in the dirt with the basil. "It says here, you're supposed to stick your finger in to see if the soil's moist before you water it."

The brothers, grimly silent, move to flank the aspiring horticulturist and block any path of escape. Magoo removes his finger and sighs as he studies the tiny specks of black dirt clinging to the digit. "I mean, what the fuck?" A shrug, "Feels like dirt to me. How am I supposed to know whether or not to water the damn—"

He lunges for the magnetic rack of knives over the stove but Jack is ready for him. Utilizing what the play-by-play guys might call a "compact swing" he shatters Magoo's elbow with a hard shot from the wooden bat.

Magoo doubles over with the spastic lurch of a man rocked by a Taser. Then, clutching his broken arm, howling in agony and rage, he busts out of his crouch to sweep the knives from the overhead rack. He's already off-balance, a wide receiver lunging for an overthrown ball, when Marty drops him with a vicious blow to the knee. The solid thwack of wood on bone makes it clear there's been some serious damage done.

Crippled now, pounding the floor with his one functioning fist, Magoo eyes the gleaming clutch of fallen knives. "We shouda taken care of you punks a long time ago. I told him! I fucking told him!" Gasping in pain, he humps his crippled bulk across the linoleum like a beached sea lion until Jack kicks the knives out of his reach. Then, with a barely perceptible nod, the hitman turns the proceedings over to his brother.

Marty puts his shoe on Magoo's head and presses his face into the floor. He's gripping the handle of the bat with both hands and taking the short, circular test swings of a batter waiting on a fastball. His eyes burn with pure, unadulterated hate. "Coulda, shoulda, woulda." Magoo grabs his tormentor's ankle with his good hand in a pointless effort to reduce the pressure on his skull.

Marty raises the bat high over his shoulder. His voice is emotionless. "You may experience a little discomfort with this procedure." He brings the barrel of the bat down on Magoo's elbow with tremendous force, snapping the outstretched arm like a tree limb. Magoo screams and the arm flops uselessly on the floor.

Marty proceeds to hammer away at the battered limb with the fierce intensity of a convict breaking rocks. Finally, when the arm has been reduced to a bloody mash of flesh and bone, he removes his foot from Magoo's head and steps to the side.

Magoo's drooling mouth emits something between a wheeze and a sob as he attempts to crawl away on his stomach, propelling himself with his one good leg and dragging his pulverized limbs like flippers.

Marty follows behind the creeping gangster with the benign patience of a proud papa watching his toddler learn to crawl. He takes careful aim and brings the bat down to shatter the ankle of Magoo's good leg. Magoo shrieks with the shrill intensity of a creature that has abandoned any pretense to dignity. He slithers sideways to press his face into the baseboard of one of the counters while Marty watches with cruel satisfaction. "Any port in a storm."

He places his foot between Magoo's shoulder blades and presses the big man's chest and neck into the linoleum. He grips the handle with both hands like a plunger and uses the blunt end of the bat to methodically pound his victim's nose, cheek, ear, and jaw, laboring conscientiously until the face is an unrecognizable mass of pulverized meat. Then, he backs off and delivers a bone-splintering shot to Magoo's hip. The blow elicits nothing more than a gasping whimper and Marty follows up with powerful, bone-cracking assaults on each of his shoulder blades.

Magoo is making muffled, gurgling sounds into the floor. The pool of blood around his head has spread to encircle his entire body and his battered bulk shimmies in the gory mess like a freshly hooked fish. Marty, careful to avoid the creeping puddle, twists the bat in his hands as he ponders his next target.

Jack taps the countertop with his bat to get his brother's attention. "Stick a fork in it already." Marty ignores him. Raising the bat high above his head, he emits a high-pitched scream of rage while delivering a powerful blow to Magoo's tailbone. The thug's entire body shudders but he makes no sound. Still not finished, Marty reloads and delivers another crushing blow to Magoo's rectum.

Marty steps back to admire his handiwork. The burly, bald-headed thug has been reduced to a mound of moist, quivering meat in a thin polyester casing. Marty looks to his brother. "Finish him."

Jack unholsters the Glock. He takes the silencer out of his pocket and screws it onto the barrel. He holds the gun out to his brother. "You do it." Marty makes no effort to take the weapon, so Jack sets it on the counter. "I'm done with this. With killing."

Marty stares at his brother in disbelief. Then, realizing that Jack means it, he picks up the Glock. He meets his brother's steady, appraising gaze with a challenging glare. "Fuck him if he can't take a joke."

Jack is about to leave him to it when he realizes his brother is staring at the partially open silverware drawer in the kitchen island. He looks at his brother in astonishment. "No. Fuck no."

Marty, responding in kind to his brother's challenging look, steps over Magoo's blubbering form and carefully closes the silverware drawer. Jack shakes his head. "You are one sick son of a bitch."

Jack walks outside. He leans against the wall and takes the small glassine bag of dope out of his shirt pocket. He lights up a joint and silently counts the muffled shots coming from inside the house: Marty is emptying the entire clip.

Marty joins him a few minutes later. He leans back against the wall beside his brother. He has a bat in either hand, their bloody barrels resting in the dirt. He could be a gladiator at rest, stunned by the realization he has once again survived the ordeal of the arena. Jack reaches over to take the Glock from his brother's pocket. Marty, with a slight tilt of his head, indicates the opposite pocket. "I got the shells." Jack nods. Sucking on the joint gripped in his teeth, he whistles inadvertently as he removes the silencer, clears the chamber, and returns the gun to the holster.

Jack returns to a resting position against the brick wall. It's at least a minute before he breaks the silence. "You still with me?"

Marty's eyes are closed. He looks as if he'd rather be anywhere else but here. "Do I have a fucking choice?"

Jack glances down at the gory baseball bats. He almost sounds regretful. "Not anymore." He pushes himself away from the wall but Marty doesn't move. Jack stops and stares at him. "What?"

Marty's still trying to work this all out. He nods in the direction of the condo. "In there... You said you were done with all this."

"Yeah?"

Marty is perplexed. "But now you wanna go do this other guy."

"This one doesn't count. Guy took a fucking rain check." Jack moves off in the direction of the car. "Let's go fix this thing."

50

THE FLAMES ERUPTING FROM the blazing dumpster fire are feasting on the swirling gusts of powdery snow. Aside from Jack's car, there's nothing within a thousand yards in any direction but desolation. The siblings have stripped down to their boxer shorts and are tossing their clothing into the inferno. Jack grins at his brother. "We must look like a couple of fucking meth heads." Marty, staring morosely into the flames as he incinerates his trousers, ignores him.

Jack tosses the bloody baseball bats into the fire. Then he stoops to remove the Glock from the holster at his feet. He checks to make sure there's not a round in the chamber and tosses the gun and holster into the inferno. Marty looks at him as if he's lost his mind. "What the fuck?"

Jack is already struggling into a fresh pair of jeans. "Trust me, wouldn't do us any good anyway. Not with this guy."

They finish dressing and warm themselves by the fire. Marty stares morosely into the fiery pyre. He turns to look at his brother; he's distraught, beaten down by the events of the past few days. "We're killers, Jack. We fucking kill people." His eyes are moist with tears. "How did this fucking happen?"

Jack shakes his head.

Marty stares at his brother, his distress turning to disgust. "That's it? That's all you got?"

Jack has nothing. Marty turns and heads for the car. "Let's do this thing."

Jack finally finds his voice, calling after his brother: "Few more hours, Marty. It'll be over. Done. Like it never happened. I swear to god." He follows his brother. "Hey, did I ever tell you the one about Beowulf?"

Marty stops when he reaches the car. "You always got a fucking story."

Jack stops by the trunk. "I wanna show you something."

He's fishing for his keys as Marty joins him. "Beowulf... Is it about a wolf or something?"

Jack unlocks the trunk. He turns to look at his brother, dead serious. "No. It's about a guy trying to kill a monster."

Marty looks away. "Not sure I wanna hear that one right now."

Jack turns back to the car and opens the trunk. Inside are two long-handled fire axes. Marty stares at them in disbelief. "You're fucking with me, right?"

Jack picks up one of the axes and takes a few practice swings. "Whadaya think? Do some serious damage with this puppy."

Marty, not quite convinced, leans into the trunk and hefts the other axe. "So what's the plan?"

Jack holds his axe straight out in front of him, eyes fixed on the middle distance, a Crusader knight sizing up his opponent. "There's that tunnel behind the train station. At Newark Street. Remember?"

Marty takes a few tentative swings. "That still there? We were frigging kids."

Jack executes a few slick movie samurai moves. "Guess we'll find out, huh?"

Marty advances on an imaginary opponent with some vicious figure eight parries and thrusts. "That's way the other side of the tracks. Why don't we just park at the station? Nobody gives a shit, it's a goddamned abandoned building."

Jack dispatches a vanquished foe with a vicious head chop. "What we don't want is for this guy to see us coming. Alright?"

They turn and face each other, axes raised high in front of them. Marty is still looking for reassurance. "So, this Beowulf dude... Does he kill it? The monster?"

They close and tap the metal axe heads together as if preparing for a bout. "Yeah. He kills it. Fixes everything."

Marty seems satisfied with this answer. The brothers move a safe distance from each other and begin taking roundhouse swings at imaginary opponents. From a distance, they could be two boys at play, two very large, very dangerous boys.

51

THE KILLEEN BROTHERS ARE slogging through the partially flooded baggage tunnel. The tunnel goes underneath the wide expanse of abandoned passenger and freight platforms behind the Michigan Central complex. Rusting grids of rebar tendons erupt from the crumbling concrete walls. There is standing water, mud, and sludge underfoot.

The two men trail behind the roving beam from Jack's flashlight. Jack's axe is slung casually over his shoulder. Marty follows close behind with his axe at the ready. He's on the lookout for rats. Something spooks him. "What was that?"

Jack briefly directs his light in the direction Marty indicated. "There's no rats down here—they'd fucking drown. That shit only happens in the movies. Like alligators in the sub—" He stops mid-sentence, struck by a disturbing image from a dream.

"What? You see something?"

Jack shakes it off. "Yeah, guy in a hockey mask with a chainsaw." He slogs forward through the muck. "Let's do this."

Marty becomes talkative when he's nervous. "So, your guy Alvin, he do the train station too?"

Jack stops so abruptly Marty nearly stumbles into him. He turns to glare at his brother, carefully enunciating both words: "Albert Kahn." Each subsequent word is accompanied by a tomahawk chop hand gesture: "Albert. Fucking. Kahn."

Jack waits until Marty looks sufficiently contrite before moving on. "Some other guy did the train station. Supposed to look like a Roman bath or something." He walks a little further before stopping and plays the beam from the flashlight over the muddy ground to study the path ahead. He turns the flashlight off and pockets it. "Getting close."

Moonlight leaking in from the tunnel entrance provides enough illumination to guide them the rest of the way. They step out of the old baggage tunnel and pause for a moment to orient themselves. To their left, the squat mass of brick and masonry containing the station's baggage and passenger loading areas rises out of the earth. In front of them, the dark office tower looms over the landscape like a bleak fortress.

Jack gazes into the gloom, momentarily lost in thought. He snaps out of his reverie when Marty whispers ominously into his ear, in his best scary voice, "The dark tower. Mordor..."

"Just shut the fuck up already. Wasn't funny when you were eight."

They cut across a wide expanse of hard-packed dirt and gravel that forms a sort of courtyard alongside the rear southeast corner of the dark station complex. To their left is a dirt embankment they'd have to scale to reach the baggage and passenger areas that once funneled throngs of passengers onto the loading platforms. Ahead of them is the stone base that serves as the foundation for the main body of the station and the office tower above it. The gravel courtyard jogs to the right at that point and narrows as it passes beneath a pedestrian bridge that leads to a side entrance of the station, overhead at ground level.

They move along the side of the station complex, parallel with a row of large, rectangular basement windows. Some of the windows are boarded up but many are completely open to the elements.

Jack uses the flashlight to search for an opening they can climb through without encountering too much broken glass. "He's probably holed up somewhere in the office tower."

Marty steps back to gaze up at the massive structure. In the darkness, it could be a watchtower built by a race of giants. "That's a fuck of a lot of territory to cover with just two guys."

"He's not gonna be hard to find." Jack hefts his axe and prepares to move forward. Before Marty can respond the two men are caught in the glare of headlights from a car parked beneath the pedestrian bridge. Standing alongside the car, guns pointed at them, are Detectives Chambers and her partner, Detective Michael Searcy. Searcy, a tall Black man with close-cropped hair, is younger, leaner, and more stylish than his partner.

"Drop the weapons!"

"Let me see your hands!"

The Killeen brothers drop the axes into the dirt and the detectives stride forward with their guns at the ready. "On your knees! On your fucking knees! Now!"

The brothers comply and are pushed face down on the ground. The detectives handcuff the two men behind their backs and search them. Searcy finishes frisking Jack and turns to his partner with barely concealed surprise. "He's clean."

Chambers gives Jack some side-eye. "Not as dumb as he looks." In the process of going through Marty's pockets, she finds his cellphone. She examines it under the beam from her flashlight. She sounds impressed. "My, my, aren't we all on the cutting edge and shit? Direct line to your Shylock?"

Marty twists his head to look up at her. "I was calling Crime Stoppers. Wanted to report a couple cops cooping up here by the train station."

Searcy kicks him. Chambers holds out a hand to stop him. "Easy." She indicates the bloody bandage on Marty's head. "They'll go trying to pin that shit on us." She pulls Jack to his feet and leaves Marty for her partner. "You take Free Willy."

Searcy hauls Marty to his feet and hustles him over to the unmarked police car beneath the bridge.

Before doing the same with Jack, Chambers reaches into his shirt pocket and pulls out his stash. She holds the clear sandwich bag up in front of Jack's face. There are three tight, thin joints inside. "Boogie Bear Blue?"

He nods.

"Good as they say?"

"You tell me."

Chambers smiles and stuffs the baggie into her pocket. "I'll let you know."

She grips his elbow and guides him over to the car. They could be a couple of old friends, up until the moment she slams him face down on the hood next to his brother. Searcy keeps his gun pointed at them while Chambers walks back to retrieve the axes. Returning to the car, she opens the trunk and throws them inside.

Searcy is shining his flashlight around the barren landscape. "You guys take the bus? Where's your vehicle?"

Chambers has rejoined her partner. "Only bus these two'll be riding is the one upstate. I thought you two clowns got out of the scavenging business?"

Jack twists his shoulders to get eyes on her. "Looking for railroad ties. Kids nowadays, they get high smoking the creosote." He gives her a sly smile. "It's a harm reduction thing."

Marty is growing annoyed. "You gonna charge us for hanging around an empty building? Write me a ticket already. For what? Trespassing?"

Chambers ignores him and turns to study the desolate ruins of the train station. "You two maybe thinking about settling a few scores?" She turns back to Jack. "Maybe you got a line on Grizzly Adams? Maybe you're looking for a little payback?"

Jack hasn't got a clue. "Who the fuck is Grizzly Adams?"

The two detectives exchange glances. Chambers comes to a decision. "I guess you got a right to know. Our perp, the newspapers,
they're calling him Grizzly Adams now."

Searcy grabs Marty by his collar and shines the light in his face.
"Maybe we should be looking at Chewbacca here." He pokes Marty's
bloody bandage, making the big man wince. "Could be, one of the
vics got a few licks in." He pushes Marty's head back onto the hood
and grins at Chambers. "Peckerwood this ugly's probably got a taste
for beaver too."

Jack presses his forehead against the hood in an unsuccessful effort
to smother his snorting laughter. It takes him a moment to find his
voice. "You call yourself a fucking detective? Marty'd rather put a
gun to his head than—"

Marty body slams his brother in anger. "Shut the fuck up!" Jack,
still laughing, slides off the hood to the ground.

Jack is still chuckling when Chambers pulls him back onto the
hood. She shakes her head and sighs. "The perp likes to eat beavers,
you dumbass. You know, the ones with the teeth?"

Searcy shakes his head in disgust. "Who the fuck eats beavers?
That is some nasty shit."

Chambers ignores her partner. "At the Broderick Tower crime
scene, there was a partially eaten animal carcass. North American
Beaver. Castor Canadensis."

Searcy is still shaking his head. "Gotta be a white guy. Gotta be."

Chambers leans in close to Jack. "You here working for Pompey?
Or you here looking for Pompey?"

Jack smiles. "Creosote. We're gonna corner the market. You wanna piece of the action, you're too late. You missed the bus."

Searcy joins his partner. He glares at Jack. "What does that ass
clown need you for? He could hire a hundred hungry niggers for
what he pays you."

Jack rests his face on the hood. He's enjoying this. "I don't know how to break it to you, detective... Even in Detroit, there are places an Irishman can go that a..." Jack, opting for discretion over valor, chooses his next words carefully. "That a brother can't."

Searcy hooks his foot under Jack's ankles and yanks his feet out from under him. Jack manages to twist his body on the way down so his shoulder slams into the ground before his face does.

Chambers almost looks impressed. "Nice save."

Jack, his face pressed against the ground, spits out a few pieces of gravel. "Done this before."

Searcy pulls Jack back to his feet by his handcuffed wrists and deposits him next to his brother. Chambers stiff-arms his face into the hood. "You're about as much goddamned Irish as the Irish Spring soap I use to wash my coochie."

She steps away from the car so she has more room to expound. "When you gonna get with the program, Jack? There's no more Irish in Corktown. There's no more Greeks in Greektown. There's no Polacks in Poletown. No Italians on the east side. No Jews on the west side. There's not even any Chinamen in Chinatown no more. Hell, there's no Chinatown in Chinatown no more."

She returns to lean over Jack's prostrate form. "Nobody here but us Black folks, Jack. Maybe it's time to relocate your hinky white ass."

Jack is unimpressed. "It's like the NBA, y'all. Players are Black. Owners are white."

Chambers's voice is full of contempt. "What the fuck does that make you? Ball boy?"

Searcy grins. "Larry Bird."

Chambers turns to stare at her partner in befuddlement. Jack and Marty would do the same if they could.

Searcy gapes at her as if it's completely obvious. "Larry. Fucking. Bird." He indicates Jack. "This bitch, he's like the Larry Bird of Detroit hitmen. Now, I wouldn't put him up there with Bird when it comes to the trash talk." He indicates Jack's cuffed hands. "But, he is a step slow." He gives Marty a swift kick. "Knows how to pass the ball. And I bet he's got one hell of an outside shot."

Chambers is not quite sold. "Larry Bird? That's pretty old school."

He throws her a challenging look. "Alright, who then?"

Chambers is at a loss. "I don't know. You got your Kobe, your Grant Hill, Shaquille, Dikembe, MJ..." She lands on one. "What about that guy Dieter... Dieter Shrimpf?"

Searcy corrects her. "Detlef Schrempf. He doesn't count. He's German."

Chambers doesn't get the distinction. "So? That's white."

"How bout we keep this to English as a first language?"

"Alright, fine. Jeff Hornacek."

It's Searcy's turn to roll his eyes.

Chambers is clearly grasping at straws now. "Bill Lambier?"

Searcy snorts in derision. "You must be trippin."

Her grin indicates Chambers finally has a winner. "John Stockton."

Searcy has to give that one some respect. "Yeah, I forgot about him."

Marty is beginning to feel left out. "Hey, if he gets to be Larry Bird, then I'm Kevin McHale."

Searcy gives him a dismissive look. "You look like you just ate Kevin McHale."

Chambers takes the manacle off one of Jack's wrists and secures it to the door handle. She holds her hand out to Searcy for his key. She frees one of Marty's wrists and links that manacle to the one attached to the car door, leaving each brother secured by one wrist to the door handle.

"You sure about this?" asks Searcy.

Chambers smiles confidently and takes out her flashlight. "Let's go see who else was invited to the party."

Searcy takes a skeptical look at the towering train station. "Why don't we let the uniforms check it out?"

She's not smiling anymore. "This is our collar."

Jack is uneasy at the prospect of Chambers running into Victor. "You might want to call for backup."

Chambers looks expectantly at him. "Is there something we should know?"

Jack is conflicted. He's not sure if he's concerned for her safety, afraid he'll lose out on his chance at revenge, or both. In the end, the fact that she's a cop short-circuits any other considerations. He lowers his head and stares at the ground.

Chambers opens the car door to turn the headlights off. "Suit yourself." Leaning into the car, she hesitates for a moment, eyeing the shotgun in the locked rack between the seats. She leaves it and closes the door. She turns her attention to Searcy. "Detective?"

He's looking down at his shoes. They are nice shoes. Mephisto's. He looks annoyed and goes to open the trunk. He pulls out a pair of rubber boots, leans against the fender, and starts to pull them on over his shoes.

Detective Chambers is already walking toward the nearest window. Hopping on one foot as he struggles into the boots, Searcy gestures at the pedestrian bridge overhead that leads to a side entrance at ground level. "There is a door up top, you know. Real big-ass door."

Chambers ignores him. She shines her light inside a window before pocketing it. She straddles the sill and climbs inside.

52

CHAMBERS DROPS TO THE basement floor. She takes out her flashlight and service Glock and examines her surroundings. The basement is a vast industrial catacomb that extends under the entire station complex. Moonlight streaming in from the large windows on the east wall illuminates the first several rows of burly concrete pillars supporting the station overhead. Once beyond the reach of the pale lunar glow from the windows the vast subterranean grotto quickly descends into pitch darkness.

Chambers grins at the sounds of cursing and rubber boots skidding across a hard surface as Detective Searcy clambers through the window. A moment later he is at her side. He has the shotgun.

Chambers eyes the weapon skeptically. "How you gonna hold your flashlight? With your dick?"

He gives her a sour look. "Could. If I had to." He cradles the gun in the crook of his arm while taking out his flashlight. He grips the shotgun with both hands, holding the flashlight to the barrel like a bayonet. The slightest hint of a smile creases his lips.

Chambers gives him a little stink-eye and leaves it at that.

Once they move away from the windows the detectives find themselves in complete darkness. The narrow beams from their flashlights skip and dance like a pair of dueling lightsabers as they pick their way through a regimented forest of pillars.

At one point Searcy stops and rotates in place. His flashlight illuminates evenly spaced rows of concrete columns in every direction. He raises the beam of the flashlight to reveal the damp concrete overhead. Chambers points her flashlight in the same direction. "Find something?"

He's pondering one particular section where the concrete is drizzled with moisture. The worn surface is etched with a network of meandering cracks that resembles a topographical map. "Do you know how many tens of thousands of tons of concrete, bricks, steel, and Krylon spray paint there are directly over our heads?"

Chambers shakes her head in annoyance. "No, but I'm sure you're gonna tell me." She moves on without him.

Searcy uses his light to examine several nearby columns. The concrete is fractured and crumbling beneath the immense weight of the station overhead. Searcy whispers to himself, "Buncha damn toothpicks." He calls after his rapidly disappearing partner. "We're like a couple of cockroaches walking underneath a hairbrush with a damn elephant standing on it."

Chambers calls back over her shoulder. "Can't nothin' kill a cockroach. You know that."

As they move forward the seemingly endless colonnade of pillars merges with and is eventually replaced by a warren of chambers and passages. The detectives find themselves traversing a labyrinth of abandoned workshops, baggage handling rooms, and machine shops. Everything of value has been stripped away and the ground is littered with debris.

The muck underfoot turns to standing water as they move deeper into the bowels of the building. Searcy stops. He makes a point of shining the light on his booted feet, ankle-deep in water, as if to confirm his shoes are still dry.

Chambers doesn't need to see his face to know there's a smirk on it. She turns away from him and shines her light through an open archway.

Searcy, moving forward without her, opens a battered wooden door at the end of the corridor. "Got a staircase here."

"So?"

"So? It goes upstairs."

She shines her light around a yawning boiler room that no longer contains any boilers. Water six inches deep covers the entire floor except for the rectangular raised concrete islands where boilers and heavy equipment have been removed. She moves into the room, yelling over her shoulder to Searcy. "Did those two clowns out there look like they were going upstairs?" She answers her own question. "No? I didn't think so."

Detective Searcy is out of earshot by now and doesn't respond. Chambers steps onto one of the concrete platforms and tries to stomp the water out of her shoes. All around her, vandals, leaking pipes, and the elements have transformed every surface into that familiar rustbelt mélange of rust, crumbling concrete, soggy plaster, and grunge.

She shines the light down into the wading pool that has turned the boiler room into a subterranean water feature. Despite the dank surroundings, the water lapping up against the platform is surprisingly clear. Something about the existence of this pristine body of water in the midst of all this decay causes Chambers to flash onto her youngest child's upcoming science project. Maybe there's something here that could be the basis for some kind of an experiment? *Lord Jesus and his apostles, anything but another goddamned model of the solar system.*

Searcy has moved past the staircase and entered some sort of a workshop. Sturdy workbenches, their surfaces scarred from years of heavy use, line the walls. The detective hears a scraping sound overhead. He uses the beam of his flashlight to follow the noise to its apparent source: a jagged hole in a dropped ceiling of plaster and lathe.

Searcy grabs one end of a heavy workbench and walks it away from the wall until it is directly beneath the opening. He looks around the room until he finds an old stepstool hammered together from scrap wood. He sets it on top of the table, holsters his gun, climbs up on the table, and mounts the stool. He's a bit wobbly in the rubber boots and reaches up to grab one of the boards framing the hole to steady himself.

He shines his flashlight through the opening but can't quite get the right angle to see what is up there. He hesitates, singing softly to himself, Ray Parker Jr. "I ain't afraid. I ain't afraid. I ain't afraid of no ghosts." He continues humming the lyrics after he sticks the flashlight into his mouth to free up his hands. He grips both sides of the crater in the ceiling, rises up on his tiptoes, and pokes his head through.

There is a stifled scream. Searcy's arms and legs begin to thrash wildly and the stool is knocked to the floor. The flashlight falls, bounces once, and rolls to the edge of the table before its progress is arrested by the bench's raised metal lip.

Searcy continues to struggle fiercely and one of the rubber boots is flung across the room. After a few moments, he grows still. His head is still jammed into the hole. His limp body is a softly swaying pendulum of flesh and blood.

Chambers is working her way back to Searcy, calling out as she goes. "Mike? Mike! Where the fuck are you?" The floor of the corridor is silted over with a layer of dried mud and Chambers stops when she spots the imprint of a horseshoe in the muck. She stares at it in amazement, shouting out to her partner. "Someone had a freaking horse down here." Then she looks more closely. The imprint she took for that of a horseshoe is actually the track left in the mud by the heel of a shoe, a very big shoe.

Chambers is beginning to wish she'd never heard of Michigan Central Station. She plays the beam of her flashlight inside a series of cramped work stalls that line one side of the hallway. Something in one of the stalls catches her attention and she goes inside.

The stall appears to be inhabited by a derelict. There is a tangle of old blankets where someone has been sleeping and the remains of a cook fire.

Crouching down by the jerry-rigged grill, her flashlight illuminates the charred bones of a small animal. The skull has prominent front teeth. "Oh shit." She hears a noise behind her and exhales in relief. She pockets her gun as she stands. "Mike, you almost gave me a damn—"

Chambers turns to find the monster—a humanoid gargoyle the size of an ox—blocking the doorway. The brute grabs her by the throat with one powerful hand and lifts her off her feet. The detective struggles to breathe while kicking futilely at her attacker. She reaches for her gun but the rear sight gets snagged in the hem of her coat pocket. She fights fiercely to free it and manages to work the gun out of the pocket. The rear sight is still tangled in the fabric and pulls the lining of the pocket out with it.

The beast watches impassively as she slowly, painfully, inch by inch, manages to raise her arm until the gun breaks free from the stubborn threads.

Detective Chambers finally, triumphantly, raises the gun to point at the creature's head. Her last conscious act is to place her finger on the trigger. She's dead before she can manage the eight pounds of force required to pull it. The gun drops soundlessly into the muck.

———————— • ————————

Marty is tugging at the handcuff chain attached to the car door handle. "Two of us together, we could pop this thing right off."

Jack, focused on the tower, is not interested. "They'll just come looking for us. And I don't want them to come looking for us. For me at least."

Marty ignores him and tugs on the handcuff chain. Jack turns angrily on him. "We deal with it here. Alright?"

Marty has his knee pressed against the car door, bracing himself to try again. Jack grabs the door handle. "They got nothin'."

Marty relents and settles back against the car. Jack does the same. "I don't have a fancy fucking phone, but I do have a good goddamn lawyer."

Marty shrugs. "Nobody but you and Timmy had the number anyway."

"I'm touched."

Marty stretches, raising his free arm above his head. "Got something to take the edge off?"

Jack instinctively reaches for his shirt pocket before he remembers. He shakes his head. "Fresh out."

Marty turns to him, amused. "That's gotta be a first."

Jack shrugs. "Lot of that going around these days."

The two of them settle back against the side of the car. Marty looks to his brother. "Kinda like old times, you know? Us working together. Like we're on the same team or something."

Jack glares at his brother. "Let me tell you something, Marty. We are not and have never been on the same fucking team."

Marty's had enough. "Fuck it. Forget it. Forget I said anything."

"Fine by me."

They settle back against the side of the car, as far from each other as the cuffs will allow. They both react to the sounds of scraping and scuffling as someone struggles to climb out of a basement window. They can hear loose bricks clacking together and glass being crushed underfoot but can see nothing in the gloom.

A moment later the beast comes lumbering out of the darkness. Marty stares at the approaching creature in astonishment. "We're gonna need a bigger fucking—"

The beast is already on them, slamming into them with such force the car skids sideways into the bridge abutment.

There is a brutal hand-to-hand struggle between the enraged beast and the manacled men. The combined weight of the grappling scrum of bodies on the handcuffs rips the handle from the door. Marty is beaten to the ground and Jack is hurled onto the roof of the car. Victor starts to drag Jack from the roof and Marty leaps onto his back. The creature turns and slams Marty repeatedly into the side of the car to the accompaniment of shattering glass and buckling metal. Jack leaps onto the beast from the other side.

The struggling pile lurches away from the car on six legs and collapses in a frenetic, brawling heap. Jack and Marty are still manacled together at the wrist as the three combatants grapple in the darkness.

At such close quarters the brothers, both powerfully built men, are no match for the creature. In their desperate struggle to draw just one more breath, they punch, scratch, kick, gouge, and strike out with any weapon that comes to hand.

Marty picks up a jagged board and drives it into the beast's back with all of his strength. The beast screams in rage and slams Marty to the ground, knocking him unconscious.

Jack grabs a broken bottle and drives the raw edges into the side of the creature's head. The demon howls in agony and hurls Jack into a ditch with such force his unconscious brother is pulled along with him. Jack comes to rest on the bottom of the ditch and Marty's dead weight tumbles in on top of him.

The hideous face of the beast moves close to his. "Not yet, hitman. Not yet."

Jack loses consciousness.

———— • ————

Jack is listening to the angry twittering from a knot of quarreling sparrows. "Too damn stupid to fly south," he mutters, tasting dirt as he finds his face pressed against the cold ground. He opens his eyes to find that the sun is rising on a frigid, clear day.

The rail station's office tower, its brick and masonry gleaming in the chill winter light, rises into the crisp blue sky like some lost Elvish citadel. A single handcuff manacle attached to a few links of broken chain is still fastened to Jack's wrist. He looks around but there is no sign of his brother.

Jack tries to stand but immediately sinks back to the ground. His arms and legs feel as if they've been beaten with a ball-peen hammer. One side of his face is so swollen he can't see out of that eye. He crawls on his hands and knees to the car and clutches the rear fender to pull himself to his feet. He leans against the car for support as he circles it, hands sliding over the cold metal body, peering around with his one good eye in search of his brother.

Then he sees him. Marty's body is hanging upside down from the side of the pedestrian bridge.

Jack limps over to his brother's dangling corpse. He stumbles on the uneven ground just before he gets there, staggering forward to grab onto his brother's arms to keep from falling. There is some give in the rope and Jack pulls the corpse downward until he is able to wrap his arms around his brother's chest.

He stands like that for a long time, vaguely aware of the scent of sweat and aftershave that will always remind him of Marty. Eventually, the pain racking his body becomes too much and he collapses to his knees. As he sinks to the ground, he can feel his brother's broad shoulders slipping forever from his grasp.

53

MARLENE HAS THE BUSINESS end of a large wooden mixing spoon lodged beneath the head of the metal pin in the basement door hinge. She hammers at the spoon's handle with the base of a hardwood knife block until she dislodges the pin. She allows the makeshift tools to clatter to the floor and holds the door level while she removes the pin and tosses it in the corner with the others.

Marlene wrestles the solid wood door out of the hinge brackets and levers it away from the doorjamb so that the lock assembly twists and warps until it is ripped completely from the door frame. She drags the heavy door away from the opening and leans it against the wall.

She hits the light switch on the landing and moves cautiously down the stairs. The basement looks its age, with a rough concrete floor, grimy iron support posts, cobwebbed ceiling joists, and bare light bulbs. Off to one side is a spartan workout space with a sagging heavy bag, an array of free weights on racks, and a weight bench.

At the rear of the building, the long narrow cellar is equipped with a workbench, various hand tools, and a bench vice. Against an adjoining wall is a padlocked antique steel mesh gym locker that Marlene immediately pegs for Jack's gun cabinet.

At the other end of the basement is the target for Jack's makeshift gun range: the anonymous black silhouette of a man peppered with bullet holes. Marlene can only shake her head in bemusement when she realizes it is backstopped by cartons of old books, now shredded by gunfire.

Marlene goes to the locker but it is securely padlocked. Peering through the steel mesh she can make out the shapes of several guns and boxes of ammunition. She sifts through the drawers beneath the workbench but there is no key to be found. There's a tall metal swivel stool by the bench and she takes a seat to ponder her next move.

A variety of tools hang from a sheet of pegboard attached to the paneling behind the bench. Examining them, Marlene experiences a fleeting sense of superiority when she realizes that her own home workbench is better equipped.

When she told Victor she wanted to work on the house he thought she meant he was going to be writing checks while she pored over paint and fabric swatches with some blue-haired lady in Bloomfield Hills. So he was surprised when she assembled her tools and set up a workbench in the three-season room. When, after many months, she had made little progress, he began teasingly referring to it as "Geppetto's workshop." *Fuck him*, she thinks. So what if she never completed any projects? She would have. Eventually. She will.

As a child, she'd spend hours in a sort of fugue state studying her father's workbench in the basement. She was obsessed with the methodical array of tools lined up on pegs like artifacts in a museum. She examined them, testing their weight in her hands, wanting so desperately to put them to use, to make something with them, but having no idea where to begin and no one to ask.

In college the stacks of textbooks in the bookstore with their trim covers and crisp, white pages mesmerized her. She devoured the thick course catalogs with their ordered columns of condensed course descriptions, each a teasing invitation to another, more fulfilling world. But she was paralyzed by the multitude of choices. She never seemed to manage to take that next step. She floundered, always planning, always preparing, researching, regretting, until she'd worn the subject out, until it was time to move on.

And she always moved on. Directionless. Going with the flow. But, sometimes, that flow, that formless current, carried you, like a leaf floating in a stream into a little sheltered cove someplace that wasn't really so bad. Someplace where you might even see yourself hanging out for a while. Maybe even staying. Maybe, like with nursing, just by stupid dumb luck you landed on something that just somehow worked. At least for a while. Until it didn't. Or, sometimes, like with Victor, it all just landed on you.

Marlene notices a long, vertical seam in the wall behind the pegboard. She leans across the bench to trace the seam with her fingers as it joins with a horizontal seam to form the corner outline of a door. She pulls down a rack of screwdrivers as she follows the channel cut into the beadboard. She removes the rest of the tools from the pegboard but there's no sign of a handle, just an incision in the beadboard in the shape of a door. She doesn't see the point of it. The workbench is bolted to the wall, straddling and blocking any possible opening. *Why would there be a fucking door here?*

She finds a pry bar and contemplates ripping down the pegboard to see what's behind it. Then she decides it makes a lot more sense to take some of these tools upstairs to see what she can do with the padlock on the outside door. As she turns away from the workbench Marlene is startled by the sound of something striking the wall from the other side. She knocks over the stool in her haste to get away. *Now what?*

She grips the pry bar in both hands like a weapon as she takes another step back. She can't decide if it's a trapped animal, some crazy construction project, or the onset of a fucking earthquake.

It soon becomes clear that someone is smacking the wall from the other side. The violence of the attack intensifies, and the remaining tools are knocked from their hooks to clatter to the table. Then, the pegboard covering the door cut into the beadboard begins to give way under the assault, forming cracks as it bulges outward.

Seemingly emboldened, the unseen attacker's blows increase in ferocity and the cracks in the pegboard widen into ragged seams as the door behind it is forced open. Then, the thin membrane of perforated wood shatters like a sheet of ice.

Marlene's first thought is that it's the cops forcing their way in. She drops the pry bar in a panic, shouting, "I'm alone in here! I don't have a weapon! I'm not armed!"

The door cut into the beadboard is now clearly defined as it slams repeatedly into the workbench. The screws attaching the workbench to the wall give way, allowing the door to be forced open about six inches.

Marlene backs away, holding her arms away from her sides, terrified of being shot by some adrenaline-hyped cop come to rescue her.

An arm and a shoulder wedge their way out from behind the door, followed by the almost unrecognizable head of Jack Killeen.

Marlene continues backing up, more slowly now. "Jack?"

He puts his shoulder to the door and the table vice hits the floor with a tremendous crash as the workbench topples forward. Jack forces the door completely open and stumbles into the room, nearly falling forward before catching himself on the upturned edge of the workbench.

He stands there, gripping the table, staring uncomprehendingly at her. His knuckles are battered and bloody. One side of his face is a raw, swollen mass of bruised and pulverized flesh. There's a handcuff manacle on his right wrist. There are bits of gravel and tar embedded in his coat like shrapnel. He looks as if he was thrown from a moving car.

"Jack... My god... What happened to you?"

Jack ignores her. He reaches up and runs his hand along the top surface of an overhead rafter until he finds what he's looking for: a key. He goes to the gun locker and opens the padlock. Marlene flinches as he hurls the padlock to carom through the wreckage of the workbench.

Jack pulls out a Sig Sauer automatic. He stuffs the gun into one coat pocket and shoves a box of shells into the other. He reaches deep into the locker and removes a sawed-off shotgun, gripping it by the barrel. He leans it against the wall and jams a carton of shotgun shells into his coat pocket.

Marlene takes a few hesitant steps forward. "Jack, what's going on?"

He ignores her, pawing frantically through the locker until he finds a large tactical knife in a leather sheath. She approaches him warily as he unsheathes and examines the lethal-looking double-edged blade. "Where's your phone? You need to go to the hospital."

He slides the blade back into the sheath and pockets it as well. Only then does he respond to her question. "Gone."

"You're scaring the shit out of me, Jack."

He doesn't seem to hear her; his mind is racing in another direction. He goes and peers into the doorway he just kicked open. When he turns back to her his eyes are wild. "I've got to get you out of here."

"What are you talking about?" She tries to peer through the doorway. "What is that?"

He grabs her arm. "Goes to the garage across the alley. Pompey's people are watching the front." She holds her ground and he grows frantic. "Don't you understand? You've got to get out of here. Now!"

She yanks her arm free and backs up against the wall, defiant. "I'm not running anymore. And I'm sure as hell not going anywhere with you."

Jack slumps back against the opposite wall, like a man who has suddenly reached the limits of his endurance. He seems somehow diminished, no longer fearsome but defeated. His voice is not much more than a hoarse whisper. "Marty's dead."

She starts to go to him. "Oh my god, Jack... I'm sorry. I'm so sorry..."

She stops short. Jack is staring at the floor, fists clenched. His moment of weakness has passed and his entire being is throbbing with pent up desperation and anger. Instead of embracing him, she stands there, tentative, unsure what to do next.

He comes off the wall like he's received an electric shock and grips her arms. He speaks with chilling certainty. "He killed Marty. He killed Rhonda. He butchered my little girl. Now he wants you."

She tries to pull away but his grip is too strong. "What are you talking about? Who?"

Jack stares at her with such ferocity she has to avert her eyes.

"You're hurting me."

This is the first time her words appear to reach him. He seems surprised to find his hands wrapped tightly around her wrists. He releases her and she backs up against the opposite wall, suddenly afraid of him. "Who is after me, Jack? I have a right to know that much."

He takes a step back as if increasing the distance between them will make this easier to say. "Victor. Victor Moravian. Your husband."

Marlene, stunned, slides to the floor with her back against the wall. "Victor... He's alive?"

"No."

"But you just said...?"

Jack watches her warily. "He's coming for you. To kill you."

Suddenly hopeful, she presses her hands against the concrete wall and struggles to her feet. She pushes off from the wall, moving to him. Her eyes never leave his. "Then he must be alive."

He reaches out to grab her shoulders, not to hold her but to keep her at a safe distance. "He's dead. Victor Moravian is dead."

She struggles to free herself from his grip. She's wound up now, desperate. "How can you be so sure? Maybe Pompey lied. Maybe there's been some..."

He grips her with such violence she freezes, eyeing him fearfully. He struggles to find the courage to say the words he will never be able to take back. "I know he's dead because I killed him."

Jack releases his grip and Marlene backs away from him as if he has suddenly become something repulsive. He makes a move toward her, desperate to explain, but she waves him off. Her voice is icy cold. "Where is he?"

"Don't you understand? He's the one doing this... Killing these people."

She's trembling, rocketing between anger, hope, and confusion. "But you said it was that... thing."

Jack stares at her. Marlene realizes the creature that burst into the kitchen was Victor. "That night in my kitchen... He knew my name..." The realization horrifies her. "Oh my god! Victor! My poor Victor. What have you done to him?"

Jack is desperate to make her understand. "He's not Victor anymore. Can't you understand that? He'll kill you."

He puts his hand on her arm but she pulls away. "I'm going to find him."

She lunges toward the tunnel but Jack moves to block her. "I can't let you do that."

"How dare you! How fucking dare you! After what you've done?" She tries to get by him and he grabs her. The grief and anger suddenly overwhelm her and she attacks him with a flurry of blows. Jack makes no attempt to ward them off. "You bastard! Goddamn you!"

Her anger spent, she leans against the wall and sobs. She doesn't resist as Jack picks up the swivel stool and makes her sit. He stands in front of her. "You can hate me, god knows you've got the right, but I'm not going to let him get to you. He's not Victor Moravian anymore. He's not your husband. He's a..." He catches himself before saying the word that has become a double-edged sword.

She slumps forward in the stool and rests her head on his chest. "I promised myself I would never let you touch me again. And if you did, it would mean nothing to me. Nothing."

He reaches out and rests his hand lightly on her back. She embraces him.

"Why do you keep doing this to me, Jack Killeen? Why do you keep coming back into my life? Why?"

He slowly wraps her in his arms. "I won't let anything happen to you. I swear..."

He realizes she is trying to get the gun in his coat pocket. He grabs her arm and yanks her violently to her feet.

"You're hurting me!"

He releases her and secures the gun in his pocket. He looks at her incredulously. "What were you gonna do? Shoot me?"

She knocks the stool over in front of him and tries to dart past but he grabs her in a bear hug. She fights him. She's hysterical. "I have to find him! I have to find him!"

Just when he thinks he's got her under control she screams. "Help! Police! Help! Rape!"

He attempts to shush her and she bites his hand. "Son of a bitch!"

He presses her up against the wall in an effort to contain her but she continues to struggle. "Help! Help! Someone help! Rape! I'm being raped!"

He hauls off and slugs her. He catches her as she falls, easing her limp body to the floor. He stands there for a moment, stunned by what he's done. "I'm sorry, Marlene. I'm so sorry. It wasn't my fault. I swear to god, it wasn't my fault."

You'd almost think he believes it.

54

J ACK AWAKENS IN A chair outside the upstairs room where Marlene is sleeping. He sits quietly for a moment, trying to assess
what it was that woke him. His coat is hanging on the back of the
chair and he reaches into the pocket for the Sig Sauer. He rises slowly
and opens the bedroom door. Marlene is asleep, gathered in a tight
heap in the center of the mattress, as if she'd been dropped there
from a great height.

He pads to the bedroom window. Outside, the street is deserted.
There is no sign of Pompey's men or the police.

Jack goes downstairs and looks through the peephole in the steel
outside door. There's no sign of activity in or around Haddad's
market. He checks to make sure both the gun and the combat knife
are within easy reach before opening the padlock. After slipping
outside, he locks the door behind him and crosses to the market.

The placard on the door has been flipped to the "CLOSED" side,
but when Jack presses on the glass, he finds it unlocked.

Inside, Haddad has ventured out from his plexiglass pillbox to re-
stock the shelves. His father is asleep on the balcony with the shotgun
across his lap. Haddad is on his knees, pricing cans of SpaghettiOs.
He looks up from his work as Jack enters the store. "I'm sorry, my
friend. We are closed."

The condition of Jack's face and the look in his eyes makes Haddad
realize something is wrong. He rises slowly to his feet, a man being careful

not to spook a wild animal. He moves cautiously to the plexiglass barrier, opens the door, and enters the protected area.

Haddad allows the door to slam shut behind him with a loud bang, like a gunshot, and the old man on the balcony is startled awake. He leans forward in his chair, screaming at Jack in Arabic and pointing the shotgun at him. Haddad shouts angrily at his father and the two of them yell at each other in Arabic. The old man's finger is on the trigger.

Acting on instinct, Jack pulls his gun and shoots the old man in one smooth, deadly motion. Haddad watches in horror as his father topples backward in his chair and disappears from sight. He turns to Jack and their eyes meet through the scarred plexiglass as Haddad fumbles for the gun in his waistband.

Jack sees the partition door is still ajar and kicks it open. Haddad is knocked back against the wall, toppling wire racks of cigarettes, lighters, and assorted bric-a-brac. Taking no chances, Jack fires twice in rapid succession: one to the heart, one to the head.

Haddad crumples to the floor and Jack robotically closes the plexiglass hatch. He returns the gun to his coat pocket and stands frozen in the store aisle. Both bodies are out of sight now, but the eerily empty store is haunted by their presence.

Jack motivates his frozen legs into motion and staggers toward the front door. He knocks over a display of canned goods in passing and stops to watch the tumbling cans roll across the wood plank floor.

His eyes follow one particular can as it rolls down the aisle and he blocks it with his foot. He stoops to grab the can and is startled to find it warm to the touch, like some small, metallic creature. Nausea creeps up the back of his throat as he takes out the combat knife, punctures the lid, peels it back, and holds the can up to the light. The can is filled with flesh, the sallow, blue-veined flesh of the dead: wrinkled fingers, bone, eyes, hair, tissue; all immersed in a viscous stew of coagulated blood.

He drops the can in disgust but is immediately compelled to open another. Inside he finds more of the same foul ingredients. He continues to open cans, one by one, until the knife is slippery with gore. He remains rooted to the spot, puncturing and peeling back the tin lids until the blood is soaking his shirtsleeves.

The knife slips from his hands and drops into the sodden mess that covers the floor. Stooping to retrieve the knife he spots large burlap sacks of flour and rice in the adjoining aisle. He strides over to them and rips one open with the blade. A mixture of bones and ashes spills from the gaping wound onto the floor.

Around him, the shelves are piled high with boxes, bags, and cans. He knows what is in them. And he knows he must open each and every one of them.

Jack awakens with a gasp. He's seated in the chair outside the upstairs room where Marlene is sleeping. He grips the arms of the chair, wary, trying to determine if he actually is awake, if the nightmare is really over. The sound of traffic on Trumbull is somehow reassuring and he listens carefully for anything that sounds out of place. Satisfied, he stands and opens the bedroom door. Marlene is asleep, gathered in a tight heap in the center of the mattress.

Jack goes and looks through the window. As he does, he notices the debris on the sill and the gouged mortar around the glass from her earlier escape attempt. The street outside is deserted but there are two cardboard carryout coffee cups set casually atop the dumpster in the alley behind Haddad's—as if the men drinking them had just stepped away for a moment. He watches for several minutes but there is no sign of movement save for the occasional car passing by on Trumbull. Then, he looks further into the alley. There is a man's shoe lying on the gravel. There is no sign of the shoe's former occupant.

Jack goes downstairs and moves to the steel exit door. He peers through the peephole but can't see anything. He steps back and reaches for the padlock just as the door explodes inward.

Everything goes black.

———————— • ————————

When Jack regains consciousness, the door is resting in the middle of the floor like a bent steel throw rug. Outside, the sun is shining on a cold, clear day. Three little Black boys are riding their bikes in circles in the street while peering curiously into the gaping doorway of the building that has probably been a neighborhood mystery their entire lives. Seeing Jack, they peddle off, unzipped parkas flapping at their sides.

Jack ignores them and charges upstairs. The bedroom door stands wide open. The bedding is strewn across the floor. Marlene is gone.

Jack is standing at a payphone in front of a boarded-up storefront. He has the receiver pressed to his ear. "JJ? Yeah, it's me, Jack. What was the name of that building? The one by the beaver dam?"

He loses it when JJ fails to get right to the point. "Just the fucking name! Alright?" He repeats the name he is given "Detroit Gray Iron Works," and hangs up the phone. He speaks absently to the now silent receiver as he searches his pockets for more change. "I owe you one."

He drops another quarter into the coin slot and dials. Someone picks up almost immediately, announcing the Pompey residence. Jack doesn't wait for him to finish. "I want to speak to him." Jack listens impatiently for a moment before cutting off the person on the other end. "Put him on the fucking phone. Tell him it's Jack Killeen. Tell him I've got Victor Moravian."

55

DeRon sits forlornly at his workbench watching the two baby mice caught in a glue trap. The creatures squeak pitifully as their efforts to pull free mire them more deeply in the treacherous glop.

DeRon's workstation sits beneath one of the two balconies on either side of the industrial loft space. Above him, he can hear the steady thump of footsteps, approaching and receding as the beast paces above the object of his fevered desire.

DeRon avoids looking in the direction of the surgery suite where the beast's latest trophy, the most beautiful woman the lab assistant has ever seen, lies unconscious on an operating table. Her name is Marlene. And she is oblivious to the unspeakable horrors he and the Professor are about to inflict on her.

The hideous female mate created from Victor's victims is strapped to the adjoining operating table. The horrifying mosaic of human limbs, composites, metal strapping, and hydraulic lines is nearly obscured beneath a thin casing of clear plastic vinyl sheeting that is swollen and distended by the mounds of dry ice heaped over the monstrosity.

Drettmann's powder blue lab coat glides through DeRon's peripheral vision as the Professor checks the diagnostic monitors attached to the carcass. "Good, excellent: eighteen Celsius. The host continues to maintain a core temperature in the therapeutic range."

DeRon cringes at the sound of the Professor's approach. The man's proximity chills him and DeRon attempts to focus on the work in front of him, until the Professor's hand on his shoulder turns him to stone.

Drettmann spots the glue trap on the floor and stoops to pick it up. He holds the trap in both hands as if preparing to fold it in on the two quivering captives and crush them. "You should put them out of their misery." Then, grinning at DeRon's horrified reaction, he sets the trap back on the floor with the doomed mice unharmed. He looks up at the sound of the beast passing overhead and nods in satisfaction. "Excellent. Bipedal mobility is quite robust." He pats DeRon affectionately on the shoulder. "We are having an excellent day, young man. A very excellent day."

DeRon stays focused on the work in front of him. "What happens when it's done? When he doesn't need you—us, anymore?"

Drettmann's smile is that of a patient adult responding to a rebellious child. "One day, you will understand. This is only the beginning."

DeRon shocks himself with the audacity of his reply. "I don't think there is anything to understand. I think you're just a..." He stifles at the sound of the beast passing overhead.

The Professor smiles and pushes past his assistant's chair to peer through the gap where the exhaust fan is mounted in the outside wall. In the distance, across Jefferson Boulevard, a posse of machines is demolishing a pair of vacant homes. "When you look out there, what do you see?"

DeRon doesn't need to look. "More abandoned buildings being knocked down. It never stops."

Drettmann continues to watch the demolition. "I'll tell you what I see. I see an untreated open wound extending over an area of one hundred and forty-three square miles. I see once healthy tissue that has suffered extensive third-degree burns. To such an extent it has compro-

mised the entire dermis and the epidermis and extends into the fat
cells. I see rot and putrefaction. I see decay, violence, and depravity."

He turns to glare at his assistant. "I see a raging, unchecked in-
fection. Because the wound has been infected with necrotic tissue."
His eyes are shining now. "And, as you know, if I've taught you
anything, a wound with necrotic tissue present will not heal. Dead
tissue cannot be salvaged. The necrotic tissue must be excised in
order to allow healthy tissue to grow in its place."

DeRon stares at the Professor in astonishment. "Dead tissue?
People live here. I live here."

Drettmann moves away from the fan opening. He pauses to check
the metal bike cable that confines DeRon to the rolling chair. Confident of his captive audience, he takes a seat opposite him. He
studies DeRon carefully, a researcher examining his subject for any
indication of observable change. "I realized long ago that such sen-
timents as yours—as universal as they are fallacious—could never
be overcome with logic." He sighs at the absurdity of it all. "So,
obviously, surgical debridement was out of the question."

DeRon is stunned. "Debridement?" He forces a smile, hoping,
against all evidence, that the Professor is making a joke. "What were
you going to do? Nuke the city?"

Drettmann is not smiling. "I determined that the only remaining
option was larval therapy."

DeRon can't believe what he's hearing. "Maggots? Your solution..." He waves his arm in the direction of Jefferson Boulevard.
"Your solution to all this was maggots?"

They both look up as the heavy tread of the beast passes overhead.
Drettmann shrugs. "Mechanized maggots perhaps. I prefer bots.
Bots on a massive scale."

DeRon, not wanting to attract the beast's attention, hisses. "You're not healing this city, you're the one infecting it. With monsters! With, with... atrocities! With abominations!"

His words draw a fleeting smile from the Professor. "Abominations. How very biblical of you." His tone is dismissive. "My course of treatment, by design, is extremely localized. There is little danger to the wider ecosystem."

DeRon responds with a sneer. "What?" His eyes follow the beast's retreating footsteps. "Have you programmed that thing to stop at Eight Mile Road?"

The Professor remains unconcerned. "Like maggots, they feed only on necrotic tissue. They cannot survive outside the infected region. However, unlike maggots," he tilts his head in the direction of the pacing beast, "they cannot reproduce."

DeRon indicates the creature in the operating room. Whispering hoarsely, he emphasizes each individual word: "But. You. Are. Making. Another. One."

Drettmann stares at his assistant. He seems sincerely puzzled by the younger man's inability to grasp such a basic concept. "Obviously, we must scale up proportionately to effectively treat an open wound of this magnitude."

DeRon, enraged, strains against the cable confining him to the chair. "What about all these people? What about me?"

Drettmann is staring at DeRon's hands like a hungry dog focused on a treat. "Any surgeon in the world would kill to have those hands. Your hands."

DeRon, uncomfortable, folds his hands on his lap.

His excitement growing, the Professor reaches across the table to grasp the arm of DeRon's chair. "This is only the beginning. We, you and I, we are the future. With those hands... with my genius... we will create a pure partnership of man and machine." He stops, struggling to find the right words. "You will be whole again." He clasps his hands into fists, frustrated by his inability to capture and articulate the concepts rocketing through his brain. "No, no, more than whole. You will be a part of me! You and I..." He gestures in the direction of the beast. "We will be like them."

DeRon has only a vague notion of what Drettmann is referring to but it's enough to terrify him. He looks into the Professor's crazed eyes and backs his chair away from him. He doesn't want to go anywhere with this guy, even metaphorically.

The beast passes overhead and Drettmann nods to himself, as if engaged in some intense internal dialogue. He rises from his chair and returns to the operating theater.

DeRon picks up the glue trap with its quivering captives. Both mice are welded head to tail to the adhesive sludge. He folds the flat plastic trap in half, entombing the mice in the glutinous mass. He closes his eyes tight and crumples the entire mess into a silent, plastic-encased capsule of glue, fur, and tissue before dropping it into the trash.

56

J ACK IS ON THE roof of an abandoned warehouse overlooking the sprawling ruins of the Detroit Gray Iron Works. A heavy cloud cover cloaks the city like a shroud. The crust of snow coating everything reminds Jack of old book illustrations depicting ancient Pompeii smothered beneath a blanket of ash.

Jack double-checks his arsenal. The Sig Sauer in his right coat pocket is in easy reach and the left pocket is jammed with extra clips. The sawed-off hangs from his shoulder on a sling studded with shotgun shells. A seven-foot section of oak banister rail, bound tightly with muffler clamps to an equal length of 3/16th inch angle iron, is leaning against the low retaining wall at the roof's edge. The tactical knife is bolted to one end like a spear point and reinforced with additional muffler clamps and duct tape. It looks like it could stop a charging rhino.

Jack settles in to wait. Across the street, the western face of the Detroit Gray Iron Works rises nearly four stories and extends over a hundred yards in either direction. The battered facade, once an orderly grid of iron, brick, and glass, is now a patchwork bastion of sheet metal, tin cladding, plywood, brick, and cinderblock, all threaded with ducts and scaffolding, and marinated in rust, industrial waste, bird shit, and graffiti. It's as if Hadrian's Wall had been cobbled together by cyberpunks and welders.

That same hundred years of industrial ebb and flow has churned the blocks immediately west of the foundry complex into a confounding maze of deserted factories and warehouses, dead-end alleys, orphan walls, pointless rail sidings, and bricked up doorways.

To the east, beyond the flat, snow-covered roofs of the ironworks, decades of urban clear-cutting have reduced what was once a vast forest of smokestacks into a bleak, icy steppe that extends all the way to the Belle Isle Bridge.

South of the abandoned ironworks is an isolated expanse of parkland. A fresh coating of snow has merged the fields, the frozen streams, and the beaver dam into a scruffy white post-it note clinging inexplicably to the banks of the Detroit River.

Directly north, behind the thin parapet of bleak storefronts lining Jefferson Boulevard, a trio of excavators is hunched over the gutted ruins of an elementary school like a gang of giant carrion birds. Their bucket heads plunge deep into the carcass, articulated steel necks rising and falling with a lurching, mechanical precision as the serrated teeth rip out tangled clumps of entrails.

Jack studies the patchwork quilt of vacant lots, burned-out structures, and occupied buildings surrounding the demolition site. He feels as if he's watching his world, the harsh but familiar landscape of this rustbelt city, being methodically erased and returned to nature.

He doesn't have long to ponder the implications. He sees a convoy of SUV's approaching the ironworks from the east and goes to gather up his armaments. Then he walks along the warehouse roof parallel to the ironworks to study the terrain.

From above, the massive foundry barns resemble four long, narrow river barges lashed together in two separate, parallel pairs. A long, narrow strip of land that once provided truck access and staging divides the two paired foundry spans. A fifth diagonal foundry span bridges the four parallel segments about a third of the way down, so that the entire lower section of the complex forms a rough, double-legged H. At the northern end, toward Jefferson Boulevard, the four parallel foundry runs are capped by an additional four stories of office and workspace that loom over the rest of the complex like the bridge of a freighter.

The long narrow strip between the two paired foundry sections is littered with the snow-covered shapes of abandoned trucks and trailers. At the northern end of the strip, closest to the "bridge" tower, the gap is filled with half a dozen broken-down semi-trailers in a neat row. Unlike the other vehicles, something inside them is generating enough warmth to keep them free of snow. Jack studies the tower section closest to the parked trailers for any signs of activity but the windows are all boarded up.

Pompey's convoy has reached a snowy field just south of the ironworks and Jack continues to watch as the vehicles park haphazardly around a clump of scraggly trees. Ten car doors are flung open and a determined group of large men in bulky coats emerges from the vehicles. As they gather around the rear hatch of a black Cadillac Escalade, their boots stomp the snow like steers jostling at a feed station, their mouths venting steam flares into the cold air.

Even from this distance, Jack can see that Pompey has assembled an all-star team. Borneo, wearing a blue UAW windbreaker, stands by the open hatch distributing the goodies.

In the scrum of bodies, Jack makes out Leon "Deadhead" Degenhardt and Vince "Grease Trap" Turco, as well as a guy they call "Bonedigger" something or other, out of Jersey. There's Leon "The Gonad" Bonaduce, out of Chicago, and some of Pompey's local talent from the city: Ed "Brickhouse" Jones and a big guy they call "Slomotion" whose real name Jack can't remember. There are a few others new to him.

Once equipped, the men move away from the Caddy to form a ragged skirmish line. Each man is armed with an AR-16, a shotgun, or a hunting rifle. Borneo has a military assault rifle with a grenade launcher mounted beneath the barrel. Jack can feel the adrenaline coursing through his body. Things just got real.

Pompey and his men move off in the direction of the most easterly of the four foundry wings and Jack decides to find a way in from the west. He goes to the fire escape and begins his descent from the warehouse roof. He stops on a landing halfway down and smacks the butt of the spear into the iron deck at his feet. The deadly weight of the homemade lance in his grip is immensely satisfying and Jack continues down the stairs, smiling grimly. *This will definitely do some damage.*

57

MARLENE IS TRYING HARD not to panic. Her head is clamped so securely she can only move her eyes. The crisp chill of polished metal pressing against her scalp makes her wonder if her head has been shaved. And she's been intubated! *What in god's name is going on?*

She's desperately trying to remember how the hell she got here. From the little she can see it's not like any hospital she's ever been in, more like a lab of some sort—a creepy, do-it-yourself kind of lab—like in some fucking horror movie. She remembers from her time as a nurse: sometimes people, they lose their short-term memory after a traumatic event. Is that what's happening to her?

Did I get hit by a car? Oh my god! Was I shot? Am I paralyzed? She takes a deep breath-—no, just sedated—she can feel her hands and legs, move them a little, but she's restrained. *What the hell?*

She closes her eyes and tries to relax. What was that technique the therapist tried to teach her? The one Victor sent her to? What was it? Sense memory? That's right: think of a happy memory, a calming event. If she can make herself relax, maybe she'll be able to work this out.

She squeezes her eyes shut, trying to remember what it felt like to be happy once. There was that time on vacation... Lying on that velvety thin towel pressed into the hot beach sand... and the sun... Oh my Lord, that sun! She can almost hear the waves lapping against the shore. A soft, gentle breeze is coming off the water. From out there where Victor is... somewhere... floating... watching her. What did he call himself? A voyeur. And I was his damn bikini Bond girl. God, I'd forgotten that. Fuck, whatever.

There's a gentle, almost imperceptible spray of water spritzing her bare skin. The tiny droplets peppering her legs feel like he's caressing her with his eyes. It feels so good...

Then, the jagged sound of squealing caster wheels blows it all to hell. Just like those fucking shrieking birds that always startled her from her beach naps—like a bawling mob of babies from hell, screaming for their momma's titties.

No more happy place.

She opens her eyes. Someone's here, leaning over her. He's wearing a powder blue smock and a surgical mask. A Black dude. In a rolling chair. Rolling around her like some damn dental technician. *What am I doing at the fucking dentist? Did I get my teeth knocked out? Did he...? Fucking Jack!*

She's blinking her eyes now, trying to get his attention, but all of his focus is on something at the back of her head. He's holding something in his hand. *What the fuck? Is he going to cut me? Why isn't he talking to me? Asking questions? Isn't there supposed to be a protocol? Blink once for yes? Twice for get me a fucking bedpan?*

She knows it's useless with the tube down her throat, but she tries to speak. A pathetic mewling sound is all she can manage.

That gets his attention, and he leans in close to her. He looks young. His eyes are red, bloodshot. But soft. These are gentle eyes. Wounded even.

He reads the growing panic in her eyes and holds up the object in his hand for her to see, as if to reassure her. It's a black sharpie marker. He's looking at her with concern and she wonders if he's going to write something with the marker for her to read. Then something startles him and he rolls backward, out of her field of vision.

Now some old white dude is peering down at her. He has a beard under his surgical mask. It makes him look like one of the guys behind the counter at Subway, with their beards scrunched up under hairnets like dead animals. Not with those eyes though. If she'd ever encountered someone behind a counter with those eyes, she'd have run, not walked, in the other damn direction. Those eyes are lifeless.

The other guy is back now, leaning in close, drawing on the side of her head, stubbornly refusing to make eye contact with her. The bearded one watches intensely, focused on the sharpie in the Black guy's hand. The Black guy rolls his chair from one side of her head to the other, casters squibbling, using the edge of the table as a grab bar.

There's no longer any doubt about her head being shaved when she feels the greasy hard felt tip as it circles her head. *What the fuck? Isn't this what they do before brain surgery? As a guide for the initial incision? Oh my dear Lord. What in god's name is happening to me?*

Both men react to something off to the side. The Black guy puts the cap back on the sharpie and rolls out of her line of sight again. The old white dude leans in to study the Black guy's artwork and then moves away as well.

Then, standing at the foot of the operating table—because now there's no doubt: this is a fucking operating table—is the biggest dude she's ever seen. He's wearing a hooded sweatshirt the size of a damn pup tent and she can't see his face. He looks like one of those NFL linemen on the TV with the winter capes draped over their pads. But bigger. Way bigger. *This guy can't be for real. Can he?*

He moves closer until he is standing beside her, blocking out everything else, like the damn monster truck next to you at the stoplight. She feels a giant hand next to her face, cold and solid, like a piece of luggage. Then, the Jolly Green Giant leans over her, and she can see his face. If that's what it is. She can't quite make sense of it as a face. It must be the drugs they've given her, but it's not a face, it's the front end of an old-timey car or something. The grille or whatever you call it. All smashed in after a head-on collision.

But those eyes, there's something about those eyes looking down at her. They don't belong to that face. They don't fit with the rest of it. She knows those eyes. *Oh my god! Victor? My poor, dear Victor? But that's impossible...*

He—it—Victor, turns away, reacting to something, and the face disappears behind the hood again.

Marlene is relieved when the voice that comes from those lips is not Victor's. It's the coarse, guttural growl of something not quite human but not quite animal either. "They have come for me."

And he is gone.

And, suddenly, so is everything else.

Marlene realizes they've put something over her eyes. And, for some reason, she doesn't really give a damn. She can sense a flurry of activity around her but she feels calm, chill, like she's floating.

She can hear voices drifting in from far away. "Twenty cc's... Good... Excellent... Her vitals... Trending... Yes... Excellent..."

She knows this feeling, the sharp little bite from the needle, almost like a kiss. And then, express bus to the happy place!

Marlene tumbles weightlessly, silently, happily, into a deep, dark well.

58

J ACK HIKES THROUGH THE crossbar of the H, the diagonal east/west
foundry span that bridges the four parallel north/south foundry
barns. He moves cautiously through a dune-scape of scrap metal mounds
until he reaches the first of the four intersections. He finds the passageway leading into the first of the four foundry barns blocked by a solid
barricade of crushed vehicles, so he moves on to the next intersection.
Once there, he weaves his way through a jumble of dumpster-sized steel
bins filled with scrap metal until he finds a narrow corridor leading into
the second foundry wing.

The cramped corridor, not much more than a gangway, leads to a
doorway in a heavy steel bulkhead that resembles the watertight compartment on a ship. The massive steel bulkhead door sits uselessly off to
the side and Jack steps through the opening to find himself in the main
expanse of the second foundry barn.

Jack moves through a gaping, man-made cavern framed in rusted steel
girders. The latticework banks of windows on either side have been covered up with sheet metal or plywood but sunlight leaks in from the gaps
overhead where parts of the roof have collapsed, illuminating a towering
labyrinth of machinery, hopper bins, conveyors, and cranes.

Jack stops, holding the spear like a staff, as he readjusts the sling for
the shotgun. The mossy metal gorge he's moving through—with dead
winter foliage and rust coating every surface like coral—could be the
floor of a vast undersea trench. Looking around, he can see scaly gears

and wheel handles clinging to the mechanical monoliths like fossilized sea urchins. He grips the spear with both hands and moves on.

———— • ————

Pompey and his soldiers are sweeping through the foundry wing furthest to the east. As they range through the vast industrial-age barn of rusted steel girders, brick, and glass, the gang boss uses hand signals to direct them into the jumble of corridors, tunnels, and ramps that lead over, under, around, and through the long rows of silent furnaces and foundry equipment.

Scattered groups of armed men slog through flooded tunnels and clamber over mounds of rusted machinery as they make their way through the foundry span.

Borneo stops in the center of the yawning space and takes in his surroundings. Shafts of light from the ruined ceiling reveal a bewildering mesh of steam pipes, girders, and catwalks overhead. A tangled carpet of dead foliage covers everything below, reducing massive presses, crucibles, and shakeout machines to anonymous rust belt artifacts.

Borneo playfully aims the grenade launcher at an ossified boiler. There is admiration in his voice as he peers through the gunsights and caresses the trigger. "Stop a freight train with this son of a bitch." He turns to Pompey, who has stopped, hands resting on his knees, to catch his breath. "This big enough to stop your boogie man?"

Pompey straightens up. "It'll do." He moves forward, clearly struggling, his voice raspy. "Let's do this thing."

The various groups of gunmen compress into a thin, meandering string of bodies as they move out of the main foundry space and enter a long, low passageway with few windows and a mostly intact ceiling.

Three of the gunmen have moved ahead of the rest of the pack, nervously fingering their weapons as they make their way through the dank corridor. Dagenhardt, unlit cigar clamped in his teeth, leads the way with his hunting rifle at the ready.

The three lead goons are forced to hug the wall to skirt a gaping pit where a section of the floor has given way. A few dozen yards beyond the pit the corridor dead-ends at a steel warehouse-style fire door. Dagenhardt slings the hunting rifle over his shoulder and grasps the door handle with both hands to roll it open. He has barely gripped the latch when something big slams into the door from the other side.

Dagenhardt backs away from the door as the entire upper track and its rollers are ripped out from the wall by the force of a second blow. Then, he backpedals furiously to avoid being crushed by the armored hatch as it topples forward.

The massive slab of steel-clad old-growth lumber hits the floor hard, and a shockwave cloud of dust and grit momentarily blinds the gangster. When it clears, he finds himself confronting a towering apparition, a two-legged conglomeration of flesh, body parts, and hydraulics. With his target in clear view, a tight smile forms on the hood's face. He takes a step back and unslings the rifle. "The bigger they are..." He fires point-blank at the beast.

The beast seems unfazed by the gunshot and the smile freezes on Dagenhardt's face. He grabs the rifle like a club, but the beast is on him before he can react. The creature grabs the thug, slams him violently against the concrete wall, and tosses the broken body aside.

The remaining two gunmen back down the passageway, firing as they retreat, until they find themselves backed up against the edge of the pit. They've both emptied their clips and the creature charges before they can reload. He slams into them, and the three struggling figures topple into the void.

———— • ————

Jack reaches the point where the foundry barn dead-ends at a row of sturdy brick piers supporting the exterior wall of the tower annex at the northern end of the complex. The gaps between the piers are piled high with scrap metal and ruined machinery, presenting what appears to be an impenetrable barrier between the foundry barn and the attached wing.

Jack focuses his efforts on the niche between the two most central piers, using the butt of the homemade spear to poke through the debris until he discovers the edge of a doorframe behind the rubble.

Jack momentarily freezes at the sound of distant gunfire. Then, he leans the spear against the wall and sets to work clearing a path to the door.

———— • ————

Pompey, Borneo, and the remaining gunmen move cautiously through the dark passageway. The entire group comes to a halt at the sound of a loud grinding noise from up ahead. Pompey shouts into the darkness. "Dagenhardt? Hey, Dead Head... What the fuck's going on?"

A moment later, an avalanche of steel comes bearing down on them from out of the darkness, sending off sparks as it scrapes the concrete floor and walls. The gangsters realize that the beast is pushing the steel fire door ahead of him as a shield and they let loose with a barrage of gunfire, creating an ear-shattering din in the confined space of the passageway. The slugs tear into the steel face of the fire door but fail to pierce it as the beast moves inexorably forward.

Pompey gestures frantically to his lieutenant. "The bazooka! Goddamn it, use the bazooka!"

Borneo crouches in the passageway. Muttering under his breath, he draws a bead on the approaching iron landslide with the grenade launcher. "I don't think so, motherfucker."

Suffice to say, the closest Borneo ever came to military service is the time he nearly beat his little sister to death with his prized GI Joe Cobra Night Raven jet fighter. His aim is off and the grenade slams into the ceiling, exploding harmlessly in front of the advancing fire door.

There is no time to reload and the entire posse retreats down the passageway. The fleeing gunmen burst into the main space of the foundry barn and scatter to take up firing positions. The enraged demon emerges from the passageway, pushing the fire door ahead of him, and is immediately met with a barrage of gunfire. The beast crouches behind the door and lets the steel plate absorb most of the punishment.

Borneo and Grease Trap are working frantically to reload the grenade launcher. Meanwhile, Bonedigger has taken up a position in the shack-like dispatcher's office and stands in the open doorway blasting away with a hunting rifle. The beast puts his shoulder to the steel door and bears down on the shack. Bonedigger ducks inside and the creature plows through the flimsy wooden structure like a bulldozer. The rifle fire stops.

Borneo fires another round but the grenade slams into the wall over the beast's head. Bricks and debris rain down on the creature, but he is unharmed.

The other gangsters maintain a withering fire on the beast. The creature holds the shield upright with one hand and uses the other to grab various objects—metal drums, girders, machinery—and fling them over the makeshift parapet at his attackers.

One of the gunmen darts from cover in an attempt to get a clear shot. The beast cuts him down with a ragged piece of machinery hurled with the velocity of a missile.

Slomotion moves along a catwalk high above the creature's head. He braces himself against the railing and opens up with an assault rifle. The demon hurls a heavy metal lathe table with such force it takes out the gunman along with the catwalk.

Brickhouse Jones provides cover fire with a pump shotgun while Borneo lines up another shot. He fires and the projectile screams across the foundry to score a direct hit on the steel barricade. There is a tremendous explosion and the fire door is pulverized. The beast is hurled backward by the blast and everything around him is obscured by smoke and debris.

Borneo leaps to his feet and raises the grenade launcher over his head in triumph. "I got him! I got the son of a bitch!"

As the smoke dissipates it becomes clear that the shattered door has absorbed most of the blast. The beast struggles to his feet with a steaming sooty vapor rising from his charred body.

Borneo is looking over his shoulder at Pompey, in full grinning, fist-pumping Eminem mode. "You heard of hell? Well, I was sent from it."

Behind him, the beast has picked up a twisted fragment of the fire door the size of a manhole cover. He hurls it like a giant discus and Pompey dives for cover. Borneo turns to see what spooked the gang boss and the deadly projectile cuts him in half.

The beast seems exhausted by the effort and leans heavily on a steel girder support post. Pompey crawls forward on his hands and knees to retrieve the launcher. Grease Trap crawls up behind him with the canvas bag of grenades. He slides one into the barrel of the launcher and tosses the empty bag aside. "That's it. Last shot."

Pompey raises the launcher to fire. "What if I miss?"

Grease Trap is already moving away to take cover. "Don't fucking miss."

Pompey wipes the sweat from his eyes and peers through the sights of the grenade launcher. The beast is only partially visible behind the girder and the gangster waits for him to show himself. "C'mon, you ugly son of a bitch. Come ta papa. I got a fucking enema for ya."

The gang boss begins to have tremors. The onset of the attack enrages him even more. "No! No!" Soon he is in the grip of a full-fledged seizure and the grenade launcher clatters noisily to the ground. "Aarrrhhhhg-gg—"

Grease Trap and Brickhouse Jones rush forward to drag Pompey to safety.

59

J ACK STALKS A GROUND floor corridor in the brick tower anchoring
the northern end of the ironworks. The structure has not been abandoned as long as the rest of the foundry complex and remains relatively
intact. The long, narrow, railway tunnel of a corridor is lined with heavy
steel rolling doors opening into loft-like manufacturing spaces. There is
still power in the building and the sporadic, still-functioning fluorescent
tubes reveal vast, derelict chambers that have been mostly stripped bare.

The hallway's ancient wood plank floor has been overlaid with a pathway of steel plates down the center, polished smooth as glass by decades
of forklifts and work boots. Jack stops when he sees that the corridor
ends in a T-intersection twenty yards ahead.

Suddenly, he's back at Standish, in max, caged, staring down another
narrow corridor, at another distant wall. Once again, he's filled with an
overwhelming urge to launch himself at that barrier, convinced he can
run right through it.

Jack readies himself. The steel carpet at his feet is a running track and
he is a sprinter gearing up to explode out of the blocks and accelerate all
the way through the tape at the finish line. The tape, in this case, being
the solid plaster and lathe that he will power through, picking up speed
right up to and through contact, arms and legs pumping like pistons,
muscles and tendons stiffening and contracting until he has become a
dense, invulnerable, speeding projectile as he bursts through the solid
wall unharmed.

There was a time when his obsession with running full force into plasterboard walls earned him time in isolation. If not the infirmary. Now, in this place, fueled by adrenaline and armored with a hard shell of hate and rage, Jack is convinced he can really do it this time. If he runs fast enough and braces himself firmly enough...

He crouches, gripping the spear in both hands. "Ready." He's rocking on his heels. "Set." He takes a deep breath, tensing, just about to launch himself...

Jack is startled by the sound of something being dragged across the steel floor plates behind him. He swivels to find the beast standing at the other end of the corridor, framed by the open freight elevator at his back. The creature is listing to one side. His flesh has been ripped by bullets and charred by the exploding shells.

Jack leans the spear against his left shoulder and holds it there in the crook of his elbow while he slips the shotgun off his right shoulder and chambers a shell.

The beast takes a few shuffling steps forward. Something resembling a sneer emerges from that wreckage of a face. "I have taken them all, hitman. Now I have come for you." The beast moves closer. "I will be quick. Merciful." The sneer hardens. "Like you."

Jack loses his nerve and backs off, the butt of the spear scraping the metal plate at his feet as he drags it with him. He can't get his brain around the sheer, malignant bulk of this jerry-rigged, rustbelt golem that has somehow risen from the horrors of his past.

The beast continues to close the gap between them. He shapes his mouth into a hideous gash of a smile. Then, he carefully forms one word with those blistered lips: "Marlene."

Jack is done retreating. He tosses the shotgun aside. He screams something unintelligible and grips the spear with both hands, a caveman confronting a hobbled but still dangerous cave bear.

The beast moves closer, picking up a wooden pallet that he grips like a shield. His gait is unsteady. His breath erupts in the rapid, syncopated bursts of a faltering diesel. Each word seems to take enormous effort. "Now. As we speak. She is being prepared for me. She will be even more hideous than I. She will be mine once more. Always."

Jack no longer cares how big, hideous, and seemingly indestructible this thing is. He, too, is indestructible.

He raises the spear and charges.

Jack is still accelerating when he collides with the pallet. The point of the spear smashes through the wooden slats and the beast's forward momentum is momentarily checked by the ferocity of the assault. The hitman attempts to drive the blade home, but the beast swings the skid to the side and slams him into the wall. Jack slides to the floor and the beast raises the wooden skid over his head to strike. Jack rolls out of the way as the pallet splinters harmlessly against the wall.

The spear has skimmed across the steel floor plates in the direction of the elevator and Jack scrambles after it. He snatches the weapon on the move and sprints for the open freight elevator with the beast lumbering after him.

Jack barrels into the elevator car and pulls the telescoping doors shut behind him. He frantically punches the button for the top floor as he peers at the approaching beast through the small glass panel in the door.

The powerful creature slams into the door and Jack starts looking for a way out. He pops the ceiling escape hatch open with the butt of the spear. He tosses the weapon through the opening and climbs out on top as the elevator car finally shudders into motion.

The enraged beast forces the telescoping doors open and hurls itself into the moving car, barely avoiding being caught between the rising floor of the elevator and the top of the doorframe.

The creature claws at the hitman through the overhead hatch and Jack jabs at him with the spear. The beast dodges the blade and attempts to wrench the lance out of Jack's hands. Jack maintains his grip and the beast thrusts the weapon back with such force it knocks Jack to the ground and propels the butt of the spear into the wall of the elevator shaft.

Jack attempts to recover the spear but it becomes wedged between one of the horizontal supports for the elevator guide rails and the ascending car. He watches helplessly as the angle iron is bent out of shape and the oak railing splinters. The muffler clamps snap like rubber bands, allowing the angle iron and combat knife to plunge into the elevator shaft.

The beast drags his bulk through the hatch and crawls onto the roof of the elevator. His hand finds a broken section of the oak bannister and he uses it for support as he struggles to his knees.

Jack tries to crawl out of reach but the beast drags him back. Propping himself up with the wood shaft, the beast holds Jack down with one powerful hand. "Prepare a place for us in hell. Hitman."

The elevator reaches the end of the line and the steel bulkhead at the top of the shaft slams into the beast's broad back, sandwiching the creature between the unforgiving steel bulwark and the rising elevator car.

The butt of the oak railing slams into the roof of the elevator. The beast screams in agony as the broken end of the wooden shaft is driven into and then through his shoulder. The wooden shaft arrests the car's movement for a brief moment before shattering.

The car continues its ascent and the beast is driven to the ground beside Jack as the space between the top of the car and the bulkhead slowly shrinks. The creature's immense bulk prevents Jack from being pinned as well.

The beast, being crushed between the bulkhead and the elevator, reaches out to rip the power cable from its mooring. The elevator lurches to a halt.

Still pinned, the beast jabs at Jack with the live cable. Jack moves as far as he can without rolling off the top of the elevator. He grabs another fragment of the spear and blocks the beast's next thrust.

The creature flails at him with the cable and Jack uses the wooden shaft to press the live end into the side of the beast's skull. The monster screams and thrashes wildly as the current surges through him, then lies still.

Jack uses the wooden shaft to push the live cable off the edge of the elevator. He fumbles in his coat pocket for the iron rail spike and crawls over to the beast. He is determined to drive the spike into the creature's heart, but the beast is wedged so tightly between the bulkhead and the top of the elevator that Jack has no target or even room to raise his arm to strike. He stares into the creature's eyes but there is no satisfaction to be found there either as the beast stares past him, glassy-eyed and uncomprehending. Then the eyes close and the creature is still.

Jack tosses the spike away and listens as it tumbles through the open hatch and rattles across the floor of the elevator car below. He rolls painfully over to the hatch and drops down into the elevator car. He lands awkwardly and crumples to the floor in a heap. He lies there without moving, not sure he'd be able to get back up even if he wanted to.

Above him, the beast snaps out of his stupor and begins to thrash about in the spastic terror of a trapped animal. Jack digs into his pocket for the Sig Sauer but it has been lost during the struggle. He rotates on his side in a wide, desperate circle until his hand closes on the iron spike. He uses the wall to climb to his feet as the elevator car is rocked by the creature's violent contortions.

The beast explodes in one, final, furious, convulsive frenzy and the elevator car breaks free from the bulkhead. Jack hugs the wall as the elevator plunges several floors before the emergency brake kicks in to stop its descent.

The elevator car stabilizes at a lower floor with the creature's arm dangling limply through the open hatch. Blood and hydraulic fluid drip down from the ceiling but the beast is still.

Jack pushes himself off from the wall and grabs the creature's wrist to hold himself erect. He plunges the spike into the cadaverous tree limb of an arm. Blood drips down the rusty iron shaft of the spike but the arm remains inert. Jack sinks to the floor.

60

TWO OPERATING TABLES ARE arranged head-to-head in the makeshift surgery suite. One holds the slender form of Marlene, a shorn and intubated Sleeping Beauty, serene and still beneath a thin sheet. She is dwarfed by the entity on the adjoining table: the monstrous, bloated carcass of the mate.

Drettmann is fussing with the dials on a tower of rack-mounted diagnostic devices. A tangle of cables and hoses spill out the back of the rack like the entrails of some gutted alien creature. Most lead to the heart/lung machine that will be used to infuse the assemblage of dead flesh on the operating table with some semblance of life.

DeRon sits beside Marlene. He stares at her, horrified by what they are preparing to do. "Look at her. How can we do this?"

Drettmann joins his assistant. He looks at Marlene without emotion. "The subject is an excellent donor: Fit. Healthy. Alert."

DeRon is outraged. "She's not a donor. She's not dead. Or dying." His manner turns wistful. "She's beautiful. She's beautiful and she's alive."

Drettmann inspects the grim array of surgical instruments laid out on a small rolling table, dominated by the lethal shape of a craniotomy saw. The Professor guides the table over to DeRon's chair and locks the wheels in place.

DeRon stares at him in confusion. "What are you doing?"

Drettmann seems unusually subdued. "You will be my hands for the skin incision." He rests a hand lightly on the saw. "Perhaps the craniotomy as well. We'll see how it goes."

DeRon stares at the tray of instruments in a panic. "This is crazy. I've never done any of this before. I'm a... I'm a tech, not a surgeon."

The Professor studies the fingers of his own two hands splayed out on the surgical tray. They are steady. "It's not that I'm not capable. For the present at least." He brightens and turns his attention to DeRon's hands, eyeing them hungrily. "I've done everything in my power to make you ready. And you are ready."

DeRon attempts to push the table away, but the wheels are locked in place. He rolls his chair backward until he bumps up against a rack of equipment. He gestures helplessly at Marlene. "I can't do it." He turns defiant. "I won't do it."

Drettmann speaks with calm, reassuring authority. "We are going to make history here, you and I. As a team." He taps the side of his head with a finger. "My brain." He tilts his head in the direction of his assistant. "Your hands." He gestures to the array of surgical instruments, like a salesman presenting his sample display. "I'll talk you through it. Every step of the way."

DeRon holds up his hands in front of him and glares at the Professor. "You don't want to know what I'm wanting to do with these digits, Professor."

Drettmann, realizing his assistant is not going to bend to his will, sighs in resignation. "Fine. Then you will assist me as usual."

DeRon folds his arms across his chest. "No. Never."

Drettmann's voice goes cold. "Then she will die on the table."

DeRon can't meet his gaze. "Maybe... Maybe that's better. Better than..." He falls silent. He can't go there.

Drettmann studies his assistant. "You will never allow that to happen." He tilts his head in the direction of the balcony. "He will never allow that to happen."

DeRon peers nervously up at the balcony as if the beast might return at any moment. Drettmann's voice is suddenly all malice. "He will pull your arms from your body like an insect."

DeRon turns to take another look at Marlene. Lightly sedated and in her happy place, she has only a vague interest in her surroundings. DeRon takes another apprehensive look up to the balcony, then rolls his chair over to where the two operating tables come together. He sets to work arranging the tent-like panels around the shaved heads of the two patients.

Drettmann carefully surveys the surgical gear. "Don't worry, after this, I..." He pauses to correct himself. "We. We will find another way."

The Professor raises the craniotomy saw and fires it up. He watches the whirring blade with obvious satisfaction, then switches it off and sets it back on the table. He turns to his assistant, who is preparing to insert the anesthesia feed into Marlene's intravenous line. "The host must be enabled at precisely the same moment the living brain is severed from the donor. We will not get a second chance."

They both freeze at the sound of heavy footsteps stomping across the balcony. A frantic Jack appears at the railing. He quickly surveys the scene below and screams at Drettmann. "No! He's dead! Victor is dead!"

Drettmann looks up at the hitman and smiles. "Then I must create another." He turns back to the surgical tray and selects a scalpel for the initial incision. Suddenly, a row of bullet holes erupts in stutter-step across his back. The Professor carefully returns the scalpel to its assigned spot, then sinks lifeless to the floor.

Pompey is standing on the balcony opposite Jack. He blows dramatically into the smoking barrel of his M-16. Grease Trap is already hustling down the stairs to cover DeRon. Brickhouse Jones stands beside Pompey and points his shotgun at Jack.

Pompey glares at the hitman. "You promised me Victor Moravian."

61

VICTOR MORAVIAN OPENS HIS eyes on a world that is nothing more than a blurry montage of gray textures and ghostly scrims. He can't tell if it's the light or if there's something gone wrong with his vision. He can't even decipher if it is night or day.

Victor squeezes his eyes shut and then opens them again. He can make out some detail now. There are tiny, fluttering objects high overhead, diminutive black shapes flitting rapidly through the gauzy, shifting membranes that fill his line of sight. Swirling leaves? No... Bats? Can't be. He focuses on them. *They must be swallows,* he decides. *They have to be swallows.*

He can feel himself starting to relax. This must be the charming little outdoor terrace at that hotel in Sette. The one right on the Mediterranean. The one where the swallows come each morning, gliding silently across the turquoise sky, diving and dipping into the lush foliage surrounding the little patio while he and Marlene enjoy their pain au chocolat.

But why can't he see the sky? And where is Marlene? Growing anxious, Victor squints, attempting to focus on the tiny, agile creatures crisscrossing overhead. *No, they're not soaring, not gliding—it's more of a darting, wheeling motion. And the flapping wings are articulated. Reptilian even.* His heart sinks. *No. Those are not swallows. Those are bats. This is not the south of France. This is Detroit.*

He squeezes his eyes shut. He needs to think. He needs to work this out somehow. He needs to remember what the hell has happened to him. But where is he now? Somehow, for some reason, this place feels like a prison courtyard. But why would he be in prison? And why does he feel such dread? Such foreboding? Like he should be in prison? Or worse. Because of something he's done, something unspeakable, unforgivable. *Why can't I remember? What the hell have I done? Where in god's name is Marlene?*

Victor senses movement around him but resists opening his eyes. He's not going to be fooled this time. There will be no rescue. No EMT. No false hope.

There's a fitful, oddly rhythmic sound close by, like someone pumping a jack handle. No, it's too big for that; it's a winch. There are men working nearby. Someone is grunting, cursing, cranking the handle. And that muffled scraping sound is a heavy chain being dragged and cinched around something.

And then he hears the tinny, stubborn groan of metal pipes, rigid, inflexible, until, suddenly, with an almost operatic sob, they buckle and give way.

Victor is startled by the shrill whine of a power saw. Close. Too close. The piercing whine of the saw builds to an ear-splitting shriek, now backing off, now growing in intensity, as the reciprocating blade, strident, relentless, unbearably loud, bites through steel plate.

Finally, blessedly, the racket comes to an end. But the silence doesn't last. There are voices again, urgent, wary. "Get back! It's going! Watch it!" Then the air around him erupts with the sound of splintering wood, metal being ripped and torn, heavy objects grinding and scraping together. He feels himself falling. Then, he slams into the ground with tremendous force.

And the world ends. Again.

Victor is dragged back into consciousness by the distinctive beeping signal tone of a forklift moving in reverse. He doesn't know how long he's been out. He opens his eyes to find something is covering them and he sees nothing but darkness. Rough hands are grabbing him. Lifting him. There is the familiar, cloying scent of aftershave. And an acrid mix of perspiration, burnt metal, and smoke that reminds him of the locker room at the plant. *How is that possible?*

He can sense himself moving. Rolling. Something has shifted and he can see out of one eye, through a gap or a tear in the covering. He's moving! It's a fucking gurney! And overhead... *Oh Jesus!* Overhead is the grimy industrial blur of pipes, flaking paint, and rust from a suddenly remembered waking nightmare. *Oh dear god! Not again! Dear god, please, somebody help me!*

———— • ————

Marlene, still groggy, wrapped in a sheet, sits on the edge of the operating table with her head in her hands. DeRon wheels his chair over and offers her a paper cup with water. She takes it without acknowledging him. Instead of drinking the water she splashes it in her face to clear her head. They both turn to watch as Pompey rolls the massive warehouse door open.

Jack and Grease Trap roll in a four-wheeled industrial dolly bearing the slack and broken figure of the beast that is Victor Moravian. Brickhouse Jones follows close behind with the shotgun.

They park the dolly next to the operating table bearing the mate. Brickhouse prods Jack with the shotgun and he goes to join DeRon and Marlene.

Victor moans softly. Marlene gets unsteadily to her feet and goes to him. Jack attempts to intercept her, "Marlene, no!" but is blocked by Grease Trap.

She ignores him, reaching out for Victor's massive lawn rake of a hand as Jack watches in horror. "He'll kill you..."

At her touch, Victor instinctively searches out and entwines his fingers with hers. Elated, she grasps his hand in both of hers and leans over to speak softly into his ear. "April come she will. When streams are ripe and swelled with rain."

Victor's voice is little more than a whispered growl. "May, she will stay, resting in my arms again." His eyes open, barely, just slits. "Marlene...?"

"Victor, I'm sorry. I'm so, so sorry."

He turns his head away from her. "How can you even bear to look at me?"

She smiles despite her tears, trying to make a joke of it. "I've seen worse hanging on our walls, sweetheart." She grips his hand even more tightly. "You are my husband. You are my love."

Already exhausted, he closes his eyes again. "Stay with me..."

She holds the massive paw to the side of her face. "I'll never leave you. Never. I swear."

Victor has lapsed into unconsciousness. Pompey moves in for a closer look and Grease Trap pushes Marlene out of the way. Pompey looks over to DeRon. "You're telling me this is Victor Moravian?"

DeRon's attention is focused on the body of his former mentor, Professor Drettmann. "The brain of Victor Moravian."

Pompey stares at the battered creature in astonishment. "You put Victor Moravian's brain into this... thing?"

DeRon nods.

Pompey is thoughtful now. The gears are turning. "If you did it once, you could do it again. Right? You could transplant a brain into a normal body. A body that doesn't..." He begins to tremble violently and grips the handle of the dolly to brace himself.

The attack is a mild one and passes quickly. Pompey straightens up, pale but in control. He moves to Jack, who is closely guarded by Brickhouse, but his attention remains focused on DeRon. "It would still be me... my mind? My thoughts? My memories?"

DeRon, reluctant to acknowledge this fresh horror, barely nods.

Pompey runs his hand appraisingly over the hitman's arms and shoulders. "My brain in a healthy body." He gets right in Jack's face, grinning. "Your body, Jack."

Jack spits in Pompey's face. Brickhouse clubs Jack to the floor with the sawed-off. He raises the gun to deliver a second blow but Pompey stops him. "Easy there." He pulls Jack to his feet and slaps him affectionately on the cheek. "I don't want no damaged merchandise now."

The gangster turns and grins wickedly at DeRon. The little man tries to wheel his chair away but has nowhere to go. "I won't do it."

Pompey shoves Marlene roughly aside as he goes after DeRon. She stumbles into the wall and DeRon nearly falls out of his chair in a futile attempt to help her.

Pompey, seeing DeRon's reaction to Marlene's distress, stops short. He smiles at DeRon while he unholsters his automatic pistol. He places the barrel of the gun against Marlene's head. "Want to see how I perform a brain transplant?" He releases the safety. "Boom! Splat! Her brain transplanted to that wall."

DeRon's defiance evaporates. Pompey grins in triumph and holsters the gun. He moves over to admire the array of surgical instruments. "First things first. I want Victor Moravian." He picks up the craniotomy saw and thrusts it at DeRon. "Give me his brain—the lousy chiseler—I'm gonna bronze it and use it for a doorstop."

Marlene throws herself across Victor's body. "No! Leave him alone. Please, dear god, leave him be." Grease Trap pulls her away and she looks desperately to Jack. "You can't let them do this. You can't let them take him away from me again."

Brickhouse trains the shotgun on Jack. The hitman calmly surveys the scene around him. He reaches into his shirt pocket and Brickhouse tenses, pressing his finger against the trigger. Jack removes his hand to reveal a plastic baggy with several joints and a book of matches. He ignores Marlene's angry glare and lights up.

DeRon has the saw in his lap as he rolls his chair over to Victor's side. Grease Trap grabs Marlene to prevent her from interfering. DeRon fires up the saw and Victor, conscious again, begins to thrash around in an effort to move away from the whirring blade. DeRon gestures to Brickhouse. "I need you to hold him still."

The gunman, eyeing the beast's massive bulk, hesitates. Pompey, impatient, barks at him. "Let's do this thing already."

Grease Trap is holding Marlene in a throttlehold with one arm. He uses his free hand to point his gun at Jack, who is sucking on the joint. He nods to Brickhouse. "I got this."

Brickhouse reluctantly sets the shotgun aside. "I don't know, boss..."

Pompey seems hypnotized by the spinning saw blade. "Just do it."

Brickhouse pokes around the lab until he finds a length of metal cable. He runs it underneath the dolly and then loops it several times around Victor's chest and shoulders. He moves off to the side, close to DeRon, and pulls the cable tight, pinning Victor to the dolly. Marlene struggles fiercely but Grease Trap holds her fast.

DeRon moves the whirring blade closer and closer to Victor's skull. Then, he suddenly spins around and plunges the spinning blade into Brickhouse's chest. The gunman screams and staggers backward until he hits the wall. He stares in amazement at the blood soaking the front of his shirt. The cable ends slip from his lifeless hands and his body slumps down the wall to the floor.

DeRon, horrified at what he's done, drops the bloody saw. Grease Trap swivels to take aim at DeRon and Marlene digs her teeth into his arm. He screams and drops the gun while Marlene breaks free.

Jack dives for the gun, grabs it, rolls onto his back, and points it at Grease Trap. The gangster backs off, gripping his injured arm. "Jack... Buddy... It's me." He smiles with the pathetic hopefulness of a drunk cadging a drink. "Remember? We used to sit around drinking forties? Go down to Harpo's trolling for pussy..."

Jack's not in the mood for reminiscing. He shoots. By the time he turns his attention to Pompey, the mob boss is holding a scalpel to Marlene's throat. "Drop it or I'll cut her tonsils out."

Jack does as he's told. Pompey unholsters his gun and moves toward Jack with Marlene in tow. He has the gun pointed at the hitman's head. "I should have done this a long time ago."

As he moves past the dolly, a powerful hand reaches out to grab him by the throat. Marlene slips from his grasp and Victor slowly crushes the life out of the gangster. Then, exhausted by the effort, Victor lies back on the dolly and allows Pompey's limp body to drop to the floor.

Marlene throws herself, sobbing, across her husband's chest. She looks up to see Jack approaching and grows hysterical. "Don't you dare touch him! Don't you dare fucking touch him!"

Jack backs off. Her face is a trembling mask of rage. "Don't you understand? You can't fix this! You can't fix anything!" She glares at him until he removes himself to a safe distance. Then, still muttering angrily under her breath, she turns her attention back to Victor.

DeRon has wheeled his chair over to Drettmann and is draping a sheet over the body. He notices Jack watching him. He takes one more lingering look at the Professor's now placid countenance before covering his face. There is something approaching tenderness in his voice. "He wasn't always that way."

Jack doesn't respond. He looks at the carnage around them and then back to DeRon. He takes one final toke and pinches the joint out before carefully returning it to the plastic baggy. "We got work to do."

62

J ACK RETURNS TO THE surgery suite after dragging the last of
the bodies out. DeRon is hobbling around with a crutch and a
mop as he works to clean up the gore. He stops and follows Jack's
gaze to where Marlene has fallen asleep in a chair next to Victor.
He responds to Jack's unspoken question. "I can repair most of the
physical damage. But he'll still be..." He shrugs. "What he is."

Jack stares at Marlene and Victor for a long time. He seems to reach
some sort of a decision and walks over to pull the rolling factory door
shut. There's a padlock hanging by the door latch and he secures it,
locking them in. He turns back to DeRon. "I'm gonna fix this."

DeRon has returned to his mopping. "She's right, there's nothing
you can do. There's nothing anyone can do."

Jack goes and grabs him by the arm. "I'm not talking about fixing
him."

DeRon stares angrily at the hand on his shoulder. "You killed my
dog."

Jack removes his hand from DeRon's shoulder. He tilts his head
in the direction of the operating table that once held Marlene. "You
did it before."

DeRon is horrified when he realizes what Jack is suggesting. He
looks at him in disbelief. "You want it to be you?"

Jack's unflinching gaze is his answer.

DeRon shakes his head. "You can't! I won't..."

Jack is a man possessed. The certainty of his words is a demand backed by the unspoken threat of violence. "I'm going to give him back to her."

DeRon can't believe what he's hearing. "But why? Why would you do that for her?"

"I'm not doing it for her."

The confusion in the smaller man's eyes curdles into rage. He flings the mop to the ground. "No! No! No! I will not be a part of this! No way! No fucking way!"

He flails his arm in the direction of Victor, sputtering. "He has done things... He has done so many things, so much evil, to so many people." He glares at the beast. His voice is suffused with hate. With pain. "To me. To mine." He turns his anger on Jack. "Things no one can ever fix." He shakes his head. "No. Just no."

Jack remains calm, determined. "He didn't know what he was doing."

DeRon explodes again. "Fuck him!" He gesticulates wildly in Marlene's direction. "And fuck her! I don't care how much she fucking loves him! Let her be fucking alone!" He runs out of steam and his voice drops to a defeated whisper. "That's just the way it is: some of us are just fucking alone." He pulls a chair close and sits down. "Doesn't matter. I could never do it by myself, without the Professor."

They both turn to see Marlene standing there. She has Pompey's pistol and it's pointing at DeRon's head. The look in her eyes is pure, crazed, weaponized love. "I was an ER nurse. A good one." She bites her lip before continuing; this is not a particularly pleasant memory. "Once."

Jack, moving with practiced ease, snatches the gun away from her. DeRon looks relieved, until Jack releases the safety and returns the weapon to Marlene. "Won't do you much good with the safety on." She eyes Jack quizzically for a moment, then moves forward until the gun is inches from DeRon's head. "We can do this. We will do this."

Jack settles into a seat next to him. "Trust me, she will pull that trigger."

DeRon, staring into the barrel of the gun, nods. "Okay. Alright. But you better be as good as you say you are."

Jack looks up to see Marlene eyeing him with cold intensity. "Don't even think this makes things right. Not even fucking close."

Jack looks away. He slaps DeRon sympathetically on the back, then waves his arm in an expansive gesture. "When you're done, burn it all. Burn this fucking place down."

———— • ————

Jack can see his reflection in the chrome collar of the goose lamp overhead. His shaved scalp is a topographical map of bruises, scrapes, scars, and cuts documenting the violent confrontations of the preceding weeks. A gloved hand pushes the lamp aside and DeRon leans in close. He's wearing a powder blue surgical mask. The lamp at his back endows him with the vaporous golden halo of an archangel or a saint. The eyes are kind. The voice is gentle. "Are you ready?"

In his peripheral vision, Jack can see Marlene opening and closing various drawers in search of something. He tries to stay focused on DeRon. He knows there is only one way he can do this: he must completely wall off from his conscious mind any hint of the terrifying reality of what he is about to do. He has to ignore the surgical instruments, the saw, the machines, the monitors, and, most importantly, the hulking form of the beast on the adjoining table.

Jack remembers the poker games with the Italians. The endless rounds of drinks you couldn't say no to: scotch, brandy, Sambuca, sickly sweet Limoncello. He steels himself by recalling the ferocious, mind-bending discipline that allowed him to remain alert and ready for anything. He could match them all night, drink for drink, and never give the slightest indication that he was getting drunk, never lose the ability to react with complete confidence, never lose his edge. Through sheer force of will, he banished the alcohol and its effects from his system for as long as he needed to. He, Jack Killeen, created his own reality.

But now, strapped to this table unable to move, without the holstered Glock pressing against the small of his back, without the ability to bully, intimidate, improvise, or run through fucking walls if he has to, he can feel his resolve cracking. Something completely alien, completely beyond his control, is seeping through those cracks and worming its way into his psyche. Jack Killeen is afraid. No, not afraid; Jack Killeen is teetering on the edge of panic.

Jack is startled by the sound of his own voice. He can hear himself speaking words he has not consciously formed, words that have somehow bypassed his brain and escaped from his lips unbidden. "I don't know... Maybe I need to think about this some more..."

Marlene is standing beside DeRon now. The surgical mask reveals only her eyes. She's holding a piece of cotton gauze and a tiny glass medicinal bottle in her gloved hands. She drips some liquid from the bottle onto the gauze and her eyes meet Jack's. There is nothing there: no love, no hate, no pity, no tenderness, no anger.

Emptiness.

Jack is panicking, searching for the right words to say to make this stop. Before he can speak, she covers his mouth and nostrils with the gauze.

The last thing Jack hears is DeRon's voice, still kind, still gentle. "His name was Babyface. I just think you should know."

Then, it's lights out.

63

J ACK IS WIDE-AWAKE THE instant the Big Fat Fuck pokes him in the ribs. He sits up and swings his legs over the edge of the bunk. The Big Fat Fuck sets a bright yellow Detroit Edison hardhat on the mattress next to him. Marty, propped up against the bedpost on the lower bunk, is sleepily jamming an identical hardhat over his lopsided bed-head bouffant.

The Big Fat Fuck has not yet fully ballooned into something resembling his epithet, but the once roomy army fatigue jacket looks like a vest on him now. He has a dishtowel tied around his head like a ninja. The machete is tucked into his belt and there are kitchen implements sticking out of his back pocket. He has a thick forehead and brows seemingly endowed by nature to go head-to-head with a rutting mountain goat. His pale blue eyes have a frightening intensity as he presses a finger to his lips to ensure the boys' silence.

Jack puts the hardhat on and slides down to the floor next to Marty. The Big Fat Fuck gestures for the two small boys to take their shoes and they follow him along the pitch-dark hallway to the kitchen. He raises his hand to bring the little patrol to a halt and the boys press their shoulders into the wall as they step into their shoes. The Big Fat Fuck hands Marty a spatula and Jack a wooden serving spoon. Jack wrestles the spatula away from a grimacing Marty and gives him the spoon. The Big Fat Fuck unsheathes his machete. The boys raise their weapons and stare into the darkness.

Then, the Big Fat Fuck flips on the kitchen light.

The kitchen floor and countertops are moving. The cairn of dirty dishes in the sink, the battered Formica table, the cracked linoleum floor, pots, pans; everything is coated with a churning, roiling, oily brown veneer of cockroaches. The three of them set upon their prey with whoops and shrieks, smashing, chopping, smushing, and killing.

The two boys ferociously pound the scuttling insects into gloppy paste with their implements. The Big Fat Fuck, pausing for the occasional kung fu pose, alternately smashes the frothing, brindled mounds of insects with the flat side of the machete blade and the butt end of the handle. He sweeps them off countertops by the dozen and the boys, their weapons now hopelessly encrusted with granulated insect mush, stomp them in a gleeful jig.

The Big Fat Fuck, in a frenzy now, falls to his knees, howling as he maniacally dices squirming mounds of roaches with the machete.

Jack can't remember ever being so happy.

64

I T'S POURING RAIN AS Marlene and DeRon struggle to guide the
heavily laden gurney up the ramp to the loading dock at the rear
of Detroit Receiving Hospital. Several miles to the southeast there is
a reddish glow on the horizon where the ironworks are fully engulfed
despite the downpour.

DeRon is at the back, leaning into the gurney with all his weight as
he hobbles along on a homemade prosthesis. She's leaning into the
rolling cart with her hip and guiding it with one hand while wielding
an umbrella with the other in an effort to protect their patient from
the deluge. Her hair has grown out into a fairly respectable baby-afro.

They are both drenched by the time they reach the shelter of
the loading dock overhang. DeRon locks the gurney's wheels in
place. He retrieves the walking stick he had deposited on the gurney
and gazes out at the torrents of water. "Spring showers bring May
flowers."

Marlene smiles as she shakes out the umbrella. "Raining cats and
dogs out there, that's for damn sure."

A low moan escapes from the blanketed figure on the gurney and
Marlene turns to comfort their patient. "Don't try to talk, baby."

The head, heavily bandaged, is clearly that of Jack Killeen. Marlene tenderly strokes his cheek. "Go to sleep, Victor, my love. Folks
here gonna help you get well again."

DeRon is already moving back down the ramp. "I'll start the van."

Marlene waits until he gets into his van and the engine turns over. She presses her fingertips to her lips and uses them to plant a kiss on the shrouded figure's bandaged forehead. Then, she stands there, frozen in indecision, her hand clenching the rail on the side of the gurney.

DeRon rolls down his window and gestures urgently for her to hurry up. Marlene turns reluctantly away from the man on the gurney. She presses the buzzer by the door and hurries down the steps. She jumps into the passenger seat of the van and DeRon pulls away.

DeRon parks down the street and they watch from a distance. Marlene peers anxiously through the sheets of rain gusting over the windshield. "What's taking so long?"

"Don't worry, they're used to folks dumping..." He catches himself. "Sorry, I mean—"

A security guard comes out onto the dock and Marlene nearly straight-arms DeRon to shush him. The guard looks under the sheet and rushes back inside. Soon the dock is swarming with orderlies and nurses who hustle the gurney inside.

Marlene stares at the now deserted loading dock. "Is he gonna be okay?"

"He's gonna live. I don't know if he's gonna be okay." He can't help grinning. "He is gonna be really fucking confused."

DeRon realizes she's staring at him. He thinks he's really screwed up this time and begins to stammer an apology.

She stops him with an upraised hand. DeRon watches with concern as her eyes widen and her body goes rigid as if she's fighting the urge to vomit. Then, some extraordinary blockage seems to break deep inside her lungs, bursting from her mouth like an explosive, barking cough as she erupts in an uncontrollable gale of laughter.

Marlene laughs hysterically, hacking, gulping, whelping until her voice is hoarse and tears are streaming down her cheeks. The attack finally begins to subside, and she grips the dash with both hands while the strangled snorts and guffaws mutate into gasping sobs.

DeRon goes to grasp her shoulder but can't quite muster the courage. "You... You did the right thing."

She's gulping for breath now, wiping her eyes with her sleeve. She desperately wants this to be true. "I really wanted to stay with him. I did. I really did."

DeRon turns on the wipers and the headlights. "We should go. Before someone, you know..."

She takes a final look at the loading dock. "I can always come back. Right? There's no reason..." Her voice trails off and she turns back to DeRon, still sniffling. "What will you do?"

He shrugs.

She turns her attention back to the barren loading dock. "Can we stay? Just a little longer?"

He shuts the van down. "Absolutely. No problem."

She's gazing into the rain now, at the distant glow from the fire. "We were at the zoo. You ever been there?"

"Naw."

"Detroit Zoo. Lions and tigers and bears... And, I don't know, giraffes, I guess. And rhinos. Every kind of damn animal you can think of." She smiles at the memory. "So Victor, what does he do? He sees this little old seed fluttering down from a tree..." She demonstrates, twirling her index finger. "You know, one of those helicopter thingies?"

DeRon does know. "Maple tree. Or Sycamore maybe."

She shakes her head in bemusement. "Damn, Urkel in the house. Anyways, he grabbed for it, tried to snatch it outta the air. Stepped off the path and broke his damn ankle. They had to send one of those golf carts for us. I think it had tiger stripes." She gives DeRon a searching look. "Pretty pathetic, huh?"

DeRon, suddenly shy, can't meet her gaze. "Yeah... I guess."

Marlene takes a plastic baggie out of her coat pocket and lights up a joint. She inhales deeply and offers it to DeRon.

He instinctively demurs. "I don't... I never..."

She starts to pull the blunt away but he grabs her wrist. He gives her a challenging look as he moves her fingers close to his lips and sucks on the joint. He releases her wrist and presses his lips together to hold in the smoke.

She watches him, appraisingly, as she exhales, smiling through the smoke. "I'm old enough to be your momma."

He grins, leaking smoke. "Yeah, if you had me when you were, like, six."

She holds his gaze, smiling, until he looks away in embarrassment. They share the rest of the joint in silence. She watches him the entire time, looking thoughtful. Finally, she stubs the glowing nub out in the ashtray. "Okay. I'm ready."

His hands are on the wheel. "Where? We spent all the money."

She smiles. "Don't sweat it. I got me a whole damn warehouse full of art."

DeRon turns the key in the ignition. "Cool." He fires up the wipers and the headlights. Then he leans back in the seat, suddenly serious, and looks at Marlene. "Why'd he do it?"

She's leaning her head against the side window. She closes her eyes. "Just go. Please."

DeRon looks at her, smiling. He mumbles to himself, too softly for her to hear. "Birds of a feather." He throws the van into gear and pulls away.

65

FR. PAUL'S FINGERTIPS LINGER near the toggle switch as he prepares to turn on the penitent light. Then, he pulls his hand away, annoyed. The jangling, doddering chorus line of walkers, canes, and oxygen tanks outside his confessional will just have to wait.

He leans back in his seat, arms crossed, in a mood. He can't believe the TV news has featured yet another elderly nun who is a "super fan" of the Tigers. Where do they find these women? He's been buying season tickets since before he got out of the seminary. Well, splitting them with Nick over at St. Pius. And Fr. Polidori at Holy Redeemer, when they can wrestle the bloody mousetrap out of his wallet that is. But still, no one ever came to his rectory with a camera crew.

And now, who knows what they'll do? The way they've jacked up the prices in the new stadium for that pitiful excuse for a major league baseball team, even a three-way split is going to be a stretch.

The coughing and hacking outside the confessional is getting hard to ignore. Fr. Paul sighs and reaches for the toggle switch just as the massive church portal is flung open like a storm door in a hurricane. For a brief moment, a stunned silence falls over the gaggle of parishioners on the other side of the confessional curtain. Then, all hell breaks loose as they suddenly erupt in a panicked melee of screams, flailing bodies, and clanging metal cylinders.

The priest, paralyzed by fear, cowers in his cubicle. Outside, the ruckus recedes and then fades away completely as the geriatric scrum makes a ragged retreat through the side exit.

The church has fallen completely silent by the time Fr. Paul peeks through the curtained opening to see Mrs. Zelinski out cold among the litter of purses, shoes, and canes left behind in the panic.

Then, Jesus on his wee cross begins to tremble as something quite large moves slowly down the aisle toward the confessional. To the priest hiding in his dark cubicle, it sounds as if the devil himself has entered his church. It, whatever it is, takes deep, raspy breaths that are somehow not quite human. And it makes a scraping noise as it slouches toward the confessional as if it is dragging fiendish claws across the tiles.

Fr. Paul presses himself against the backrest and watches in terror as a giant foot shoves Mrs. Z's limp body aside like a candy wrapper. Then, the entire confessional shakes and the wood paneling in the adjoining cubicle splinters as the intruder settles heavily into it.

The frightened priest's hand trembles as he reaches out to open the door that covers the screen separating the two cubicles. The awful breathing is close now and Father Paul has to endure several false starts before he's able to get the words out of his dry mouth. "Yes... my son?"

The voice that answers is the raspy croak from the mouth of a corpse. "Bless me, Father, for I have sinned."

Then, a massive paw rips away the thin panel that separates them.

Fr. Paul gazes in horror upon the face of the beast. His first awful impression is that of a jumble of ravaged, flayed human faces somehow stuffed all together into a giant pickle jar. He tries to look away but finds himself riveted by the eyes, the eyes of Jack Killeen.

"I've come for your absolution, Father."

CONTENT WARNING

This is a horror novel in every sense of the word. Bad things happen to good people, good dogs and innocent children. Awful people say hurtful things about race, gender, and disability. Be forewarned.

Author's Note

Counted With the Dead is a period piece. The Detroit Gray Iron Foundry is long gone, and the old Packard plant is slated to follow it into oblivion. However, I'm happy to report that all of the other major buildings depicted in various states of abandonment or ruin in this book have been restored to their former glory. These structures include the Central Train Station, the Metropolitan Building, the Wurlitzer, the Farwell, the GAR, and the David Broderick Tower, among others.

ACKNOWLEDGMENTS

Much love to my wife Lesley Walker who has always supported me in whatever the hell it is I do. To friends and family, Mark Manos, R. Michael Beatty, Catherine Borshuk, Stephen Gill, 'Professore' Steve Shore, my siblings: Michael, Kathy, Dennis, Mary, Diane, Gary, Patrick, and too many nieces and nephews to list here. To Katy Heins and Pat Clifford, Sarah Jean Heins, Judith McGee, Jonathan Nashel, Rebecca Brittenham, Elaine Roth, Steven Gerencser, Erika and Lyle Zinda, David Blum, Andrea and Donnie Rogers.

Thanks to my editor Gabino Iglesias, whose dark sensibility outstrips even my own.

To the folks at Grendel Press for taking a chance on one very tough piece of work (I'm talking about the book, not me.)

To Trace Chiodo, a great sounding board, office mate, and friend.

To the mentors, agents, and producers who were there at the beginning of the journey: George Malko, Tom Allen, Lyndon Chubbuck, Robert Mozejewski, Matt Keener, Dana Cioffi, and John Marsh.

Thank you.

About the Author

Counted With the Dead is Peter O'Keefe's first published novel. Peter started out writing for George Romero's *Tales From the Darkside* and has since worked as a Hollywood screenwriter, optioned numerous original screenplays, and written TV movies for German networks. His narrative short films have screened at a variety of film festivals and Peter's documentary about visual artists in the Midwest, *Dreaming In Public, Making Art In the Real World* was awarded a Chicago Regional Emmy. His short stories and essays have appeared in various literary and online journals.